SWEET PROMISE

"I think you like more than a few things about me, Jennifer Mainwaring. Just as I like more than a few things about you."

"Like what?" she asked shyly.

"Your hair." John shifted his hand to tug lightly on one of the ringlets.

"My plain brown hair?"

"Your hair is a deep, rich brown, Jennie, with red and golden highlights that shine in sun or candlelight. I have often dreamed of what it would look like falling free around your shoulders and down your back."

There was a curious possessiveness to John's tone that sent a shiver of excitement racing through Jennifer. "What else do you like?"

"Your eyes." John moved his hand from her neck to her cheek. "I like your spirit, and your loyalty." His gaze travelled up to her face. "And I like to kiss you, so much so that I am tempted to kiss you again, right on the mouth, right now."

"John!" Jennifer moved to fan her face again, but he stilled her hand.

He leaned closer and took her other hand as well, his voice dropping to a whisper. "And there are other places I would very much like to kiss besides your tempting mouth, other things I would very much like to do to your lovely body, and someday, Jennie, someday soon, I promise you, I will . . ."

The Wild Rose
Jessica Wulf

ZEBRA BOOKS
KENSINGTON PUBLISHING CORP.

ZEBRA BOOKS are published by

Kensington Publishing Corp.
850 Third Avenue
New York, NY 10022

First Printing: October, 1995

Printed in the United States of America

In memory of my beloved grandmother,

Marian Hamm Henning
1907-1995

See you later, Gram. ♥

Acknowledgements

There are a few people I wish to thank for their contributions to this book:

Thanks to my new editor, John Scognamiglio, for your patience and guidance. You are a pleasure to work with.

A great big thanks to my art director, Mike Capobianco, for a fantastic cover!

Thanks to my dear friend, Loretta, in Santa Maria, and my brother, Tony, in San Jose, for their kindness and assistance on my research trip to California. You both took good care of me.

As always, thanks to "the Girls"—Barbara, Denée, Mary, Margaret, Sandie and Carol. What would I do without you?

Thanks to Katie and Jake, two special and gentle souls who touched my heart and gave me hope during a very difficult time of my life.

A special thanks to Dad and Jesse for sticking around. I'm not sure I could have finished this book otherwise. I love you both.

And finally, I want to acknowledge my parents, Neil and Sharlene, to whom I dedicate this book. You taught me how to dream, Mom, and Dad, your loving acceptance helped give me the courage to stick with it. Thank you both for believing in me.

—J.W.

Prologue

Ciudad de Mexico, June 1873

The sound of the dirt hitting the top of the simple pine casket pulled the tall man at the grave side from his painful reverie. John Novales Cantrell blinked, but allowed no emotion to show on his face. Elena, his strong-willed, beloved grandmother, was gone.

His gaze shifted to the two headstones next to the slowly filling hole. They marked the final resting places of Juan, his grandfather, and Ana Maria, his mother. Farther away, over a small rise in the crowded cemetery, he could find the grave of Benito Juarez, the Patriot of Mexico, for whom he had fought so long and so hard. They were all gone.

"Is there anything I can do for you, my son?" Although the old priest had lived in Mexico for over forty years, his flawless Spanish still carried a faint French accent. He placed a gentle hand on John's forearm.

John remained silent, watching as the grave digger continued his task of filling the grave of Elena Novales with a monotonous rhythm. Scoop, dump. Scoop, dump. For some reason, John found the sounds irritating.

Finally, he shook his head and patted the priest's gnarled hand, answering in the language of his mother and grandparents. *"No, gracias, Padre.* There is nothing more to do here. I appreciate the fine service you read for Grandmother." He did not comment on the lack of mourners. Only two ancient nuns had come from the convent to pay their respects, and even now, they tottered away, holding onto each other for support.

The priest pulled a handkerchief from his sleeve and mopped his face. "So hot already, and it is only June." He shook his head in disgust. "Come back to the kitchen with me, where it is cool. We will speak French and share a glass of wine and talk about the days when you were a youth and your mother was alive."

John's jaw tightened, but he kept his tone calm. *"Non, merci, Père Michel,"* he responded, and continued speaking in French. "There is much yet to do at home. I must prepare for my journey. But I would be honored if you would join me for supper this evening."

"Eh bien. I would enjoy that."

The two men turned from the grave and moved slowly along the path that wound through the headstones toward the church. After a few moments of silence, the old priest turned his rheumy eyes to John, his expression one of deep concern. "Are you so determined to travel to California, then?"

"I must."

Evidently his grim tone gave the priest pause, for the old man hesitated before he spoke again. "Better you should believe the compassionate words of your dear mother than the bitter ones of Elena Novales. Your grandmother lacked understanding; she believed only what she chose to believe, and, on occasion, the truth had little impact on which belief she chose."

When John did not answer, the priest shrugged. "I will pray for you, my son."

"Gracias, Padre. No doubt I will need your prayers."

John Cantrell wandered through the rooms of the spacious apartments he had called home for the past six years, ever since Benito Juarez had successfully reclaimed the ruling

power of Mexico from the French. Although the furniture remained, all personal effects had been removed and packed,
giving the rooms a lonely air. He paused at one of the narrow,
floor-to-ceiling windows that overlooked a small square. The
panes had been opened in a futile attempt to catch an errant
breeze.

The noise of the city called out to him, and John braced
his hands on the ornate wrought-iron railing which prevented
the careless from plummeting to the ground three stories below. The streets surrounding the square were crowded with
all manner of traffic, including people of many races and
nationalities, as was evidenced by the sounds of several languages floating up to his ears. Fancy carriages and rude
wooden carts jostled one another, while the drivers of each
sweated and cursed.

As he looked over the city, the Juarez rebellion to drive
Maximilian and the French army from Mexico seemed long
ago and of another world—a world of danger and passion,
of *El Lobo* and *La Serpiente,* a world now come to an end.
John had been prepared to die for Benito Juarez, but he had
lived, had lived even longer than Juarez, who had been his
leader, mentor, and friend.

The strange exhilaration of living in constant danger, of
knowing that at any moment he could be asked to give his
life for a cause he found noble, had given way to a high-
ranking and surprisingly boring government post where the
only excitement to be found was in the never-ending political
intrigues, of which he had grown weary. With Juarez dead
this year past, John's position no longer held interest for him,
and now, having buried his grandmother, he had no reason
to stay in Mexico. He did not know how to live in peace.

John needed a new challenge. He had considerable money
saved; perhaps it was time to buy his own land, think about
settling down, take up the battle against the elements and
wrest a living from the earth. But first, he had one matter to
see to.

His mouth set in a grim line, John turned from the window and marched through the silent rooms to the jumble of trunks and boxes waiting near the front doors. He dropped to one knee beside a battered trunk and pulled the opened padlock from its ring. After raising the lid, he rummaged through the contents until he found an oak letter box, which he pulled from its place. He straightened, allowing the trunk lid to slam shut, and moved to a chair.

His dark eyebrows drew together in fierce concentration as he searched the contents of the box, then finally he held up a battered letter. A piece of the old, cracked sealing wax fell to the floor. He stared at his mother's neat handwriting on the outside fold of the letter. Although the ink was faded, he could easily make out the name written there: *Preston Cantrell.* Had the words been no longer legible, he would have known them by heart. Preston Cantrell. His father. An *Americano* whose language Ana Maria had insisted her son learn. A man he had never met, a man who had turned his mother away when she'd become pregnant. A man he hated.

His mother, on her deathbed, had extracted John's promise that one day he would seek his father out and deliver her last letter to him. His grandmother, on her deathbed, had demanded that he find Preston Cantrell and avenge the Novales family honor. John Novales Cantrell placed the letter in his breast pocket, his jaw tight, his eyes blazing with determination. He would do both.

One

"To Jennie, my lovely goddaughter. I can't tell you how good it is to see you at my table again." With a wide smile, Preston Cantrell raised his glass to the young woman seated next to him.

Jennifer Mainwaring's answering smile was warm with affection. "And I cannot tell you how good it is to once again be at your table, Preston." She sipped from her glass and savored the excellent wine, welcoming the warmth the liquid offered on its way to her stomach. Even after two days of rest, she had not completely recovered from the long days of travel that had brought her to California, and she knew the wine would help ensure a good night's sleep.

The sound of a sigh caused her to face the man on her right. Her uncle, Oliver Mainwaring, made no attempt to hide his boredom. She sent him a pleading look, then returned her attention to her godfather at the head of the table. He was a tall and robust man, and the lines fanning from his piercing blue eyes and the fair hair now turned white were the only indications that the still-handsome Preston Cantrell was approaching his sixtieth birthday.

"I am anxious to see what changes you have made to the Santa Maria since I was last here," Jennifer said, hoping Preston hadn't noticed Oliver's expression. "After all, it has been fourteen years. Perhaps tomorrow you or Bill can take me riding." She smiled at Preston's attractive twenty-seven-year-old son, who sat across the table from her. With his wavy blond hair and blue eyes, Bill Cantrell bore a strong resemblance to his father. They shared no blood ties, but Jennifer considered Bill her cousin.

Bill nodded in agreement. "I'll take her, Pa. For weeks I've been promising Barbara I would show her the new dam we built in the foothills." He took the hand of his plump, pretty, brown-haired wife and planted a kiss on the back of it. "We'll all go together."

"I'd like that, Bill." The sound of Barbara's voice was soft and melodious as she smiled at her husband.

"The dam is an engineering marvel, Jennie, and vital to our plans to improve the grasslands on the ranch's eastern border," Preston said proudly. "I want you to see it." He arched an eyebrow at Oliver. "And perhaps Oliver would like to join you. He may find a ride more entertaining than he has our company so far."

Jennifer looked warily from one man to the other. There was no mistaking the challenge in Preston's tone, just as there was no mistaking the arrogance in Oliver's answering one.

"I think not."

Jennifer felt a blush climb her neck and cheeks as she struggled to hold her tongue, knowing that in Oliver's present mood, anything she said could very well lead to an ugly and embarrassing scene. She lowered her gaze to her hands. They lay tightly entwined in her lap, appearing very white against the deep burgundy of her satin evening gown. Whatever was wrong with her uncle? At twenty-nine, he was six years her senior, but she felt he often acted like a petulant schoolboy. Tonight he was surpassing himself.

She glanced at him. The light from the two silver candelabras on the table bathed Oliver's patrician features and highlighted his sandy-brown hair and trimmed mustache. She wondered, as she often did, how someone so attractive could be so unpleasant.

Preston, too, struggled with his temper. He was sorely tempted to escort Oliver Mainwaring from the table and give him a lesson in manners, but his gaze fell on his goddaughter, and for her sake, he kept quiet.

The fact that Jennifer had grown into a lovely woman did not surprise Preston, for he had seen the promise of her beauty even when she was a child. Candlelight played off the gold and amber highlights in her dark-brown hair, now coaxed into a charming arrangement that allowed soft curls to trail down the sides of her face and neck. The style of Jennifer's costly and fashionable evening gown bared her shoulders, emphasizing the elaborate ruby necklace that encircled her graceful neck. Preston tried to ignore the fact that her collarbone and shoulder blades were too prominent, that her clear skin was too pale, that shadows of unhappiness lurked within her large green eyes. His beloved goddaughter attempted to hide it, but all was not well with her. He hoped his concern did not show; now was not the time to speak of it, not with her disagreeable uncle present.

Preston stiffened as the uncomfortable silence was suddenly filled with the sharp staccato of approaching hoofbeats. Whoever it was, the rider came at a full gallop. He exchanged a glance with Bill.

"I'm not expecting anyone," Bill said.

"Neither am I." Preston set his napkin on the table.

The sound of the hoofbeats steadily rose in volume, until it seemed to Jennifer that the visitor intended to ride right into the dining room. A feeling of foreboding rushed through her as the hoofbeats finally stopped. A horse whinnied, loudly, angrily.

Preston pushed back from the table. "Something must be wrong."

At that moment, Preston's name was shouted from the yard by a male voice as loud and angry as the horse's whinny had been. Jennifer stood without waiting for Oliver to pull her chair back and followed Preston and Bill into the foyer. The furious voice called again.

"Preston Cantrell!"

Preston opened the massive Spanish-style oak door and stepped out onto the wide, covered veranda. Jennifer, Bill, and Barbara followed. A few of the hired men had gathered in the yard, watching the visitor with apprehension-tinged curiosity; two carried rifles. Gabriel Horn, the foreman of the Santa Maria, appeared protectively at Preston's left, while Bill stepped up to his right.

Jennifer could not take her eyes off the horseman in the yard. Riding a stallion as black as his clothes, he made an impressive picture in the light of the full moon. He easily controlled the excited, prancing animal, who occasionally rose up to paw at the sky. Moonlight winked off the silver studs decorating the saddle and bridle and down the row of silver conchos that lined the outside of the man's pants leg. The ominous-looking pistol at his hip seemed to glow.

"Which of you is Preston Cantrell?" the man demanded.

Preston stepped forward. "I am. State your business."

The stallion danced in a tight half circle as its rider stared at Preston for a long moment. When the man spoke, his low voice, filled with a fierce hatred, carried across the yard. "I am John Novales Cantrell, your bastard son by Ana Maria Novales, and I have come to kill you."

The only sounds that could be heard were those of the horse as it shifted and chewed its bit. Jennifer stared at John Cantrell, uncertain she had heard him correctly. He had come to kill Preston? His own father? She turned to Preston and was not at all comforted by the stunned look on his face. As she watched, he stepped down off the veranda and finally spoke.

"What did you say?"

"You heard me, *Father.* It is time you paid for what you did to my mother."

"I don't understand." Preston took a step closer to the man on the horse. "Ana Maria disappeared over thirty years ago."

"Because you sent her away!"

"No, I did not." Preston looked around the yard, then back at the horseman. "Come inside. We must talk."

"We'll talk here."

Preston turned away and walked toward the house, speaking over his shoulder. "We'll talk inside, privately."

"I could shoot you now, and be finished with it," John warned.

Preston paused, only for a moment, then continued walking. "No son of mine would shoot a man in the back. Come inside. If you don't like what I have to say, you can kill me just as easily there as here. Gabe, see to his horse. The rest of you stand aside and let him pass. Leave us alone in my study."

John watched Preston disappear through the wide doorway and felt a grudging respect for the man. He swung down from the saddle and handed the reins to the wiry, middle-aged man waiting by his side.

Gabe accepted the reins. "I don't much care what your reasons are," he warned. "If you harm a hair on Preston Cantrell's head, you won't leave the Santa Maria alive."

John met Gabe's intense gaze, measuring the man's worth. Again, he felt the stirrings of respect. He would guess that Gabe was a man of few words, but a man who meant what he said when he did speak. "No, sir, I am sure I won't. And I am prepared for that. Thank you for seeing to my horse." He turned and walked toward the house, leaving Gabe to stare after him in astonishment.

Jennifer followed Barbara and Bill into the foyer, where Oliver waited. They made a semi-circle around the open door to Preston's study and watched John Cantrell enter the house.

He removed his hat as he stepped through the door, and Jennifer saw he had thick black hair that hung over his collar. His clean-shaven face boasted a strong jaw and chin, a straight nose, and very blue eyes that stood out in sharp contrast to his tanned skin. Those eyes were the only resemblance John bore to Preston, but they were a striking resemblance. Could he really be Preston's son?

John fearlessly met the hostile stares of the people in the foyer—the young man who stood next to the door, his hand resting on the butt of his pistol; the dark-haired woman at his side, her eyes wide with apprehension; the insolently curious, well-dressed man at the foot of the stairs; and the slender woman in the elegant burgundy ball gown who waved him toward an open door as she spoke.

"He's waiting for you in there."

Her green eyes reminded John of glittering emeralds, for they were as sharp and as cold as any jewel he had ever seen. Her lips had pressed into a tight line, and her distrust of him was evident in the rigid stance of her body. He held her gaze a moment longer, then turned into the room, closing the door behind him.

Bill immediately took up a post at the door. "I hate leaving my father alone in there with that man," he said through gritted teeth.

"Oh, Bill, can it be true?" Barbara came to her husband's side. "Can he be Preston's son?"

"I don't know." Bill shook his head in bewilderment. "I just don't know." He met his wife's gaze. "Why don't you go check on the children? They may have been awakened by all the commotion."

Jennifer glanced up the stairs. The nursery that Bill and Barbara's two young children shared was on the second floor above the foyer where she now stood. She hoped that David and Molly had not been awakened.

"All right." Barbara kissed his cheek, then moved to the stairs and grasped the banister. After climbing a few steps, she hesitated long enough to send a worried glance over her shoulder toward her husband. At his reassuring nod, she continued up the stairs.

"I believe I shall retire." Oliver placed a foot on the lower step, then paused. "Be a good man," he said to Bill, "and send some brandy to my room." Without waiting for a response, he climbed the stairs.

Jennifer stared after him in disbelief, then turned to Bill, whose face was flushed with anger. "I apologize for my uncle's lack of manners, Bill. I don't know what is wrong with him tonight."

Before Bill could answer, Gabriel Horn came in through the front door.

"Where are they?" the foreman demanded.

Bill jerked his head toward the closed study door.

Gabe leaned against the wall on the other side of the door and pushed his hat back on his head. "Then I reckon we just have to wait."

"There's nothing else we can do." Bill rubbed a hand over his face. "You heard what Preston said."

"I'll take Oliver his brandy if you'll tell me where it is," Jennifer offered.

Bill shrugged ruefully. "Preston keeps it in the study, along with the snifters." He hesitated, then added, "But Rosa may have some in the kitchen."

Jennifer nodded and made her way to the dining room, passing the long table, still covered with supper dishes. It didn't seem possible that only a few minutes ago she had been enjoying a quiet meal with Preston and his family, Oliver's rudeness notwithstanding. Now, her stomach was twisted with fear, and she wondered if, before this night was over, the angry man in black would make good on his threat to kill Preston.

She pushed through the swinging door that led to the big, spotlessly clean kitchen and was relieved to find Rosa at the stove, muttering over a pot.

"Excuse me, Rosa. May I trouble you for some brandy?"

The short, trim Mexican woman, who was as neat and clean as her kitchen, turned and waved a spoon, causing her long black braid to swing against her hips. "Of course, Miss Jennifer. I get it for you. You can have anything you want. Has that man left yet?"

"No."

"Madre de Dios." Rosa quickly crossed herself as she moved to a cabinet, took down a bottle of amber liquid and poured some into a cup. "Did you see him?"

"Yes."

"Quickly, tell me how he looks."

Jennifer shrugged. "Tall, dark, dressed all in black. With very blue eyes."

"Ah. Eyes like *Señor* Cantrell, no?" Rosa took a swallow from the cup she held. "Is he beautiful?"

The cook's question startled Jennifer. Was John Cantrell beautiful? She did not find him so, but it was hard to tell when he was so angry. "He is a handsome man," she reluctantly allowed.

"Ana Maria was beautiful," Rosa said softly. "Her son would be beautiful, too."

Jennifer stared at her. "You knew her?"

"No, but my mother did. She told me that Ana Maria's beauty was legendary. You know, Ana Maria was *Señor* Preston's housekeeper when he first built this house. My mother said they were deeply in love, but *Señor* Preston was already engaged to a woman from the East—Bill's mother. It was so long ago." With a faraway look in her large brown eyes, Rosa again sipped from the cup. Suddenly she started. "I am drinking your brandy!"

"Actually, it's for my uncle." Jennifer smiled as Rosa bustled over to the cabinet and poured more brandy into a clean cup.

The woman turned with a derisive sniff. "That one, he will want a fancy crystal glass, no?"

"He will use the cup," Jennifer said firmly. "Now is not the time to be concerned about my uncle's whims. Preston's life could be in danger."

Rosa's brown forehead puckered with worry. "Surely that

man would not kill his own father," she whispered, hurriedly crossing herself again.

"I don't know, Rosa," Jennifer said soberly. "He was very angry."

"I will pray," Rosa announced.

"That is all any of us can do for now." Jennifer flashed a small, encouraging smile at the concerned cook as she held out her hand for the cup.

"And I will take this to *Señor* Mainwaring," Rosa added, keeping the cup from Jennifer's reach. "You should not be waiting on that man." She sniffed again, making clear her opinion of Oliver Mainwaring, then pushed through the door into the dining room, giving Jennifer no choice but to follow.

When they reached the foyer, Rosa continued on up the stairs, nodding at Bill's request that she check on Barbara and the children. Bill and Gabriel had not moved from their posts on either side of the study door. In answer to Jennifer's questioning look, Bill shook his head and shrugged. She could hear the sound of raised voices coming from the study, but she could not make out the words. Until Preston came safely from that study, Jennifer knew sleep would be impossible. She settled onto a hard wooden settee that rested along the wall opposite the study door, determined to stay there all night if necessary.

"She was eighteen and pregnant when you sent her away." John Cantrell's voice was hard with fury. As he paced the bright Mexican-style woven rug on the stone floor in front of the fireplace, his hand opened and closed, repeatedly making a fist he longed to use on the man seated behind the impressive mahogany desk.

"I know how old she was, but I didn't know she was pregnant," Preston snapped. "As I told you before, I did not send her away. Did she tell you I did?"

John whirled around. "No! My grandmother told me the

truth. I don't know why, but my mother defended you always! You seduced her, ruined her, and sent her away when she became pregnant. Still she defended you, insisted that my father was a good and powerful man, that he would one day be a great man." He put his hands on his hips. "I do not see a great man before me. I do not see even a good man. A good man does not shirk his responsibilities."

Livid with rage, Preston rose out of his chair and, bracing his hands on the desk, leaned forward. "I did not seduce your mother! We willingly and freely became lovers, but I will not discuss the intimate details of our relationship with you. I loved Ana Maria with all my heart, so much so that I decided to break my engagement to Bill's mother and send her back to her family in Boston. I intended to marry your mother."

John snorted in disbelief and crossed his arms over his chest. "So the great *Americano* landowner would marry his lowly Mexican housekeeper? I'm not a fool, Cantrell."

"I was not great and she was not lowly!"

John continued as if Preston had not spoken. "Do you know what life is like for an unwed mother in a small, Catholic, Mexican village? For a bastard child who bears the unmistakable mark of his *Americano* father?" He stabbed a finger in the direction of his own eyes. "Her parents tried to shield us from the scorn and cruelty of the villagers, but they could not be there all the time. She had a hard life, Preston Cantrell, thanks to you."

"And so did you," Preston remarked quietly.

Stunned into momentary silence, John looked down at the floor. The first stirrings of doubt nagged him. Preston was not reacting the way John had expected him to. There were no denials, no excuses, and perhaps most surprisingly, no fear.

Preston spoke again. "Where is your mother now? I want to see her."

"You're too late. She is long dead." John's cold words seemed to echo in the room.

Preston slumped back down into his chair. "Somehow I

knew that," he whispered. He turned his swivel chair to stare out the uncurtained window into the black night.

After a moment, he continued speaking. "I was just starting out, and I needed a housekeeper until my fiancée arrived from the East. Ana Maria was lovely beyond anything I have ever seen, before or since. I didn't intend to fall in love with her, but I did. I thought she loved me, too. I thought she would be willing to stand by my side, work with me to build a future. I named this ranch after her, for God's sake! But she left me, with no more explanation than a short note, telling me that she loved me too much to stay." Preston shook his head in confusion. "How can you love someone too much to stay?"

The anguish in Preston's voice was unmistakable. John watched him intently, wondering if Preston could be telling the truth. Had his mother been truthful all along? Had his grandmother's deep hatred for the *gringo* who ruined her daughter's life caused her to lie to him?

"If you loved her so much, why didn't you come after her?"

"I did." Preston turned around in the chair to face him again. "I searched for months, all through California and even into Mexico. She had vanished." He paused. "Did she ever marry?"

John's mouth tightened. "Yes. When I was nine. My mother was still young and lovely, and her suitor did not seem to care that I was a bastard."

Preston nodded, surprised that the idea of Ana Maria marrying another man could hurt after so many years. "Were they happy?"

"He was, as long as we behaved as he wanted us to. When we did not, he would beat us. My mother was not happy."

Chilled by the cold, dispassionate tone of John's voice and sickened by his words, Preston stared at the younger man, dreading the next question he had to ask. "When and how did she die?"

"In 1855. She did not recover from that last beating."

Preston buried his face in his hands as raw agony tore through him. He remembered Ana Maria's beautiful face; her huge, dark eyes so full of life and love; her long, glorious hair and lovely body; her comforting serenity. It was unthinkable that anyone could want to harm her, that anyone could want to trample her spirit. A black rage filled him at the thought of a man striking her. He raised his eyes to John. "Where is he?" Preston demanded roughly.

"Dead. When he wouldn't stop hitting her that night, I shot him."

Speechless, Preston could only stare at John once again. In 1855, John could have been no more than a boy, perhaps thirteen. Ravaged by guilt, Preston dropped his gaze. He should have searched for Ana Maria until he found her. He should have raised his son. Startled, Preston looked again at the angry man in front of him. Did he then accept that John was his son?

"She wrote you a letter before she died." John pulled a yellowed, wrinkled piece of paper from his vest pocket. "The sealing wax came off somewhere along the way, but I swear I haven't read it. No one has read it but her, and now you."

Preston accepted the letter with a trembling hand, not noticing that John turned away from the desk. His heart pounding, he spread the paper out and began to read.

"April 6, 1855

"My dearest Preston,

"I will soon be with the Virgin in Heaven, and there are things I must tell you before I go. Please believe that I have never stopped loving you. Forgive me for not having the strength to stay with you, but I could not bear to see you wed to another woman, nor could I force you to marry me by telling you I carried your child. I thought it best for all of us if I left. Now I think perhaps I was wrong, but it is too late.

"If you are reading this letter, then John has honored my wishes and has delivered it to you. He is your son, Preston. He is a proud and angry boy, but a good one. I hope that father and son may have the chance to know each other and that you grow to love each other, as I have loved you both. I also hope you both can forgive me for the pain my long-ago decision caused all of us.

"The one thing Death cannot conquer is love. Please know that I love you with all my heart and soul, and I will forever. I will be waiting for you.

"Ana Maria"

Once again, Preston buried his face in his hands. "Oh, Ana," he moaned, fighting tears. Thirty years had not dimmed his memory of her, or his love. Apparently her love for him had not died, either. As he struggled with his emotions, it seemed that he felt her calming presence. He raised his eyes to the man who waited by the fireplace. Ana Maria's son. His son. Their son. The living proof of the love they had shared.

Preston stared at John as if seeing him for the first time. He was tall, probably as tall as Preston himself, and lean. There was a subtle grace about him, evident in the way he carried himself. He had his mother's thick dark hair and his father's blue eyes. Ana Maria had given him a beautiful son.

There were other characteristics as well, ones that did not show on the outside. John had been loyal to, and protective of, his mother. He was also courageous, and perhaps a little headstrong, as proven by his bold appearance here tonight. All in all, John Novales Cantrell was a son to be proud of. And Preston was proud.

"For what it's worth, you were conceived in love," Preston said quietly.

Startled, John met his eyes, then looked away.

Preston held out the letter. "I want you to read this."

"No. That's between you and her."

"Please. You will see that it was her decision to leave."

Preston waited, but John did not move. "Your mother and I deeply loved each other, John."

John took a steadying breath. "I'm beginning to believe that." He crossed the room and accepted the letter. Fresh pain twisted his gut at the sight of his mother's handwriting. Even after all this time, he missed her.

Ana Maria's gentle, loving words brought tears to his eyes, as they had to his father's. He set the letter back down on the desk and turned away.

"Do you still intend to kill me?" Preston asked calmly.

John braced his hands on the fireplace mantel and looked down, unable to face Preston. "Foolish threat, huh? I'm surprised you didn't shoot me the minute it came out of my mouth."

Preston stood up and came around the desk. "I don't blame you for feeling that way, believing what you did about me."

John turned to look at him. "Did you know my grandmother?"

"No. I never met any of Ana Maria's family. Perhaps if I had known them, where they came from, I could have found her."

"My grandmother hated you. If she were still alive, she'd have insisted on coming with me, and she would have shot you on sight. You're lucky I waited so long to find you. Grandmother was a very determined woman."

Preston smiled. "It runs in the family, I think."

John did not return the smile, but he felt some of the tension leave his body. Suddenly he was very tired. "Grandmother was convinced you ruined her daughter, broke her heart, sent her away in disgrace. She never believed it was my mother's decision to leave. She told me Mama was just protecting you, because she still loved you. And I wanted to believe my grandmother." He shrugged. "I guess I did believe her."

"And now?"

"And now I don't believe her." John turned away and

walked over to the window. As Preston had done earlier, he stared out into the black night. *Now what?* he demanded of himself. He had been traveling for months, across hundreds of miles, by train when possible, by horseback when trains were not available. From *Ciudad de Mexico* to the Santa Maria Ranch, he had traveled with one goal in mind: to find his father, confront him, and if he felt it necessary, kill him. He had not lied to Gabriel in the yard—he had been prepared to die. But now everything was changed. Preston Cantrell would not die tonight, and neither would he.

John's shoulders sagged with resignation and weariness. The desire for revenge had kept him going for a long time, for years, for most of his life. What would he do now?

Preston echoed his thoughts. "What will you do now?"

"I'm not sure." John faced Preston. "But I will not bother you again. I kept my word to my mother—I delivered the letter." He reached for his hat, which rested on a chair. "I'll be on my way." He started for the door.

"Wait, son. You don't have to leave."

John stopped, but did not turn around. He clenched his teeth so tightly that he could feel a muscle twitch along his jaw. "Do not call me that. And yes, I do have to leave."

"Why?" Preston demanded. "Why do you have to leave right now? It's very late; at least stay the night. I'd like you to stay longer, for as long as you want. You have a brother and a sister-in-law, a nephew and a niece. Meet them; get to know them. They are your family."

An unreasonable fury rushed through him. "Like you are?" John sneered as he whirled to face Preston.

"Yes. Whether you like it or not, John Novales Cantrell, I am your father. Nothing will change that." Preston crossed his arms over his chest, a challenge flashing in his blue eyes. "You had the courage to come here. You were ready to kill me, which would have cost you your own life, and I'm sure you knew it. You were prepared to die. Are you also prepared to live? Do you have the courage to stay, at least for a while?"

John was quiet, surprised at Preston's words, troubled by them. Finally he met Preston's gaze. "Why do you care whether I live or die? Why do you want me to stay?"

"Purely selfish reasons. You are my son, and I want to know you."

"You already have a son."

"I have two sons," Preston corrected.

John smiled cynically and walked around the room. "Are you telling me that you intend to welcome me into the bosom of your fine family, share all this with me?" He waved a hand to encompass the study and the ranch beyond its walls.

Preston shrugged. "Welcome you, yes. Share the ranch? That remains to be seen. But it is a big ranch. There is room for two sons."

"I wonder if my brother is as generous as you are," John mused. "What is his name?"

"William. We call him Bill."

"How will my dear brother Bill feel when he learns his new brother is a half-Mexican bastard?"

"I don't know how Bill will feel, and don't call yourself a bastard."

"But I am one, *Father,* whether you like it or not, and nothing will change that," John retorted in a deliberate mimic of Preston's earlier words. He put his hat on and again moved toward the door. "It's best that I leave."

"You're a coward, John Cantrell."

Once again, Preston's words stopped John in his tracks.

Preston continued. "You don't have the guts to find out who was right about me, your mother or your grandmother. Aren't you the least bit curious about what and who your father really is? Am I the horrible, selfish man your grandmother told you I was or am I a man who was worthy of your mother's undying love? I challenge you to stay and find out."

John turned on him. "Why do you care what I think of you?"

"I care because you are my son. I care because I loved your mother; I still do. We created you, she and I. I want to know you, just as I want you to know your father and his side of your family. You have a right to know us." Preston took a step toward John. "Please stay."

Powerful emotions churned within John as he stared at the man he had hated for so long. His mother had loved Preston Cantrell with all her heart; she had never stopped longing for him. There must have been good reasons, for his mother was not a foolish woman. Surely she could not have been entirely wrong about the man. And John knew Ana Maria would have wanted him to stay.

He raised his gaze to his father's blue eyes, eyes so eerily like his own. Preston Cantrell was a proud man, but he was also vulnerable. John could see it, could see the hope. He took his hat off again with a sigh of resignation. "I'll stay for a few days."

A surge of relief rushed through Preston, and a cautious joy. He longed to reach out his hand, but something in John's defensive stance warned him that it was too soon. "Good," he said simply. He moved past John to the door and flung it open.

Bill pushed away from the wall, as did Gabriel, while Jennifer jumped up from her seat. They stared at Preston.

"Bill, come in here. We need to talk." Preston turned back to John as Bill worked his way around the two men into the study. "Give Bill and me some time alone. I'll call you in a bit, if you don't mind waiting."

John shrugged and stepped into the foyer. "I'll wait."

"Gabe, you can go on to bed," Preston said to his foreman. "Everything's all right here. I'd appreciate it if you'd make sure John's horse is settled for the night. They'll both be staying with us for a few days."

Gabe nodded and left without a word.

Preston's gaze fell on Jennifer. "Come here, Jennie." He held his hand out to her.

She moved to Preston's side, and he draped an arm around her shoulder, turning so they both faced John. "John, this is my goddaughter, Jennifer Mainwaring. She and her uncle are visiting from Philadelphia. Jennie, this is my son, John Novales Cantrell." There was no mistaking the pride in Preston's voice.

Both John and Jennifer glanced at Preston in surprise, then Jennifer turned back to John. He met her gaze with those blue eyes so like Preston's. In the light of the chandelier over John's head, she could see that he was indeed beautiful, as Rosa had suspected. Suddenly she remembered her manners and held out her hand.

"How nice to meet you." She hoped she sounded somewhat polite for Preston's sake, but it was proving very difficult to disguise the hostility she felt toward the man in black.

John accepted her hand and bowed over it. "I am delighted as well, Miss Mainwaring," he said smoothly, although the cold expression in his eyes told her he lied. He was no more delighted to meet her than she was to meet him.

She pulled her hand away as Preston spoke again.

"Did Barbara go up to bed?"

Jennifer shook her head. "She's with the children. David and Molly were both awakened and frightened by all the noise." She kept her reproachful gaze on John. "Rosa took them some warm milk a little while ago; she thinks that will help. Oliver has retired."

"You go on, too, honey." Preston kissed her forehead. "Thank you for waiting up, but as you can see, all is well." He looked at John. "I'll call you in a few minutes. I want you to meet your brother." At John's nod, he again went into the study and closed the door.

Jennifer had no interest in going to bed just yet. She crossed her arms over her chest and studied John as he wandered around the foyer with his hat in one hand. He moved with an animal-like grace, yet she could sense his tension. He was wound like a spring, ready to snap. Her distrust of him grew, heightened by renewed fear for her godfather. John Cantrell was a dangerous man; she had no doubt he was capable of killing. He did not seem to notice her intense perusal of him. As she watched, he looked into the darkened dining room, then stepped back as Rosa entered the foyer.

The Mexican woman stared up at him in shock. *"Madre de Dios,"* she whispered, crossing herself. "You have the eyes of *Señor* Cantrell." Her own expressive brown eyes narrowed. "Are you going to kill him?" she demanded.

"No," John answered wearily.

"Good." Rosa nodded with satisfaction, then stabbed John in the chest with a finger. "Otherwise, you answer to me, Rosa Garcia, and you won't like what I do to you if you hurt the *señor.*" She peered up at him. "You look tired, John Cantrell. You want some coffee?"

"Yes, ma'am, that would be nice."

Rosa turned her penetrating gaze on Jennifer. "And you, Miss Jennifer? You need some coffee, too, I think."

"No, thank you, Rosa, but Preston and Bill might. Mr. Cantrell will soon be joining them in the study."

Rosa nodded and turned back into the dining room. "I make a big pot then," she said as she walked away.

Jennifer kept her hostile gaze on John until he finally looked at her.

"Is there a problem, Miss Mainwaring?" he asked mildly. He hung his hat on the elaborate hat rack next to the door. It irritated Jennifer that he had chosen the hook next to Preston's hat.

"You ride in here like an avenging angel, or a denizen of hell—I'm not sure which—announce yourself as Preston's son, threaten to kill him, then have the nerve to ask if there is a problem?" Jennifer planted her hands on her hips and advanced toward him. "Yes, Mr. Cantrell, there is a problem. Many people, myself included, love Preston Cantrell, and we will not stand by and watch you harm him."

John glared at her. "I won't harm him."

"You said you'd *kill* him. I saw your face, the hatred and fury in your eyes. You had every intention of killing him."

"I no longer do."

Jennifer came to a stop right in front of him. "I don't believe you. That kind of rage doesn't just go away." She waved a hand to emphasize her statement, then pointed her finger at him. "If you harm Preston, I promise you will regret it."

John laughed harshly, with no humor. "Gabriel Horn has already threatened to kill me, and Rosa Garcia has just promised me hell if I hurt him." He derisively looked her up and down. "You're a skinny little rich girl, probably spoiled rotten. I've met your type before, too many times. You talk big, but what can you possibly do to me?"

Jennifer stiffened, then her hand whipped out and slapped his cheek, hard. "That's just the point," she spat. "I *am* rich, rich enough to hound you to the ends of the earth if I have to. I repeat—if you harm my godfather in any way, you will rue the day you met me."

The flare of rage in John's eyes made Jennifer want to step back, but she would not, nor would she lower her own gaze. She watched as he struggled to control himself, almost wishing he would make a move toward her. She would love to hit him again.

"I suppose I deserved that," he finally said. "It was very rude of me to insult your person. Please accept my apologies." He bowed stiffly.

"I won't accept anything from you, John Cantrell." Jennifer turned toward the stairs. "Just remember what I said. I can make your life miserable, and if you give me any reason to, so help me, I will."

"I'm sure you will, Miss Mainwaring." John stroked his stinging cheek and watched as she started up the stairs, leaving in her wake the faint, pleasing scent of orange blossom water. For all she was so thin, she carried herself with regal grace, and he appreciated the way her satin skirts swayed in time with the gentle movement of her hips. "If it's any comfort to you, I already regret meeting you," he impulsively called out.

The intriguing sway of the burgundy skirt stopped. Jennifer did not look back at him as she spoke coldly over her shoulder. "And I regret meeting you, Mr. Cantrell." She continued on up the stairs and disappeared down the hall.

John watched her go. Weariness set in, and he slumped down onto the uncomfortable bench she had vacated. What was wrong with him? He had never before insulted a lady to her face. Jennifer Mainwaring had threatened him because she was afraid for her godfather; her actions were understandable. His were not.

Nothing was going as he had planned, and now he was committed to remaining at the ranch for a day or two. He would suffer through it, then leave as diplomatically and as quickly as he could, avoiding the touchy Miss Mainwaring whenever possible.

Rosa came from the dining room with a tray just as the door to the study opened. Preston stepped into the foyer and beckoned to John. "Come on in," he said.

"I made coffee, *Señor* Preston." Rosa bustled past Preston into the study and came out a moment later without the tray. "I go to bed now. *Buenas noches, señores.*" She shot a warning glance at John before she again disappeared into the dining room.

"Good night, Rosa, and thank you," Preston called after her.

John rose, stifling a sigh, and followed Preston into the study. It was time to meet his brother. He hoped he would get along better with Bill than he had the others he had met tonight, but he wasn't counting on it.

Two

Engaged in a struggle to control her anger, Jennifer marched down the hall toward her room, her hands clenched into fists. She and John Cantrell were not going to get along, of that there was no doubt. She hoped the man did not plan to stay more than a day or two. Her much-anticipated and long-awaited visit with Preston would be ruined if she had to share him with John.

She slowed as Barbara backed into the hall from the children's room and quietly closed the door.

"Did they settle down?" Jennifer whispered.

"At last." Barbara's lips curved in a tired smile. "Molly went right to sleep after drinking her milk, but David is old enough to understand that we have a visitor, and he wanted to meet him. Although he is only three, he can be very stubborn." Her smile faded. "Is that man still here?"

Jennifer nodded. "But all is well, at least for now. He is talking with Bill and Preston."

"Is he Preston's son?"

"Evidently so. Preston introduced him as such. I guess he will be staying for a few days."

Barbara shook her head. "So Bill has a brother. I wonder how he's taking it."

Jennifer shrugged. "I don't know. He seemed fairly calm; certainly he is more calm than I am. I don't care much for John Cantrell, myself."

"He does seem very angry, almost dangerous." Barbara

glanced longingly toward the stairs. "I wish I could speak to Bill, but it might be best to leave them alone."

"I think so," Jennifer agreed. "You look tired, Barbara. Maybe you should wait for Bill in your room; you can rest there."

Barbara nodded. "You're right, I'm sure." She reached for Jennifer's hand. "I'm so glad to have finally met you, after hearing about you for so many years. I think we will be good friends."

"I know we will," Jennifer said with a smile. "Good night." She watched as Barbara went down the hall, then turned in the opposite direction, toward her own room. Ahead of her, a door opened, and Oliver stepped into the hall. He motioned impatiently.

"Come here at once," he commanded.

"Shh!" Jennifer put a finger to her lips and hurried to his side. "The children are finally asleep again, Oliver. Please don't awaken them. What is it?"

Oliver ushered her into his room, then closed the door with a strong push.

"Shh!" Jennifer repeated. "The children!"

"Forget the children, Jennifer." Oliver's face was flushed with anger as he glared at her. "That woman, that . . . *cook,* served my brandy in a cup!"

Jennifer gaped at him, unable to believe her ears. "What did you say?"

"My reaction exactly." Oliver straightened the belt at the waist of his expensive smoking jacket, then crossed his arms over his chest in self-righteous indignation.

"I can't believe you are serious," Jennifer said in a voice heavy with disgust.

Oliver's eyes narrowed. "What do you mean?"

Jennifer put her hands on her hips. "The brandy snifters are kept in Preston's study, a room into which Rosa could not go, on Preston's orders. This may come as a shock to you, Oliver, but there are more important things in this world than your desire for properly served brandy."

"Not to me." Oliver settled into the wing chair in front of the open window.

"What is the matter with you tonight?" Jennifer demanded. "Your attitude is embarrassing, to me as well as to you, although you don't seem to be aware of it."

Oliver raised an eyebrow. "It is quite inappropriate for you to speak to me in such a manner, Jennifer." His tone was soft, but there was no mistaking the warning in his cold eyes. "I trust you will not do so again."

Jennifer flushed. How she hated his condescending tone and vaguely threatening manner! She was tempted to defend herself, but she knew, as she had known at supper, that if she did, the situation would escalate into another of their heated battles. The hour was too late for that, and she would not risk waking the children.

"I apologize, Oliver." She paused, gritting her teeth when he arrogantly nodded, then continued. "These people are dear friends of mine, family, really. I do wish you would make an effort to be civil."

Oliver took a sip from the despised cup of brandy, his attractive face twisting in a grimace. He gave a dramatic sigh. "Very well, Jennifer. I shall make an effort—if you make certain that I am never again served brandy in a cup."

Jennifer eyed him warily, wondering if he was teasing her. She doubted it; Oliver did not have much of a sense of humor. "Very well," she said.

"Then go." Oliver waved her toward the door. "See how the little drama downstairs unfolds." He chuckled, the sound strangely humorless. "How interesting that Preston Cantrell's ill-conceived chicken has come home to roost. Wouldn't it be amusing if that Mexican bastard does indeed kill him? That would liven things up around here."

Jennifer stared at him, aghast. "The drama *has* unfolded, Oliver, and John Cantrell will not kill Preston."

His shoulders fell in mock disappointment. "How unfortunate. I shall have to seek entertainment elsewhere, then." His gaze fell on Jennifer's outraged face, and he chuckled again. "Go on, silly girl. Get out of here."

She whirled and stormed out into the hall. Only the knowledge that the children slept nearby kept her from slamming the door when she closed it behind her. As she made her way to her room, Jennifer tried to put Oliver and his twisted comments out of her mind. She would have a hard enough time sleeping tonight as it was.

Much later, Jennifer restlessly shifted against the pile of pillows behind her head, pulling her heavy braid forward over her shoulder as she did. In answer to a bothersome itch, she slipped a finger under the edge of her nightcap and scratched, irritated to find her hair damp with sweat. She gazed longingly at the opened French doors, hoping to see a breeze stir the curtains, but the filmy material hung limp and motionless. Surely it was as hot and as miserable here in August as it was in Philadelphia.

She had extinguished the lamp well over an hour ago, and still she could not get comfortable, nor would her troubled thoughts let her rest. The heat, combined with the unsettling appearance of John Cantrell, conspired to keep her awake. In exasperation, she threw back the sheet and scrambled out of bed. Perhaps some relief could be found on the balcony.

She crossed the darkened room to the French doors and slipped outside. It was still warm, but out here there did seem to be a bit of a breeze. She leaned against the wrought-iron railing and looked up at the moon, toying with the long ribbon of the nightcap that was tied under her chin.

The night sky was beautifully clear, without a hint of a cloud. Cheerful sparkling stars dotted the darkened canopy of the heavens. From faraway she heard the call of what she now recognized as a coyote, to whose plaintive song she had been introduced in Wyoming during the journey west. Her gaze wandered over the moonlit hills that surrounded the ranch compound. She would enjoy a ride in the morning. She had been cooped up in railroad cars and horse-drawn coaches for too long. The seemingly endless days of travel had wearied her mind as well as her body.

Jennifer laughed at herself at that thought. As a child of eight, she had traveled to California with her father in 1858 shortly after her mother's death; they had come by ship around Cape Horn and had returned to Philadelphia that same way two years later. The trip then had taken just over three months. Why had three weeks of train travel seemed so much more tiring? This recent trip had even been broken by a short stay in Wyoming.

Perhaps her young age had contributed to her enjoyment of that long-ago sea voyage, for she had found the journey fascinating. The days had been restful, as had the nights, when she had been lulled to sleep by the endless rocking of the ship. She remembered missing her mother terribly, but did not remember arriving at Preston's ranch in such an exhausted state.

Jennifer stretched her hands over her head and took a deep breath of the sweet-smelling air. The scent was familiar to her, stirring long-forgotten memories of the many months she had lived here as a child. A sense of peace settled over her, a sense of homecoming. After all, she had been born in California, so it really was her home. She leaned against the iron railing and let her gaze wander over the moonlit Spanish-style courtyard around which Preston's *hacienda* was built.

The courtyard was centered with an elaborate fountain, whose gentle whisper of falling water she found soothing. A riot of flowers—azaleas and bougainvillea, roses and alyssum—offered their scent to the night, along with that of flowering herbs such as lavender and chamomile. The courtyard was an inviting place, one that Jennifer intended to explore more fully in the morning. She was curious to see what changes, if any, had been made in the fourteen years since she had last been here.

A yawn escaped her. Perhaps now she would be able to sleep. She pushed away from the railing and turned toward the French doors just as she heard another door open on the floor below. She remained on the balcony, but ducked back into the shadows along the wall. Preston and John moved into view.

"The room will be yours as long as you want it." The sound of Preston's voice drifted up to Jennifer's ears. She could not make out the words of John's low reply. As she watched, the two men crossed the quiet courtyard to what Jennifer knew was a guest room in the single-storied west wing. A flood of light soon came through the opened door, as well as from the multi-paned window. She could hear a murmur of voices; a moment later, Preston came out and closed the door behind him.

He retraced his steps across the courtyard. Just before he passed from Jennifer's view, Preston turned and looked back in the direction of the guest room, then continued on his way. Jennifer heard the click of the door below closing.

She let out her breath, surprised to realize she had been holding it. Her jaw tightened with determination as she stared at John Cantrell's room. She would watch his every move. The memory of his panther-like pacing of the foyer came to her mind, reinforcing her assessment of him as a dangerous man. Even if he had been sincere when he said he no longer intended to kill Preston, Jennifer knew there were other ways to settle old scores. He could try to hurt Preston by sabotaging the ranch in some way, or he could attempt to destroy him financially. Mentally, she repeated the words she had earlier said to John: *That kind of rage doesn't just go away.*

His shadow moved across the lighted window, then the lamp was abruptly extinguished. Jennifer yawned again. She heard a sound from the hallway outside her other door, suggesting that Preston had retired to his own room. The house settled into silence. It was late; surely now she could sleep. Again she moved toward the French doors, pausing to glance

back one last time at John Cantrell's room. Her eyes widened
as she realized the door was opening. She darted to a position
against the stuccoed wall and pressed against its coolness,
her heart pounding.

John stepped outside and closed his door, then waited for
several moments. Apparently satisfied he was alone, he
crossed the courtyard to a gate set in the opposite wall and
disappeared from view.

Again, Jennifer let herself breathe. John wasn't wearing his
hat, nor was he carrying it, so she knew he wasn't simply
leaving. What should she do? Convinced he was up to no
good, she hurried across her room, pausing only to grab a
thin shawl from the wing chair in front of the fireplace. She
slipped out into the hall. A glance in both directions revealed
no one. She draped the shawl over her shoulders and made
her silent way down to the first floor and into Preston's study.

Moonlight poured in through the big, uncurtained window
behind Preston's desk. If Jennifer remembered the layout of
the *hacienda* correctly, the gate through which John had
passed led to a yard that could be seen from this window.
She crept to one side of the window and frantically searched
every visible corner of the yard.

Nothing.

Where did he go? Was there any way he could get to Preston's room without coming through the house? Jennifer leaned
against the wall, shaking her head, suddenly feeling foolish.
There was no way John could know which room was Preston's; she would have heard them if Preston had given him
a tour of the house, just as she had heard Bill come up to
his room earlier.

She again searched the yard, looking for any sign of the
man. Her shoulders slumped in disappointment. She was
about to give up when she noticed a furtive movement by
the barn doors. A figure in black appeared, then vanished. A
moment later, lantern light flowed around the slightly opened
door, but it instantly dimmed. A grim smile curved her lips.

Jennifer left the house through the main door, grateful to Rosa for keeping the wide black iron hinges well oiled. She darted across the yard, wincing at the small stones that dug into her bare feet, and paused at the barn door. The low murmur of a man's voice reached her ears. Who could John Cantrell be meeting in the barn in the middle of the night?

Convinced that the sound of her racing heart would give her away, Jennifer took a few deep breaths to calm herself. Her stomach twisted with fear, and she could feel small beads of perspiration on her forehead. If she had any sense at all, she would return to the house and awaken Preston, or go to the bunkhouse and get Mr. Horn. But then John Cantrell would have a chance to get away, to do whatever he intended to do.

Almost soundlessly, she slipped into the barn, where she was greeted by the pleasant, familiar smell of horses and fresh straw. She loved animals, and under other circumstances would have enjoyed coming here, but now the barn seemed an ominous place, filled with shadows. And it seemed even warmer here than in her bedroom. Jennifer shook off her thoughts and crept forward.

The lighted lantern was a distance away, placed on a nail protruding from a support post of one of the stalls. The low sound of a man's voice continued. As stealthily as she could, Jennifer made her way past several empty stalls, ignoring the scratchy pieces of straw that pricked her feet. Finally, she neared the lantern and saw John in a stall with the huge black stallion. He spoke to the horse as he brushed the animal's glossy coat with long, rhythmic strokes.

Jennifer silently berated herself for a fool. He had only come to check on his horse, as any decent man would have done.

A trickle of moisture ran down the side of her face, and she tugged at the high neck of her nightdress. It was time to return to her bed. She was too hot and too tired to deal with John Cantrell tonight.

The sound of his voice softened, then ceased. Jennifer glanced back at the stall, and her heart stopped. The horse tossed its head and whickered, but the man had disappeared.

Now her heart started pounding again, and she backed toward the door. Her gaze flew around the dimly lit cavern of the barn, searching, finding nothing. The complete silence was unnerving.

She hesitated near the door, and suddenly a powerful arm wrapped around her from behind at the same moment a hand clapped over her mouth. The terrified scream in her throat came out as a muffled squeak.

"Never try to sneak up on a wolf." The man's voice was low and dangerous, a voice Jennifer recognized immediately. She grabbed the hand at her mouth and tried to pull it away as she struggled uselessly against John Cantrell's far superior strength. He released her mouth and wrapped his other arm around her, pulling her tightly against the length of his body.

"Get . . . your hands . . . off . . . me," Jennifer ordered breathlessly. She twisted and fought to no avail.

He strode back toward the lantern, easily carrying her along with him. When they reached the pale circle of light, he relaxed his grip and pushed her back against a stall gate.

"Miss Mainwaring. How lovely to see you again." John folded his arms across his chest. Despite his polite words, he sounded anything but pleased.

He seemed very tall to her, and lean. A pearl-handled pistol rested in the holster of a black gunbelt strapped around his narrow hips. The silver conchos that ran down the long lengths of his legs reflected the feeble light of the lantern and contrasted sharply with his black clothes. The way his blue eyes glittered did indeed remind Jennifer of a wolf. A beautiful, dangerous wolf. She felt trapped. It was not a comfortable feeling, and to disguise it, she rebuked him.

"You have no right to manhandle me, Mr. Cantrell!" She straightened the shawl around her shoulders and pulled it across her breasts, suddenly very aware that she wore little more than her nightdress. The ribbon at her throat had come untied, and it felt as if her nightcap were slipping off to one side, but she resisted the temptation to straighten it as well. She raised her chin and glared at him, determined that he would not intimidate her.

John raised a mocking eyebrow. "And you have no right to follow me, to spy on me. I am a guest in my father's home, just as you are. Free to come and go as I choose."

"You are not free to harm him! When I saw you sneak out of your room, I followed to make certain that was not your intention." She tossed her long braid back over her shoulder. "Since I am now reasonably assured that Preston will sleep unmolested, I shall leave you to your horse." With all the dignity she could muster, Jennifer stepped carefully on the prickly straw, headed toward the door.

"Miss Mainwaring, have you heard of *El Lobo?*"

Jennifer stopped, but did not look back at him. His words sounded familiar. Although she had been fluent in Spanish years ago, she had lost much of it. "My Spanish is a little rusty. What does it mean?"

"Le loup?"

Her French was not rusty. *The wolf.* She turned and faced him. "Why do you keep referring to a wolf?"

"In Mexico, I was known as *El Lobo.* I earned my name, Miss Mainwaring, through six long years as an agent for the Juarez revolution against the French." John started toward her. "Think of a wolf."

It took all of Jennifer's considerable willpower to force herself not to move as he slowly circled her. He was close. Too close. Another trickle of sweat made its way down her cheek.

"A wolf is not only smart, but cunning as well. Strong, fearless, a good hunter. A wolf is . . . dangerous." He stopped behind her, so near that Jennifer could feel his breath on her neck. His voice was seductively low. "Very dangerous, Miss Mainwaring." Suddenly his tone harshened. "Do not ever follow me again. You cannot do so without my knowing

you are there. And do not suddenly come up behind me."
His hands clamped down on her shoulders. "There's no telling
how I will react if I am startled, what I might do."

Jennifer shivered.

"Are you cold?" he asked with mock concern.

"No," she snapped, and jerked away from him. "I'm very
warm, although I doubt you care." She glared at him. "I understand your warning quite clearly, Mr. Cantrell. You watch
your step around my godfather, and I won't be forced to follow you. But I will be watching you." She marched toward
the door.

"You don't really sleep in that, do you?"

Jennifer was so surprised by his question that she whirled
to face him. "I beg your pardon?" she demanded frostily.

John advanced on her, and when he was close enough, he
reached out to finger the long sleeve of her nightdress. "This.
And that cap. Surely you don't sleep in them."

Jennifer pulled her arm from his reach and drew herself
up to take advantage of every inch her slight frame would
allow. She still had to look up into his face. "Mr. Cantrell."
In Philadelphia, the cold tone of her voice would have socially
ruined the recipient of her ire. "A gentleman never refers to
a lady's nightwear. But then, you have not exhibited much of
the manner of a gentleman."

"Miss Mainwaring." John crossed his arms over his chest
and looked down at her, the suspicion of a smile tugging at
the corner of his mouth. "A lady would never leave the privacy and safety of her boudoir wearing only a nightdress, a
cap, and a flimsy shawl." Her peered down at her feet. "My
God, miss. You are even barefoot."

Startled, Jennifer dropped her gaze to where her naked toes
peeked out from under the hem of her nightdress. She felt
the warmth of embarrassment flood her face. Before she
could think of anything to say, John reached out and touched
her cheek.

"And you are overheated." His voice curiously softened.

"Your loyalty and protectiveness toward Preston Cantrell are admirable. Go back to bed and rest easy; no harm will come to him tonight by my hand." His hand fell to his side.

Jennifer eyed him warily, then finally nodded. "Thank you for the reassurance, Mr. Cantrell." She turned toward the door and had almost reached that welcoming portal when John spoke again.

"Your nightdress is too heavy for this season and this climate, and your nightcap only makes you warmer still. You will never sleep comfortably if you insist on wearing them. I advise you to sleep naked, as I do."

Unable to stifle a gasp, Jennifer looked back over her shoulder. John had not moved, except that now the hinted smile had burst forth in all its glory. She clamped her mouth shut and stomped from the barn, refusing to give any indication that her tender feet were tormented by cruel pebbles and stabbing pieces of straw.

John Cantrell's irritating laugh followed her.

Three

"Good morning, Miss Jennifer."

Rosa's cheerful voice came to Jennifer from what seemed far away. She moaned and buried her face in the pillows. Surely she had fallen asleep only moments ago.

"If you are going riding with Bill and Barbara, you must get ready. I brought you coffee, and fruit and bread. Did you sleep well?" Bright sunlight filled the room when Rosa swept back the curtains at the window.

Jennifer sat up and rubbed her eyes. "Not really," she admitted. "It seemed very hot." She pulled at the ribbons of the nightcap and, when they released, jerked the cap from her head.

Rosa advanced on the bed, a frown on her normally cheerful face. She placed a hand on Jennifer's forehead. "Are you sick?"

"No, just hot."

Dropping her hand to the sleeve of Jennifer's heavy cotton nightdress, Rosa nodded. "Of course you are. You cannot wear this in the summer and sleep comfortably."

Jennifer found Rosa's innocent repeat of John Cantrell's words very annoying. She scrambled off the bed and over to the commode where the washbasin awaited. "This is what I sleep in, Rosa, all the time. It is a proper nightdress for a lady."

"Perhaps in Philadelphia it is proper, but here in California, it is foolish—just as that cap is," Rosa retorted, crossing her arms over her chest. "This summer has been especially hot, and we are having a drought." She eyed Jennifer's nightdress. "Do you want to sleep or no?"

Surprised by Rosa's tone, Jennifer turned to look at her. No disrespect showed on the Mexican woman's face, only honest concern. Jennifer sighed and tugged irritably at the high neck of the offending nightdress. "I want to sleep."

Rosa nodded in satisfaction. "I will have my daughter Francisca make you a sleeping shift this very day. She is only twelve, but she is very gifted with a needle. You will sleep better tonight." She approached Jennifer and touched her shoulder, examining her from head to foot, then moved her hand from Jennifer's shoulder in a straight line and touched her own forehead. "Francisca must know how long to make the shift," she explained. She planted her hands at Jennifer's waist, measuring, then pulled out the sides of the nightdress. "You must also have room to move."

Jennifer waited patiently as Rosa made a circle around her. She doubted that the woman was much over five feet tall. Somehow, she had seemed much taller when Jennifer was a child. Rosa had filled out since then and now carried her neat hourglass figure with the dignity and confidence of a woman secure in her place in the world. She exuded a sense of peace that Jennifer envied.

"You are tall, Miss Jennifer, and very beautiful," she squeezed Jennifer's hand lightly, "but you are much too thin, and perhaps a little unhappy."

Jennifer pulled her hand away. "I beg your pardon?"

Rosa shrugged unapologetically. "For those who care enough to look, it shows in your eyes. I care, and *Señor* Preston, he cares, but that uncle of yours," she snorted in disgust, "he does not care for anyone but himself. By the way, how does one so young as he come to be your uncle?"

"Oliver is my father's much younger brother," Jennifer explained. "When my grandparents died, he came to live with us. I was ten; he, sixteen. It was shortly after we returned to Philadelphia in 1860."

"Well, he and his airs do not impress me," Rosa said firmly. "I also do not like how he treats you. You should throw him out."

"Throw him out where?" Jennifer asked in exasperation. "He is my uncle. One does not just throw one's relatives away."

"That one you should. He is not good for you."

"I do not wish to discuss it further," Jennifer said stiffly. Rosa's words stung, because Jennifer privately agreed with her. She had never been close to her uncle, and the volatile nature of their relationship had worsened over the past few years. She moved to the bureau as she yanked the thin ribbon from the end of her braid, then picked up her brush.

Rosa pulled Jennifer's green riding habit from the huge mahogany wardrobe. *"Señor* Preston always says I am not one to mince the words, Miss Jennifer. I remember when you were a child; you were happier then. You lost your mama when you were too young." She turned with an affectionate smile. "I will be like your mama while you are here, just as before."

At that, Jennifer laughed. "Rosa, you are not old enough to be my mama."

"I have reached thirty years now, and you . . ."

"Twenty-three," Jennifer supplied helpfully.

"Sooo—" Rosa's brow furrowed as she calculated, then her eyes widened and she shrugged again, with a big smile. "So, I am a very young mama. I will teach you to live comfortably in the heat of this land, and I will feed you well." She looked doubtfully at the garments in her arms. "Like the nightdress, these are too heavy. You will be too warm if you ride in these clothes."

Jennifer's smile faded and she clenched her jaw, peevishly wondering if any of her wardrobe would meet with Rosa's approval. She dropped the brush on the bureau and snatched the riding habit from Rosa's arms. "I will wear it anyway," she snapped, then noticed the other woman's hurt expression. She softened her tone. "Thank you for your concern, Rosa, but I don't need a mama. I do need help dressing, however."

Rosa marched to the door. "I will send Francisca," she announced, and swept out into the hall, her short body held with stiff pride. The door closed behind her.

With a troubled sigh, Jennifer sat on the edge of the rumpled bed, the riding habit still in her arms. "I am just as nasty as Oliver," she muttered.

A half an hour later, Jennifer descended the stairs, resplendent in her forest-green riding habit, with the overlong skirt draped over one arm and carrying a parasol in one gloved hand. She also wore a pert hat of matching green decorated with a white silk scarf, and her hair was pulled into a smooth chignon at the back of her head. She paused at the open double doors of the great room, or *sala,* as Preston called it, but no one was there, and the study also stood empty. The sound of voices reached her from the front veranda. She stepped outside, a little disconcerted to find Preston, Bill, and Barbara waiting for her. Several saddled horses were tied to the railing that encircled most of the veranda.

"Good morning, Jennie." Preston came to her side to place a kiss on her cheek.

"Good morning. I apologize for keeping you all waiting." She nodded to each in turn.

"You haven't kept us," Bill assured her. "We are also waiting for John and your uncle."

Jennifer's heart sank. "So they will be joining us." Try as she might, she could not keep a note of dismay from her voice.

"I will be." John Cantrell's mocking voice came from the side of the house. A moment later, he walked into view, leading his stallion. "Unless you have objections, Miss Mainwaring?"

"Of course not, Mr. Cantrell." Jennifer's grip on the parasol tightened as she struggled to be civil for Preston's sake. She made the mistake of glancing at John Cantrell's handsome face, where the taunting expression in his blue eyes was easy to read. "I'm quite certain I don't care what you do."

John merely grinned.

Jennifer tried to ignore the startled expression on Preston's face and was saved from trying to explain her rudeness, or worse yet, apologize for it, when Oliver came out onto the veranda. He frowned as he looked over the waiting horses.

"Surely you do not expect me to ride one of those . . . cow ponies, with a Western saddle." He struck the side of one of his highly polished boots with his quirt.

Preston raised an eyebrow as he took in Oliver's proper English riding outfit, a movement Jennifer could not help but notice was identical to the one John used with such derisive excellence. She found the resemblance in the two men's expressions disturbing.

"You *are* in the West now, Mr. Mainwaring," said Preston. "And you are on a cattle ranch. Most of our horses are 'cow ponies,' and we have only Western saddles. If that will not suit you, you may have to amuse yourself in another way this morning."

Oliver's quirt struck his boot again. "I will manage," he said tightly. "Which of these nags has been assigned to me?"

"The paint." Preston gestured toward a sturdy animal tied at the end of the railing. "Jennie, the sorrel mare is yours. I'll help you up."

Jennifer moved toward the beautiful mare, stopping at her head. "Hello, sweetheart," she crooned as she held her hand under the animal's nostrils. She stroked the mare's neck and saw that her saddle also was a Western-style one. Suddenly, wearing her fancy riding habit did not seem like a good idea.

"Jennifer needs a sidesaddle," Oliver declared.

"There are none to be found on the ranch, Mr. Mainwaring. They are impractical and dangerous," Bill explained. "Our horses are not trained to them." He and John had already mounted, as had Barbara, who rode astride in comfort thanks to the wide-legged split skirt she wore. Jennifer could not help but admire the practicality of Barbara's skirt.

"No proper lady would ride astride, and my niece certainly will not." Oliver moved away from his horse. "Jennifer and I will remain here."

Jennifer looked at Barbara's pretty face, now flushed with embarrassment. Oliver did not seem to even notice that he had insulted Barbara. Bill, however, did, judging from the black look on his normally easygoing features, as did the scowling Preston.

Perhaps it was John Cantrell's irritating presence. Perhaps it was the fact that Rosa's prediction that she would be too warm in her riding habit was already threatening to prove true. Perhaps it was Oliver's continuing rudeness. Whatever the reason, Jennifer no longer cared if her actions or her uncurbed tongue triggered an argument with her uncle. The man had gone too far.

She glared at Oliver as she handed her parasol to Preston and, in one easy motion, gathered the reins and swung up into the saddle. She arranged her long skirts to cover her legs, draping the extra folds of green velvet over the horse's rump and flanks, then reached for the parasol Preston held up to her. She turned the mare toward Barbara. "My uncle is mistaken, Barbara. Please forgive his thoughtlessness. Proper ladies ride astride when the occasion calls for it."

"Jennifer!" Oliver barked. "I forbid you to ride like that. Where is your sense of decorum?"

Jennifer opened the parasol and shaded her face from the sun before she turned back to her uncle. "In Philadelphia, Oliver, where I suggest you send yours," she said coolly. "We are in California now and shall not offend our hosts by criticizing their way of life. Are you coming with us or not?"

The mare tossed her head and chewed nervously on the bit, anxious to go. Jennifer easily controlled the animal with one hand on the reins, holding her parasol with the other, her defiant gaze never leaving Oliver's face.

Oliver hesitated, staring in angry astonishment at his rebellious niece. "I will not be joining you," he answered finally. "And if you insist on behaving in such an unladylike fashion, we will discuss this in private when you return."

Bill and Barbara headed their mounts toward the gate, while John and Preston waited for Jennifer.

"We will discuss it when I return," Jennifer repeated.

"I did not know you could ride astride, Jennifer."

"There is much you don't know about me."

Oliver's mouth tightened. "Who taught you?" he demanded. "If it was the stableman at home, I'll fire him."

Jennifer glared at him. "Preston and Bill taught me, when Father and I lived here those two years after my mother died." The mare turned in a half circle, eager to follow the others. Jennifer looked back over her shoulder at Oliver. "Good day, uncle." She touched her heels to the mare's sides. John and Preston took a position on either side of her, and they headed toward the impressive gate that heralded the entrance to the compound.

Oliver watched her go, striking the side of his boot with the quirt again and again, his jaw clenched. Jennifer had changed in the week since the short visit he had allowed her with her friends in Wyoming. Alarmingly so. She had never before dared to talk to him in such a manner in front of other people.

He wondered if he had made a mistake by agreeing to postpone their journey long enough to stop in Laramie City so that Jennifer could attend the wedding of Susannah Duncan and Conor O'Rourke. At the same time, he knew that if he hadn't allowed her to attend the wedding, he would have never heard the end of it. Jennifer's two closest friends were Susannah and Alina Parker, Conor's cousin. Oliver was convinced that Jennifer would have found a way to be there for that damned wedding, even if it had meant running away, as absurd as that seemed. But it disturbed him that since leaving Wyoming and continuing west, Jennifer seemed moody and dissatisfied, prone to arguing with him over the slightest matters.

Oliver turned back into the house. Perhaps it was just the fatigue of the journey, for they had left Philadelphia almost three weeks ago. Jennifer would revert to her usually pleasant, pliable self when they returned home. He would encourage Bradley Ames to ask for her hand, and see her married into one of the wealthiest and most influential families in Philadelphia. She had balked on that subject long enough. Then he would find a wife for himself, one wealthy enough to free him from the financial worries that plagued him now. He would settle down, finished at last with his responsibilities toward his argumentative and unappreciative niece.

The group of five riders left the *hacienda* compound and headed east. Jennifer rode at Preston's right, John at his left, while Bill and Barbara brought up the rear. Preston explained to Jennifer and John that the ranch extended to the mountains of the Diablo range in the distance. The *Rancho de Buena Ventura,* owned by the Noriega family, bordered the Santa Maria to the south, and the lands of the old Santa Clara mission lay to the west. North was the Henderson ranch and beyond that, at a distance of some thirty miles, the city of San José.

The new dam had been built in the foothills of the Diablo Mountains. Completed only a month earlier, the dam would eventually double the yield of their pastureland and allow him to support many more cattle, Preston claimed. He estimated they would reach the dam within a half an hour.

Jennifer fell back and allowed the rest of the group to pull ahead a short distance. She was content to be alone, to let her thoughts wander as her gaze roamed over the expanse of land that made up the Santa Maria. They rode through a shallow valley surrounded by gently rolling hills dotted here and there with evergreen oak trees and contented cattle. A narrow creek meandered along the base of the southern hills. It was a beautiful, pastoral scene, one that helped keep Jennifer's mind from the coming confrontation with Oliver. She refused to think about her uncle now.

She shifted in the saddle, thankful that she had ridden astride the previous week in Wyoming. With any luck, her legs would not be too sore tonight from the day's excursion. A trickle of perspiration coursed down her cheek, and she wiped at it with irritation. As she had feared, Rosa's prediction about being uncomfortable in the riding habit had come true. The tight jacket seemed plastered to her body, and she could feel a growing circle of wetness under each arm. More than ever, Jennifer envied Barbara the wide-brimmed hat and split skirt she wore.

John Cantrell still rode next to Preston. Jennifer studied the man in black. She could not help but notice that he was an expert rider, for he seemed as one with the huge stallion. His lean body moved with easy grace in response to the animal's gait. Again, she wondered what game he played. He had given up his desire for revenge too easily. As she watched, Preston laughed at something John said, and Jennifer's heart lurched. She hoped her godfather was not setting himself up for betrayal and heartbreak at the hands of his newly discovered son.

Preston drew up and waited for her, as did John. Bill and Barbara joined them.

"The dam is behind that hill to the right up ahead." Preston pointed as he spoke. "It's an earthen dam, with the latest in flow control equipment. Cost me a pretty penny, I'll tell you, but it will be worth it. Although the reservoir won't be full because of the dry summer we've had, I think you'll find it impressive."

Jennifer smiled at his enthusiasm. "Let's go see it, then."

"All right." Preston eagerly led the way at a gallop. John held back as Bill and Barbara chased after Preston.

"Isn't your arm tired from holding that parasol?" he asked.

"No, Mr. Cantrell, it is not," Jennifer lied. Her arm ached, but she dared not risk a sunburn. And now, having seen the familiar mockery in his blue eyes, she would carry the parasol into the next century if necessary. She urged the mare to a gallop, knowing as she did that John's stallion would easily keep pace with her.

The magnificent animal raced by her, throwing up clumps of mud as he passed. Jennifer cried out in outrage as the wet globs stuck to her skirt; one hit her cheek. She pulled back on the reins, curbing the mare to a walk.

John immediately slowed his mount and returned to her side. "What is it?" he demanded, then noticed the mud. Puzzled, he looked at the ground. "Where did that come from?"

"From your horse, sir!" Jennifer trembled with fury. "You could have ridden farther off to the side!" She brushed at the mud on her face.

John guided his horse alongside hers, pulling a handkerchief from his vest pocket. He leaned out of the saddle and wiped her cheek. "Miss Mainwaring, Preston mentioned that there has been a drought for months. How was I to know there would be mud?"

Surprised and disconcerted by his act of kindness, Jennifer snatched the handkerchief from his hand and rubbed her cheek. "I don't know," she admitted.

"I do apologize for dirtying your outfit," he said sincerely. "I had no idea the ground was muddy."

Jennifer sighed. "I am certain you didn't, Mr. Cantrell." She stared at the soggy earth. "Do you think there is a ground spring nearby?"

"No." John studied the surrounding terrain. "If there were a spring nearby, the grass would be green. There hasn't been any rain, yet this is like a recent rainfall." Suddenly he straightened, shading his eyes with a gloved hand as he stared in the direction of the other riders. "Or a broken dam," he whispered.

"Oh, no." Horrified, Jennifer followed his gaze; as she watched, Preston, Bill, and Barbara rode out of sight.

"Let's go!" John shouted. His stallion jumped to a gallop. Jennifer folded the parasol shut and quickly went after him, no longer concerned about sunburn or flying mud. As she and John closed the distance to the dam, the ground became more and more saturated, until they were riding through a shallow lake. They rounded the curve of the hill and pulled to a stop.

Preston, Bill, and Barbara sat their mounts, stunned into silence, as were Jennifer and John. The earthen dam had been destroyed, literally blown apart. The stout logs that had formed the breastwork were scattered about the area, now twisted and broken. Here and there a length of pipe or a piece of metal told the fate of Preston's new flow control. A gaping hole in the center of what had been the dam showed that a lake of mud was all that remained of the small reservoir. A solitary cow had wandered into the quagmire and now bawled plaintively, unable to extricate itself.

"This had to have happened several hours ago," Bill commented quietly. "The water is well dispersed."

Preston rubbed his jaw and nodded. "Probably last night. The *hacienda* is too far away for us to have heard the blast."

Jennifer urged her horse to his side, where the look on his face caused her stomach to tighten with concern. "Are you saying someone used explosives and deliberately destroyed the dam?"

"Look at it," Preston answered, waving a hand. "This was no accident, and it was not caused by nature. Someone is trying to ruin me."

"Who would want to do such a thing?" Jennifer asked. "And why?"

"I don't know," Preston said grimly. "But I intend to find

out." He started his horse forward, speaking over his shoulder. "Let's free that cow, Bill, then get home. I want some men back here this afternoon. We'll begin rebuilding immediately. No one will scare me off my land." He rode off, followed by Bill.

Jennifer turned to Barbara. "Has something like this happened before?"

"Nothing so big." Barbara stared after the two men with an anguished expression on her face. "Little things: cut fence wire, stampeded cattle, uprooted fruit trees. Irritating, but easily fixed. This is different."

"How long ago did these acts of sabotage begin?"

"Only a few weeks." Barbara started her mount after the men. "But nothing like this," she repeated miserably, shaking her head. "Preston was so proud of his dam."

Jennifer watched as Barbara joined Preston and Bill, then she shifted her gaze to John. He had ridden up to the remains of the dam and seemed to be examining the blast site. Her mouth tightened as she remembered her own thoughts of the night before. *There were other ways to settle old scores.*

She urged her horse forward, coming to a halt at his side. "Do you know anything about this, Mr. Cantrell?" she demanded harshly.

John stiffened. He turned to face her, his eyes narrowed with hostility, his jaw set. "What are you implying?"

"I am not implying anything. I am asking you a straightforward question. Did you have anything to do with the destruction of this dam?" Jennifer did not take her eyes from his face, although her horse moved about nervously in the thick mud.

"No, I did not, and I resent your suggestion that I did."

"I am not concerned with your resentment or your ruffled feelings, John Cantrell. I am concerned with the well-being of my godfather, and I find it an interesting coincidence that these acts of destruction against Preston began shortly before your appearance here."

He glared at her, tight-lipped, his blue eyes seeming to blaze. "Think what you will, Miss Mainwaring. I'll not waste my breath trying to change your unfavorable opinion of me. Nor will I dignify this discussion by allowing it to continue." He turned his stallion's head away from her and rode off, leaving Jennifer to stare after him in helpless frustration.

Four

No one spoke on the ride back to the *hacienda*. Jennifer and Barbara left their mounts and the men at the barn and crossed the yard. As she approached the main house, Jennifer could not help but notice its elegant simplicity. Preston had built his *hacienda* of wood and stucco in the Spanish style, and when she entered the cool foyer, she once again appreciated the interior decor, done in leather and wood, accented here and there with a modern Victorian piece. The overall feel of the home was one of welcoming comfort.

Preston had worked so hard to make a lovely home for his family, had worked for over thirty years to build the ranch into the successful enterprise it now was. Even as hot as she was, Jennifer shivered with the force of the rage that roared through her at the thought that someone would deliberately try to destroy all that Preston had built.

Rosa came from the dining room. "It is true?" she asked in a troubled voice. "The dam is destroyed?"

Barbara nodded. "Yes. It was blown up."

"Madre de Dios." Rosa crossed herself. "Who is doing these things to *Señor* Preston?"

"We don't know, Rosa. But Preston and Bill will find out and put a stop to it." Barbara took her hat off and hung it on a hook. "Where are the children?"

"In the courtyard with Francisca. I fix their noon meal now."

"Thank you. I'll go see them, and we'll be in soon. Will you join us, Jennifer?"

Jennifer smiled and shook her head. "Thank you, but I think my first priority must be a bath." She indicated her soiled skirt.

"I'll see you later then." Barbara left them.

Rosa stepped closer to Jennifer, eyeing her curiously. "You do need a bath," she admitted.

"I know." Jennifer took her gloves off. "And you were right about the riding habit being too hot. You will be pleased to know that I was very uncomfortable."

"No, I am not pleased. I do not wish you to be uncomfortable. I just know when I am right." Rosa's words were stated with simple honesty.

Jennifer could not suppress a laugh. "And you were right." Then she sobered. "I'm sorry I was rude to you this morning, Rosa. You were only trying to help me."

"Is all right, Miss Jennifer." Rosa flashed a warm smile.

"No, it isn't, but I appreciate your graciousness. I was acting like my uncle." She grimaced in distaste. "Speaking of whom, where is he?"

Rosa waved toward the stairs. "His majesty is in his room. He wants to see you immediately."

Jennifer shook her head rebelliously. "He will have to wait. I must bathe first."

Rosa nodded in approval. "Good for you. You are not at his call and beck. You are the lady of his house—of your own house, really—a woman grown. He can wait for you. Go now, Miss Jennifer. I will have one of the men bring up the tub and some warm water."

"Thank you, Rosa." Jennifer gave the woman a quick hug. "And please do not call me 'Miss Jennifer.' When I was a child, you used to call me 'Jennie.' I wish you would again."

Rosa's smile widened. "Very well, Jennie. I like that better." She disappeared into the dining room.

Jennifer draped the long side of her skirt over one arm and

slowly climbed the stairs, feeling weary and discouraged. The morning had started out so promising, and had ended so badly. She would never forget the look on Preston's face as he stared at his ruined dam. He had tried to hide his emotions, but she had seen his shock, hurt, anger, and, finally, his resolve. He would not be defeated by acts of vandalism. Jennifer hoped for Preston's sake that John Cantrell was not behind them, but her suspicions about him had not been laid to rest, his heated denials notwithstanding.

She made her way to her room and took off the jaunty hat. A wad of mud had landed on the white scarf that encircled the crown. With a sigh, she looked in the mirror, then regretted she had. Her cheek was dirty, her nose sunburned, her hair dishevelled, her riding habit filthy.

"Hardly a picture of a fine lady now," she said sarcastically to her image. She unbuttoned the jacket of her outfit and had slipped it off her shoulders when a strident pounding on her door startled her.

"For heaven's sake, come in!" She allowed the jacket to fall to the floor.

The door opened, but rather than a man with the tin tub, as Jennifer expected, she saw in the mirror Oliver's reflection. He did not look pleased.

"I told that housekeeper I wanted to see you immediately," he snarled as he slammed the door.

Jennifer whirled to face him. "She gave me the message. I will speak with you after I have bathed. I am certain you can appreciate my need for a bath." She held out the folds of her mud-splattered skirt.

Oliver advanced on her, ignoring her comment. "How dare you defy me in front of those peasants?" His eyes fairly flashed with rage. Never had Jennifer seen him so angry. The thought occurred to her that he might strike her. Although he had never done so, he looked as if he could now. She drew herself up, refusing to allow him to intimidate her.

"You insulted Barbara, Oliver, unforgivably. And you didn't

even notice what you had done. I'm surprised Bill didn't come off his horse after you; he would have been within his rights. I tried to cover your dismal lapse of manners in the only way I knew how—to put myself in the same 'unladylike' class as Barbara."

"You challenged me, scolded me, *humiliated* me!" Oliver grabbed her upper arms and shook her. "In front of Preston Cantrell and his sorry family!"

Jennifer lost her tenuous hold on her already frayed temper. She twisted out of Oliver's grip. "I will tolerate no more of your vile tongue! Nor will I suffer your manhandling. How dare you touch me in such a manner? I'm not some child you can chastise at whim. You are in the wrong. You have behaved as a rude, brooding bore since the minute we arrived at the Santa Maria, and I will stand no more of it. If you are so miserable here, leave."

Oliver stared at her, then nodded slowly. "You are right. We will leave."

"You misunderstand me, uncle." She pointed at him. "I said *you* leave." She paced back and forth in front of the fireplace. "You promised me a visit with my godfather, and I shall have it. But I will not allow you, or anyone else, to ruin it." She forced the image of John Cantrell's arrogantly handsome face from her mind. "You are the one who insisted I accompany you on this entire trip, although I cannot imagine why. You don't need me along while you explore investment opportunities on the west coast. I could have easily stayed in Philadelphia or waited for you in Wyoming and enjoyed a nice long visit with Alina and Susannah. But now I am here, and here I intend to stay for several more weeks. You go on to San Francisco and Seattle by yourself if you wish."

"And leave you alone with these barbarians? Never! I would betray your sainted father's trust in me!"

Jennifer rolled her eyes. "Please, Oliver, spare me the false nobility. It has long been my deepest regret that my father made you my guardian rather than Preston. How much happier both you and I would have been."

Oliver's face flushed a dull red. "Your father showed sound judgment in leaving you in my care, Jennifer. He knew this ranch was no place for a young woman to finish her education. You never would have gone to school in England. Surely he was as concerned about the unhealthy influence of these provincial friends of yours as I am. I don't like your associating with them, not those here, nor those in Wyoming."

"How can you say that?" Jennifer demanded, her hands at her hips. "Preston was my father's friend long before he was mine. You know they were very close. And as for Alina and Susannah, they come from the same background I do; they are just as educated, and so is Bill, not that it matters to me. They are my friends, Oliver, true, lifelong friends."

"Your friends threw themselves away on mere *cowboys,*" Oliver argued. "They denied their social class and their heritage. They will live out their lives in the wilderness, working as common laborers. And William Cantrell is no better. His mother was a Fulbright, one of the finest families in Boston. He could have made a brilliant match, regardless of his paternal heritage. He could have even married you, but he chose a *schoolteacher.*" Oliver spat out the word as if it were a distasteful morsel. "And then there is Preston Cantrell. Dallying with Mexican servants, begetting bastards, working alongside his hired hands as if he were one of them." Oliver crossed his arms over his chest. "He is not fit company for a refined lady like you. None of these people are. If your father, my brother, were still alive, I am certain he would now agree with me. Obviously, Preston Cantrell somehow pulled the wool over Albert's eyes."

Jennifer held herself stiff and tall, her hands clenched in painful fists at her sides, afraid she would use those fists to wipe the arrogant sneer from her uncle's face. "Get out," she ordered hoarsely.

Oliver blinked, a baffled expression on his face. "What did you say?"

"I said get out." Jennifer marched to the door and opened it, gesturing with one hand toward the hallway. "I will listen to no more of your insults directed toward my friends."

"Very well. I can see it is pointless to discuss anything with you when you are in such a state." Oliver came to her side and grabbed her chin in one hand, forcing her to look at him. "But this is not finished, dear niece. You have grown entirely too disrespectful since we left Wyoming, and your outrageous and unacceptable behavior will not continue once we return to Philadelphia."

Jennifer jerked her head from his grasp. "You will not dictate my behavior, Oliver, ever again. I am past the age of emancipation. From now on, I make my own choices."

"Then I wash my hands of you. When we return home, you will choose a husband. It is long past time you were married, to a man who can keep you in line." Oliver stormed into the hallway.

"As I said, I will make my own choices," Jennifer called after him before she slammed the door with enough force to rattle the painting on the wall. Shaking with anger, she leaned her head against the solid wood of the door and struggled to calm her breathing.

She and Oliver had engaged in many arguments over the past few years, especially since Jennifer had reached her twenty-first birthday and had no longer been under his legal guardianship, but none as vicious as this one. Had he become more difficult, or had she grown up? Perhaps it had been easier to get along with him in Philadelphia, where they each had their own circle of friends, where they did not see that much of each other, for all they shared the same house. Oliver was right about one thing, though: she had changed since her visit with Alina and Susannah in Wyoming.

Her friends were married now; Alina was a mother and Susannah hoped she soon would be as well. They both glowed with happiness, basking in the love they shared with their adoring husbands. No man had ever looked at Jennifer as Beauregard Parker did Alina, as Conor O'Rourke did Susannah. And Jennifer had never felt about a man the way her friends did about their husbands. She wanted that kind of love in her life. She wanted a man who cherished her, a man she cherished, a family around her. Granted, Oliver was family—actually, the only blood-related family she had left. But the two of them would never be a family. Now, she doubted they even liked each other. She wanted a family like Preston's family, close-knit and loving, living together in peace, working together to build a future.

With a sigh, Jennifer turned away from the door, pulling the pins from her windblown hair. She had reached a turning point in her relationship with her uncle; no longer could they go on as they had in the past. She had taken a stand against him, a stand from which she was not willing to back down. Jennifer knew, with deep certainty, that from this day forward, her life would never be the same.

John Cantrell offered to stay long enough to help rebuild the dam. Preston was surprised and touched by his offer. Jennifer was more than surprised; she was very suspicious.

At supper that night, Preston announced his intentions to hold a *fiesta* to celebrate Jennifer's visit and John's appearance in his life. Friends and neighbors from across the valley would be invited to the party to be held the following Saturday. The next morning, Jennifer rose early and accompanied Bill and Barbara and the children into the nearby town of Gilroy to buy the supplies necessary for the *fiesta*. She was thankful she avoided seeing John.

Not long after they left, an elaborate buggy pulled into the yard, drawn by a perfectly matched pair of snow-white geldings. A man on horseback accompanied the buggy. Preston came out onto the veranda to greet his neighbors. Alejandro

Noriega y Gonzales, a distinguished-looking grey-haired man, helped his elegantly dressed daughter down from the buggy while his son dismounted and tied his horse to the railing.

"Good morning, Alejandro." Preston stepped off the veranda and extended his hand to his longtime and close friend. "Nice to see you, Constanza." He nodded to the young woman, then looked at the young man. "Arturo, I see you are riding my horse," he said with a smile, waving his free hand at the fine bay stallion. "Or it would be my horse if you would sell him to me."

Arturo only smiled in return, a thin smile that did not reach his close-set eyes. Preston idly wondered how such a gregarious and generous man as Alejandro could have spawned such a cold and discourteous son. And Alejandro's spoiled daughter was not much better behaved than her brother. Perhaps he should introduce Arturo and Constanza to Oliver Mainwaring. After all, they had much in common.

"Greetings, Preston," Alejandro said as he shook Preston's offered hand. "We heard that you have discovered you have another son. We have come to offer our congratulations and introduce ourselves to the newest member of the Cantrell family."

"Papa insisted it was the neighborly thing to do," Constanza purred. "We hope we are not intruding."

"Not at all, Constanza. Please come in." Preston stood back and let his neighbors precede him into the foyer. "Make yourselves comfortable in the *sala,* and I will join you shortly." He directed them to the main room and disappeared, calling for Rosa.

Constanza dropped her polite facade as she plopped down onto one of a matching set of camelback sofas. "Surely this visit was not necessary, Papa." Her face twisted into an unflattering pout. "I don't care to meet Preston Cantrell's bastard son, and certainly not at such an ungodly hour." She yawned without covering her mouth. "Why did you insist I come along? You and Arturo could have paid my respects."

She waved at her brother, who leaned carelessly against the wall by the fireplace with his thumbs hooked in his belt.

"Do not use that foul word in Preston's house." Alejandro glared at her. "He has found a son. That is a grand event in a man's life, and I am here to congratulate my friend. I expect you to behave yourself, daughter."

Constanza rolled her eyes, but said nothing as she leaned against the back of the sofa with another yawn.

Rosa entered the room bearing a tray laden with a fine china coffeepot and matching cups. Preston followed her in and watched as she set the tray on the low table in front of the sofa.

"Buenos días, Don Alejandro," Rosa said.

"It is nice to see you again, Rosa." Alejandro smiled warmly at her. "How is your daughter?"

"She is well, thank you. I will leave you to your visit." She nodded politely in Arturo's direction, then Preston's, and left the room, pointedly ignoring Constanza. Constanza did not miss the snub, as was evidenced by her suddenly flushed face and stiffened spine.

Making a mental note to speak to Rosa later, Preston cleared his throat. "John is seeing to his horse. I've sent for him." He settled onto the sofa opposite Constanza and poured cups of steaming coffee. "We'll be having a *fiesta* this coming Saturday in honor of John's return to his home. You may have heard my godchild is visiting as well. There's much to celebrate. I hope you'll all come." He set a cup down in front of Constanza, offering her a conciliatory smile, to which she did not respond.

"Surely you cannot mean little Jennifer Mainwaring," Alejandro commented as he accepted a cup.

"I do," Preston assured him, "but she is not so little anymore. She has grown into a lovely young woman." He glanced at Arturo. "Would you care for some coffee?"

Arturo shook his head.

"Is she that skinny little girl with the long brown braids

who lived with you many years ago?" Constanza asked as she picked up her cup.

"Yes." Preston eyed Constanza over the rim of his own cup. Constanza was three years older than Jennifer, and had tormented the younger girl mercilessly at every opportunity during Jennifer's two-year stay with the Cantrells after her mother's death. Preston suspected that Constanza would no longer find his goddaughter the easy target she had been as a child. "But as I said, she is not so little anymore."

"Is she married?"

"No."

"Where is she? I want to see her."

"She went into Gilroy with Bill and Barbara. You'll see her at the *fiesta.*"

Constanza nodded with satisfaction and sipped from her cup. "It will be interesting to see little Jennifer again," she said softly, almost to herself.

Preston did not like the predatory look on Constanza's face. A wave of protectiveness washed over him, and he was suddenly glad that Jennie was not there.

"We heard your dam was destroyed, Preston." Arturo crossed his arms over his chest. "What happened?"

Constanza glanced at her brother with a small, odd smile, then took another sip of coffee.

"Someone blew it up," Preston answered calmly, although he spoke through clenched teeth.

"Blew it up?" Alejandro demanded. "With dynamite?"

"Yes."

"Who would do this?"

"I don't know, not yet. But I will. Have you been having any trouble with vandals?"

Alejandro's brows drew together in puzzlement. "No. What are you talking about?"

Preston shrugged. "Strange things. Fence wire cut, a few young fruit trees pulled from the ground, cattle scattered. More irritating than seriously damaging, until now."

"No, we have had no trouble." Alejandro looked at his son. "Have we? Is anything happening you have not told me about?"

Arturo shook his head. "We have had no such trouble."

Alejandro nodded in satisfaction. "We will keep a lookout, Preston, and let you know if we see anything suspicious, any strangers in the area. Are you going to rebuild the dam?"

"We've started work on it already."

"I will send Arturo tomorrow with a few men to help you."

Preston smiled. "Thank you, my friend."

"Now tell us about your new son." Alejandro took a seat next to Preston. "How did you find him? How did you know to look for him?"

"He found me. I knew nothing about him until the other night." Preston paused as the memories rushed back. "He is Ana Maria's son."

"Ahhh." Alejandro nodded in understanding. "Could he tell you what happened to her, why she disappeared, where she went?"

"Yes. He explained everything."

"And Ana Maria? Where is she now?"

Bleakly, Preston met Alejandro's gaze. "She's dead."

Alejandro set his cup on the table and awkwardly patted Preston on the shoulder. "I am sorry, old friend, truly sorry. I know how you loved her."

"Thank you." Preston looked up just as John entered the room. "There you are. I would like you to meet some good friends." He stood, as did Alejandro.

"John, these are our neighbors to the south; I think I mentioned the Buena Ventura ranch on our ride yesterday. I would like to present *Don* Alejandro Noriega y Gonzales." He placed an arm around Alejandro's shoulders. "Alejandro and I received our land grants at the same time, back in 1840." He waved his free arm as he spoke. "There by the fireplace is his son, Arturo, and this is his daughter, Constanza. My friends, my son, John Novales Cantrell."

John held out a hand to Alejandro, uncomfortable with the obvious pride in Preston's voice. "How do you do, sir? I am pleased to meet you."

"Likewise, I'm sure." Alejandro pumped his hand, wearing a wide grin.

John nodded to Arturo, who nodded insolently in return. John ignored the younger man's rudeness and turned to face the woman seated on the sofa. "Miss Noriega," he said, then caught his breath in astonishment. The young woman was staring at him with wide, surprised eyes. *Constanza Gonzales.* Could it be she? He blinked, struggling to regain his composure, thankful when the long-practiced reserve from his days as an agent slid into place.

It was she. There could be no mistaking the luxuriant black hair allowed to fall freely about her shoulders, which she still covered with her signature black lace mantilla. He recognized her huge brown eyes, the stunning beauty of her face, and the voluptuous breasts swelling above the deeply veed neckline of her violet carriage dress. Only Constanza would leave her hair down and wear a low-cut dress during the day. She had not changed, except that her beauty had lost the suggestion of innocence and had matured, somehow making her even more alluring. "How nice to see you," he said, holding out a hand.

She nodded demurely as she placed her hand in his. "The pleasure is mine," she said in the low, throaty voice he remembered so well. "All mine." She ran the tip of her tongue over her bottom lip, a gesture which John also found familiar. He kissed the back of her hand and released her.

"Do you two know each other?" Alejandro asked with a puzzled frown.

"We met in *Ciudad de Mexico* several years ago, Papa," Constanza explained, not taking her eyes from John's face. "When I lived with *Tía* Ynez and attended the convent school.

I believe we actually met at a ball given by Maximilian the year before he was killed, didn't we, *John?*"

"I believe so," John said curtly.

"Of course, then I knew you as Juan Novales." Constanza toyed with the ornate gold crucifix that hung from a delicate chain around her neck. "Had I known your true name was Cantrell, I would have guessed you were related to our dear neighbors."

"And I knew you as Constanza Gonzalez."

Constanza shrugged. "My mother's name. We both carry secrets from our days in Mexico, do we not?" She taunted him with her long-lashed eyes as she again ran her tongue over her lip, seemingly oblivious to the others in the room. When John made no comment, she spoke again. "How long ago did you leave *Ciudad de Mexico?*"

"This past June. I'm sure you know that Juarez is dead."

"Yes. And I know you were close to him. I'm sorry."

John did not detect any sympathy in her tone. They had both worked to return Benito Juarez to power in Mexico, but Constanza had never shared John's fervent belief in the man. At the time, he had doubted she truly cared about anyone. He suspected that had not changed, either.

Alejandro glanced curiously from John to Constanza, then spoke to Preston. "The last time we saw each other, you mentioned you were getting a new breeding bull."

Preston nodded. "A Holstein. He was delivered last week. Come and have a look at him." He turned to John. "Perhaps you and Constanza would like to wait here. I doubt she is interested in breeding bulls, and I'm sure you two would like to talk."

"That would be lovely, *Señor* Cantrell," Constanza said smoothly. "John and I have *much* to talk about." She released the crucifix so that it fell to the end of the chain and nestled in the valley between her breasts.

"That would be fine," John answered.

Preston led Alejandro out to the foyer. Arturo pushed away

from the wall, glaring at John. "I think we met also, Juan Novales, when I came to *Ciudad de Mexico* to bring my sister home. I think I do not like you."

John studied the angry man, vaguely remembering a tall, thin youth with bad skin and worse manners. Arturo appeared to be a few years younger than Constanza. He had the same thick black hair and the same deep brown eyes, but there the similarities ended. Constanza had inherited the beauty in the family. While her full lips could be coaxed into an intriguing smile or a flirtatious pout, Arturo's were twisted into a perpetual sneer, over which a thin, scraggly mustache curled. His skin had cleared and his body had filled out, but not even the most generous of kindhearted souls could call him attractive.

"I think the feeling is mutual," John finally said.

Arturo took a threatening step toward him. "I tell you again what I told you in Mexico years ago. Stay away from my sister."

"Arturo!" Alejandro had retraced his steps to the door of the *sala*. He motioned to his son. "Come. Someday you will inherit my ranch, and you must know about breeding bulls. I wish you would show a little more interest in such things."

Arturo flushed at the scolding. He glared at John a moment longer, then spun on his heel and stomped from the room.

Alejandro shrugged apologetically in John's direction. "My son and daughter are very close, John Cantrell. Forgive Arturo if he is a little over-protective." He glanced at Constanza, then continued speaking as if she were not in the room, his voice touched with a curious note of sadness. "He does not seem to understand that my daughter is perfectly capable of taking care of herself." He turned away from the door. "We shall not be long."

John and Constanza watched each other in silence as the sound of Alejandro's footsteps faded. When they heard the front door latch click into place, Constanza launched herself from the sofa into John's arms in one swift move, locking her lips with his. She twisted her hands in his hair, rubbed her breasts against his chest, ground her hips against his. Caught by surprise, John automatically tightened his arms around her for a moment, then pulled back.

"I cannot believe you came for me, Juan Novales," Constanza whispered breathlessly, her eyes glazed with passion. "And now to find out you are a Cantrell. It is perfect."

John took a step backwards and, when she reached for him, caught her hands. "I can see your devious mind working, and I tell you to forget whatever you are thinking. I am here only for a short time."

She laughed. "Of course you are not here for only a short time. The Santa Maria is your heritage. It belongs more to you than to your weak-spined brother, for you are half-Mexican, and this is California, which rightly belongs to Mexico and one day will again. But we will talk of that later." She grabbed his hand and laid it open-palmed against her breast, then leaned forward to plant a quick, urgent kiss on his lips. Her voice dropped to a sultry whisper. "Where is your room?"

"Constanza, please." John pulled completely away from her and walked over to a set of double doors that opened onto the courtyard. "Times have changed; we have changed. Whatever was between us in Mexico is over."

"We can start it again." Constanza came up behind him and wrapped her arms around his waist, pressing her full breasts against his back. "Once you found me beautiful."

"And you still are." John turned in her arms and grabbed her shoulders. "You are more lovely than ever." He gently set her back from him. "And it is over. Long over."

Constanza folded one arm across her stomach and fingered the gold crucifix with her other hand, arching an eyebrow at him. "We were good together, Juan Novales. Do you remember? I was eighteen; you, twenty-three. So young, yet we were so good. You were my first lover."

"I was not," John corrected with a smile.

"Well, perhaps not." Constanza shrugged. "But you were the best."

Now John arched an eyebrow. "I doubt that, but thank you for the compliment."

"Juan—or should I call you John—I would not lie to you."

John laughed. "Yes, you would, my dear Constanza, in a minute. You have lied to me in the past, and surely you will lie to me again."

Constanza's mouth curved upward. "Maybe just a little." She sighed, her full lips now pouting. "That is why we would be good together again. You know me so well, and I know you so well."

At that, John sobered. "You don't know me, Constanza. No one does. Leave the past in the past. The exciting world of Maximilian's court and the Juarez revolution is long gone. We cannot go back to those days. Besides, I'd be risking my life to get involved with you again."

"Whatever do you mean?"

John touched his left side over his rib cage. "I still wear a scar from your knife, my dear."

Constanza shrugged again. "You should not have flirted with that French *ramera*. Then I would not have had to punish you." Her smile was forced, her eyes a little too bright.

"You tried to kill me," John said softly. He lifted her chin with one finger and looked into her eyes. "It is over, Constanza. Let it be over." He placed a light, gentle kiss on her lips. This time, it was she who pulled away from him.

John heard a sound and looked up to see a disapproving Rosa standing in the doorway that led to the foyer. "I think it's time I joined the men in the corral," he said lamely.

Constanza did not respond. John crossed the room and made his way around the glaring Rosa. "Thank you for the coffee, Rosa." She did not respond to him, either, just moved into the *sala* and began to collect the china cups with what seemed to John to be a great deal of force. Fearing for the unfortunate cups, he walked through the entryway, grabbing his hat from the hook as he passed, and let himself out the front door.

Five

The Noriega family left a half an hour later, declining Preston's invitation to join them for the noon meal because, as Alejandro explained, they were keeping the Cantrells from their work. Reiterating his promise to send Arturo back the next day with extra men to help, he picked up the reins and the buggy pulled away in a cloud of dust with Arturo riding alongside.

Preston and John watched them go from the shade of the veranda.

"Small world, isn't it?" Preston commented casually.

"Sometimes it is," John responded. *Sometimes too small.* He was not entirely pleased to have met Constanza again, especially in the company of her father. Although he did not know Alejandro well, he liked him, and doubted that the older man would be happy to learn that his unmarried daughter had taken a lover. Had taken many lovers, no doubt. Constanza could not be trusted to be discreet. If word of their long-ago affair got out, it could cause tension between the two families. Surprisingly, John realized that he did not want to cause trouble for Preston, especially not over an affair with the tempestuous Constanza.

"Did you know her well?" Preston asked.

"Well enough." John settled his hat more firmly on his head. "I knew she was from California, but nothing more. I had no idea she lived so near you."

"I've known her all her life. She was born and raised on

the Noriega ranch. Her mother died when she was still quite young, and I fear Alejandro spoiled her in trying to make up for the loss. She's a very headstrong woman, but you're probably already aware of that." Preston eyed him, his curiosity evident.

"I am." John abruptly changed the subject. "Their visit cost us a lot of time; do you want to head to the dam now or wait until after we eat?"

"I've already asked Rosa to pack us something to take. If you'll bring the horses around, I'll get the food."

John nodded and stepped off the veranda. He crossed the yard with his long, easy stride and disappeared into the barn. Preston watched him go, a father's pride filling him again. His heart grabbed at the thought of all the wasted years. If only he had found Ana Maria! They could have raised their son together. But then Bill would never have been born. Would he trade one son for the other? The very thought was distressing. For now, he had them both. Perhaps John would want to stay. *Not likely,* he thought, shaking his head. His newfound son had much pride and a fierce independence. Preston turned and went into the house.

"Rosa," he called as he pushed through the swinging door that led to the kitchen.

Rosa stood in front of the huge cast-iron stove, stirring something in a large pot. "*Sí, señor,* the food is in the basket." She waved the spoon in the direction of the table.

Preston ignored the basket. "Rosa, I want to talk to you. Please come over here and sit down."

Without a word, her face set like a stone, Rosa came from the stove, wiping her hands on her clean white apron. She took a seat at the end of one of the long benches that ran along each side of the massive wooden table, which was scarred from years of use as the main family dining table.

Preston sat opposite her. "You were very rude to Constanza today," he began.

"*Sí,* I was." There was no apology in her tone.

"Rosa, I know you don't like Constanza, but you can't be rude to her, especially when she is a guest in our house."

"She is rude to me," Rosa argued, crossing her arms over her chest. "She is rude to everyone, no matter where she is."

"Yes, she is, but that doesn't give you call to be rude back."

"*Señor* Preston, you told me long ago that those who deserve to be treated with respect will be treated with respect. That woman does not deserve respect, so I ignore her." She stared stonily ahead, her mouth set in an obstinate line.

Preston sighed. "Yes, I told you that, but can you understand that it makes me look bad when my people are rude to my guests?"

"I ignore only her. Her papa, he is a good man, and her brother, he would be better if he stayed away from his witch of a sister. I do not ignore them. I do not ignore anyone else, except for maybe *Señor* Oliver. Soon I ignore him, too."

Preston struggled to hide a smile and was eventually successful in schooling his features into a stern expression. "Rosa, I must ask you not to ignore anyone. For my sake, please be polite to Constanza and Oliver."

Rosa was quiet for a moment, then sighed. "Very well. I will not ignore *Señor* Oliver. But the other . . ." She shook her head despairingly, and much to Preston's surprise, her large dark eyes filled with tears. "You don't know what you ask," she whispered. "You don't know all she has done, from the time she was a child—what she did to me, to Jennie, to my baby, to my Enrique. She is evil, *señor.*" She bowed her head.

"Rosa, what are you talking about?" Preston asked in bewilderment. "She was a spoiled child, demanding and temperamental, but evil?"

"*Sí*, evil." Rosa dashed the tears away with the back of one hand and stood up. "I have lived at the Santa Maria all my life. You have given me a home, and my mother before me, and my daughter after me. You gave Enrique work so he could support his family, and now that he is dead you have given me work to support my child. I owe you much. You are the *patron*, and it is my duty to do as you ask. But this I cannot do, not even for you."

Stunned, Preston rose also. "Rosa, I had no idea you felt so strongly about this."

Rosa walked to the stove, her spine stiff. She snatched up the spoon and stirred the contents of the pot. "I will look for other work." Her tone was flat, lifeless.

"You will not." Preston came to her side and took the spoon from her hand, then placed his hands on her shoulders and turned her to face him. "This is your home, as it always has been. You will not leave."

"I cannot do as you ask!" she cried.

"Then I won't ask it of you."

Rosa's tear-filled eyes widened with hope. "Truly, *señor?*"

"Truly, Rosa. I don't know what Constanza did, but obviously it was very serious. Perhaps one day you'll tell me, so I can understand. Just don't ignore Mr. Oliver, and I'll be pleased."

"Gracias," Rosa whispered, and began to cry in earnest.

Preston took her into his arms and held her, his mind racing. He had never seen Rosa like this, had never heard such hatred in her voice. He noticed John standing in the doorway with a concerned, sober look on his face. Preston motioned with his head toward the basket on the table. John nodded and grabbed the basket, then left the room. Rosa's sobs had quieted to sniffles. She stepped back and self-consciously wiped her eyes with a corner of her apron.

"Are you all right now?" Preston asked kindly.

She nodded. *"Señor* John is waiting for you. Go now. Get out of my kitchen." She waved toward the door, her lips curved in a wobbly smile.

"That's my Rosa," Preston said with a relieved grin. "Thank you for preparing the meal."

"De nada." She turned away and once again grabbed the spoon.

Preston took the cue and left to join John in front of the house. John was already mounted on his black stallion.

"How much did you hear?" Preston asked as he adjusted his hat against the glare of the midday sun.

"Enough."

"Rosa is not given to hysterics, John." Preston swung up into his saddle. "Something awful happened, probably years ago, when Jennie and her father lived here for a while. Do you know Constanza well enough to have any idea what she may have done?"

John shook his head and turned his horse toward the gate. "I know that she can be very unpleasant when she doesn't get her way, even violent." He touched his left side.

At the gesture, Preston's eyebrows raised with curiosity. "Violent?"

John did not respond, and Preston decided not to press him. "Well, maybe Bill or Jennie knows something. I'll ask them tonight. Let's get to work." He touched his heels to his horse's flanks, and the two men left the yard at a canter.

"We had visitors today," Preston announced that night at supper. "The Noriegas came by to meet John. They are definitely coming to the *fiesta*."

"All of them?" Barbara asked quietly.

"Yes."

Jennifer looked down at her plate, her heart pounding, astonished that after all these years, the mere mention of the Noriega name could cause such a reaction in her. *Constanza Noriega.* It only figured that sooner or later she would have to deal with the woman. She glanced at Barbara, noticed her friend's subdued expression. Perhaps Barbara did not care for Constanza Noriega any more than she did.

Preston continued. "It turns out that John and Constanza knew each other in the City of Mexico a few years back."

Jennifer looked at John in surprise. Because Oliver was still sulking and had insisted on taking supper in his room, John was seated next to her. He suddenly seemed very interested in his supper. Jennifer had not seen Constanza Noriega in fourteen years, but, based on Barbara's reaction, it was doubtful that the woman was much improvement over the girl Jennifer had known. If John Cantrell considered Constanza a friend, Jennifer's already low opinion of him slipped another notch.

"You remember, Bill, when she went to convent school in Mexico," Preston said.

"I remember. Things were much more peaceful when she was gone." He winked at Barbara, who smiled at him gratefully. "How is Alejandro?"

"Just fine. He was intrigued by the new bull. Even Arturo seemed impressed. They may be interested in some of the calves come spring."

"Tell Arturo he has to sell us his stallion first. Or at least let us breed him with some of our mares."

Preston shook his head. "I asked him again, offered a generous stud fee. He won't share the horse, said something about not wanting to ruin the line."

Bill snorted. "He doesn't know what he's talking about. Our mares are of finer stock than his."

Preston nodded in agreement, then went on to briefly explain what had happened earlier with Rosa. "Jennie, Rosa mentioned that you had some trouble with Constanza when you were younger. Can you shed any light on the reason for Rosa's distress?"

Jennifer paused with her fork halfway to her mouth, then set it down, suddenly very uncomfortable. She did not want to discuss Constanza Noriega, especially if the woman was a friend of John Cantrell. "I don't know. Rosa was maybe fifteen, Constanza was eleven, and I, only eight, so it was Rosa's responsibility to watch us when the Noriegas came to visit, which wasn't that often." *Thankfully,* she added silently.

"Go on," Preston encouraged her.

Jennifer glanced around the table. Bill, Barbara, and John watched her, waiting for her to continue. She shrugged, feeling like a child telling tales out of school. "It was a long time ago. I don't remember all the specifics." *Liar!* her mind screamed. *You remember everything!* "Constanza constantly tried to get Rosa in trouble. She was often successful."

"How so?"

"I'd rather not say, Preston. She is Mr. Cantrell's friend." Jennifer glanced nervously at the quiet man seated next to her.

"Thank you for your concern, Miss Mainwaring, but I am well aware of Constanza's faults," John said. "You may speak freely."

"Please, Jennie, this is important," Preston urged. "I don't like to see Rosa so upset."

Jennifer sighed. "It was mostly childish pranks. Hiding from her, putting kittens in buckets of water, that sort of thing. Constanza was a bully, but I don't know of anything she did that would lead to such strong and long-lasting feelings on Rosa's part. Perhaps something happened after my father and I returned to Philadelphia."

"Bill, do you know anything?" Preston asked.

"No more than the rest of you." Bill leaned over and draped an arm across the back of Barbara's chair. "I avoided her as much as possible, especially once she got it in her head that she was going to marry me and join the Cantrell and Noriega land grants into one."

"You never told me that!" Barbara gasped.

Bill moved his arm from her chair to her shoulders. "You didn't realize your husband was in such demand, did you?" he teased.

"I didn't realize my husband was so full of himself," she retorted in a very sweet voice.

Bill laughed and planted an enthusiastic kiss on Barbara's cheek. "I married the right woman," he said lovingly.

"You certainly did," Preston agreed with a smile. His expression sobered as he looked around the table. "Constanza will be here on Saturday, so let's all try to shield Rosa from her as much as possible." Bill and Barbara nodded their agreement.

Jennifer stared at Preston, surprised and touched that he would be so concerned for his cook. Oliver would have fired Rosa for being rude to a guest, no matter how long she had worked for him. Then Jennifer glanced at John. From his expression, she could tell he was surprised, also. Perhaps John Cantrell was learning that his father was not the man he had thought. As she reached for her wineglass, Jennifer hoped that was the case.

It was customary for the family to gather in the *sala* after supper, but Jennifer begged off, claiming fatigue, which was not entirely false. Sore muscles from the ride the day before added to her discomfort, as did John Cantrell's presence. She climbed the stairs, determined to get to bed early. The new sleeping shift that Rosa's daughter Francisca had made for her was so comfortable that she couldn't wait to get out of her heavy clothes.

As she passed the open door to Bill and Barbara's room, she glanced in and saw Barbara sitting on the edge of the bed, her brow furrowed with concern. Jennifer knocked lightly on the door.

"Is everything all right?" she asked when Barbara looked up. "You seem troubled about something."

"I'm just being silly." Barbara's mouth curved in an obviously forced smile.

"May I come in?"

Barbara nodded. "Are the men still in the *sala?*"

"Yes. They started talking about the new bull again, and now they'll probably talk for hours." Jennifer joined Barbara on the edge of the bed.

"Was John with them?"

"Yes, and Mr. Horn."

"What do you think of John?" Barbara asked.

Jennifer sighed. "I don't know what to make of him. He seems to be trying to fit in, helping with the chores and all, but I don't know." She shook her head. "There's something about him I don't trust. I cannot forget how he looked that night, Barbara. I felt that he *hated* Preston, just as I believe he fully intended to kill him. Now he's the ideal son, making an effort to get along with everyone . . ."

"Except you," Barbara interjected softly. "He doesn't get along with you."

"No, he doesn't, any more than I do with him. We've had a few arguments; he knows I don't trust him. And I know he doesn't like me, which is fine. I would just as soon not have to speak with him."

"Oh, dear, and I sat him next to you at supper tonight. I'm sorry."

"It's all right, Barbara. We managed to be civil with each other. I do wish he'd leave, though. Then I see the joy on Preston's face, and I feel guilty for wanting that."

Barbara sighed. "I know. I feel the same way. For Bill's sake, I wish he'd leave, too. These past few days have been difficult for him, even though Preston has assured him that his future—and mine and that of the children—is secure, no matter what John decides to do. But John isn't very talkative, except with David and Molly. And they seem to really like him. I guess he can't be all bad if the children like him."

"I guess not. Is that what is bothering you?"

"Actually, no. I'm worried about the *fiesta.*"

"Why? I think we'll have plenty of food, and Rosa and Francisca will help us."

Barbara jumped off the bed and began to pace the floor. "As I said, it's silly. I don't have a really nice dress to wear, and there's no time to have one made. Constanza Noriega will be here, and all of the most influential people in the valley. I'm afraid I won't make a good impression on Bill's friends and business acquaintances."

"Surely you've met them before now."

"Yes, but not with her there. She'll make sure everyone notices my dress."

Jennie nodded in understanding. "It has been a long time since I've seen her, but that sounds like Constanza." She pursed her lips in thought, then stood up and grabbed Barbara's hand. "Come with me. I have an idea."

The two women hurried down the hall to Jennifer's room and slipped inside. The lamps had been lit earlier and filled the inviting room with soft light, but Jennifer turned them up high. She pulled open the wardrobe door and rifled through the clothes inside, finally pulling out a garment.

"Here!" she said triumphantly. She held up a beautiful evening gown made of rose-colored faille with an overskirt of Valenciennes lace.

Barbara gasped. "Jennie, it's lovely! I've never seen anything like it. You'll be stunning in it."

"Not me, you goose," Jennie said with a laugh. "This is for you. I've never worn it. It's yours." She put the dress in Barbara's arms.

"Thank you," Barbara whispered as she stared down at the exquisite dress. "What a thoughtful gesture. But you're forgetting one thing."

Jennifer's head was buried once again in the wardrobe. "You're right. We have to find you some matching shoes."

Barbara laughed. "Now you're the goose. Jennie, you are much more slender than I am. This dress will never fit me."

Jennifer backed out of the wardrobe. "Let me see." She took the dress from Barbara and held it up in front of her friend, then examined the side seams. "This won't be difficult to let out. I think Francisca can help us—that child is a positive wizard with a needle. Do you think the train is too long?"

"Yes, now that you mention it."

"So do I. We'll go to work on this first thing in the morning. It's two days until Saturday. We have plenty of time."

"How can I thank you?" Barbara asked quietly, her eyes filled with gratitude and affection.

"You can carry yourself like a queen, which you are, and don't let that horrid Constanza shake your confidence. The Santa Maria is your home; you have a husband who adores you, two beautiful children, and Preston loves you like a daughter. Constanza is just jealous."

Barbara looked down at the floor, then blurted out, "When I was carrying David, she invited Bill to her bed."

"What?" Jennifer looked up from the dress to stare at her friend, aghast.

"We were at a Christmas party at the Noriega ranch. She pulled him into an alcove that opens onto a small balcony. Neither of them knew I was on the other side of the curtain, seeking a breath of fresh air. She threw herself at him, told him in detail the things they could do together, to each other." Barbara shuddered. "He refused her, vehemently and rudely, and told her to never approach him again, but she still frightens me. She has no morals, Jennie, no conscience."

"Well, you have nothing to worry about with Bill. You know that, don't you?"

"Yes. He about went crazy when he realized I had heard everything, fell over himself apologizing, as if it had been his fault. But she is so beautiful. I don't know how any man can resist her."

"I suspect many can, Barbara, and Bill is one of them. Not all men are blinded by beauty. Unless Constanza has changed a great deal from when we were children, her beauty hides the soul of a snake. She can't fool everyone, and certainly not Bill." Jennifer smiled in encouragement and held out the dress. "Now take your dress; we'll start on the alterations in the morning."

"May I leave it here? I'd like to surprise Bill with it on Saturday."

"What a good idea. It will be our secret."

Barbara gave her a hug. "Thank you," she said sincerely.

"You're welcome. Now get some rest. Those children kept you running all day."

"Good night." Barbara let herself out the door.

Deep in thought, Jennifer stroked the smooth material of the underskirt. So the wicked child Constanza had grown to a wicked woman. Suddenly Jennifer was very anxious to see her childhood tormentor again. Their meeting would no doubt be very interesting. She smiled grimly. Very interesting, indeed.

Later that night, Jennifer was awakened by a dream, a nightmare, actually, involving John Cantrell and Constanza as a child and yards of rose-colored faille. She lay quietly for a while, trying to shake off the lingering grips of the dream. Finally, she climbed out of bed, drawn again to the balcony that overlooked the courtyard.

It was a lovely night, as it had been the other night when she visited the balcony. A horse whinnied from the direction of the barn, then fell silent, leaving Jennifer to appreciate the peaceful stillness.

Although the drought had not eased, there seemed to be a hint of coolness to the air she had not felt before. Perhaps rain was on the way. Or perhaps it was that she wore only the light cotton batiste shift Francisca had made for her. Reluctantly, she had even followed John's advice about the nightcap, and her uncovered hair hung down her back in a long braid. As much as she hated to admit it—and she would never admit it to him—she was much more comfortable, and sleep came much easier, albeit sometimes accompanied by disturbing dreams.

With a sigh, she leaned against the railing and thought over the last few days. So much had happened that it didn't seem possible she and Oliver had arrived only five days earlier. If she could persuade Oliver to continue his journey without her, and if John Cantrell would leave, things would settle down and she would be able to truly enjoy her time with Preston's family. Perhaps John and Oliver would both leave after the *fiesta;* she could only hope so.

A yawn escaped her lips. Just as she turned to go back into the bedroom, she caught a movement from the corner of her eye. It was John Cantrell, again furtively leaving his room under cover of darkness. He retraced his steps of the other night, then disappeared through the wall gate. Jennifer's eyes narrowed with suspicion, but she repressed the urge to follow him. She had no desire to repeat their meeting in the barn. Resolutely, she made her way back to the bed and climbed in, pulling the sheet up over her legs. John Cantrell could enjoy the company of his horse all he wished.

A short time later, something pulled her back from the brink of sleep. Confused, she lay still, blinking, trying to figure out what had disturbed her. The sound of voices reached her through the open French doors. She jumped from the bed and ran to the balcony railing. The voices came from the direction of the barn, and now she could see lights as well. Something had happened.

Jennifer hurried back into her room and snatched her linen wrapper from the bench at the foot of her bed, tying the belt as she slipped out into the hall. She raced silently down the stairs on bare feet, meeting no one on the way. Not until she was halfway across the yard did she see another person. One of the cowhands trotted toward the barn with a lighted lantern in one hand and a leather satchel in the other. He stopped and waited for her to catch up to him. When she neared, Jennifer recognized Gabriel Horn.

"What has happened?" she asked breathlessly.

"Buford has been hurt," Gabe answered in a gruff, angry tone. He marched toward the barn, holding the lantern high so Jennifer could see by its feeble light.

"Buford?"

"The new bull. Little David insisted the bull had to have a name, and that's what he named him."

Jennifer hurried along at his side, ignoring her protesting feet. She and Gabe joined the small group of men in the large pen at the back of the barn. The combined light of three lanterns on posts around the pen revealed Preston, his features set and grim, a robe covering his nightshirt. Bill stood next to him, wearing only boots and a pair of pants. John waited off to one side, and the fourth man, one of the Mexican hands named Pedro, stroked his full mustache thoughtfully. All eyes were on the magnificent bull standing in the corner.

Jennifer came up to Preston's side and stared at the bull. The halter on his head was tied by a short lead to the stall fence, and he snorted as he looked at the group of people, his eyes wide and wild. He pawed the ground in agitation and struggled in vain to pull free from the lead. From where she stood, Jennifer could see the slow drip of blood from several wounds on his flank and stomach.

"My God," she whispered, her heart aching for the frightened animal. "What happened?"

Preston shook his head, too angry and upset to speak.

"Someone tried to castrate him," Bill said quietly. "Thankfully, he fought and made enough noise to waken Pedro, but not before the knife got him a few times."

Jennifer looked at Bill in horror. "This was done on purpose?"

He nodded, his features grim and tense.

A wild rage roared through Jennifer at the thought of someone deliberately injuring an animal. "Is he badly hurt?"

"I don't think so, but we'll know more in a minute." He nodded toward Gabe, who was easing closer to the bull.

Impulsively, Jennifer stepped forward. "I want to help."

Preston pulled her back. "I know, but an injured animal is dangerous. Gabe and the boys will take care of him."

Jennifer stared at the bull in helpless frustration, sensing its pain and fear, and spoke almost to herself. "We need car-

bolic acid to cleanse the wounds, and it looks as if some
need to be stitched. It'll be hard to keep him clean until the
skin closes again. He must have fresh straw at all times—his
droppings must be cleaned up immediately—and we have to
try to keep him from rolling." She looked up at Preston.
"Someone should stay with him around the clock for a few
days. His greatest enemy now is infection."

She realized Preston was staring at her in amazement, that
indeed all the men were, including John Cantrell, who stood
nearby. A few more hands had come in during the last few
minutes, and they now lined the fence of the pen.

"How do you know all that?" Preston asked.

Suddenly self-conscious, Jennifer stepped back and
shrugged, stuffing her hands into the deep pockets of her wrapper. "I've studied books, and the stablehand at home taught
me some things when I helped him care for one of our horses
when it injured itself in a bramble thicket."

"I'm gonna need some help, boys," Gabe called from the
bull's side, effectively drawing attention from Jennifer. "He's
too skittish to let me do much by myself."

Several of the men filed through the gate into the pen, one
pausing to grab a loop of rope from a nail.

Jennifer's heart went out to the upset bull. She longed to
try to soothe him. "Is there anything I can do?" she pleaded.

Preston shook his head, a gentle smile softening his tense
features. "Thank you, honey, but no. I've sent one of the
boys for Doc Lafferty, and he'll be here by first light. All
Gabe can do now is clean the wounds and see how deep they
are. Buford will be all right until the doc gets here."

Disappointed, Jennifer looked away from him to the group
of men surrounding the bull. "I'm glad the doctor is willing
to treat animals," she commented.

"He's a veterinary doctor," Bill explained.

"Really?" Jennifer's eyes widened in interest. "I would like
to meet him."

"You will," Preston assured her. He faced Pedro. "You're certain you couldn't make out who did this?"

"No, *señor*." Pedro shook his graying head sadly. "I hear the noise, the kicking of the wall and the bellowing, and I come quickly. I see someone run off, and I chase, but he get away. When I come back, the new *señor* is with the bull." He nodded in John's direction.

"Can you describe the man you chased?"

Pedro held out his hands in a helpless gesture. "He was dressed in black. It is dark. I did not see much. I am sorry, *patron*."

Preston clapped him on the shoulder. "Don't worry about it. You were of great help, Pedro. Between you and Buford, a tragedy was averted. Let's see how Gabe is making out." The two men crossed the pen, followed by Bill.

Jennifer turned suspicious eyes on John, who was dressed all in black. He stood back from the group of men.

He met her eyes and immediately stiffened. "Don't say it," he warned in a chilling tone.

She advanced on him. "I saw you leave your room, Mr. Cantrell, well before anything happened. What were you doing? Going for a stroll? Visiting your horse?"

"As a matter of fact, I was. He called me, not that I expect you to believe me."

Although Jennifer vaguely remembered hearing the whinny of a horse from her balcony earlier, she folded her arms over her chest and raised a disbelieving eyebrow. "He called you," she repeated derisively.

"That's right, Miss Mainwaring," John said through clenched teeth. "Horses make great watchdogs, especially nervous stallions like Diamante."

"Perhaps." She was not convinced, but she had no hard evidence to indicate that John Cantrell was the culprit. "I'll not let down my guard, Mr. Cantrell. You have an ulterior motive for staying here; I'm certain of it. I will take whatever steps I feel necessary to protect my godfather and his interests, if it means hiring guards for his stable and his dam, if it means watching you day and night." Her breath came fast with the force of her angry warning.

"That does it." John grabbed her hand and marched toward the barn door, leaving Jennifer no choice but to follow him.

"Let go of me this instant! I'll call for Preston!" She pried at his immovable fingers.

"Preston, I'm escorting Miss Mainwaring back to the house," John called.

"Thank you, John," Preston called in return, much to Jennifer's chagrin. She tried to twist from John's grasp, giving a small yelp of pain as one of her tender feet found a merciless rock.

John stopped and looked back at her, then down at her feet. Without a word, he swept her into his arms and carried her out of the barn.

"Put me down!" Jennifer shrieked, struggling against his powerful chest to no avail. His arms only tightened more. He carried her easily, as if she weighed nothing. For some irritating reason, she was aware of a clean masculine scent emanating from him, one of soap and leather and sage.

"I will listen to no more of your accusations, Miss Mainwaring," John ground out. "I am weary of defending myself to you. From now on, mind your own business, and your business does not include any relationship I may have with my father. I wish him no harm."

"I don't believe you," she snapped breathlessly.

"I don't give a damn if you do or not. Just stay out of my way." He stopped and released her legs so that her feet found the smooth wooden floor of the veranda. He still held her close against his body, with one arm around her back and ribs.

Her eyes closed. Jennifer could feel his heart pounding against her breast, could feel his breath on her temple. And she could feel his power, of will and of muscle. A strange, unwelcome excitement coursed through her stomach, leaving her trembling. She had never been held in a man's arms like this, had never been so physically close to a man like John Cantrell, had never even known a man like John Cantrell. She raised her eyes to his face, which was highlighted by the glow of the lantern hanging outside the front door.

He stared down at her, his lips slightly parted, his expression unreadable. But something flashed in his eyes, in his blue, blue eyes, eyes made even more blue by the dark stubble covering his cheeks and chin—anger, irritation, perhaps something else? She couldn't be sure. She pushed against him again, and this time he released her. He raised a hand to lightly touch her hair, then jerked it away.

"For God's sake, wear something on your feet when you leave the house," he ordered, and abruptly strode back toward the barn.

Jennifer felt her face flush hot. "You'll not order me about, John Cantrell," she swore softly to his retreating form. "And God help you if I find out you are behind these attacks." She watched until he disappeared into the barn, acutely troubled by her physical and emotional reaction to the man. He had manhandled her, for heaven's sake, had carried her off, and yet some deep, traitorous part of her had responded to him, to his power, had responded *favorably*. She turned and crossed the veranda, letting herself into the house.

What on earth was wrong with her? There was a very real possibility that John Cantrell intended to harm Preston, in one way or another, and she felt some kind of strange attraction for the man! Granted, he was handsome. But he was also arrogant, bossy, irritating, rude, and sometimes downright unpleasant. She didn't even *like* him.

Jennifer grabbed the banister and started up the stairs. Perhaps she was simply tired, too tired for her body to resist the call of his rugged, masculine beauty. Whatever had caused her response to him, she could not let down her guard because of it. There were simply too many coincidences to believe that John Cantrell was completely innocent. He still posed a threat to Preston.

By the time she reached her room, her mind was made up. In the morning, she would take Bill into her confidence, share her suspicions with him. Perhaps he could help her come up with a plan to protect Preston and find out what his newly discovered half-brother truly wanted. And absolutely, under no circumstances, would she think of John again tonight. She would not remember the feel of his arms around her, the strength and confidence exuded by his tall, lean body. She would not see his handsome face in her mind, with its strong jaw, sensuous lips, and arresting eyes.

"Who are you fooling?" Jennifer demanded of herself in a soft, sad voice as she settled under the sheet. "Of course you will think of him. You will probably dream of him."

Six

When he at last climbed into bed, John folded his arms under his head and stared into the blackness of the room. The bull was resting easily now, or at least as easily as the poor beast could, considering his injuries. John's jaw clenched. He wished he had taken Diamante's warning a little more seriously, had gotten to the barn a little sooner. If he, rather than Pedro, had seen the man who attacked the bull in the pen, the man would not have escaped.

Perhaps then he would not have had to face the accusations in Jennifer Mainwaring's eyes, in her tone and words and stance. Damn the woman! She insisted on thinking the worst of him. He wondered if she had shared her suspicions with the others, if they all watched him as closely as she did. The instant the thought came to him, he discarded it. He would know if they were watching him.

Preston treated him with the same easy acceptance and respect he did Bill. In fact, he could be accused of trusting too easily, of being too vulnerable, at least where Ana Maria's son was concerned. John sighed. As much as he hated to admit it, his father seemed an honorable man, a likeable man, a sire of whom any man would be proud.

His grandmother had been wrong. John suspected that even Elena Novales would have liked Preston Cantrell if she had ever had the opportunity to meet him. He smiled to think of the two of them together—the tall, imposing *Americano,* the short, feisty Mexican matron. Elena would have been impressed that Preston spoke fluent Spanish, that most of his employees were of Mexican descent, that he treated all people, regardless of race, age, or gender, with the same respect. His father and his grandmother would have liked each other.

Bill was more reserved, as was Barbara. They weren't sure of him, he knew. They wanted to like him, for Preston's sake, he suspected, but they were also protective of Preston, as Jennifer was. He wondered how Bill truly felt, having a brother show up, an older brother, who could legally lay claim to half of everything Preston owned, thanks to their father claiming John as his son. It probably didn't help that Bill's endearing children had taken to their "Unca' John" like ducks to water. John smiled in the darkness. More than anyone, David and Molly made him feel like part of the family.

John continued down his mental list. Rosa and Gabe treated him with the same respect they accorded guests—polite and distant. They, too, were very protective of Preston. The rest of the hands seemed noncommittal; none had challenged him, none had befriended him.

Then there was Jennifer. Surely she was one of the most confusing, irritating women he had ever met—tall and cool, intelligent and suspicious, elegant and combative, and as sharp-tongued as a harpy. She could carry herself with gracious dignity while wearing the most fashionable evening gown, yet run around the barn barefoot in the middle of the night wearing little more than a nightdress. And she disliked him, if not hated him. Distrusted him. Wanted him gone.

Why did he care?

He remembered the feel of her in his arms. She was so light, too light for a woman of her height, but there was surprising strength in her also, in her body and in her spirit. Behind her cool demeanor, he sensed a barely restrained passion, saw the promise of it in the way she stood up to him, fearlessly challenging him, accusing him, arguing with him. The thought of that passion being channeled into an outlet other than anger was intriguing.

And she is beautiful.

John sat up straight, allowing the sheet to fall to his hips. Had he lost his mind? Jennifer Mainwaring, *beautiful?*

Yes. With her green eyes and shining brown hair, her tall, lithe body and commanding presence, she was beautiful.

He fell back on the pillow. What did he want? A place at Preston's side as his son, as Bill's brother? To lay claim to half an empire he had not helped build? Jennifer in his bed?

John rolled onto his side and punched the pillow before he laid his head down again. Things were spiraling out of control. He had come prepared to kill Preston, and instead was growing to care for him. Constanza had reappeared in his life, and he knew she would not easily let him go. The children were entwining themselves around his heart, and he genuinely liked his brother and his gentle sister-in-law. Then there was Jennifer. . . . Things were getting too complicated.

It was time to go; all of his finely honed instincts told him so. After the *fiesta,* he would take his leave, slip away without a word if he had to.

You are a coward, John Novales Cantrell. His father's words came back to haunt him. John punched the pillow again, fearing Preston was right.

Jennifer awakened early the next morning and immediately scrambled out of bed, determined to check on the injured bull and, if possible, speak to Bill. After washing up, she dressed as quickly as she could, which was not all that quickly because she did not call Francisca to help her. Once in her chemise and drawers, she struggled into her corset, chose a light bustle of ruffled crinoline over one lined with steel-spring, and, in a fit of exasperation, decided to forego the last of three petticoats. Over all that, she put on the simplest dress she had brought, a russet poplin day dress trimmed with gold braid.

Again she pulled her hair into a chignon at the back of

her head and secured the style with hairpins. She stared at her reflection in the dressing table mirror, discouraged. With her hair pulled away from her face in the almost severe arrangement, the thinness of her face could not be disguised. Nor could the unnatural paleness of her complexion, the faint shadows under her eyes. It was John Cantrell's fault, she thought irritably. Since his arrival, she had not had a decent night's sleep, and her face was paying the price. She sighed in frustration and resignation as she wrapped a light shawl around her shoulders. She had done the best she could with what she had to work with; it would have to do.

The house was quiet as she hurried down the hall, descended the stairs, and went out the front door. Judging by the buggy parked in front of the barn, a chestnut mare waiting patiently in the traces, the doctor had arrived.

Jennifer eased the heavy barn door open far enough to accommodate her skirts and slipped inside. The sound of voices came to her from the pen at the back of the barn. As she approached the group of men surrounding the bull, she saw that Preston and Bill were there, and John. He turned and stared at her, his handsome, recently shaved face expressionless, then his gaze dropped pointedly to her feet. Startled, Jennifer looked down as well, saw the exposed toes of her black kid boots because she held her skirts up from the straw-strewn floor. She looked back at him. He nodded approvingly, then turned away, but not before she saw the sparkle of humor in his eyes.

Her jaw set in irritation, Jennifer made her way to Preston's side, struggling to resist the urge to introduce John Cantrell's shin to her boots as she passed him.

"How is Buford?" Jennifer asked Preston. She saw a wiry man with a head of white hair and a matching mustache standing at Buford's side and decided he must be the doctor.

Preston frowned at her. "You shouldn't be here, Jennie, not while Emmett is working."

Jennifer was stunned. "Why not? I want to check on Buford, and besides, you told me I could meet the doctor."

"This isn't a sight for a lady to see." Preston took her arm and turned her toward the door. "You can meet Emmett at breakfast."

"Preston, please do not make me leave." She raised her pleading gaze to his set face. "You know how much I care about animals. I'll stand back and just watch."

"Not while Emmett sews up Buford's privates," Preston said firmly. At that moment, Buford let out a bellow of protest. A chorus of swear words followed as the men struggled to restrain the unhappy bull. Preston grimaced, then, with renewed determination, propelled Jennifer toward the door.

Jennifer's face burned. She felt like an errant child being sent from the schoolroom for misbehaving, and the knowledge that John Cantrell probably witnessed the scene only added to her humiliation.

When Preston guided her out into the cool morning, she whirled on him. "I never expected you to treat me in such a manner." She could not prevent the tears that formed in her eyes. "Oliver, maybe, but not you."

Preston sighed. "Jennie, you don't belong in there right now; no lady would."

"I am tired of being a lady!" Jennifer angrily brushed at a stray tear that trailed down her cheek. "I want to be of some help to you; I want to take care of Buford, and any other injured animal I come across. I thought you understood that about me." The pain of Preston's perceived betrayal cut deep.

His rugged features softened with affection. "I do understand. I remember how devoted you were to the animals when you lived here as a child, and I see now that hasn't changed. But I will not allow you into a pen with an upset bull who is injured in a delicate place and surrounded by swearing *vaqueros*. I would not allow any woman in there."

Jennifer looked away from him. "I just want to help."

"I know." Preston drew her into his arms for a fatherly hug. "Your compassion is one of the many things I love about you."

With a sigh, Jennifer returned the hug. "Isn't there something I can do?"

"I'll ask Emmett," Preston promised.

The barn door emitted a groan as it was pushed further open, and Bill stuck his head out.

"Dr. Lafferty is finished, Pa. He'd like to talk to you."

"All right." Preston dropped an affectionate kiss on Jennifer's head and went back inside. Bill eyed her curiously, then stepped out to join her.

"What's wrong?" he asked kindly.

She scowled. "I do not appreciate being treated like a lady."

Bill smiled. "No?"

"Or a child. Preston expelled me from the barn, said it wasn't proper for a lady to be there."

"Well—"

"Don't you dare agree with him, Bill Cantrell, or I will never forgive you," she warned.

Bill held up his hands in a defensive gesture. "Let's just say I can see both sides," he said cautiously. "I guess your interest in animals didn't lessen as you grew up."

"No. If anything, it is stronger than ever, perhaps because I rarely have the opportunity to be around animals of any kind." Jennifer sighed. "I expected Preston to understand."

"Most men wouldn't have, Jennie."

"I know. But Preston isn't like most men."

"No, he isn't." Bill hesitated a moment. "Are you hungry?"

She managed a small smile. "Yes. Do you think Rosa would mind if I ate downstairs this morning?"

"Why would she mind?"

"She brings a tray up to me every day. I assumed that was easier for her."

"No, Jennie. She's done that because Oliver instructed her to, just as he insists on having his breakfast brought to his room. It makes additional work for her."

Jennifer stared at him, stricken with guilt. "I didn't know, Bill. If I had, I would have stopped it the first day. I will stop it today. I would much rather eat with all of you."

"Good."

They started across the yard. After a moment, Jennifer spoke again, in a lower tone.

"What do you think of John?"

"I don't know." Bill ran a hand through his thick blond hair. "It's strange to find I have a brother after living all my life without one. I can't make him out, Jennie. I don't know what he wants from Preston, or from me."

"Are you convinced he means Preston no harm?"

"I don't think he does." Bill studied her face. "Are you convinced?"

Jennifer stepped up onto the veranda. "No, I'm not, Bill. I am deeply concerned that all this trouble started just before John Cantrell made himself known to us. He could have been in the area for weeks, studying the ranch, watching."

Bill pulled her farther back from the door. "I thought the same thing, but haven't mentioned it to anyone except Barb."

"There's more." She quickly explained her theory that such deep hatred as she had seen in John's expression that first night did not just go away, that there were other ways to exact revenge. She told him how she'd caught John in the barn the night the dam was destroyed and how she had seen John leave his room minutes before all the commotion started with the bull. "He claims his horse warned him something was wrong, and in fairness, I did hear a horse. But it sure seems convenient."

Bill expelled his breath in a long sigh. "I can't tell Preston this, not now. But I'll warn Gabe and Rosa. We'll all be careful. And I hope to God our fears are groundless." He stared in the direction of the barn, his expression distant. "Preston is so happy John is here. I guess he deeply loved Ana Maria. He never felt that way about my mother, at least not that I ever saw. Of course, my mother may not have felt that way about him, either."

Jennifer placed a hand on his arm. "Bill, I know Preston cared for your mother a great deal; I saw them together. There was a genuine affection between them. He just may not have felt the depth of passion he felt for John's mother." She tightened her fingers. "Perhaps a love like that happens only once in anyone's life."

"Perhaps."

John came from the barn and started across the yard toward them, and at the same time, the door behind them opened. Bill turned just as a small boy threw himself at his legs. With a laugh, Bill caught the child in his arms and hoisted him high. "What have we here?" he growled playfully. "I think it's a David-bug. What do you think, Jennie?"

"I think it is," Jennie answered with mock seriousness, struggling to contain a smile. "What are you going to do with it?"

Bill draped the giggling child over his shoulder. "I think I'll cook it for breakfast."

David shouted with laughter. "No, Papa! Mama Rosa already made breakfast! That's what I came to tell you! She made flapjacks!"

"We'll see," Bill said suspiciously. "If she did, then I guess you're off the hook—for today, anyway." He shifted the boy down from his shoulder and kissed the top of his blond, curly head. "If not . . ." His voice trailed off ominously. David burst into fresh peals of laughter. Bill laughed, also, and carried his son into the house.

Jennifer turned to follow them, then caught a glimpse of John as he advanced on her. There was a strange, guarded expression on his face. Had he guessed that she and Bill were talking about him? A twinge of guilt assailed her. She had no proof that John Cantrell had committed any of the acts she suspected him of, yet she had shared her suspicions with Bill. Was that fair? She raised her chin defiantly and went into the house without waiting for him. What was fairness in comparison to Preston's safety and the survival of the Santa Maria?

As she passed the entrance to the dining room, she noticed the room was empty. Perhaps breakfast was not quite ready yet. She hurried up to her room to deposit her shawl, then came back downstairs to find the dining room still empty. The polished oak table was bare of everything save the candelabras. Where was everyone? Where was breakfast? Following the sound of numerous voices, she pushed through the swinging door into the kitchen. Her eyes widened in amazement at the sight that greeted her.

Several people were gathered around the scarred pine table, crowded onto the two long benches. Preston sat at the end of one bench, in deep conversation with the white-haired man from the barn, who sat across from him. Bill held little Molly on his lap, while Barbara helped David cut his flapjacks. Francisca smiled up at her, closemouthed, her slightly puffed cheeks indicating that she had a mouthful of food, and John, who was seated next to David, merely glanced at her, then away. Gabe and Rosa sat at the other end of the table, arguing good-naturedly over who was going to get up and bring the coffeepot from the stove, only a few feet away.

"I'll get the coffee," Jennifer offered. She motioned to Rosa to stay in her seat and retrieved the pot from the stove, then worked her way around the table refilling cups. John nodded his thanks when she poured coffee into the cup he held up for her, but he did not say anything.

She approached Preston, who offered her a wide, conciliatory smile. Unable to resist, she smiled back and noticed the relief that flashed in his eyes.

"Jennie, this is Dr. Emmett Lafferty, the veterinarian I told you about," he said. "Emmett, my goddaughter, Jennifer Mainwaring."

Emmett stood up. "How do you do, Miss Mainwaring?"

"Hello, Doctor," Jennifer said shyly. She looked into warm brown eyes that belied the doctor's age. He was not a tall man, perhaps only an inch taller than she was, but he carried himself with dignity. She immediately liked him.

"I am pleased to make your acquaintance, sir, honored, actually," she said. "You are the first veterinarian I have ever met."

"Honored, huh? That's a strong word." Emmett raised a teasing eyebrow while his lips curved in a smile beneath his thick white mustache.

Jennifer smiled in return. "Well, I am. I so admire what you do, working to ease the suffering of innocent creatures."

"Yes, Preston mentioned that you have a strong interest in animals and some knowledge of their medical care—most unusual for a young lady. You may like to know that your advice on Buford's treatment matched mine exactly."

A pleased blush warmed Jennifer's cheeks. "How is Buford?"

"Barring any unforeseen complications, he should live to sire a herd for Preston. Perhaps you would be willing to help keep an eye on Buford over the next few days."

Jennifer nodded eagerly. "I would be happy to." Her arm was beginning to ache from holding the heavy coffeepot, and she turned to fill the doctor's cup as he sat down again.

"Have more flapjacks, Emmett," Preston urged. "You could use some meat on those old bones."

"I reckon I could." Emmett reached for the platter of flapjacks. "My cooking just can't measure up to Grace's, and sometimes I lose interest in eating altogether. Mealtime is lonely around my house now."

Preston nodded in sympathy. "It's been, what, maybe six months since Grace passed on? How are you adjusting to losing her?"

"It's hard, Preston. Me and the old gal were together for over forty years. I miss her like the dickens. Don't have anyone to argue with anymore." Emmett paused and cleared his throat. "I sure did love that woman."

"I know, old friend. I know."

Jennifer was saddened by Emmett's words and touched his shoulder in a gesture of sympathy before she moved on to fill Barbara's cup.

"Is this where you always eat breakfast?" she asked Barbara in a low voice.

"This is where we always eat everything, 'cept when we have comp'ny," David piped up. "When we have comp'ny, me'n Molly can't eat with the grown-ups."

"It's not polite to answer a question asked of someone else, honey," Barbara informed him gently.

"Is it like interruptin'?" David asked.

"Sort of." Barbara smiled at her son.

Jennifer returned the pot to the stove, her brow furrowed in thought. How much trouble had she and her uncle caused the Cantrell household? And, short of leaving, what could she do to return things to normal for them?

Although there was more room next to John, she took a seat at the end of the bench next to Rosa, who promptly handed her a plate piled high with flapjacks.

"You will eat all of them," Rosa ordered as Jennifer eyed the tall stack with dismay. "You must keep up your strength, especially if you and Barbara will drive the wagon to the dam today." She pushed a pitcher of maple syrup closer.

Jennifer raised a questioning eyebrow at Barbara.

"I promised the children we would meet Bill at the dam for lunch today, and I thought you might like to come with us," Barbara explained.

"I would love to." Jennifer poured syrup over her flapjacks, knowing that she would be lucky to eat one quarter of the food on her plate.

Barbara hesitated a moment. "Do you think Oliver would like to join us?"

"I think he would be bored, but I will ask him."

Barbara nodded in satisfaction and reached out to wipe the corner of Molly's mouth.

Jennifer took a small bite of food, looking around the table as she chewed. Although the noise level was high, everyone appeared to be enjoying themselves. Talk ran from discussions of the progress made on the dam to speculation on whether it would rain to which friends were coming to the *fiesta* on Saturday.

She could not help comparing this meal to those she had shared with Preston and his family in the formal dining room. The evening meals had been pleasant enough, but in retrospect, they seemed reserved and almost stilted. Perhaps she and Oliver were responsible for that. The thought disturbed her. This meal was much more relaxed, much more fun. She did not like to think that Preston had changed his routine, and that of his family, to suit some vague notion of etiquette for her sake. She would speak to him about it when the opportunity arose.

She caught Rosa's warning glance and dutifully took another bite of food, smiling all the while.

Seven

The late morning sun beat down unmercifully upon the occupants of the farm wagon that was pulled along the dusty, rutted road by two sturdy draft horses. Oliver had rudely declined Jennifer's invitation to join them, as she had suspected he would, and she was thankful he had. Everyone would have a much more enjoyable time without him along.

She was also thankful for the wide-brimmed straw garden hat Barbara had loaned her. Occupied as she was with the animated Molly on her lap, it would have been impossible for her to hold a shielding parasol against the glare of the sun. David sat between her and Barbara, chattering joyously about anything and everything, while Barbara handled the reins with a confident ease that Jennifer envied. Oliver, as her parents had before him, considered handling a team unladylike, so she had little experience in driving, a situation she longed to change.

Jennifer dropped a kiss on the cotton sunbonnet that protected Molly's head. At fifteen months, Molly was a beautiful child, with golden curls, her father's clear blue eyes, and her mother's serene features. She chattered on with as much enthusiasm as her brother, only her words could not yet be understood.

Barbara glanced at her daughter. "She's a talker, isn't she? Just like her brother."

"She is," Jennifer agreed with a smile. "And she is so serious, as if what she is saying makes perfect sense to her."

"David did the same thing when he was her age. Sometimes they carry on entire conversations with each other in those incomprehensible words, and I *know* they are communicating. Children are very wise, Jennie, much wiser than most adults give them credit for." Barbara's gaze dropped down to David. "The responsibility is overwhelming sometimes. How do I teach them all they need to know? How do I prepare them for life?"

"I think the most important thing is that you love them, Barbara." Jennifer reached over David's small, hat-covered head to pat her friend's shoulder. "All parents make mistakes, but love will overcome a lot of mistakes. You and Bill are doing a wonderful job. You have lovely children."

"Thank you," David interjected, then looked up at his mother, his little face wreathed in doubt. "I'm s'posed to say 'thank you' when someone says somethin' nice 'bout me, but I interrupted again, huh, Mama?"

Barbara hugged him against her side. "Yes, you interrupted, but I did teach you to say 'thank you.' You did fine."

Jennifer looked up and saw that they had come around the final hill before the dam. Her mouth fell open in astonishment.

All traces of the destruction wrought by the explosion were gone. In two short days, Preston and his men had cleared away the mangled logs and the destroyed flow system. A new foundation was already taking recognizable shape. Jennifer hated to think how much earth had been moved by sheer manual labor, and in such heat.

Barbara drew the wagon to a halt, and for a few minutes they watched the activity. From the direction of the forested hills in the distance, Bill approached the work site on horseback, towing a log. When he reached a place near Preston, several hands released the log from the ropes that held it. Preston studied a paper in his hand, periodically raising his head to examine the dam. He shouted out a measurement, and Pedro stepped forward with a length of thin rope knotted in even increments. After making quick marks with his knife, he stepped back and two men moved into position with the long, mean-bladed bucking saw.

Jennifer recognized one man as Gabriel Horn, but it took her a minute to realize who the other man was because his face was hidden by the shadow of his black hat and he wore no shirt. Her breath caught. It was John.

The tantalizing promise of broad shoulders, muscular torso, and tapered waist—always before hidden by his shirt—was fulfilled. As he pushed and pulled the saw blade across the thick log, the muscles in his back tensed and relaxed, tensed and relaxed, with an even rhythm. A sheen of sweat covered his skin, making him almost glow in the bright sunlight. His gunbelt drew attention to his narrow hips, while the snug-fitting denims he wore revealed the movements of his powerful flanks and legs as he rocked back and forth with the saw. John Cantrell's body was as handsome as his face. Unconsciously, Jennifer caught her lower lip in her teeth.

The two men rested for a minute, and John straightened, removing his hat. He ran a gloved hand over his forehead, then noticed the wagon. His face split in a wide grin and he raised a hand in greeting, his blue eyes seeming to sparkle. Startled and ridiculously pleased, Jennifer moved to wave back. She caught herself as David jumped to his feet and raised both his arms over his head.

"Hi, Unca' John! Hi, Papa! Hi, Grampa! We brung you lemonade!"

Quickly, Jennifer shifted her rising hand to smooth the ruffle on Molly's bonnet. She felt foolish and was grateful that she had not actually waved. What was she thinking? she asked herself in irritation. John Cantrell had no reason to wave at her, had no reason to be glad to see her, as he was to see David and Molly.

John settled his hat on his head and swiftly crossed the distance to the wagon. He nodded to Jennifer.

"Miss Mainwaring. No parasol today?"

Jennifer clamped her mouth shut, cutting off her cordial response to the first part of his greeting. She would not look at his face, but she was very aware of the close proximity of his naked chest. Fine dark hair covered the muscled expanse, narrowing down his stomach, and a thin white scar, perhaps three inches long, stood out in stark relief on his left side. She wondered how he had come by the scar, surprised that it troubled her to think of him being wounded.

David maneuvered around Jennifer's knees and held his arms out to John, who obligingly lifted the boy from the wagon.

"You want some lemonade, Unca' John?" David asked.

"Later, partner, when Gabe and I are finished with the log. Will you save me some?"

David nodded solemnly. "Molly wants to come, too," he pointed out. Molly squirmed on Jennifer's lap, reaching for John.

John plucked the child from her grasp, brushing Jennifer's breast with his forearm as he did. "My apologies, Miss Mainwaring," he murmured, then turned away with the children.

Jennifer's face flamed, although she knew no one had seen John's accidental indiscretion. She watched as he handed Molly up to her father, who still sat his horse, then carried David over to the log. He set the boy down, said something to him about standing back, and once again took up the saw.

Preston approached and assisted Barbara down from the wagon. "Is it true you brought lemonade?" he asked hopefully.

Barbara nodded with a smile and waved toward the large ceramic crock in the wagon bed. "Rosa insisted, said she had to do something with the lemons before they spoiled. She said we had better not bring any back."

Preston circled the wagon and lifted Jennifer to the ground. "You don't have to worry about that." He tapped the top of her head. "Nice hat, Jennie. It looks good on you."

Jennifer smiled. "It's much more practical than a parasol.

Barbara loaned it to me; I'll get my own the next time we go into town." She indicated a basket in the wagon bed. "Rosa sent along a couple of pies, too, complaining that the plums were also beginning to spoil. She said to be sure Mr. Horn got some, because plum pie is his favorite." She lowered her voice to a conspiratorial whisper. "I think Rosa likes Mr. Horn."

"We think so, too," Barbara whispered back. "And we think Gabe likes Rosa. He's been spending more and more time around the kitchen. It's been six years since Rosa's husband died. Maybe she's ready for Gabe now."

"It would be good for both of them," Preston commented. "But don't you two play at matchmaking and try to hurry things along; let Rosa and Gabe work this out for themselves." He winked at them and headed back toward the dam.

Barbara laughed and lifted the pie basket from the wagon bed, while Jennifer grabbed the lunch basket and a folded blanket. The two women fell into step and by unspoken agreement walked to a sprawling oak tree a few yards away.

"How did Enrique die?" Jennifer asked. "Rosa never told me, and I didn't want to ask." She spread the blanket in the shade of the tree and they both sat down, arranging their skirts around their legs.

"He drowned in the river," Barbara answered. "Evidently he had gone for a swim; his horse waited on the bank, his clothes were neatly folded. But the river was running very high, and Enrique was never a strong swimmer. We found his body downstream a day later." She shook her head. "It was so sad. You know, he was only twenty-seven, and he and Rosa truly loved each other. She was devastated. For a while, we weren't sure she would recover. Finally, Gabe helped her realize how much Francisca needed her. Enrique was his best friend, and he has always been a good friend to Rosa."

"Poor Rosa," Jennifer murmured, her heart heavy with grief.

Both women lapsed into silence for a few minutes. When she spoke, Barbara's voice was soft and thoughtful.

"Life is so fleeting. One day Enrique was here, alive and laughing and loving, and the next day he was gone." She turned her eyes on Jennifer, their hazel-green depths shining in the dappled sunlight. "It terrifies me sometimes, how deeply I love Bill and the children. I don't know if I would survive losing one of them. Rosa is so brave."

Jennifer reached for Barbara's hand. "It is awful to contemplate, isn't it?"

Barbara nodded. "My parents died in a cholera epidemic shortly after I was born, and I was raised in an orphanage. I had no real family until I married Bill, and I've never lost anyone I was close to." She looked at Jennifer curiously. "How did you adjust to losing your parents, if you don't mind talking about it?"

"I don't mind." Jennifer stared off in the distance. "It was devastating when my mother died, for both me and my father. I was only a child. Later, my father and stepmother were killed when the boiler on the pleasure ship they were on exploded. But after being sent away to school for years, I was no longer close to my father, and my stepmother and I despised each other. Since I felt that I had lost my father long before, I remember feeling only a terrible numbness, but no real grief. Then Oliver was named my guardian, and I think I just put it all away." Her voice dropped to a whisper. "It seems like such a long time ago." She removed her hat. "It was a long time ago," she repeated with forced cheerfulness.

Barbara smiled. "Enough of such serious subjects. Let's talk about the *fiesta,* and how you think Francisca is coming along with my dress."

At that moment, a chorus of cheers and shouts rose from the dam site, signaling that John and Gabe had successfully sawed through the log. Preston called for the noon meal break. The men trooped toward the wagon, each carrying a burlap lunch sack. Bill rode up and handed Molly to Barbara, while John, now wearing his shirt and again carrying David, galloped from the log to the blanket, where he deposited the giggling boy. People settled in small, companionable groups around the wagon and began to eat.

Jennifer concentrated on the piece of bread she held, determined to ignore John. Yet, after a moment, she could not stop herself from stealing a glance at him. He had taken his hat off and leaned back against one of the wagon wheels. He seemed to be watching her, but surely it was the children he watched as they tumbled around on the blanket. Jennifer felt hot; she wished she had left off the second petticoat as well as the third. She used a linen handkerchief to pat a fine sweat from her upper lip, longing for the coolness and solitude of her room, anywhere away from the presence of John Cantrell.

Suddenly, all heads turned at the sound of approaching horses. Jennifer saw a group of five riders come up to the wagon, led by a young man on a magnificent bay stallion. Something about him was familiar.

"My father sends his greetings, *Señor* Cantrell," the man said with no warmth in his manner or his tone. "We have come to offer our assistance with the rebuilding of the dam."

Preston stood up. "Welcome, and thank you, Arturo. Please help yourselves to the lemonade." He waved toward the crock. "We'll be finished eating soon, and then we'll all get to work." He settled back down on the blanket.

Arturo. It had to be Arturo Noriega. Jennifer stared at the man as he and his companions dismounted and took advantage of the lemonade. She remembered Arturo Noriega as an insolent and rude boy who doggedly followed his older sister Constanza everywhere, eagerly partaking in her cruel plots and games. Now, the bored expression on his thin face, combined with his curled, sneering lip, led Jennifer to believe that Arturo was no more pleasant as a man than he had been as a boy. She turned her face away when he noticed her, for his eyebrows rose in curiosity; she wondered if he remembered her.

The easy comfort of the gathering had disappeared. The Cantrell hands seemed in a hurry to finish their meal, even declining Barbara's offer of plum pie. Gabe muttered something about waiting until the afternoon break and walked off in the direction of the dam. Gradually, the men finished and followed him. John stood up and dusted the seat of his denims, then adjusted his hat, prepared to follow Gabe.

One of the Noriega hands, a big, red-haired brute of a man, eyed John. "You must be the new Cantrell," he said, a curious note of taunting in his gruff voice.

John slowly turned to face him. "I am. What of it?"

"Forgive me, Lewis," Arturo interjected, a calculating smile twisting his lips. "I did not introduce you. This is John Novales Cantrell, *Señor* Cantrell's bastard son by a Mexican woman." He faced John. "John Cantrell, meet Baxter Lewis. His parents were married."

Jennifer caught her breath at the deliberate insult. She could tell that both Arturo and Lewis were challenging John, but challenging him to what? And why? As little as she cared for John, she found herself wanting to slap the smirk off Arturo's unattractive face in his defense.

Preston rose to his feet, as did Bill; both men moved closer to John. As Molly crawled by, Jennifer pulled the child onto her lap, while Barbara secured David against her side. The air suddenly seemed very still.

"How nice for him," John responded tightly. He turned away.

One of the Noriega men approached Arturo. "Come on, Arturo, leave him alone. *Señor* Noriega sent us here to work, not cause trouble."

Arturo glared at him and waved him away. The man stepped back, shaking his head.

"Don't think I seen no blue-eyed Mex before," Lewis commented loudly, hooking his thumbs in his gunbelt.

John whirled around. "If you're not careful, Mr. Lewis, this blue-eyed Mexican will be the last thing you'll ever see."

His eyes glittered dangerously, and his jaw was set and stiff, reminding Jennifer again of a wolf, a cornered wolf. John's right hand hovered over the pearl-handled pistol at his hip.

Lewis threw back his shoulders, which had the effect of causing his protruding belly to stick out even further. "You threatenin' me, half-breed?" He spoke over his shoulder to Arturo. "I think he's threatenin' me, boss."

"I think he is," Arturo agreed. He moved to Lewis's side, his eyes narrowed with malevolence.

John took a calming breath and shot an apologetic look at Preston, deeply regretting this had happened with women and children nearby. He noted his position in regards to the sun and the people around him. Thankfully, Barbara, Jennifer, and the children were out of the direct line of fire. A part of his mind registered the horrified expression on Jennifer's face, and he idly wondered if she would care if he were shot.

"It's no threat, Lewis," John said almost conversationally. "It is a promise. You have no call coming here and upsetting everyone. Either mind your manners or go home." He noticed that Preston and Bill had taken positions on either side of him. Surprisingly, reluctantly, his heart warmed; his father and his brother were backing him up.

"No half-breed is gonna be tellin' me what to do," Lewis growled.

"Then I will!" Preston thundered in a voice that caused Jennifer to quake inside and Molly to whimper. "How dare you come on my land and insult my family? And you." He stepped forward and pointed his finger at Arturo. "You have shamed your father. He'll be shocked to learn what you did, and in front of women and children. Take your men and get off my land. *Now.*"

Arturo stared at Preston, his expression a curious combination of hatred and fear. "As you wish, *Señor* Cantrell," he said stiffly. "I will tell my father you did not want our help." He swung up into his saddle.

"You tell your father the truth, Arturo, or by God, I will.

You are not welcome in my house until you apologize to my son, and only then because of the respect and friendship I have for your father. And you," he pointed at Lewis, "will never set foot on my property again, for any reason. If you do, you'll be escorted off at gunpoint. Is that clear?"

Lewis only glared at him as he mounted his horse. Arturo led him away at a gallop, followed by the other men, with the exception of the one who had tried to defuse the situation. That man mounted up and guided his horse to a stop in front of the Cantrell men.

"For what it's worth, Mr. Cantrell, I'm sorry. I'll be collecting my pay after this, and I'll make certain *Señor* Noriega knows what happened; I can't stomach working with that damned Arturo any longer." He tipped his hat in the direction of the women on the blanket. "Beg your pardon, ladies, for swearing, but the word fits the man, and I always speak my mind."

"Thank you, sir." Preston held out his hand, which the man accepted. "What's your name?"

"Ross Latham, late of Wyoming Territory." He smiled ruefully. "Reckon I'll soon be late of Santa Clara County as well."

"If you want to stay in Santa Clara County a while longer, Mr. Latham, stop by the Santa Maria after you leave the Noriega ranch," Preston said. "We could use another hand, especially one who isn't afraid to speak his mind."

Ross settled his hat more firmly on his head. "Thank you, Mr. Cantrell. I just might do that." He looked at John. "Arturo holds a powerful grudge against you, and that's always dangerous coming from a cocky, small-minded man. I'd watch my back."

John nodded his thanks. Ross touched his heels to his horse's flanks and rode off.

The three Cantrell men watched him go, then Preston led his sons farther away from the women and children.

"We may need to strengthen the watch around the ranch," he said in a low tone.

"Might not be a bad idea, at least around the house and outbuildings." Bill pushed his hat back on his head. "I hate to say this, Pa, but do you think it's possible the Noriegas are behind all the trouble we've been having?"

"No." Preston shook his head vehemently. "I'd stake my life on Alejandro's trustworthiness. For God's sake, he's one of my oldest friends."

"I'm damned sorry about all this, Preston," John said quietly.

"It wasn't your fault. The man challenged you; both of them did." Preston clapped him on the shoulder.

"I've been called worse things in my life. I could have walked away, should have, with the women and kids here. It won't happen again." He hesitated. "I appreciate your both standing with me."

"The Cantrells stand together, John," said Preston. "You don't have to tolerate insults on Cantrell land, or in my house. You are my son, and any who do not treat you with respect will not be welcome." He looked up at the sky. "We're wasting time. Let's get back to work." He strode off toward the dam.

Bill turned to John. "Do you think Arturo is behind the trouble we've been having?"

John shook his head. "Not by himself—he's not smart enough." He looked Bill in the eye. "You don't think I'm behind it?"

His brother met his gaze without flinching. "I don't know, John. I sure as hell hope not, for my father's sake. If it turns out you are, I swear I'll take you apart with my bare hands. But I can't think of what you'd gain from it, just as I can't figure out what Arturo Noriega would gain from it."

John sighed. "I don't know what he'd have to gain, either. Let's all keep a careful watch on everything." He followed Preston.

Bill turned back to Barbara. He hefted David up onto one hip and pulled his wife to her feet with his free hand. "Why don't you take the children on home, honey?"

"All right." She took Molly from Jennifer and raised her eyes to her husband's face. "That was frightening, Bill."

"I know. But I doubt it will ever happen again." He held out a hand to Jennifer and helped her up.

"So that was Arturo Noriega," she commented.

"It sure was. He grew up to become a charming fellow, didn't he?"

Jennifer set the straw hat on her head. "Somehow, I am not surprised." She folded the blanket and followed Bill to the wagon.

When everyone was settled in their places, Bill gave Barbara a kiss. "Save those pies for us," he said, then winked at David. "You make sure all these girls get home safely, son."

"I will, Papa," David said, then promptly yawned.

Bill laughed and handed Barbara the reins. "We'll be home by sundown, and we'll be hungry," he said. " 'Bye, Jennie." He stepped back from the wagon and waved them on their way, then turned toward the dam, his brow furrowed with worry.

Had John Cantrell brought more trouble upon them? Bill took his hat off and slapped it against his thigh in frustration. He agreed with his father that John had done the right thing standing up to Arturo and Baxter, but in the end, would he make things worse? Was John setting their father up for a big fall?

Everything had changed. John's arrival had upset the balance of the family. Preston had welcomed him, was practically doting on him. Bill could not miss the joy and pride Preston felt toward John, and it stung. He recognized his feelings for the jealousy they were and had the sense to recognize those feelings as normal. Preston Cantrell had raised no fool.

But John's presence was causing other changes. Arturo

Noriega had never before spoken to any member of the Cantrell clan with such disrespect. Bill suspected that Arturo had often been tempted to, but had never dared risk the certain wrath of Alejandro, his formidable father, by doing so. That Arturo had behaved so abominably in front of Preston and so many other people indicated a depth of hatred for John that was puzzling in its intensity. And as Jennifer had said, such hatred did not just go away.

Bill squinted up at the sun and crammed his hat back on his head. Trouble was brewing; he could feel it. And even if it were eventually proven that his newfound brother was not the direct cause of it, John Novales Cantrell was most certainly the catalyst. He would not be sorry to see John leave the Santa Maria.

Barbara and Jennifer spoke little on the way home. David laid his head in his mother's lap and was quickly asleep. Jennifer held Molly cradled against her breast, and she knew the child would also soon fall asleep, if she hadn't already.

A rush of love filled Jennifer's heart for the two children, followed immediately by an intense yearning for a baby of her own. While her love for David and Molly did not surprise her, the sudden, unexpected surge of maternal longing did. Deep in thought, she rested her cheek on Molly's sweetly scented head and stared off at the surrounding hills. Why would she want a child now? she wondered. There was no man in her life with whom she wished to share her heart and her body, no man whose seed she wanted to capture in her womb and nurture into a living expression of their love.

Unbidden, the picture of John Cantrell filled her mind—John with no shirt on, working the saw against the stubborn log, his muscular back glistening in the sunlight, his thighs pressing against the confines of his denim pants. She shook her head in irritation. What did John have to do with an absurd, ill-timed wish for a child?

A shiver ran through her, one of primal excitement. On a deep level, Jennifer knew that John Cantrell would be able to care for his woman and his children in the most basic sense. Just as he had stood up to Arturo Noriega and Baxter Lewis today, he would protect his family against any threat, would provide for them, would keep his babies safe.

She compared John to Bradley Ames, the young Philadelphia man Oliver wanted her to marry. Bradley came from a fine family, one of the wealthiest and most prestigious in all of Pennsylvania. He was younger than John by a few years, educated at Yale, poised to follow his father in the family shipping business. But Jennifer could not imagine Bradley sawing a log. Or standing up to a bully. Or swinging a three-year-old boy up in his arms and galloping across a field with him. She did not know Bradley well, but to her knowledge, his greatest talent was his dancing skill.

Could John dance? She would find out at the *fiesta,* and somehow, she suspected he could. Would he dance with her? She knew what it was to be held in his arms in anger. How would it feel to be in his arms for an entirely different reason?

One of the wheels hit a rock, causing the wagon to lurch and disturbing Jennifer's train of thought. Molly stirred and fussed for a few minutes, then settled back to sleep. Jennifer resolutely pushed John Cantrell's handsome image from her mind and concentrated on the feel of Molly's small, warm body in her arms. It brought a wonderful contentment to her, a combination of love and maternal protectiveness and pride, and the child was not even hers. How would it be to hold her own child? One day she would know. Another strange thrill raced through her at the thought.

Eight

Oliver finally left his room the next morning, but he did not leave his petulant mood behind. He moped around the house all morning until Jennifer, in exasperation, begged Preston to offer him the use of the buggy. Perhaps a drive around the ranch or a trip to Gilroy would lighten Oliver's mood. If nothing else, it would get him out of everyone's way for a while.

Preston agreed, and Oliver was only too happy to venture forth on an excursion of exploration. After lunch he descended the stairs in full calling regalia, complete with a gold-tipped walking stick.

Just as he reached the bottom step, Jennifer came from the *sala*, where she had been helping Rosa rearrange the furniture in preparation for the *fiesta* the next day. Oliver's eyebrows raised in disapproval at the apron Jennifer wore over her dress, but he wisely did not comment.

"I do wish you would join me, Jennifer," he said with a pout as he pulled on his gloves. "It would do you good to get out of the house as well."

"Thank you for asking, Oliver, but I've been out. If you will remember, Barbara and I drove to the dam yesterday." She pushed back a strand of hair from her forehead, not surprised to find her skin damp with sweat. It was hot again today, as it had been every day since they had arrived in California.

"You drove in a farm wagon, with young children crawling

all over you, and they no doubt babbled the entire way. I would hardly call that a relaxing excursion."

Determined not to let him goad her into another argument, Jennifer kept her voice calm as she responded, "I had a very nice day, Oliver. Now why don't you go along? I think the buggy is ready."

"Very well." He again eyed her apron. "I hope you are not being treated as a servant, Jennifer."

"Don't be silly." She guided him toward the front door. "I want to help with the preparations for the *fiesta* as much as I can, which isn't very much. Barbara, Rosa, and Francisca are very capable." She walked him out to the veranda, watched as he settled himself in the buggy, and waved as he drove off. She marvelled that he had not complained about the fact that he was forced to drive a simple piano-box buggy rather than a stylish spider phaeton, as he drove at home. With a sigh of relief, she went back inside.

The rest of the day passed smoothly. Oliver returned late in the afternoon, and he must have enjoyed his drive, for he was in surprisingly good spirits throughout supper. Again, Jennifer was relieved, but she was also growing suspicious. Quite simply, Oliver was in too good a mood.

Saturday dawned with clear skies and the promise of continued hot weather. The morning was spent bathing. Jennifer learned that the members of the Cantrell house did not use the portable tin tub in their bedrooms, as she had been doing since her arrival. A bathing room had been constructed off the kitchen, complete with its own pump and wood-fueled water heaters. An ingenious method of draining the used bathwater from the two large, built-in clay tubs was accomplished by removing a cork from a hole in the bottom of each tub. The water was carried away from the house by a narrow canal of sorts, built of the curved clay tiles that served as roofing material for the *hacienda*. A similar bathing room had been built at one end of the bunkhouse. Jennifer decided that, in many ways, Preston was a man ahead of his time.

As the tub had already been brought to her room, Jennifer used it, but she determined it was for the last time. She would not put Preston's household to any additional trouble, no matter what Oliver said about the impropriety of roaming about the house in one's wrapper or robe.

After the noon meal, Barbara laid David and Molly down for a nap and joined Jennifer in her room, where they arranged each other's hair and helped each other dress.

A few hours later, with the children left in Francisca's care, Barbara and Jennifer hooked arms and walked down the hall. The buzz of many voices rose from the stairs; the guests were beginning to arrive.

Barbara smoothed the lace overskirt of her dress with her free hand. "Thank you again for the gown, Jennie. I feel so pretty."

"You are," Jennifer assured her with a smile. "I cannot wait until Bill sees you."

They reached the top of the stairs and looked down on the small crowd gathered in the foyer. While Jennifer did not know most of the people, she recognized the man Preston welcomed at the door as Alejandro Noriega. She straightened her shoulders; the unpleasant Arturo and his sister Constanza would not be far behind.

As the thought came to her, a dark-haired woman in a flame-red satin gown swept through the door. Jennifer heard Barbara's intake of breath and patted her friend's hand. "Remember: You're a queen," she whispered.

As they slowly descended the stairs, Jennifer stared at her childhood nemesis. Constanza had grown into a breathtaking beauty. Her black hair was pulled away from her face and secured at the back of her head with an ornate Spanish-style hair comb. A black lace mantilla covered the thick locks that were allowed to fall down her back to below her waist. Her dark eyes, lined with black, appeared very large, while the red of her lips matched the color of her gown.

And that gown. Although Jennifer recognized that the style

was copied after the latest Paris fashion, there was something almost shocking about it. Perhaps it was the startling, unrelieved red color, perhaps the plunging neckline accentuated by an ornate golden crucifix that drew attention to Constanza's generous bosom. Still, Jennifer had to admit Constanza presented an arresting picture. The woman carried herself with pride and confidence. As Jennifer watched, Constanza tapped Preston's forearm with her folded fan and said something to him, then tittered in laughter. Jennifer gritted her teeth; she remembered that laugh.

Constanza turned as Jennifer and Barbara neared the bottom of the stairs. She stared for a moment, as if amazed, then put her hands on her hips and sauntered toward them, a calculating gleam in her eyes.

"I hardly recognized you, Barbara. Your style of dress is usually so unremarkable and . . . mousy."

Barbara pulled away from Jennifer's arm. "How nice to see you again, Constanza," she said in a soft, polite tone.

Jennifer glanced at her friend and saw that Barbara's face, just moments before becomingly flushed with excitement and anticipation, was now deathly pale.

"You lie," Constanza retorted with a lazy smile. "You are not happy to see me at all, and you hope and pray your husband does not see me." She eyed Barbara's dress with a derisive glance as she smoothed her own satin skirt.

Barbara stiffened, apparently at a loss for words.

Something in Jennifer exploded. "You're quite right, Miss Noriega," she snapped. "Mrs. Cantrell merely made the mistake of attempting to be polite. She is not the least bit pleased to see you, and neither am I. Neither of us care much for the company of social bullies."

Ignoring the astonished expression on Constanza's face, Jennifer searched the foyer until she spotted Bill near the doors to the *sala*. "Bill," she called. When he looked up at her, she motioned him over.

"Who are you to be speaking to me in such a manner?" Constanza demanded.

"I think you know."

Constanza's eyes widened. "No," she breathed. "It can't be."

Jennifer fearlessly met the woman's surprised and hostile gaze. "Yes, it can."

Bill joined them, unable to take his eyes from Barbara. He held his hand out to her, which she gratefully accepted as if he had thrown her a lifeline. "Darling wife, you take my breath away," he whispered. He guided her off the last step and tucked her arm around his, then led her away, seemingly oblivious to the furious Constanza.

Jennifer stepped down from the final stair, prepared to make her way to Preston's side.

Constanza whirled on her. "I heard you were here," she snarled. "Little Jennifer Mainwaring, after all these years." She shook her head and crossed her arms over her chest, looking Jennifer up and down. "Life in the East must not agree with you; you are so thin. Even now, as a woman grown, you have nothing for a man to hold onto." She slightly raised her folded arms, causing her breasts to bulge even farther from their casing of red satin.

For a moment, Jennifer did not respond. In a deliberate mimic of Constanza's pose, she crossed her own arms and ran a slow, critical eye over Constanza from head to foot. "And you, Constanza, have too much. Perhaps that is why you feel the need to flaunt it."

Constanza gasped. *"Ramera!"* she said in a low, outraged whisper.

"And that's the other problem," Jennifer said smoothly, as if Constanza had not spoken. "You are vulgar, distressingly so. You were as a child, and you are still. It is most unbecoming." She smiled sweetly and swept away, leaving a fuming Constanza alone at the bottom of the stairs.

John Cantrell watched the interchange from the door of the

dining room. Jennifer had managed Constanza wonderfully, first in defense of Barbara, then of herself. What a picture she had made, standing there so tall and proud, steadfast against the wicked tongue of the notorious *señorita*. Jennifer and Constanza had presented him with an interesting study in contrasts.

One, voluptuous and fiery in a red satin dress, her black hair tumbling down her back in a sensuous display better reserved for the privacy of one's bedroom. The other, slender and cool in a tasteful and elegant gown of moss-green silk worn over a forest-green underskirt, her rich brown hair arranged in a flattering style of rolls and curls with two flirtatious ringlets teasing her right shoulder.

In truth, he mused, each woman's costume complemented her. Constanza's red dress emphasized her dark coloring and paid tribute to her tempestuous and often outrageous temperament, while Jennifer's green gown highlighted her beautiful eyes and regal carriage, and hinted at a calm and secure spirit, a spirit both strong and, he suspected, passionate.

At that moment, Constanza saw him and hurried to his side, furiously fanning herself with a black lace fan. "Never have I been so insulted!" she huffed. "That *ramera*. How dare she speak to me like that?" She clutched John's forearm and raised her face for an expected kiss.

He hesitated, then placed a light kiss on her powdered cheek. "She's not a bitch, dear Constanza," he murmured. "You are."

"Oh, Juan." She swatted his shoulder with the now closed fan. "Of course I am. But she is, too." She pouted prettily, and John could not contain a laugh.

"No, she isn't," he repeated, surprised at himself that he was actually defending Jennifer Mainwaring. "But I'll not argue with you." He removed her hand from his arm. "You must excuse me. My father wishes to introduce me to some of his friends." He bowed and left her, joining Preston at the door.

Constanza frowned after him, then stomped her foot and whirled around, intending to follow her father into the *sala,* when she collided with another guest. A tall, male guest, she discovered, who smelled pleasantly of cologne, whose hands were at her waist in an attempt to steady her.

"I beg your pardon, madam," a frosty, cultured voice said.

Constanza slowly raised her eyes from the expensive coat to the fine, chiseled features of the man. He was very handsome. Who could he be? She lowered her eyes in a false show of modesty and snapped her fan open. "Pray forgive me, sir, for surely it was my fault." She took a small step back and fanned herself, noting with satisfaction that his gaze had paused, however briefly, on her breasts.

"Surely not, my dear lady," the man countered, with more warmth in his voice. "I accept full responsibility."

"If you insist." Constanza gave him the considerable force of her most charming smile. "However, in order to make amends, you must introduce yourself."

"Oliver Mainwaring, at your service." He bowed, then straightened and waited, idly stroking his mustache with one hand.

"Mainwaring? You are related to Jennifer?"

"She is my niece."

"I did not know Jennifer had an uncle," Constanza purred as she batted her eyes at him over the top of her fan. "Does she also have an aunt?"

Oliver smiled fully now. "No, my dear. I beg you, tell me to whom am I having the great pleasure of speaking."

Constanza drew herself up proudly, pleased to see Oliver's gaze wander lower once again. "I am Constanza Noriega y Gonzales. My father, *Don* Alejandro, owns the *Rancho de Buena Ventura,* the largest and grandest ranch in all of the valley. We are neighbors to the Cantrells."

"I am honored to meet you, Miss Noriega. I saw you speaking with John Cantrell; clearly, he upset you, and I am certain that is what led to our fortuitous collision. I must remember to thank him." Oliver held out his arm. "I would be honored if you would allow me to find you some refreshment and perhaps offer you more enjoyable company than that of John Cantrell."

Constanza smiled coyly behind her fan and placed her hand on Oliver's offered arm. "I would be delighted, Mr. Mainwaring."

Jennifer stood at Preston's side and watched in surprise as Oliver led Constanza toward the *sala*. A moment earlier, the woman had been kissing John, and now she had latched onto Oliver. Jennifer grimaced in disgust, thinking little of either man's taste. "Fools, the both of them," she muttered under her breath.

"What did you say, Jennie?" Preston asked.

"Nothing important." She smiled up at him, then her gaze fell on John. He stood at his father's other side, playing the gracious son, modest and polite as Preston introduced him to the friends and neighbors of the Cantrell family. Perhaps he had just kissed Constanza Noriega, but his manners, unlike his taste, were above reproach. He would not embarrass himself if he were to call upon the Queen of England. When John Cantrell put his mind to it, he could be devastatingly charming.

To Jennifer's eye, he looked remarkably handsome tonight, although he was again dressed all in black. The color both complemented and suited him, she decided. It was befitting that a man as threatening and mysterious as he wore black.

He again wore the tight pants with the small silver conchos kissing the lengths of his ridiculously long legs. A short, Spanish-style jacket covered his black silk shirt, leaving his ever-present gunbelt in clear view.

Her eyes moved to his clean-shaven face and thick black hair. Suddenly, he winked at her.

Mortified to have been caught staring at him, Jennifer blushed and looked down at the floor.

"I don't think I have mentioned that you look lovely tonight, Miss Mainwaring," John said smoothly.

Astonished at his compliment, her gaze jerked back to meet his. She wondered if he was teasing her, but his blue eyes seemed to shine with sincerity. Confused, she again looked away as Preston agreed with his son.

"She does indeed, John."

Jennifer made a concentrated effort to collect her thoughts. "Thank you, gentlemen," she said tartly. "If you continue, I fear your flattery will go to my head. Therefore, before you begin to wax poetic, I believe I shall check with Rosa and see if she needs help." She gathered her skirt in one hand and made her escape, to the sound of Preston's appreciative laugh.

If Jennifer hoped to find anything resembling peace in the kitchen, she was disappointed. Because Francisca was busy with David and Molly, Rosa had commandeered the assistance of Gabriel Horn. He looked down sheepishly at the white apron tied around his waist and shrugged.

"These are my best clothes," he said in way of explanation.

Jennifer hid a smile and faced Rosa. "Is there anything I can do?"

Rosa nodded. "In one minute we take the food out to the tables set up in the courtyard. You help with that if you wish, Jennie, but only if you watch your gown. I would hate to see you get anything on it."

"I'll be careful," Jennifer promised. She noticed that instead of her usual single braid, Rosa had dressed her hair up and decorated it with a beautiful comb made of mother-of-pearl. A long apron protected Rosa's gown, but Jennifer could see that it was made of blue satin and covered with an over-skirt of black lace. It seemed to Jennifer that Rosa's eyes sparkled more than usual, that her cheeks carried a hint of a blush. Rosa was beautiful tonight, and Jennifer told her so.

"Silencio, Jennie," Rosa scolded affectionately, although she looked pleased. "Stop the nonsense and carry this bowl out to the courtyard."

"Yes, ma'am," Jennifer said with a laugh, and accepted the

bowl. When she reached the courtyard, she paused to look around in appreciation. Although it was only dusk, numerous lighted lanterns hung from the rafters of the overhangs and winked from tree branches and shrubs, casting a soft, romantic light on the gathering. The heady scent of a myriad of flowers filled the air, stirred by a miraculous early-evening breeze. The harmonious sound of the water fountain offered a nice background for the three musicians who were able to make a guitar and two violins sound surprisingly sophisticated.

A few couples were dancing, and Jennifer was pleased to see Barbara and Bill among them. They noticed her and came to her side.

"Is Rosa ready to serve?" Barbara asked breathlessly.

Bill had not released his wife's hand, and Barbara seemed to glow with happiness. The sight gladdened Jennifer's heart. "Yes," she said, as she set the bowl on the table. "I think everything is ready."

"We'll help," Bill said, and pulled Barbara toward the kitchen.

Gabe, no longer wearing the apron, approached the table with a heavy-looking cast-iron pot.

"It's kind of you to help Rosa, Mr. Horn," Jennifer said.

"It's nothing," Gabe said as he carefully set the pot down. "Rosa works hard; she deserves a little help now and then." He turned his piercing gaze on her. "You helped her, too, Miss Jennifer, with moving furniture and food preparation." His lips curved in an approving smile.

Jennifer waved his compliment away. "Everyone at the Santa Maria works hard, Mr. Horn. I can't just sit around."

"You could if you wished. Your uncle does."

"My uncle and I are very different."

"Thankfully," Gabe commented gruffly, then retreated to the kitchen.

Jennifer was ready to follow him until she spotted Constanza and Oliver seated together on a wrought-iron bench, deep in conversation. For some reason, the sight troubled her.

She had no time to further pursue her thoughts, however, for a jovial parade emerged from the kitchen, led by Rosa. Even Preston and John had been pressed into service. Soon, the long tables were covered with a tempting array of foods, from fresh fruits and vegetables to plates of *tortillas* and pots of spiced *frijoles* to bowls of the special sauce Rosa made from chiles, onions, tomatoes, and cilantro. For those less adventurous souls, there were plates of succulent roasted duck and quail surrounded with small new potatoes. To complete the feast, Pedro and several men trooped in the side gate, carrying platters of aromatic beef from the pit *barbacoa* in the yard.

Francisca brought David and Molly down to join their parents, and when all were gathered and reasonably quiet, Preston moved to the center of the courtyard.

"Welcome, friends!" he said in a ringing voice. "You have honored me and my family with your presence here tonight. Most of you have met our visiting guests, but in case anyone slipped by me, I'll introduce them now. Some of you knew my beloved goddaughter, Jennifer, when she and her father lived here fifteen years ago. As you can see, she has grown into a lovely young lady." He waved in Jennifer's direction, and she executed a small curtsey. Preston continued. "Jennifer's uncle, Oliver Mainwaring, is also here with us."

Oliver rose from Constanza's side, looking bored. He bowed briefly and sat down again.

Preston motioned to both John and Bill, and his sons joined him. "I am also proud to announce that I only recently learned that I have another son." He put an arm around John's shoulders. "John Novales Cantrell is as much my son as William Fulbright Cantrell is," he put his other arm around Bill, "and I want you to welcome him as such." Preston's voice had taken on a slightly harder edge. "And that's all the talking I'm going to do for now. I know my grandson David is hungry enough to bite my leg if I keep him any longer from the food."

From his mother's side, David stared at Preston, his blue eyes wide. "Grampa, I won't *bite* you!" he promised solemnly, much to the delight of the crowd.

"Then let's eat!" Preston shouted.

Plates were filled with food, glasses with fine wine. Conversation ebbed and flowed easily, and Jennifer found that she greatly enjoyed the meal. She loved the spicy Mexican food, its unique flavor bringing back memories of the years she and her father had spent here. As she recalled, Rosa had served such food most of the time. She wondered why this was the first she had sampled since she and Oliver had arrived, then immediately suspected she knew the reason: Oliver. She was more determined than ever to learn the extent to which her visit had disrupted the routine of the Cantrell family—and to change it back.

Jennifer was helping Rosa and Barbara spread clean cloths over the food in the event any guest wished to eat more later when she noticed Constanza approaching the table. She did not like the look on the other woman's face, the almost predatory expression in those dark eyes as Constanza closed in on Rosa.

"Were you wishing to help us, Constanza?" Jennifer stepped into her path. "It is kind of you, but you are our guest. We cannot allow you to work as if you were in your own home."

Constanza stared at her in amazement. "You think I do kitchen work in my own home?"

"How silly of me." Jennifer shook her head. "Of course you do not." The polite words came out as an insult, one that Constanza did not miss, judging from the tightening of her full lips.

"I came to speak to Rosa," she snapped, and attempted to sidestep Jennifer, unsuccessfully.

Rosa's shoulders stiffened, but she did not look up from the bowl she was covering. Jennifer noticed the woman's hands were shaking.

"You have nothing to say that Rosa wants to hear," Jennifer said firmly.

With her hands at her hips, Barbara came to Jennifer's side, glaring at Constanza. "Take your cruel remarks and your lies somewhere else, Constanza. We will not listen to you."

Constanza's glittering eyes went from Barbara to Jennifer and back again. Finally, after inviting them all to go to hell, she stormed off, her heels clicking on the flagstone floor of the courtyard, her free-falling hair bouncing in time with her furious steps.

"Gracias," Rosa said quietly. "I must go to the kitchen." She hurried away, leaving Jennifer and Barbara to stare after her with concern.

Later, when Bill and Jennifer were dancing, Jennifer asked him if he had deliberately ignored Constanza when he had met Barbara at the foot of the stairs.

"She was there?" he asked innocently.

"Right next to me, Bill."

"You were there?" he teased.

"I'll step on your foot, Bill Cantrell," Jennifer warned, struggling to keep a smile from her face.

"Please, no, not the foot stomp, Jennie, I beg you!" Bill pleaded in mock terror.

"Very well," Jennifer said with a laugh. "But you must tell me."

Bill sobered. "Of course I knew she was there. Who could miss that red dress? And I know I was deliberately rude, but Constanza once hurt Barbara very deeply, and I will do anything to protect my wife's feelings." His fingers tightened on Jennifer's hand. "Barbara must never doubt how much I love her. I want her to know that she has nothing to fear from Constanza as far as I am concerned."

"I think she knows that, Bill. Her worry tonight was that Constanza would ridicule her dress, as I gather she has done before. Barbara was afraid she would embarrass you in front of your friends."

"As if she could ever embarrass me." Bill met Jennifer's eyes, his own softening with affection. "She told me you gave her that dress. Thank you."

Jennifer shrugged. "She wanted to be beautiful for you."

"She always is, but she does look especially lovely tonight." He searched for his wife in the crowd, then smiled when he spotted her on a bench with David. The music came to an end, and Jennifer gave him a light push.

"Go to your wife, you love-crazed fool," she said teasingly. "I see I can't hold your attention."

Bill's lopsided grin seemed apologetic. "Jennie—"

"Go. You are blessed with each other, Bill. I hope I find what you two share."

He swept her up into a brotherly hug. "You will." As he released her, the music started up again, but rather than a waltz, the musicians, who had been joined by a man with a banjo, played a catchy tune, one that was familiar to Jennifer. She looked up at Bill.

"What is this song? I know it."

Bill listened intently for a moment. "So do I. Jennie, it's *The Robert E. Lee*. Do you remember the steps to that dance? We learned it on one of my visits to Philadelphia, that day in the park when the band gave a concert."

Jennifer grabbed Bill's hand. "I think so. Let's try."

After getting off to an awkward and humorous start, they found that the memory of the rather boisterous steps came back and they fell into perfect rhythm with each other. The other dancers cleared a space around them and watched with enthusiastic shouts of encouragement, clapping in time with the music.

From the shadow of a lemon tree, John eyed the dancing couple, gripped by a strange melancholy. Even in the muted light of the lanterns, the heightened color on Jennifer's cheeks and the happiness in her eyes could not be missed. Bill's face was creased in a smile; John realized it was the most relaxed he had ever seen his brother. Had his coming brought increased tension to the Cantrell household, and to Bill in particular? He immediately answered his own question: Of course it had. How could it not?

The affection and friendship Jennifer and Bill shared was obvious; they cared a great deal about each other, perhaps loved each other, albeit as brother and sister. John thought about the people who lived and worked on the Santa Maria. There seemed to be a bond shared by all of them, from Preston himself to the young man who cared for the small herd of dairy cows. A deep bond. A bond that did not include him.

Was Preston the common thread? Was it the ranch itself, or perhaps a love of the land?

No. The bond originated with Preston. Although John planned to leave the ranch soon, a part of him wanted to be bound as well, to join the extended family that was the Santa Maria. Preston had invited him. How did Bill feel about that? How deeply did the Cantrell bond with Jennifer go?

John concentrated on the dancers again. He wanted to dance with Jennifer, very badly.

The music came to an end. The crowd erupted in spirited applause as Jennifer curtseyed and Bill took a bow.

"She is making a spectacle of herself," a disapproving female voice said at John's shoulder, a voice he immediately recognized.

"You just resent that you are not the center of attention, Constanza."

She snorted and stepped to his side. "I can dance better than Jennifer Mainwaring. She does not know how to use her body as I do." She glanced up at him from the corners of her eyes.

John chose to ignore the double entendre.

Constanza suddenly grabbed his hand and pulled him farther into the light. *"El flamenco, por favor,"* she called to the musicians. "Come, Juan Novales," she said in a softer tone.

"You remember this dance." She caught his other hand and tugged at him, urging him forward.

John resisted. He did not want to dance with Constanza, but now the crowd, including Preston, called to them, urging them to perform the traditional, intricate Spanish dance. The guitarist started first, playing alone.

There was no way John could gracefully extricate himself from the situation. He caught the triumphant gleam in Constanza's eyes. Determined that this dance was all she would get from him, ever again, John forced himself to focus on the familiar and compelling music.

Jennifer watched, first in disgust that John would consent to dance with Constanza, then in fascination. Never had she seen anything like those two dancing the *flamenco*. The sensual, haunting music; the woman in red and the man in black dancing gracefully around each other, teasing, enticing, pleading, yet never touching, their heels clicking in time and counter time, faster and faster. Constanza lifted her skirts, exposing her legs to the knee, moving the red satin back and forth as she whirled in a tight circle with her hair flying around her. The tempo increased to a frantic pace, yet they never faltered. Then suddenly, abruptly, at the same instant, it all stopped—the music, the movements of bodies, the clicking of heels. Frozen in place, John and Constanza stared at each other, breathless from exertion, Constanza with an alluring expression on her flushed face, John with no emotion at all on his.

Breathless herself, Jennifer could not take her eyes from John. Surely that was the most erotic dance, the most erotic *anything* she had ever seen. Her heart pounded, and a strange excitement curled through her belly.

The crowd burst into a roar of applause. John took Constanza's hand, and she sank into a deep curtsey as he bowed. He then led her to where Preston and Alejandro stood with Jennifer.

"That was magnificent, John," Preston said, his eyes glowing with pride. "Where did you learn the dance?"

"Ciudad de Mexico, many years ago."

"I have never seen *el flamenco* performed so well," Alejandro commented, beaming at his daughter.

"Thank you, Papa," Constanza murmured demurely. It was all Jennifer could do not to roll her eyes.

"Where is Arturo, *Don* Alejandro?" John asked. "I've not seen him tonight."

"He is at home, where he will remain until his manners improve," Alejandro said stiffly. "I have already apologized to Preston, and now I will do so to you, John. My son's actions of the other day were reprehensible and have caused me deep shame. Please accept my most sincere apology."

"Thank you, sir, but it is not necessary for you to apologize. You have done nothing."

"I have raised a rude and angry son, and for that I am truly sorry." Alejandro held himself tall and proud, but Jennifer could see that it was not easy for him to say the words.

Preston spoke into the awkward silence that followed. "I hope you don't mind that I gave Ross Latham a job after he left you, Alejandro. He seems like a good hand."

Alejandro nodded. "He is. I was sorry to lose him, but I understand why he felt he had to leave. By the way, I fired Baxter Lewis. He will not be causing any further trouble."

"Good." Preston nodded in satisfaction.

"Enough of this serious talk," Constanza said with a pout that quickly changed to a flirtatious smile. She pulled on John's hand. "Dance with me, Juan."

John gently freed himself from her grasp. "Thank you, Constanza, but I promised Miss Mainwaring the very next waltz, and I believe that is what they are playing."

Jennifer looked at him, too surprised to say anything.

"Yes, I'm sure it's a waltz," John said as he took her hand. "Excuse us, please."

Jennifer allowed him to lead her away, but not before she

caught the look of unholy fury in Constanza's eyes. A shiver ran through her. What price would Constanza exact for being turned down in public? Jennifer watched as the woman in red marched over to where Oliver sat on a bench and pulled him to his feet. They disappeared through the side gate, and Jennifer gave a sigh of relief.

"Thank you for not exposing my little fabrication, Miss Mainwaring," John said as he took her in his arms. "I can tolerate Constanza only in small doses."

"I know what you mean," Jennifer murmured. She avoided John's eyes, but she could not avoid the heat and the strength emanating from him, the sure confidence as he expertly guided her in time with the music. He danced better than Bradley Ames, she decided, and it was much more enjoyable to be in his arms like this rather than being carried from the barn by force. Although that had not been entirely unpleasant, she admitted to herself.

"You handled Constanza very well earlier tonight, when she first arrived," John said, his tone conversational.

At that, Jennifer finally looked up at him. "You saw?"

"And heard. I should have applauded. I didn't like how Constanza treated Barbara. You really were magnificent."

Jennifer almost missed a step. "Do my ears deceive me, Mr. Cantrell, or are you complimenting me yet again tonight?"

John laughed. "Don't look so suspicious. I am basically a very honest man, Miss Mainwaring. I mean what I say."

"Are you saying that you have reassessed your first unfavorable impression of me?" Jennifer arched a disbelieving eyebrow.

"Yes, I guess I am."

"I'll allow no guessing here, Mr. Cantrell. Either you have or you have not."

Again, John laughed. The sound was pleasing to Jennifer, deeply so. There was no note of derision or sarcasm in his laugh tonight, as there had always been before.

"I have," he said. "And please call me 'John.' "

Jennifer pretended to ponder his request for a minute, then relented. "Very well, if you will call me 'Jennie,' as all the other Cantrells do."

John nodded in satisfaction. "I believe we have reached a truce, Jennie."

"I believe we have, John." She smiled up at him, shyly.

His fingers tightened on hers for a moment, then, much to her delight, he whirled her around the courtyard with renewed fervor. When the music ended, Jennifer was again breathless, as much from John's nearness as the exertion of the dance.

He led her to the table where a selection of beverages were laid out, including decanters of wine and brandy, and a crystal bowl filled with fruit punch. "I promised Molly a dance," he said, without releasing her hand. "Barbara wants to get the children up to bed soon, so I must find the little darling. But perhaps later you will dance with me again."

"Perhaps I will."

Jennifer smiled at him, and the effect took John's breath away. Her lovely face seemed to light up, and those green eyes—a man could get lost in their emerald depths. It occurred to him that she had never smiled at him before. He definitely liked it.

"I hope so, Jennie." He returned her smile, then took his leave.

Jennifer watched as he made his way through the throng of people to Barbara's side. He swung little Molly up into his arms and started moving in time with the music. The child stared at him with a look of joy and wonder on her sweet face, and Jennifer's heart lurched. If the way he treated his nephew and niece was any indication, John Cantrell would be a loving and attentive father to his own children. That same primal excitement rushed through her again, an excitement she was beginning to associate with John. Confused, she turned to the punch bowl and ladled a cup of the liquid, then noticed a man standing near the end of the table.

"Good evening," she said. "Would you care for some punch?"

"Thank you, ma'am, but I think I'll stick with my beer."

Jennifer sipped from her cup, eyeing the man over the rim. Something about him was familiar. He was an attractive man, with neatly combed brown hair and steel-grey eyes, dressed in a frock coat and wearing a shoestring tie. Then she remembered. "You were out at the dam the other day, weren't you?"

"Yes, ma'am, I was. My name is Ross Latham."

"I am pleased to meet you, Mr. Latham. My name is Jennifer Mainwaring. I understand you work for Preston now."

Ross shrugged. "Can't turn down honest work. Mr. Cantrell seems like a good man. You're his goddaughter, aren't you?"

Jennifer nodded. "Did I hear you mention you were from Wyoming Territory?"

He took a swallow from the mug he held before he answered. "Yes, ma'am."

"I was there myself a few weeks ago. Some good friends live in Laramie City. Well, actually, they own land outside of town to the east. Perhaps you know Beauregard Parker or Conor O'Rourke?"

A guarded expression came over Ross Latham's face. "Wyoming is a big place, Miss Mainwaring."

Jennifer smiled. "I know. But sometimes it's a small world, too. Beau and Conor are married to my two dearest friends."

One of Ross's eyebrows raised. "I did work for a man in Laramie for a while. What are your friends' names?"

"Alina Gallagher and Susannah Duncan, though of course, now they have married names."

"I knew Alina Parker, though only well enough to say hello." Ross stared at Jennifer with a strange hope lighting his eyes. "Is she all right?"

"She's fine." Jennifer watched him curiously, noting the relief that filled his face at her words. "That's an odd question, Mr. Latham. Did you suspect she was not all right?"

"Just before I left Wyoming, I'd heard she had been hurt, but that was a year ago." He took another swig from his mug.

"A year ago, Alina was attacked and beaten, but she's fine now. Beau killed the man responsible."

Ross nodded in satisfaction. "He got there in time, then," he said softly, staring at some point beyond Jennifer's shoulder.

"I beg your pardon?" Jennifer asked.

Ross focused again on Jennifer's face. "Mrs. Parker is a remarkable woman, Miss Mainwaring. She is both lovely and brave. I'm glad Parker killed that bastard Carter. He deserved killing. I should have done it myself." He hesitated. "I apologize for my language."

"As you said out at the dam, you always speak your mind," Jennifer said with a smile. She arched an eyebrow. "You seem to know a lot about the incident with Alina."

"Not a lot." Ross appeared to be very interested in his beer mug. "Just some of the people involved—I don't really know what happened. I'm glad Mrs. Parker is fine."

"She and Beau have a little girl now."

"That's good. And did you say O'Rourke is married, too?"

"Yes, to my friend Susannah."

"I don't know her." Ross drained his mug. "Well, I'm dry. Guess I'll wander on over to the keg. It's been nice talking to you, Miss Mainwaring."

"Likewise, Mr. Latham. We'll probably see each other around the Santa Maria."

"Yes, ma'am." Ross smiled at her, then again he looked past her, his face instantly sobering. "Oh, no," he whispered. He set the mug on the table and his hand flew to his hip. With a curse, he slapped his leg. He was not wearing a gun.

Jennifer whirled to face the same direction and was horrified to see Baxter Lewis push through the side gate waving a pistol. She jumped as that pistol went off.

The music stopped abruptly and several women screamed.

"I've come for John Cantrell!" Lewis shouted, shoving people out of his way as he advanced into the courtyard. As if by magic, the crowd parted to leave John standing alone with Molly in his arms.

He glared at Lewis. "This is neither the time nor the place." His quiet, deadly voice carried across the courtyard.

"You got me fired, you bastard! This place and time is just right." He lurched closer.

"You're drunk," John snapped, "and I'm holding a child." He shifted Molly to his left arm. "Get out of here. If you have something to settle with me, we'll settle it elsewhere. Don't involve my family."

"I'm here, and I ain't leavin' 'til this is done." He pointed the gun in John's direction.

Bill and Preston moved toward Lewis. Her heart pounding in fear, Jennifer saw that neither of them was armed, as none of the men were, except John. Who would have thought a weapon would be needed at a party? Ross Latham stepped around her.

"Put down the gun, Baxter," he called. "You don't want to do this. There are women and children here."

"Shut up, Latham," Lewis snarled. "And don't any of you come no closer." He took aim at John.

Bill and Preston stopped.

In that moment, John's mind took in a hundred whirling pictures—the frightened, precious child in his arms, staring up at him with wide blue eyes; Barbara's face, terrified, holding out pleading hands for her daughter, Rosa holding her back; Bill, pale with fear, his hands clenched in helpless rage; Preston, his craggy face twisted with anguish; Jennifer, her eyes huge, her hands clasped together as if she were praying. All of them too far away to catch the child if he threw her.

Lewis laughed. "Guess I'm holdin' all the cards this time, Cantrell. All you're holding is a damned kid." He cocked the hammer with a loud click, the ominous sound seeming to echo around the enclosed courtyard.

In one fluid motion, John tightened his hold on Molly and dropped to one knee, twisting at the waist to shield the child with the upper half of his body, while his right hand flew to his holster to pull the pearl-handled gun free. He fired at the same instant Lewis did.

Lewis missed.

John did not.

Baxter crashed to the ground. John wrapped his gun arm around Molly and cradled her against his chest, his eyes closed in silent thanksgiving.

A stillness settled over the courtyard for a moment, broken only by Molly's muffled whimpering. Bill rushed forward and fell to his knees at John's side, his eyes filled with tears. He grasped John's shoulders.

"Thank you," he whispered. Barbara stood behind him, crying.

John nodded tiredly and allowed Bill to take Molly from his arms. A murmur of voices started and rose steadily in volume, excited and appreciative. Preston motioned to a few men to remove Lewis's body, then came to John's side as he stood up.

"Are you hurt?" he demanded.

"No." John slid his gun back into the holster. "I'm sorry about this, Preston. I didn't want to bring trouble down on you." He glanced over his shoulder at Bill and Molly. "Or on anyone in your family."

"It's your family, too, John," Preston said. "This wasn't your fault, any more than the incident at the dam. You did the only thing you could, and you did it well. I'm proud of you."

John met his eyes. "I don't feel proud."

"No, I'm sure you don't. Killing is never easy. It's necessary sometimes, but it's never easy."

Jennifer stood off to one side in shocked confusion, thankful that Molly and John were unharmed, unnerved to have seen a man die. She was torn, wanting to go to John, not sure he wanted her there, fighting an absurd desire to touch him, his face, his arms, his chest, to make certain he truly was uninjured. The weariness and devastation in his eyes broke her heart. He looked up then, right at her. His grim expression softened a little, and without thinking about it further, Jennifer went to him.

"Are you all right?" she asked as, hesitantly, she placed a hand on his forearm.

He nodded. "But I could use some brandy."

"I'll get it."

"I'd be obliged."

Jennifer backed away, reluctant to take her eyes from him. The knowledge that he could have so easily been hurt or killed slammed into her brain, that Molly could have suffered as well. She had seen a man shot dead, yet felt no sadness for him. She wasn't sure Baxter Lewis deserved to die, but there had been no other choice. Somehow, the man's violent death was not as horrifying as the thought of what might have happened to John or Molly. Jennifer's intense relief overpowered any horror she felt.

The subdued crowd closed around John, blocking him from her view. With a troubled sigh, Jennifer turned toward the kitchen. Preston's *fiesta* was over. The atmosphere and camaraderie of the evening was irrevocably destroyed. It had been only a few minutes earlier, but somehow, the waltz she had shared with John seemed like a lifetime ago. She felt a strange sense of loss, as if something precious had been taken from her.

Nine

The *fiesta* ended abruptly, as Jennifer had known it would. The guests departed for home, and the last to leave were the Noriegas, because Constanza was nowhere to be found. Finally she appeared on Oliver's arm, looking flushed and oddly smug. Oliver explained that he had been showing Miss Noriega the new bull, which would account for the pieces of straw clinging to Constanza's skirt, but Jennifer wondered about the one in her hair. She stared at Oliver; he seemed very jovial. Had Constanza allowed him to do more than kiss her? Jennifer was not sorry to see the woman leave.

She did not have an opportunity to speak privately with John before she retired for the night, and wasn't sure what she would have said to him if she had. For some reason, she could not get him out of her mind. She tossed and turned in her dark room, seeing again and again the terrible incident in the courtyard. Why did the thought of John being hurt bother her so much? While she had never wished him harm, she had often wished he would leave the Santa Maria. No longer did she feel that way, and the realization bothered her.

When had her feelings changed? It pained her to admit she actually liked the man now, cared for his well-being. She punched her pillow in frustration. The last thing she wanted to do was harbor special feelings for John Cantrell. Such feelings would only complicate things. She would be plagued with the nagging question of whether or not he felt the same way about her, for she already wondered that. And what if he left?

John's relationship with Constanza raised questions, also. How close had they been in the past? He had kissed her tonight, and danced the *flamenco* with her. Surely one did not engage in such an intimate and erotic dance with a mere acquaintance. If John did have strong feelings for Constanza, Jennifer's opinion of him would drop dramatically. Only two types of men would be attracted to a woman like Constanza Noriega: those too foolish to see her for what she was, and those who shared her selfish and sometimes cruel traits. John Cantrell was certainly no fool. And although he could be stubborn and arrogant, Jennifer had not seen any evidence of selfishness or cruelty on his part.

With a heavy sigh, Jennifer lay back against the pillows. She had anticipated a relaxing and peaceful visit with Preston and his family. So far, her stay at the Santa Maria had been anything but.

"I will be leaving for San Francisco tomorrow morning," Oliver announced the next day. As it was Sunday and, Preston insisted, a day of rest, the family had gathered in the *sala* before dinner. Oliver had not come down from his room before now, and Jennifer noticed he still wore a strangely secretive smile. A part of her mind wondered at that, while her heart jumped in fear at his words. Did he expect her to join him?

"So soon?" she asked cautiously.

"Yes, I really must. We've been here for a week now, and I can dally no longer. Not that I haven't enjoyed myself," he added to Preston, his tone cordial and seemingly sincere.

Jennifer stared at him. What had gotten into the man? Her gaze briefly wandered to John, who sat across the coffee table from her. For some maddening reason, she was thrilled to find him watching her, his expression calm, his eyes warm.

She quickly looked back at her uncle. "I am not yet ready to leave."

"Jennie, please stay with us for as long as you wish," Preston interjected.

Before she could respond, Oliver spoke again. "Actually, Preston, I was going to ask if you would mind keeping her. But I must warn you that I plan to be gone for several weeks, perhaps even a month." He brushed an imaginary fleck from his immaculate sleeve.

'Mind keeping her'? Like I'm some horse he wants to stable? Jennifer seethed at Oliver's condescending manner, but bit her lip to keep from commenting. She did not want to start an argument with the children in the room, nor did she want to jeopardize the possibility that he would so easily agree to extending her visit. It comforted her that Preston seemed as put out by Oliver's choice of words as she was.

"I don't mind 'keeping her,' Oliver," he said, his jaw tight with irritation. "But Jennie is a woman grown, a fact it seems you often forget. The choice is hers. Why don't you ask her what she would like to do?"

Jennifer held her breath, dreading the explosion she knew was coming. She saw the flare of anger in Oliver's eyes, saw the way he schooled his expression into one of solicitous patience. But her uncle surprised her again; the explosion did not come.

"You're right, of course, Preston. How thoughtless of me. Jennifer, would you prefer to accompany me to San Francisco, Portland, Seattle, and Vancouver, or would you rather remain here with your friends?"

Startled and suspicious, Jennifer stared at him. She was probably the only one who detected the tension in his voice, masked so well by his polite words. What was his game? Only a few days ago he had denounced her friends as provincial and inappropriate. His apparent change of heart as well as his overly courteous manner made her nervous.

"I would prefer to stay here," she answered quietly.

"Very well. I shall miss you, of course, but I want you to be happy." He turned and headed for the door. "I must pack."

The group in the room watched him leave, stunned into momentary silence.

"What happened to him?" Bill finally asked from his position on the floor with his children.

"I don't know," Jennifer said, shaking her head. "But I do not like it."

"Perhaps he's just being kind, Jennie," Barbara suggested.

Jennifer shook her head again. "No. I know my uncle. He is never this kind without an ulterior motive."

"His personality change is refreshing, but suspicious," John commented.

"It certainly is." Jennifer rose from the sofa. John and Preston stood as well. "I think I will try to find out what is really going on here," she said. "Do not wait dinner for me. I know the children are getting hungry."

"Call if you need help," Bill suggested, smiling.

"I can handle my uncle," she said firmly. "Usually," she added with a grin, then left the room.

The door to Oliver's room stood open, but she knocked anyway.

"Come in."

A trunk stood open near the wardrobe, where Oliver was removing articles of clothing, while a valise rested on the bed. Oliver turned around. "Oh, hello, Jennifer. You know, the greatest mistake I made was deciding not to bring my valet along on this trip. I suppose you miss your maid, as well. Do you think I should send for them?"

"Not on my account, but thank you." Jennifer advanced into the room.

"Yes, I suppose it is much too late for that. Your woman could get here in time to be of some use to you, but my man could never reach San Francisco before I leave for Portland. He would be chasing me up the coast."

"Oliver, what is going on?"

"I think that is quite obvious, dear girl." He waved a hand at the various pieces of clothing scattered about the room. "Or perhaps I should say 'dear woman.' After all, as Preston so *kindly* reminded me, you are all grown up."

Jennifer was almost relieved to hear a hint of Oliver's familiar sneer in his words. "Why are you suddenly so polite?"

"Jennifer, I have told you many times that such bluntness is unbecoming in a lady of quality."

"A few days ago, my friends were unacceptable. Now, with no argument, you are leaving me alone with them for several weeks. Also, you have never before expressed concern about my happiness. What are you up to?" Jennifer folded her arms and waited.

Oliver stared at her for a long moment, his expression and his eyes growing cold and hard. "I will tell you nothing. Your rudeness and insubordination toward me over the last week have irrevocably altered our relationship. You will no longer be taken into my confidence."

His tone sent a chill through Jennifer. Somehow, Oliver's calm rage was far more disturbing than any of his angry and emotional outbursts over the years had been. He continued.

"You had best enjoy my congeniality while you can, for it will not last one moment longer than I deem necessary. Now get out." Oliver pointed toward the door.

A nervous fear unfolded in Jennifer's stomach. Her dislike and distrust of Oliver Mainwaring flared to new heights, but she said nothing. There was nothing to say. She did as he instructed, quietly closing the door behind her.

"I'll be in San Francisco for only a week or so, Arturo." Constanza spoke to her brother, but did not take her eyes from the young maid who was carefully laying a ball gown in an open trunk. "Be certain the lace isn't crushed, you stupid girl," she snapped.

The maid's jaw tightened, but she said nothing.

"I will go with you," Arturo insisted.

"You will not. I do not need you along while I shop, and you would be bored. You are unpleasant when you are bored, Arturo. Besides, I need you here. There are things you must see to." Constanza pulled another gown from the wardrobe and threw it on the bed.

"You can't go alone, Constanza."

"I'll not be alone. Brigit will be with me." She waved a hand in the direction of the young Irish maid.

Arturo slumped into a chair by the window. "I don't like it."

"I don't care," Constanza said with a laugh. She sauntered over to her brother's side and ran a finger along his jaw. "Now don't pout, little brother. As I said, I need you here."

Arturo jerked away from her touch. "For what?" he demanded petulantly.

Constanza turned to Brigit. "Leave us."

Without word or facial expression, Brigit dropped a curtsey and left the room, closing the door behind her.

"You must continue with my plan, Arturo. Like a mosquito, you must irritate Preston Cantrell. Make his life miserable. He is growing old, and will weary of the fight. I have almost persuaded Papa to offer for Preston's land."

"I've told you before; it won't work, sister. Preston has lived on that land for thirty years, has nurtured it through drought and flood, has survived cattle and sheep epidemics. He won't sell, not for any reason or any price." He watched as Constanza began to pace the floor.

"He *must* sell," she hissed, her hands clenched into fists. "He has no right here. None of the *Americanos* do. California belongs to Mexico, and I intend to see it returned to her. I helped rid Mexico of the French; I will help rid California of the *Americanos*. Preston Cantrell is only the beginning." Her face flushed with the force of her emotions. "Our people need the Santa Maria."

Arturo hesitated, then spoke cautiously. "The Mexican gov-

ernment granted Cantrell the Santa Maria at the same time
Father was granted the Buena Ventura. He has as much right
to his land as Father does to ours. You know that." He watched
his sister's expression harden and shook his head. There was
no arguing with Constanza when she was in one of her moods.
"What do you want me to do?" he asked wearily.

Constanza smiled. "You will think of something, Arturo."

"Should I go after the bull again?"

"Imbécil!" Constanza spat. "Of course not! They will be
watching him now." She slammed a fist into the palm of her
other hand. "If only that damned Pedro hadn't come along!
Another minute and I would have had the job done."

Arturo stood. "I told you it was a stupid idea. We were
lucky to get away."

With no warning, Constanza's hand cracked sharply across
his cheek with enough force to stagger him. "It was not a
stupid idea," she said, her voice ugly with rage. "It was a
wonderful idea—the perfect way to hurt Preston. With luck
and God's help, it would have worked."

His hand to his stinging cheek, Arturo backed away from
the fury in his sister's eyes. "Forgive me, Constanza," he
whispered, desperate to make amends, his heart pounding in
fear. "You are right, as you always are."

"Of course I am." Appeased for the moment, Constanza
resumed her pacing, this time thoughtful. "If Preston cannot
be persuaded to sell, more serious measures may have to be
considered. And then there is Juan Cantrell."

"He is nothing," Arturo growled. "An arrogant bastard with
no legal claim to the land."

"Unless Preston treats him on an equal footing with William, which he may very well do. If he is made a legitimate
heir, that will change everything." Constanza approached Arturo and stroked his reddened cheek. "I wish you would not
make me strike you," she whispered sadly.

Arturo lowered his eyes. "I'm sorry."

Constanza whirled away from him and spoke as if the tender exchange had not happened. "And you must remember that Juan Novales Cantrell is of Mexican blood, which makes him far more worthy of the land than his foolish *Americano* brother." She swept to the wardrobe and began throwing clothes out of it, her mood changing yet again. "I do not wish to think of Preston Cantrell for now, so you must do it for me. Think of the mosquito, Arturo. Stinging little assaults that get on one's nerves and wear one down. That is what you must do."

"I will think of something," Arturo mumbled, edging toward the door.

"I'm sure you will, brother. I'm counting on you. Now go." She waved at the door. "I must pack. And send that stupid girl back to me."

Arturo gratefully made his escape, his mind filled with ideas of what he could do to Preston Cantrell and the Santa Maria.

The atmosphere in the Cantrell house changed dramatically with Oliver Mainwaring's departure. Jennifer implored Preston to return the household to its normal way of life, to treat her as a member of the family, and he, as well as everyone else, did.

Jennifer joined Barbara on a trip to Gilroy and purchased a broad-brimmed hat and materials for new, more appropriate clothes. With the help of Francisca and Barbara, Jennifer soon had a much more practical, although limited wardrobe. She packed her parasol and riding habit away in her trunk, along with the heavy nightdresses, nightcaps, and bustles—indeed, most of what she had brought from Philadelphia. All except her undergarments and corsets. As much as she would have loved to pack her corsets away, she did not feel that was proper, despite Rosa's remarks to the contrary.

Jennifer revelled in her newfound freedom. She helped with the housework, the gardening, and the care of the children.

Preston allowed her to assist, minimally, with the recovering Buford's care, and Rosa tutored her, both in Spanish and in cooking the wonderful Mexican-style foods that were once again a staple of the Cantrell menu.

It was customary for the extended family to gather in the *sala* each evening after supper. In a break with the prevailing social traditions, the men enjoyed their brandy and the women their sherry in the same room. They read or played chess or simply talked. Jennifer grew to love those hours spent in comfortable companionship when the work of the day was finished. Her relationship with Bill was a deep, brotherly one, renewed again after so many years apart. Barbara was like a sister to her; Preston, a father. John, however, was none of those.

She enjoyed a growing friendship with him, one that was touched with a tinge of excitement, for her, at least. She found herself looking for him when she entered a room, when the men returned from a day of hard work, when she stood at her balcony railing in the quiet of the night, and she wondered if he ever looked for her.

Late one restless night, she decided to find a book to read before turning out the lamp. After slipping her wrapper over her sleeping shift, she trod down the dark stairs on silent feet.

To her surprise, lamplight shone from under the nearly closed door of Preston's study, where his impressive collection of books was kept. She peeked into the room to see John seated in one of the tall-backed, tufted leather chairs in front of the fireplace, intent upon the book he held in his hands.

"Excuse me for disturbing you," she said quietly. "I want to choose something to read and won't be but a minute."

John looked up, his face warm with a welcoming smile. "Hello, Jennie. You're not disturbing me." He set his book on a side table and stood up. "What are you interested in?"

"Tonight I think I would enjoy a novel more than poetry or a history." Jennifer stepped toward a tall bookcase, very conscious of the fact that once again, she was with John Cantrell in the middle of the night wearing only her nightclothes. She stifled a sigh. She was also barefoot and hoped he did not notice.

"Any author you are particularly fond of?"

"I like Dickens and Cooper, but I'm more in the mood for Austen. I wonder if Preston has any of her books." She peered at the row of books directly in front of her. "Is there any particular order to these?"

John stepped up behind her, very close, and reached over her head. "Alphabetical by author."

Jennifer inched out of his way, feeling as she had that first night in the barn when he had so closely circled her, warning her of *El Lobo*. Tonight he wore only a pair of denims and a shirt, the shirt hanging open over his pants, as if he had thrown it on in haste. His chest, covered with fine dark hair, was very close. Jennifer had an absurd, powerful desire to touch him, to see if that hair was as soft as it looked, if his skin was as warm. She dropped her gaze to the floor, feeling the heat of a blush climb her cheeks. What on earth was she thinking of? Her eyes widened to realize that he was barefoot, also.

A book suddenly blocked her vision. *"Emma,"* he said.

Jennifer blinked and looked at him, confused. "I beg your pardon?"

"The book." He waved it at her. "Unless you would prefer *Pride and Prejudice* or *Mansfield Park.* Preston has those as well. While *Pride and Prejudice* is usually considered Miss Austen's best work, I find *Emma* more complex in terms of plot. Of course, *Mansfield Park* is complex as well, but it is rather melancholic. What do you think?"

Momentarily speechless with surprise, Jennifer could do no more than accept the book from him.

"Perhaps you've not read all of them." John moved away from her, back toward his chair.

Jennifer finally found her tongue. "I have, and *Emma* will be fine. I have never compared them in such a thorough manner, and it has been awhile since I read them, but I think I would agree with you." She watched as John bent and took up his book. "What are you reading?" she asked.

"Dumas." He held up the book so she could read the spine. *Les Trois Mousquetaires. The Three Musketeers.* In the original French.

"So you are fluent in French as well as Spanish and English," Jennifer commented as she hugged her book to her chest.

"Yes."

Was it her imagination or was John staring at her? "I am certain that ability made you extremely valuable in the court of Maximilian." She bit her bottom lip, suddenly very uncomfortable. He was definitely staring at her. She felt as if his blue eyes were peeling away her wrapper and shift. A bolt of excitement shot through her.

"Yes, my language skills were helpful."

"I speak French," she blurted out. "In fact, I've read *Les Trois Mousquetaires.* And Rosa is helping me with my Spanish. I was fluent when I lived here as a child, but since I had no one to practice with in Philadelphia, I lost most of it."

"It will come back quickly," John assured her.

Jennifer nodded and again looked at the floor, feeling like a chattering idiot. She did not know what else to say, afraid something foolish would come out of her mouth. John Cantrell had unnerved her, and she was not certain how to regain her composure. It seemed that she could not think, but only feel. And she felt his hot gaze on her.

"You are barefoot yet again, Jennie." There was no mistaking the warm, teasing note in his voice.

Jennifer jerked her head up to glare at him. "So are you," she retorted.

"So I am." After a moment of awkward silence, he waved toward the other chair. "Would you like to sit down? You are welcome to read here."

Without hesitation, she shook her head. On some level, she

knew he presented a subtle danger tonight, like that of a circling wolf. "It would be better if I went upstairs. Thank you anyway," she added, belatedly remembering her manners. She backed toward the door, reluctant to take her eyes from him. There was something mesmerizing about him tonight. Perhaps it was because it was clear to her that he had come from his own bed to read and the thought of him in bed, without the shirt or the pants, made her breath stick in her throat. After all, he had told her he slept naked.

John nodded. "It's just as well. I fear if you stay much longer I will be forced to kiss you."

Jennifer stiffened with surprise and wariness. "I beg your pardon?" she said again.

"I think you heard me." John folded his arms across his chest, his challenging gaze piercing her, his sensual mouth curved in an inviting smile. "Perhaps you have no idea what a picture you present in your nightclothes with your braid hanging down over your breast and soft wisps of hair caressing your cheek. And you smell so good, like orange blossoms. Your big, beautiful eyes could rival the clearest emeralds, and your mouth . . ." He hesitated. "Your lovely, tempting mouth is the reason I want to kiss you."

His words started her heart pounding with that irritating, familiar excitement and something akin to hope. Also, her stomach clutched, but Jennifer disguised her reaction by pulling herself up to stand tall and rigid. "Mr. Cantrell, you forget yourself."

"Uh-oh. You're sliding back into your proper Philadelphia 'Miss Mainwaring' role. That's not good, Jennie." He took a few slow steps toward her. "And I am not forgetting anything. I know exactly what I am doing."

"I am certain you do, sir," she said coldly, now more sure of herself. The situation had shifted into one she could handle. "And I find your modesty so charming." She turned and marched to the door. "I think I liked it better when we did not get along. Then I was not so foolish as to let my guard down."

John laughed, not with sarcasm, but with annoying confidence. "Your guard cannot stand against me. Now that I have the idea of kissing you in my mind, I'll not let it go until I have followed through. I am very determined."

"You are also insufferable, Mr. Cantrell. Good night." Jennifer did not look back at him before she closed the door, none too quietly.

She stormed up the stairs to her room, resisting the temptation to slam her own door. The man was infuriating! She threw the book on the bed. What a conceited rogue! Her wrapper sailed across the room in the direction of the bench at the foot of the bed, but landed on the floor. Who did he think he was? Jennifer plopped down on the bed. A gentleman would not threaten to kiss a lady!

Oh, but the thought of his kiss. Jennifer slumped back against the pillows. Her anger dissipated and was replaced by a longing so intense it was almost painful. She *wanted* John Cantrell to kiss her. Wanted it very much. And the realization confused and frightened her.

Did he truly find her attractive? She tentatively touched her lips, not daring to believe a man like John Cantrell would want to kiss them. Perhaps he was toying with her. The idea caused her heart to plummet. She decided that, at the first opportunity, she would outright ask John if that was his intention. And if it was? She did not want to consider that, did not want to admit how disappointed she would be.

With a deep sigh, she realized that Jane Austen's work held no interest for her now. She suspected it would be another long night with little sleep, again thanks to John Cantrell.

The next morning after breakfast, Jennifer timed her visit with Buford when she knew John was saddling his horse for

the day's work. She approached him as he threw the saddle
over the stallion's back.

"Good morning," he said, then reached under the horse's
belly for the cinch strap.

"Good morning."

"How was your book?" He pulled the cinch tight and buck-
led it.

"Fine," she said, although she hadn't lifted the cover, let
alone read a single page. "I'll get straight to the point. All
your talk last night—are you toying with me, Mr. Cantrell?"

John straightened and looked at her, obviously surprised.
"Toying with you?"

"About the kiss." Jennifer crossed her arms over her chest,
hating the blush that she could feel heat her cheeks.

John's expression curiously softened. "No, Jennie, I'm not
toying with you. I told you I am an honest man, although I
do tease sometimes. I wasn't teasing last night. I wanted to
kiss you then, and I do now, and," he looked up over her
shoulder for a moment, "if Preston and Bill had not just come
in, I would do just that." He winked at her, then turned back
to his horse. "And call me 'John.' "

Jennifer whirled and hurried toward the door, flustered.
"Good day," she said tersely to Preston and Bill in passing.

"How is Buford?" Preston called after her.

She spoke over her shoulder as she hurried across the yard.
"I don't know. I'll check on him later."

The two men just looked at each other in surprise.

Ten

Jennifer was watchful for the next few days, afraid John would try to kiss her, afraid he would not. He did not, as it seemed there were always other people around, but he would wink at her sometimes, and she knew he had not forgotten his promise.

The unrelenting drought continued, and with all the problems at the Santa Maria, the accompanying heat seemed to make things worse. Late one morning, Jennifer sat in the *sala* fanning herself, fearful that the heat was sucking the very breath out of her. She wondered if she was coming down with something, because she had been feeling breathless and light-headed for the past few days. Only at night, when she was lying down, did she find relief from the puzzling symptoms. Perhaps she should go lie down now, as the children had.

Suddenly, the quiet of the morning was disturbed by the sound of a galloping horse. When John shouted, Jennifer was reminded of the night he had first made his appearance. She hurried to the front door, arriving there the same time Rosa did. Both women stepped out onto the veranda to see John in the center of the yard on his lathered stallion.

"Wildfire!" he shouted. "We need all hands!"

"Madre de Dios!" Rosa's face paled. She hurried off the veranda toward John.

Barbara came from the house. "What is it?"

"He said a wildfire," Jennifer answered.

"Oh, my God." Barbara ran toward John with Jennifer at her heels. The few men still at the compound gathered from the bunkhouse and the barn.

"Where, John?" Barbara asked fearfully.

"The south range. It's moving north, slow so far; thankfully, there's not much wind. But we need all hands. The herd has to be moved across the river." He stepped down from the saddle.

Ross Latham pushed through the small crowd that had formed. "Let me see to your horse, Mr. Cantrell."

John eyed the man with surprise, but handed him the reins. "Thank you. Would you mind saddling me another? I'll be heading right back out."

"No problem." Ross led the weary horse away.

Barbara twisted her hands in worry. "Where is Bill?"

"At the fire line with Preston and Gabe. Preston asked if you ladies can bring out the water wagon. We'll get it loaded and hitched up for you. Be sure to keep at least one of the barrels covered in case we need drinking water; there's a lot of ash in the air." He waved at the men. "Get saddled up, then help with the water wagon. Don't worry about taking food. Rosa will send some with the wagon. Bring shovels and axes, and blankets. Hurry!"

The men took off at a run.

"Is a wildfire different from a regular fire?" Jennifer asked nervously as she followed Barbara back to the house.

"A taste of hell," Barbara answered, her voice grim. "A brush fire, which doesn't sound that bad, but they're very dangerous. If the wind kicks up, a wildfire can move faster than anything can run, human or animal. And it's been so dry for so long. If the fire reaches the canyons and arroyos, the flames will shoot through them as if they were shot out of a cannon, devouring everything in their path."

"How terrible," Jennifer breathed. "Does this happen often?"

"Often enough that we have developed a system." Barbara

led the way into the kitchen. "The men fight the fire. The women cook and haul water."

"What can I do?" Jennifer asked.

Barbara flashed her a grateful smile. "You and I will take the wagon out. Rosa will stay here and cook; Francisca will help her mother and watch my children. Fighting a fire is exhausting work; the men need a lot of food and water to keep their strength up." She hesitated. "Firefighting is also hot, dirty work, Jennie. Perhaps you would rather stay here with the children."

"I will help you with the water," Jennifer said firmly.

"Good. Be sure to bring a scarf or neckerchief, and wear your oldest clothes. You'll be covered with soot and smelling like a campfire by the time we get home."

Jennifer could not suppress a rueful smile as she hastened back through the dining room. She did not have any old clothes.

She reached the bottom of the stairs just as another wave of the mysterious light-headedness washed over her, causing her to stumble against the stair post.

"Jennie!" John hurried across the foyer from the front door. "Are you all right?" His strong hands clamped around her waist, steadying her.

"I think so." Jennifer grabbed the stair post. "I just can't seem to catch my breath." She could smell smoke on his clothes.

John frowned. He moved his hands over her rather loose-fitting basque waist, up her rib cage almost to her breasts and back down to her hips.

Jennifer slapped at his hands. "Stop it!"

Muttering something about foolish women, John lifted Jennifer into his arms and carried her across the foyer into Preston's study, kicking the door closed behind them.

Her heart pounded. If she had felt light-headed before, now she felt positively faint. She struggled against him. "Put me down," she ordered weakly.

To Jennifer's surprise, John obeyed her, setting her carefully on her feet. He glared at her as he pulled off his gloves.
Without a word, he spun her around to face the wall and, to
her outraged astonishment, opened the buttons down the back
of her cotton waist, revealing her corset.

"John—Mr. Cantrell, what are you doing?" she cried.

"Something I should have done weeks ago," he snapped.
He pulled a wicked-looking knife from his boot and neatly
sliced the laces up the back of the corset, exposing the cami-
sole she wore underneath.

Jennifer shrieked and struggled against his strength.

"Hold still!" he commanded. He snaked a hand around her
stomach to work the lower portion of the corset from the
waistband of her skirt, then pulled the offending garment free.
"No woman could breathe with this band of steel around her
middle, not as tight as you lace it." He held the corset up
for a moment before throwing it to the floor.

After drawing a deep breath, Jennifer jerked away from
him, reaching a hand back over her shoulder to pull the open
neck of her waist together. "I did not tighten the laces any
more than I always do," she retorted. "I have worn them that
way for years." She was so angry that it did not occur to her
she was discussing an intimate piece of her apparel with a
man who irritated her beyond endurance.

"You have been eating Rosa's good cooking for a month
now, Jennie. Some of your other clothes probably don't fit
anymore, either, and I, for one, am glad to see it." John strode
over to Preston's desk and opened a drawer to rifle through
the contents. "You look much healthier now than when I first
arrived at the Santa Maria." He pulled a rolled-up piece of
paper from the drawer and, after unrolling it far enough to
peruse it, allowed the paper to snap back into place.

"You had no right—" she started.

John only glared at her as he crossed the room and flung
the door open to march into the foyer.

"You could have just loosened the laces!" Jennifer shouted after him.

"Corsets are not healthy for any woman, and besides, you don't need one!" John yelled back over his shoulder. He slammed the front door behind him.

Jennifer fought with the buttons at her back, hating to admit that she did feel better. How foolish of her not to guess the problem herself! Would John ever let her live it down? With the intention of retrieving the ruined corset, she turned to go back into the study when she noticed Barbara standing on the stairs, watching her with wide eyes.

"Is everything all right?" Barbara asked cautiously.

"Everything is just fine," Jennifer answered through gritted teeth. "I will meet you outside in a few minutes." She stepped into the study and closed the door, praying Barbara would not figure out what had happened. When the last button at her back was again closed, she snatched the corset from the floor and rolled it up. She peeked out the door. Seeing no one, Jennifer held the corset within the folds of her skirt and hurried up the stairs.

An hour later, the heavily-laden wagon bounced along the ruts that passed for a road, Barbara's sure hand hurrying the horses. The day was hot and still, and Jennifer was thankful for the shade offered by her new hat. Billowing smoke rose over a hill just ahead, then the pungent odor reached her nose. With desperate hope, she looked up at the sky for what must have been the hundredth time since they had left the *hacienda*, only to be again disappointed. There was not a hint of a cloud. A breeze whispered by her cheek, and Jennifer's heart stopped. After praying for a breeze for the last month, the thought now filled her with dread.

They passed a herd of about twenty cattle being driven toward the river by two men on horseback. One was Bill. He cantered over to the wagon and rode alongside. "It's just over that next rise, Barb, to the south. Stay on this side so you don't get cut off if the fire makes a jump."

Barbara nodded. "Do you have any food?"

"I do, but Pedro doesn't." He gestured toward the other man.

Jennifer opened a basket on the seat next to her and pulled out a cloth-wrapped bundle. "Bread and cheese," she explained as Bill took it from her.

"Thanks. You two be careful." He managed to lean out of the saddle and give Barbara a quick kiss, then adjusted his hat and rode off.

Neither of the women spoke. Fear wrapped around Jennifer's heart like a heavy blanket.

The wagon topped the rise, allowing her to see the extent of the damage. The fire had burned several acres to the south and was slowly advancing on the line of men digging a firebreak along the parallel ruts that made up the road.

"Oh, good." Barbara's voice was filled with relief. "This is manageable so far."

Jennifer stared at her friend. "This is good?" she repeated. To her eye, the fire was terrifying, even from a distance.

Barbara nodded. "They can stop this one, if the wind doesn't come up."

Preston and John approached the wagon as Barbara drew the team to a halt. With their noses and the lower half of their faces hidden by neckerchiefs, the two men reminded Jennifer of the outlaws she had read about in a dime novel. Their exposed skin was covered with soot, the creases at the corners of their eyes making strange-looking white fans. She resolutely turned her face from John.

"Hello, ladies," Preston said jovially. "Nice day for a drive, huh?" He helped Barbara down from the wagon. "Did you see Bill?"

"Yes. He and Pedro and about twenty cows."

Preston's eyebrows drew together. "Only twenty? And where were Latham and Julio?"

"I don't know. Should we be worried?"

"You're already worried enough, honey. The other two are probably up an arroyo chasing out more cattle. Bill knows what he's doing."

John held a gloved hand up to Jennifer. Reluctantly, she took it and stepped to the ground.

He immediately placed his hands at her waist, again feeling her ribs. "Just to make sure you did not put another one on," he said for her ears alone.

She slapped his hands away. "And what would you have done if I had?" she demanded.

"I would have cut it off again, right here in front of God and everybody else." He touched the brim of his hat in a mock gesture and strode off, leaving Jennifer to glare after him with her hands at her hips.

"Jennie?" Barbara called.

Jennifer turned around to find both Barbara and Preston watching her from the other side of the wagon, their curiosity ill-disguised. "What are you two looking at?" she barked, more sharply than she intended.

Preston backed up. "Nothing." The corners of his eyes crinkled, telling Jennifer that he was smiling underneath that neckerchief. She merely scowled at him, and he hurried away.

"Pull your scarf up over your nose, Jennie, like this." Although her eyes twinkled, Barbara spoke with all seriousness as she demonstrated with the brightly colored piece of cloth tied around her own neck. "We'll distribute the food; the men will see to their own water needs."

"You take John his food," Jennifer said petulantly as she secured the scarf over her nose. "I won't go near him."

"All right," Barbara said with a laugh.

Jennifer watched the encroaching flames. "Are they going to throw the water on the fire?" she asked doubtfully.

"Some of it. They'll wait until the fire approaches the fire-break, then they'll wet down their blankets and have buckets of water at hand. They'll use the blankets to beat out any flames that cross over and use the buckets for bigger flare-ups. They must keep the fire from jumping the break. If it gets past them, they'll have to try and guess which direction the fire will spread, get ahead of it, and dig another break."

A breeze ruffled Jennie's skirt. "It seems like hard work," she said, her voice troubled. "And dangerous."

"It is."

Barbara's grim tone caused Jennifer to glance at her friend. Her anger toward John Cantrell faded. Somehow, the importance of her cut corset laces lessened dramatically in the face of a very real and very dangerous enemy.

Preston came back to the wagon at a run. "The wind is picking up, Barbara. Forget the food—we have to get the water distributed. You two wait here." He climbed up to the wagon seat and guided the horses toward the line of feverishly working men.

Jennifer watched with mounting fear as the men labored together to wrestle the barrels off the wagon and fill the many buckets. The breeze was steady now, and growing in force.

When the wagon was empty, Preston returned, struggling to keep the nervous horses at a trot. He brought them to a halt and jumped from the wagon. "Don't let them bolt," he warned Barbara as he helped her up to the seat and handed her the reins. "If our own horses run, we may need you to get us out of here."

"Preston, can we help?" Jennifer pleaded. "I can slap fire with a blanket."

"Thanks, Jennie, but you have no idea how heavy a wool blanket is when it's water-soaked. Besides, I'll feel a lot better if I know you're out of danger." He lifted Jennifer up to the seat. "Just stay here. If the fire jumps the break, wait for us as long as you safely can, then get out of here." He ran back down the rise and took his place on the line.

Both women turned on the seat to watch behind them. There must have been twenty men altogether standing against the flames. Four more stood back from the line, each holding the reins of several nervous horses.

"I didn't know Preston had such a large crew," Jennifer remarked. "How many men work for him?"

"Fourteen. *Don* Alejandro must have sent a few men to help."

"That was neighborly of him. I wonder why he is so nice, and his children are . . . not."

The corners of Barbara's eyes crinkled with a smile that was hidden by her neckerchief. "You are very diplomatic, Jennie. I could think of any number of more descriptive terms for both Constanza and Arturo." She sobered. "But yes, I do find it strange that such a decent man would have such unpleasant children. I often wonder what went wrong—if it would have made a difference had *Don* Alejandro's wife not died so young." She suddenly pointed. "The flames have reached the far end of the break."

Jennifer held her breath and watched as the fire raced the final few yards to the fire break, a break that now looked pathetically inadequate. On the far side, John whipped a blanket over his head to the ground, then vanished from view in the wind-driven smoke, as did all the men. Shouts and curses could be heard over the roar and crackling of the flames.

Barbara grabbed her arm. "It jumped the break!" she cried despairingly.

With watering, smoke-irritated eyes, Jennifer watched in horror as the flames took hold on the far side of the road and merrily danced up the small hill. A riderless horse raced out of the smoke toward them, followed by several with men in the saddles. One horse carried two men.

"Go! Go!" Preston shouted to them as he drew near the wagon. The draft horses needed no further encouragement than a single slap with the reins. They broke into a gallop, dragging the wagon behind them.

Jennifer held onto the edge of the seat with one hand and

her hat with the other, her heart pounding in fear. She had not seen John ride out of the smoke.

Preston called a halt to the retreat at the top of the next hill. He turned his horse in a circle, speaking as he did. "Are we missing anyone?"

"John and a few of the men with him at the far end of the break," Gabe answered. "They're not here, but maybe they got out the other side."

The group fell into an uneasy silence. Preston rode a short distance back the way they had come, and all eyes followed him. The wind had pushed the flames north rather than west—the direction in which they had come—leaving a blackened landscape. Across the smoking wasteland Jennifer saw several men on horseback top a small rise, waving their arms and shooting their pistols in the air. Preston pulled his pistol and returned the fire. "They made it!" he shouted jubilantly.

Jennifer's shoulders slumped with relief, and she pulled the scarf down off her face. John was safe, at least for now.

"We'll set up a camp near the river," Preston said as he returned his pistol to its holster. "There's no telling what this damn wind will do, so there's no way to guess the direction of the flames." He squinted up at the sky. "It'll be dark before too long. We'll work in shifts through the night and watch the fire, then decide our course of action in the morning. We may have to burn the next firebreak rather than dig it."

"Burn it?" Jennifer repeated in a whisper.

Barbara leaned toward her. "Start another fire, one we can hopefully control, so that when the wildfire reaches that place, there's nothing left to burn and it will die out."

Jennifer stared at her with wide eyes. "And if we can't control the break fire?"

"Then we're in serious trouble," Barbara said bleakly.

"Gabe, ride back and check the water barrels," Preston ordered. "Some of them should have survived the fire, as soaked as they were. Signal if there's any we can use, and we'll get the wagon down there." He looked at the small group of Noriega riders. "Thank you for your help, boys, more than I can say. Go on home and tell Alejandro we may need you again tomorrow. I don't think we can count on rain tonight."

"We'll be here, Mr. Cantrell," one of them said and, with a wave of his arm, led the small group away.

Preston pulled the neckerchief down off his nose. He looked strange with the skin around his eyes smoke-blackened and his cheeks and chin relatively clean. He smiled wearily at the two women in the wagon. "We'll see if any barrels are salvageable, then we'll get home."

Barbara nodded. "We don't mind waiting."

"Not at all," Jennifer added.

Preston touched his hat brim and cantered off to greet the men who had made their way from the far side of the burned acreage. Jennifer was relieved to see that John was indeed among them. She resigned herself to wait, watching the cruel flames top another defenseless hill to the north. A hot, north-bound wind brushed her face on its way by.

Like everyone else, with the exception of the children, Jennifer slept intermittently that night. Early the next morning she presented herself in the kitchen dressed in a dark red walking skirt and a simple white waist with a lace-edged neckline and elbow-length sleeves, no corset, her hair pulled to a chignon at the back of her head. The room was empty. Knowing Rosa could not have gone far, she donned an apron, grabbed a long-pronged fork, and turned the thick pieces of salt pork sizzling in a cast-iron skillet on the stove.

"Good morning, Jennie."

At the sound of Preston's voice, Jennifer turned with a smile. "Good morning." She was concerned to see how tired he looked. "Would you like some coffee?"

"Yes, thank you. You may as well pour some for Bill and John; they're right behind me." He sat at the table, spreading

a rolled-up paper out in front of him. Jennifer recognized it
as the roll John had taken from the study the day before; it
was a map.

She filled four cups with fresh coffee, handed one to Preston, and picked one up herself. "What happened during the
night?" she asked.

Preston rubbed a hand over his eyes. "The wind blew hard
for a while, then slowed and shifted direction. It's headed
west now."

"Toward the *hacienda?*"

"Yes."

Jennifer sank onto a bench, her heart thudding.

Bill pushed through the door from the dining room, followed closely by John. Jennifer pointed at the coffee she had
poured for them. They each grabbed a steaming cup and took
a seat on either side of their father.

Preston made stabbing motions at the map. "We have to
try a controlled burn break. We have no choice. I think the
best place is along the top of this ridge, which runs down to
the river on the west end. We'll have a chance to contain the
wildfire if it continues west, and the land to the south is
already burned. We can only pray the wind doesn't shift on
us again, because if the fire turns north or east, we won't be
able to stop it."

John met Preston's gaze. "Do you have any idea how the
fire started?"

"It wasn't lightning, I know that." Preston took a swallow
of coffee. "Maybe some drifter got careless with his campfire."

"It may have been deliberate."

Preston, Bill, and Jennifer all stared at him.

"Deliberate?" Preston repeated. "No one in these parts
would be crazy enough to deliberately start a wildfire."

John shrugged. "Perhaps he is desperate, or just plain stupid." He paused. "Or perhaps he hates you a great deal."

Jennifer's breath caught. Could John be right? Was the fire

another calculated act of violence against Preston and the Santa Maria? A picture of those terrifying flames flashed in her mind. Who could hate that much? She glanced at John, then quickly away, refusing to even consider that perhaps he did.

Rosa came in the back door carrying a bucket of milk, effectively ending the conversation. Preston looked up at her.

"You have to prepare for evacuation, Rosa. If the wind turns to the north again, the house will be in immediate danger. Have a wagon ready. You may need to load the children at a moment's notice and get out of here."

She set the bucket on the table, her serene face solemn. "We will be ready, *Señor* Preston. You fight the fire; Rosa will see to the children."

"Thank you. Jennie, I'll need you and Barbara to make at least one run with the water wagon. Bring a lot of food. Alejandro is sending every available hand and coming himself; so are some folks from town."

Jennifer nodded. "We will be there."

Preston looked from John to Bill. "Let's go, sons. We have a battle to fight, and this is one we'd better win."

The men stood up. John glanced at Jennifer, his expression sober. She knew he had been up all night, and she could sense his fatigue.

"Be careful," she said softly.

"I will." He winked at her, a small gesture, but one that gladdened her heart. He followed his father and brother out the door.

Later, Jennifer sat on the seat of the water wagon, holding on for dear life as Rosa expertly guided the horses along the rough trail leading to the ridge. Barbara had been reluctant to leave her small children in the event it became necessary to evacuate, so Rosa accompanied Jennifer to the burn site.

They spoke little on the trip out, each woman preoccupied with her own thoughts. Finally, Rosa drew the wagon to a halt about halfway up the side of a rather steep ridge. Jennifer got down from the wagon and climbed toward the top of the ridge, where she could get a clear view of the small valley she knew was on the other side. Rosa followed her.

Jennifer was now so accustomed to the smell of smoke that she did not think the strong odor unusual. When she topped the ridge, she was astonished to see that the entire other side had been burned all the way down to where the land leveled off. The burned area went west as far as the waters of the Rio Agua Dulce, sparkling in the sunlight, and about a mile north, where several men controlled the flames. To the southeast, in the distance, a grim wall of smoke signaled the pitiless approach of the wildfire.

She raised her eyes to the Diablo Mountains beyond, several miles away, hoping to see some sign of clouds. To her surprised delight, she did, hovering over the tops of the mountains. By their whiteness, she knew they had not yet developed into storm clouds, but they were clouds just the same, the first she had seen in weeks. She whispered a prayer for rain.

Preston approached at a canter, then drew to a halt near them. "Thanks for coming, ladies. We've burned about as much as we're going to. The boys are ready to eat. Then all we can do is wait and pray the wind doesn't change direction before the wildfire reaches the burn break."

"How much time do we have?" Rosa asked.

"An hour, maybe less if the wind picks up."

"I saw clouds over the Diablos, Preston," Jennifer said.

Preston nodded. "I know. The clouds bring hope, but I don't know if they carry rain, if they're coming in this direction, or if they'll get here in time. We can't count on rain to help us."

"We can count on God," Rosa said firmly, and pulled a rosary from her skirt pocket. "I will pray."

"Good. We need all the help we can get. While you're praying, Rosa, get the wagon up here; we'll place the water barrels at intervals along the top of the ridge. When the wagon is empty, take it down there and be sure the team is headed west in case we have to make a run for it again." He pointed down the unburned side of the ridge, where several saddled horses waited with a few men watching them.

"*Sí, Señor* Preston." Rosa hurried back to the wagon and climbed up to the seat. She took up the reins and looked at Jennifer, who waved her on.

"I'll walk," Jennifer called.

Rosa nodded and started the team forward. They had brought only six barrels of water, so it did not take long for the men to set them out along the ridge. The controlled fire had been extinguished. Rosa and Jennifer distributed the food, which the tired men devoured. Jennifer was surprised to see Arturo included in the Noriega contingent. She wondered if he had apologized to John.

Her eyes found John as he stood off to one side talking with Bill. She held her hand to the brim of her hat and studied him. He wore blue denims, a white shirt, and his hat, with the requisite kerchief around his neck. Outlined against the mountains and the sky as he was, he looked tall and lean and strong, like the heroes of Alexandre Dumas' books, standing against the elements. She could easily imagine him as one of the Three Musketeers, fighting for queen and country, only in this case he fought a dragon of fire for the sake of his father's land.

He met her eyes, and this time she was not embarrassed to have been caught looking at him. Instead, she was delighted when he left Bill and came to her side.

"Thank you for bringing the food," he said.

"You're welcome." Jennifer shrugged. "But Rosa actually drove the wagon."

"Still, you helped prepare it, and you came." He turned to the south and watched the approach of the fire.

Jennifer looked in the same direction, suddenly aware that the wind was pressing her skirt against her legs. "The wind is rising," she said with a note of desperation to her voice.

"It's kind of a mixed blessing," John commented. "It's bringing the clouds, but it's also bringing the fire. This will be a close race."

Jennifer raised her eyes to the sky and saw that the clouds had indeed moved over the mountains and that they were grey now. A storm was definitely building, and building quickly. She looked back at the wildfire. Fresh wisps of smoke reached her nose, and she could faintly hear the crackling, snapping sound of a hungry fire. Without taking her eyes from the flames, she asked, "Is this what it's like to be in battle?"

John watched her. "What do you mean?"

"The waiting. You know the enemy is out there; you have done your best to prepare for him, to defend yourself, and all you can do is wait and wonder if your preparations were enough, wonder if you will survive the day."

His eyes widened in surprise at her understanding. "Yes, Jennie, this is very much like preparing for battle."

She looked at him then. "I know you were an agent in *Ciudad de Mexico,* but were you ever in an actual battle during the Juarez Revolution?"

"Yes, several."

She turned her face back to the approaching wildfire. "I'm glad you survived."

John placed a light hand on her shoulder. "Thank you. I'm glad I did, too."

They said no more. A tense, expectant hush settled over the group. The wind had whipped the flames to new heights, pushing the fire to within a hundred yards of the burn break. To Jennifer, the fire seemed a thing alive, breathing its hot, foul breath over the land, destroying everything in its path. Yet, there was a fascinating beauty and power about it. How could she be horrified and fascinated at the same time? She took a step backward.

John's hand tightened momentarily on her shoulder before he released her. "Cover your nose," he said as he pulled his own neckerchief up over the lower half of his face. Jennifer did as he instructed, then followed him to the nearest water barrel.

He pulled a blanket from a pile on the ground and soaked it in the water. When he pulled the dripping thing from the barrel, Jennifer held out her hands for it. He hesitated.

"I'll not stand by and watch, John Cantrell. I'm taking my place on the line." Her determined tone brooked no argument. He handed her the heavy blanket.

"Me, too," Rosa said firmly.

John dunked another blanket into the barrel and handed it to Rosa, then took up a bucket and filled it. Jennifer was surprised when he began to slosh water on her skirt as he spoke.

"Your skirts are in much more danger from flying sparks than our denims are, but I can't soak them thoroughly or they'll be too heavy if you have to run. Wrap yourself in the blanket if you catch fire, and call for help."

Jennifer nodded in solemn understanding.

John splashed some of the water on Rosa's skirt as he continued his instructions. "If the flames jump the break, if you get into trouble and can't make it to the horses, wrap the wet blanket around you and get to ground that has already been burned." He pointed down the hill to the burn break. "Lie on your stomach, with your head uphill and covered. With luck, the fire will jump over you."

"We can hope it won't come to that," Rosa said cheerfully. With her blanket in hand, she moved off to a place on the line near Gabe.

"Yes, we can," Jennifer echoed. She clutched her heavy, dripping blanket with a death grip and faced the oncoming inferno. Her heart pounded; her eyes watered; her mouth seemed as parched as the land around her. Never had she known such fear. Never had she been in such danger as she was now. She looked in both directions at the row of silent, somber people, her view sometimes obscured by drifting smoke. What courage they had! She met John's eyes. He shook out his dripping blanket and winked at her over his face-covering, then turned toward the flames.

Jennifer smiled, knowing he couldn't see it, and shook out her own blanket. A strange twilight descended as thick smoke rolled over them all, blotting out the sun.

"Here she comes!" Preston shouted. "May God help us!"

With a roar like that of an angry beast, the wildfire threw itself at the base of the ridge. Arms of flame shot up the hill, seeking hold, finding little. The wind blew blazing embers over the top of the ridge, igniting small fires in the dry grasses that were quickly extinguished by the watchful fire-fighters. One section just over the ridge down toward the horses flared, but several men successfully contained it.

Jennifer swung her blanket again and again against every spark she saw. Preston had been right; a soaked wool blanket was very heavy. Her shoulder muscles ached, as did her arms, and her breath seemed to tear through her lungs. From somewhere came the ridiculous thought that she was very glad she had not worn a corset today, and she smiled underneath her face-covering. John would laugh at that.

A shout came from Gabe, and to Jennifer's horror, she saw that Rosa's skirt had caught fire. Gabe threw her to the ground and covered her with his blanket, beating at her legs. Preston rushed over to help, then waved his arm.

"She's not hurt!" he shouted. He and Gabe pulled Rosa to her feet; part of Rosa's skirt had burned away, exposing her white petticoats. Gabe gave her a quick hug, then all three returned to fighting the fire as if nothing had happened.

With a sigh of relief, Jennifer went back to work, stamping an errant flame here with her booted foot, whipping another there with the blanket. The thwarted blaze had turned to the west at the bottom of the ridge, and the fire crew ran along the top, fighting each spark that lit the grasses. The wind increased in speed, pushing the flames ever westward toward the waiting waters of the Rio Agua Dulce. Jennifer heard a low rumble and peered up through the thinning smoke. Tears of gratitude filled her eyes when she realized the rumbling was indeed thunder. Never had storm clouds been so welcome.

John grabbed Jennifer's hand and led her to the front of the crowd on the western end of the ridge. As she watched, the wildfire roared over the bank of the river, flared for a moment, and abruptly died. In its mindless voraciousness, the fire had left nothing behind to fall back on, and so the beast was destroyed as quickly as it had destroyed, leaving a legacy of desolation and scattered hot spots where blackened brush and ruined trees smoldered.

After a moment of stunned silence, Bill let out a shout of joy and triumph. One by one, the weary firefighters joined in the cheer, and the sound rose in volume, sounding as sweet to Jennifer's ear as any church choir. The sky thundered in accompaniment and splattered the rejoicing crowd with tiny, teasing drops of rain.

John tore his hat off and threw it into the air, then pulled his neckerchief down off his nose and held his face to the sky, laughing. Jennifer dropped her blanket, pulled her scarf down, and did the same, causing her hat to fall backward off her head. She held her arms up and danced in a circle, opening her mouth to the gradually increasing rain. John looped an arm around her waist and joyously led her in steps that resembled a polka. Gabe grabbed Rosa, and Preston hooked elbows with Alejandro, while the others kept time with clapping hands.

The rain increased to a steady fall, still accompanied by occasional thunder, and after a few minutes, everyone began retracing their steps along the ridge in the direction of the wagon and the horses.

Breathlessly, John pulled Jennifer into his arms and swung her in a circle so that her feet left the ground. Shouting with laughter, she insisted that he put her down. He did, but he still held her close, gazing into her eyes as if he could see her very soul. One hand caressed the side of her neck below her ear. Then he gently kissed her.

Jennifer's heart slammed against her ribs. Her fingers wandered up his neck to curl in his thick, wet hair, and she opened her mouth to him, revelling in the feel of his arms around her, his body close against her. His lips moved over hers, caressing and tantalizing at the same time. None of her wistful imaginings of his promised kiss came close to the reality. Surely the earth itself shook with the power of his touch as the wind and the thunder danced around them. It was as if they were alone in the world.

Finally John released her, taking her hands in his and holding them against his chest. He did not speak, but only stared at her with his beautiful blue eyes.

"You said you would kiss me," she whispered, pulling a hand free from his grasp to touch his cheek.

He smiled. "I am a man of my word."

"I am glad you are." She blinked against the falling rain.

For a moment, he stared at her with some deep emotion she could not name, then he bent to retrieve her hat. He gave it to her and grabbed up his own. Following the rest of the crowd, he led her back to the wagon with her hand firmly held in his. The men had rolled the empty barrels to the wagon and loaded them. John lifted her up to the wagon seat, and when she was settled, Preston spoke to all present.

"As good as this rain feels, I'd like to get out of it." He urged his horse to Alejandro's side. "Alejandro, my friend, my thanks to you and your men for your help. Come on back to the *hacienda* with us; it won't be fancy, but we are going to have one hell of a celebration. Beg pardon, ladies." He tipped his hat in the direction of the women in the wagon.

Alejandro nodded with a broad grin. "We will come, Preston."

"Then let's go!" Bill shouted. "I want to see my wife and children!" He set off at a gallop. With much whooping and hollering, most of the rest of the men followed.

John grabbed Jennifer's hand again and placed a kiss on the back of it. "I'll see you at the *hacienda*," he said softly, then, with his customary wink, left her to take his reins from Gabe.

Jennifer watched as he vaulted into the saddle and rode after Bill. Her eyes met Preston's. There was no misunderstanding the warm approval in his eyes, the pleased smile on his face.

"Don't you say anything, Preston Cantrell," Jennifer warned. "Not one word."

"Yes, ma'am." Preston's smile widened, and he touched the brim of his hat. "Let's go home."

Rosa slapped the reins lightly against the backs of the draft horses and the wagon lurched forward, Gabe riding on one side, Preston on the other. No one seemed to feel the need to speak.

Jennifer breathed deeply of the rain-cooled and deliciously smoke-free air and looked back over her shoulder at the ridge. Fire Ridge, she would call it from now on. There she had taken a stand against a killer fire and had helped defeat it. There John Cantrell had first kissed her, starting a fire in her heart that she doubted would ever go out.

From the corner of her eye, a movement caught her attention. She twisted further on the seat and saw a lone horseman on top of the ridge, watching them. It was Arturo Noriega, astride his stallion. Even from a distance, Jennifer could feel his malevolent stare.

Preston turned in his saddle to follow the direction of Jennifer's gaze. He waved at Arturo. "Come with us!"

Arturo did not respond. He watched them a moment longer, then forced his horse's head in the opposite direction and disappeared over the ridge.

Preston shrugged and faced forward again. "It's hard to believe he's Alejandro's son," he commented.

"Did he ever apologize to John?" Jennifer asked.

"Grudgingly so, and only at his father's insistence, I'm afraid."

Jennifer lapsed into silence. She had a bad feeling about Arturo Noriega. He wished John harm, and she wondered how far the angry young man would go to fulfill his wish. She sighed. Some of the joy had gone out of the moment.

Eleven

One afternoon a few days later, Jennifer wandered alone in the courtyard, taking delight in the soft whisperings of the fountain and the cool shade offered by the trees. She settled onto a bench and closed her eyes, breathing in the heavily scented air. The courtyard had a perfume and a sense of peace all its own that would be impossible to recreate elsewhere. How she loved this place!

Since the defeat of the fire, Jennifer had felt a new closeness with all the people of the Santa Maria. Against the fearsome forces of nature, they had fought for their home and the land, and they had won. They were her family now, just as they had been for two short years when she was a child.

Preston was like a father to her; Bill, her brother; Barbara and Rosa, her sisters; Francisca and Molly, her nieces; David her nephew. She called Gabriel Horn, Pedro, and Ross Latham her friends. What did she call John?

Her beau, she decided with a smile, although she would not tell anyone how she felt about him. There was a difference in the way he treated her now. The sarcasm was gone, replaced by affectionate teasing. He had not attempted to kiss her again, much to her disappointment, but then, there had been no opportunity for them to be alone. That she sometimes found his smoldering gaze on her, telling her without words of his interest, was enough for the time being.

She leaned over and broke off a sprig of lavender, then settled back against the bench, bringing the herb to her nose.

The scent reminded her of her friend Susannah, who used lavender oil as perfume. Susannah was happily married to Conor O'Rourke now, living in Wyoming Territory, a long way from her childhood home in the East. She had sworn to Jennifer that she did not miss Charleston, where she had grown up, for her life with Conor was too full. She was happy in Wyoming and did not wish to live anywhere else.

Jennifer knew she could be happy living in California for the rest of her life and doubted that she would miss Philadelphia at all. One or two friends she missed, but overall, her old life no longer held any appeal for her, and she was astonished to admit it. It seemed that she had been living in a fog for the last fourteen years, and the bright California sunshine had burned it away. The sunshine and the love of the Cantrell family.

Preston had said she could stay as long as she wanted to. Did he mean it? Would he allow her to live with his family forever if she wished?

Jennifer's eyes narrowed in thought as she twirled the twig of lavender between two fingers. When her father died, his vast estate had been split evenly between Jennifer and Oliver. They had each inherited a fortune, built on the gold Albert Mainwaring had coaxed from the California earth during the Gold Rush. Thanks to her hardworking father, Jennifer had the financial means to live independently, and for the first time in her life, it dawned on her that she could live wherever she chose. She was twenty-three years old, an emancipated woman, with no family ties now that her relationship with her uncle was strained to the breaking point. Why did she have to go back to Philadelphia?

An excited smile curved Jennifer's lips. She did not have to go back. Oliver could return to the East and live in that stuffy, ostentatious house of which he thought so highly; in fact, Jennifer hoped he would. She did not want him here.

Unable to sit still as an overwhelming feeling of newfound freedom rushed through her, Jennifer jumped to her feet and whirled in joy. Oliver had always handled her financial affairs, but there was no reason she could not learn to do so herself if Preston was willing to guide her. She would write to Elias Craig, her solicitor, and ask for a detailed accounting of her assets. When that came and she understood her situation, she would approach Preston and talk frankly with him. Since the time she had lived here as a child, she had felt that the Santa Maria was home. Perhaps it truly could be.

She hurried toward the side gate. As soon as she checked on Buford, she would write the wire to Mr. Craig. With luck, it would be sent tomorrow, and if he responded quickly, as she would ask him to, she could hear from him within two weeks, before Oliver returned.

And where does John fit in? As she lifted the latch on the iron gate, she was forced to admit that she did not know. Even if he were not here, she would want to stay; she knew that much. But she was honest enough to acknowledge that his presence here made life more interesting.

John had never mentioned his long-term plans. Perhaps he did not intend to stay beyond a few more weeks or months, although she knew Preston had recently invited him again to make his home here. The thought of John leaving caused Jennifer's heart to sink. She could not imagine life on the Santa Maria without him.

Well, he simply could not leave. Jennifer smiled again and slipped through the gate. She would do her best to help Preston persuade him to stay.

Burning with curiosity, John watched Jennifer leave the courtyard. He wished he could have read her mind over the past several minutes, for the most intriguing succession of emotions and expressions had paraded across her lovely face. When she jumped up and danced around, he had wanted to join her, to dance with her, but he'd decided against intruding.

It was bad enough that he spied on her from behind the curtain of his bedroom window.

With a sigh, John released the curtain and went back to cleaning his pistol. He should have left the Santa Maria right after the *fiesta,* as he had planned. Admittedly, he had been delayed for a few days in order to give the local sheriff time to complete the investigation into Baxter Lewis's death. The sheriff had ruled the shooting self-defense, as John had believed he would. But the investigation hadn't been the only thing keeping him here. That one waltz with Jennifer had filled his heart and clouded his judgment, and he had delayed for a few more days. Then the wildfire had come, threatening everything Preston held dear, everything his father had worked thirty years to build. He could not leave then.

Now he was caught by the magical bond of the Santa Maria. He had sweated and toiled with these people, had risked his life as they had theirs to battle a raging inferno. Against his will, he had been drawn into the Cantrell family, and for the first time, he admitted that he did not want to leave. Nor did he want Jennifer to leave.

John replaced the bullets in the barrel chambers of his pistol. He hoped Oliver never returned. If the man did come back for her, John knew he would take action, although at this point he wasn't certain exactly what that action would be.

Jennifer crossed the yard, surprised to see Emmett Lafferty's buggy in front of the barn. She was even more surprised to find Buford's pen empty and swept clean. Puzzled, she moved to the back doors, which were wide open. In the near pasture, she saw Buford, Preston, and Dr. Lafferty. The bull had been healing well, and she had known he would soon be turned out with the other cattle. Evidently, the time had come. While she was happy for Buford, Jennifer also felt a twinge of sadness. She had looked forward to her daily visits with the animal, had been pleased to monitor his progress.

She picked up her skirts and crossed the corral to the fence. "So he is healed, Dr. Lafferty?" she called.

The two men came over to the fence.

"Yes, Miss Mainwaring," Emmett said, his old face lighting in a smile. "He's doing quite well. I removed the stitches today; he's on his own now. Preston tells me you helped with Buford's care."

Jennifer arched an eyebrow at her godfather. "Not much, to tell the truth. Preston wouldn't let me. All I did was check on Buford, scratch his head, and make sure his water was fresh—that sort of thing."

Preston shrugged. "It was of help, Jennie." He clapped Emmett on the shoulder. "I've invited Emmett for supper, and he'll probably stay over until tomorrow."

"How nice! Then I will see you later, Dr. Lafferty." She smiled at him, then turned back toward the barn.

Jennifer entered the coolness of the interior, taking pleasure in the straw-scented air. Because there were no animals in the various stalls and pens, the place had a lonely air today, but she loved the sense of safety and peace it offered. With Buford released to the pasture, she'd have no reason to visit the building every day, although she supposed she could still come if she wished.

That was one of the nice things about living on the Santa Maria, Jennifer decided. She was free to do as she wished, knowing she was not risking censure or disapproval from her uncle. Oliver had deeply ingrained ideas about what was proper and fitting behavior for a young lady, and what was not. Over the years, Jennifer had come to fear his diatribes and lectures and, as much as possible without surrender, had modified her behavior to avoid Oliver's angry outbursts. No more. She would not live that way, *his* way, any longer. With renewed determination, Jennifer headed toward the main door. She would get to work writing her wire to Mr. Craig.

Just as she reached the door, a small sound came to her ears. Not sure what she had heard, she stood still, waiting to see if the sound repeated itself. A moment later it did. A soft whine seemed to be coming from her left, where a towering pile of fresh hay filled the corner.

The sound came again, and Jennifer was convinced it was made by an animal, a small animal. But what? A bird? A mouse? Again the sound came, a little louder, this time almost a cry.

Without another thought, Jennifer moved around the pile of hay. "Who is there?" she asked softly, then clicked her tongue. "Call out, little one. Help me find you."

She heard the sound again, and this time recognized it as mewing. A smile lit her face. One of the barn cats had probably had kittens, and if she was lucky, she would be able to see them. She picked her way carefully around the hay, peering along the wall into the dimness of the corner. "Where are you, babies?"

The mewing rose in volume and urgency. Back in the very corner, where it was secluded and dark, Jennifer's eyes fell on a black cat lying on its side, with tiny, squirming fluffs of black fur next to her stomach. "Hello," she said softly, not wanting to scare what was sure to be a very protective mama cat. She pushed against the mountain of hay and was finally able to kneel down not far from the cats. "I won't hurt your babies," she cooed.

The mother cat did not move. Jennifer frowned. Something was wrong. She blinked, trying to adjust to the dim light.

She reached out a trembling hand toward the motionless cat. When she touched the animal's side, although it was warm, she knew immediately that there was no life under the strangely matted black fur. The mother cat was dead. A lump formed in Jennifer's throat and her eyes filled with tears.

"Preston." The name came out as a hoarse sound. Jennifer swallowed and tried again. "Preston! Dr. Lafferty!" As her voice rose, it took on a note of command. "Preston! Dr. Laf-

ferty! Come at once!" She gently picked up one of the crying
kittens. It was so tiny that it fit in the palm of her hand. She
nestled the creature in her lap and reached for another. A
careful search of the area revealed no more kittens. *Only two?*

"Jennie, where are you?" Preston called urgently.

"Back here, behind the haystack in the corner."

After pushing aside more of the hay, Preston came to her
side, followed by Emmett and, she was surprised to see, John.
Her eyes teared again. "The mother cat is dead," she said
mournfully.

"Let me see." Emmett dropped to his knees and reached
for the still cat. When he brought it out into better light,
Jennifer was horrified to see that the black fur was matted
with blood, that something was terribly wrong with one of
the cat's back legs. "Yes, she's dead," Emmett said quietly.

Preston grabbed a piece of worn blanket from a stall fence
and handed it to Emmett. The old doctor gently wrapped the
cat in the material. John squeezed Jennifer's shoulder before
he leaned forward to take the sad bundle from the doctor.

Tears trailed down Jennifer's cheeks. "What happened to
her?"

"She probably had a run-in with a coyote or a dog, but
I'd say it happened somewhere else. It's amazing she was able
to get back to her babies before she died. Poor girl." The old
man shook his head in sorrow.

"What will happen to her kittens?"

Emmett paused before answering. "They will die, Miss
Mainwaring."

Jennifer stared at him, aghast. "Can't we do something?"

Without speaking, Emmett took one of the kittens from
Jennifer's lap. He held the tiny creature up to what little light
reached the corner. The kitten mewed piteously. "This one's
eyes are open." He took the other kitten from Jennifer and
examined the tiny face, then shook his head. "This one's
aren't." He set the kittens back in Jennifer's eager hands.

"They're too young—I'd guess only about ten days old. They can't survive without their mother."

"I'll not let them die," Jennifer fiercely vowed. She settled the kittens in her lap and dashed one hand across her eyes, then stared up at Preston. A burning determination had replaced her need to cry. "You can save orphaned calves, and lambs whose mothers reject them. There must be some way to save these kittens."

"They're too small, Jennie." Preston looked at her with gentle understanding. "They won't make it. It would be kinder if you let Emmett put them down. He can do so painlessly with ether. I'll get you another kitten, an older one, if that's what you want."

"I want *these* kittens," Jennifer insisted, aware that she risked sounding like a spoiled child. She did not care. "They are *alive*, Preston. As long as there is life, there is hope. I want to try. Please." She glanced at John, silently begging for his support.

Although his eyes were soft with compassion, his tone was serious when he spoke. "I raised a litter of orphaned pups when I was a boy. They were older when their mother died than these little guys are, but I was able to feed them with milk-soaked rags until they learned to drink themselves." He shrugged. "It's worth a shot."

She smiled her thanks.

Preston sighed and helped Jennifer to her feet. "Take them to the kitchen, where Emmett can better examine them. If he can assure you that the kittens won't needlessly suffer through your efforts, go ahead and try it."

"Thank you," Jennifer breathed.

"I've got to check the irrigation pump in the orchard, so I'll be in later," Preston said.

Jennifer nodded, then looked at John. Her eyes again filled with tears when she saw the wrapped bundle in his arms.

"I'll bury her and be right in," he said kindly. "You go on with Dr. Lafferty."

She gave him a watery smile, then allowed Emmett to lead her from the barn, the two kittens snuggled against her breast.

"There were only two?" Emmett asked.

"That's all I could find. Is that not a small litter?"

"Yes, but perhaps others were stillborn or died."

"Wouldn't we have found their bodies?"

Emmett shook his head. "The mother would have disposed of them. Cats keep their nests very clean." He led the way into the kitchen.

"What is this?" Rosa demanded good-naturedly as her domain was invaded. Francisca left her mother's side to run to Jennifer.

"Orphaned kittens," Jennifer answered. "We are going to try to save them."

"Oh, may I help?" Francisca begged. She looked up with wide, hopeful eyes, and it struck Jennifer how pretty the girl was, with her big brown eyes and long black hair pulled into two thick braids. She placed one of the kittens in Francisca's outstretched hands.

"Of course," she said with a smile. Both of the squirming kittens mewed loudly.

Rosa arched an eyebrow. "They sound hungry. I will get milk."

"Goat's milk, preferably," Emmett interjected. "And a couple of clean rags, please." He turned to Jennifer. "Make a roll of the cloth and stick it in the neck of a bottle filled with warm milk. When they get a little bigger, you may be able to feed them with a rubber baby nipple, but chances are the nipples are much too big for them now." He settled a pair of spectacles on his nose. "I'll also leave you a syringe. If all else fails, shoot the milk down their throats. It'll be slow going if that's the way you have to feed them, but it'll work. Now let's examine these little guys." He reached for the kitten Jennifer held out to him.

John came in a few minutes later to find Jennifer seated on one of the benches with a kitten wrapped in a cloth and cuddled on her lap. A lovely peace kissed her features. She guided a pint whiskey bottle filled with milk to the mouth of the little creature she held and squeezed the cloth protruding from the neck of the bottle. The kitten eagerly latched onto the dripping cloth and began to suckle. Jennifer smiled in delight, although to John's eye, more of the milk ran over the kitten's face than down its throat.

Jennifer extended her smile to him when he sat next to her. His breath caught at the dazzling beauty the smile brought to her face. It struck him that it took very little to make her happy.

Across the table, Emmett instructed Francisca in the feeding of the other kitten. "They will have to be fed several times a day, and they may wake you in the night," he warned.

"I don't mind," Jennifer assured him. "I will make a nest for them in a box and keep them in my room."

"There is one other thing."

Jennifer looked at him. "Yes?"

Emmett cleared his throat. "The reason newborn kittens are so clean is because their mamas keep them that way. They are not able to clean themselves or empty their bladders without help."

Jennifer fervently wished John had come in just a few minutes later. She could not stop the blush that crept up her cheeks, but she refused to look away from the doctor's kind eyes. "What do I need to do?"

"You need to wipe their little fannies with a warm, wet cloth. It will stimulate them to release their bladders and, later, their bowels. It won't be long before they are able to tend to themselves, but they need help for a while. You must keep them clean."

"I can do that."

Emmett nodded and stood up. "Preston wanted me to check a few of the sheep, so I'll go find him now. I'll be here until tomorrow; if you have any questions, just ask."

"I will, Dr. Lafferty. And thank you. I'll take good care of these kittens."

"And I'll help," Francisca piped in.

Emmett laid a hand on the child's head. "They are very lucky kittens," he commented, then left the room.

John watched Jennifer, marvelling at the gentleness with which she treated the kitten. "Have you seen these kittens before?" he asked. "Is that why they are so important to you?"

She shook her head, not looking at him. "No. I had no idea they were there before today."

"Why are you so attached to them?"

She shrugged. "I don't know. Maybe it's because they are so young and so helpless, and no one wants them." She stroked the tiny head of the sleepy kitten. "I know there are plenty of cats in the world. As Preston said, I could have others, ones that would not require as much care. But each life is precious, John, animal as well as human. Just because there are plenty of other cats doesn't lessen the value of these two. I want to give them a chance."

John stared at her bent head. How could he have ever thought her to be a cold, unfeeling woman?

At breakfast the next morning, Emmett asked Jennifer how the night had gone.

"They awakened twice—once just after midnight and again at three o'clock," she said brightly. "I brought the box down here, fed and tended to them, and they went right back to sleep." She glanced over her shoulder at the wooden fruit box next to the stove, where the kittens slept snuggled together among the folds of an old blanket.

John sat across the table, unable to take his eyes from her. There was a special life to her this morning. She had opted to wear her hair in a simple braid, leaving it to hang down her back. He liked her hair that way, liked the soft tendrils that curled around her face, the glow of health in her cheeks, the shine of happiness in her green eyes. Could this be the same cool, elegant woman who had so arrogantly challenged him that first night they'd met? Then he had written her off as just another spoiled, rich female who cared for little more than her social calendar and wardrobe. How wrong he had been.

"I must admit, Miss Mainwaring, they are doing better than I thought they would," Emmett said. "You are a patient, caring nurse."

Jennifer smiled with pleasure. "Thank you, doctor. I just love them."

He nodded. "It shows. Have you named them?"

"Katie and Jake. For now, anyway. As near as I can determine, one is a boy and one is a girl. Jake is the one whose eyes haven't opened yet. Will they soon?"

"I'll be surprised if they aren't open by tonight."

"How can you tell which is the boy?" David asked around a mouthful of cornmeal mush.

"Don't speak with your mouth full, honey," Barbara murmured.

Jennifer blushed, not sure how to answer the child, and was grateful when John spoke.

"His eyes aren't open yet, David. That's how you can tell which is the boy. But there are other ways. I'll show you later."

David nodded with excitement, his mouth still full. The kittens were popular with all of the children in the household.

Jennifer looked up to find Emmett's gaze on her.

"You care a great deal about animals, don't you?" he asked.

She nodded.

"She always has," Bill put in. "You should have seen her as a child. When she and her father stayed here, she had a virtual menagerie."

"I didn't have that many," Jennifer objected, somewhat defensive about Bill's teasing tone. "And some of them had been injured." She faced Emmett. "That's why I so admire what you do," she said fervently. "Animals have no one to speak for them, no one to care for them when they are seriously injured or ill, or orphaned too young. They are simply put to death. I want to help those I can."

"And that desire should be encouraged," Emmett said. "Have you thought of pursuing a course of study?"

Startled, Jennifer stared into Emmett's kind old eyes. After a moment, she nodded, for the first time admitting her dream to someone else. "I have studied some on my own—the few books I could buy, or borrow from the public library—and the stableman at home taught me what he knows. But my parents disapproved, as does my uncle."

"Not appropriate for a young lady— that was their reasoning, I'll wager," Emmett commented.

Again Jennifer nodded, a familiar band of pain tightening around her heart at the memory of the disrespect her family had always shown toward her dream. In Philadelphia, she had not even been allowed to keep a cat or dog as a pet.

"Many people seem taken aback by the idea of a woman studying animal husbandry, let alone veterinary sciences," she said quietly, with an accusing glance at Preston.

Preston shifted in his seat, but when he spoke, his tone was unapologetic. "Nursing orphaned kittens or studying is one thing, Jennie. Getting too close to an injured bull when you have no experience in such things is quite another."

"True," Emmett agreed, then he looked at Jennifer. "You were not prepared to deal with Buford. But I still think your interest should be encouraged. Remember your own words, my dear: If there is life, there is hope."

"I was talking about the kittens."

"The same can also apply to you. You are alive, so don't give up hope. If you have a dream, pursue it, no matter how farfetched it may seem. Don't let the disapproving attitudes of other people keep you from your heart's desire. The ani-

mals need you. I'm sure you will find a way to help them."
He smiled at her.

Jennifer looked at the people around the table. She read
encouragement on the faces of the women and, with the exception of Dr. Lafferty, doubt on the faces of the men, but
no one voiced an objection. That in itself was a refreshing
change from the heated discussions she had endured with her
father, her stepmother, and her uncle.

John even smiled at her. She wanted to talk to him about
this, to learn what he truly thought, for, with each passing
day, his opinion was becoming more important to her.

The conversation turned to more general subjects, but Jennifer did not pay much attention. It seemed whole new vistas
were opening up before her. Did she dare believe that she
could make her life what she had previously only dreamed it
could be? Her heart soared with hope. The future, stretching
off through the years, looked promising, for the first time in
her life.

"You burned it?" Constanza screamed the words as she
advanced across her bedroom toward her brother. "That was
your idea while I was gone? You started a wildfire and destroyed the land?"

Arturo backed away from the fury in his sister's eyes.
Never had he seen her so upset. "You were gone too long,
almost two weeks. I couldn't think of anything else." He hated
that his words came out in a whine.

She stopped in front of him, very close. "This whole thing
is about the land, Arturo, the very cause we are fighting for.
The precious land. Land that belongs to Mexico. You dese-
crated it!" Her fist found his chin before he had time to react.

Arturo staggered backward from the force of the blow.
Constanza followed him, striking him again and again. He
held up his arms in an attempt to protect himself. Never did
it occur to him to strike her back.

"Please, Constanza, stop," he pleaded. "The land will recover. Fire burns out the bad as well the good."

Constanza halted abruptly, one arm raised in midair. She stared at him, her breath coming hard, the wildness in her eyes gradually fading. "You are right." She turned and walked away from him. "You are right. Fire will cleanse the land of the stench of the *Americanos*. How unfortunate the fire was defeated before it reached Cantrell's *hacienda*."

"I helped defeat it," Arturo said bitterly.

"You fought the fire?" Constanza demanded as she faced him, her hands at her hips.

Arturo shrugged. "Father insisted, just as he sent me to work on the destroyed dam. I couldn't very well refuse and tell him I had started the fire."

"Poor Arturo." Constanza came to his side and laid a hand on his cheek. "It isn't right that you should have to work so hard to undo what we have so far accomplished. We must be more clever in the future."

"Don't burn the house," Arturo warned morosely. He moved away from her and slumped into the chair by the window. "Father will have us all over there to help Preston rebuild." He shook his head. "I don't understand why he considers the Cantrells such good friends."

"Papa is a fool." Constanza stalked the rug next to her bed, curling a long strand of hair around one finger. "He has lived too long with *Americanos*. But he will see that we are right, Arturo. When the flag of the Republic of Mexico again flies over California, he will see that we are right."

With a frown, Arturo watched silently as his sister paced. He suffered no illusions that California would ever be returned to Mexico, but he dared not voice his doubts to Constanza. He would be satisfied to add the Cantrell land grant to that of his father. The combination of the Buena Ventura and Santa Maria ranches would make the holding one of the largest in the state, a holding he and Constanza would someday inherit. That was enough for him.

Constanza broke into his thoughts. "If the Cantrell *hacienda* burned with everyone inside, there would be no need to rebuild it, would there?"

Arturo tilted his head, not sure he had heard her correctly. "What?"

"No." Constanza did not seem to hear him. She pursed her lips in thought for a moment, then continued. "That would be hard to do. There are too many *vaqueros* working for the Santa Maria. We would need an army to fight them all, and it will be some time before our army can come."

"Constanza, you can't seriously be thinking of killing the Cantrells." Arturo stared at her, disturbed that he was not at all sure of his sister's answer.

"Don't be foolish, Arturo. We certainly wouldn't kill *all* of them." She looked at him, then laughed, a high, tittering sound. "And we *can't* kill Juan Cantrell."

Arturo scowled. "He is the one *I* want to kill."

"But you mustn't." Constanza fell to her knees in front of him and took his hand. She wore a strange smile. "Not Juan. I have decided that I will marry Juan."

"You will not!" Arturo pushed her away and jumped to his feet. "I forbid you!"

Constanza settled into a more comfortable position on the floor and arranged her skirts around her bent legs. She looked up at Arturo with a calculating look in her eyes. "You forbid me?" she asked quietly, ominously.

Arturo ignored her tone. "Anyone but him, sister." Now he paced the rug. "He seduced you when we were in Mexico, nearly ruined you, then walked away. I should have killed him then."

That laugh came again, high-pitched and taunting. *"Imbécil!* You were but sixteen. Juan could have killed you in his sleep with his hands tied behind his back. He was *El Lobo."* She leaned back against the chair, her expression growing soft. "He was magnificent, and still is."

Arturo glared at her. "He is an unprincipled bastard who

took my sister's virginity without benefit of marriage, thereby taking my family's honor. If Father knew, he would kill him. But John Cantrell is mine. He deserves to die by my hand."

"Perhaps, but you will not kill him, little brother." Constanza held a hand up to him, which he took and pulled her to her feet. When he made to release her, she tightened her hold on him. "My marriage to Juan will ensure the union of the Cantrell and Noriega land grants, Arturo," she whispered, moving closer. With her free hand, she touched Arturo's swelling cheek.

Arturo swallowed nervously and closed his eyes. "And what do you propose to do with Preston and William Cantrell?"

"They must die."

Startled, Arturo opened his eyes and stared down at his sister, his beautiful, beautiful sister. As always, when she was so close—too close—he became confused, struggling to resist the evil desires. In a desperate attempt to escape the path down which his traitorous mind and body were leading him, he asked sarcastically, "And I suppose you want to kill William's son, as well?"

Constanza only smiled. "If necessary," she whispered. Her gentle fingers brushed over his brow. "I hurt you again. I think your eye will blacken, Arturo." She kissed his jaw. "I am sorry." Her words were a mere breath against his mouth.

Arturo grabbed both of Constanza's hands in his and crushed them to his chest. Shaking from the force of his unholy emotions, he closed his eyes. He could feel her heart pounding where her soft breasts pressed against the backs of his hands. "What do you want of me, Constanza?" he begged in a broken whisper.

Except for her accelerated breathing, she stood motionless and said nothing, offering no resistance, offering no assistance.

After an agonized moment, Arturo pushed her away and strode to the door. Constanza's malicious laugh reached his ears before he could close the door behind him.

Twelve

"I'm glad Rosa would not come with us." Jennifer fanned herself as she spoke to Barbara in a low tone. The two women shared an uncomfortable wrought-iron settee in Alejandro Noriega's courtyard. Although an olive tree behind them offered shade, the September afternoon was still warm. "Constanza is in her element today, especially since this is her birthday celebration." Even in the crowd of guests, the woman was clearly visible, thanks to her dress of brilliant turquoise satin.

Barbara nodded her agreement. "It's best to keep them apart. Rosa coming here would be like a fly visiting a spider's web. I do wonder what Constanza did to cause such hard feelings." She looked up with a welcoming smile as Gabe joined them. "We were just commenting that it's best Rosa didn't come today."

"It is," he said. He pushed his hat back on his head. "I didn't want to come myself, but Preston felt I should pay my respects to *Don* Alejandro, especially after all he did to help us fight the fire. Rosa is under no such obligation."

"Rosa is usually so sweet and forgiving," Jennifer remarked, not taking her thoughtful gaze from Constanza. "Constanza had to have done something terrible to her."

"She did," Gabe muttered darkly.

Jennifer looked at him in surprise. Gabe had made no attempt to disguise the hatred in his voice. She knew by the set of his jaw that he would say no more, even if she or

Barbara pressed him. "It seems warm today," she said brightly, in order to change the subject.

Barbara fanned herself. "It certainly does. So warm that I think I'm in need of refreshment."

"I'd be happy to bring you some lemonade," Gabe offered.

"I'll go with you. I should offer *Don* Alejandro my compliments on his lovely *fiesta.*" Barbara stood up and took Gabe's extended arm. "Jennie, would you like to join us?"

"No, thank you. I promised John I would wait here for him. He shouldn't be too much longer."

"I don't know." Gabe shook his head. "He and Preston were discussing horses with *Don* Alejandro the last time I saw him. They could talk for hours." His eyes glinted with humor.

"I'll send him to you," Barbara promised with a knowing smile.

Jennifer felt her cheeks warm. "Go on with you both," she said affectionately as she waved them off.

She was in a strangely pensive mood. Two weeks had passed since the fire, ten days since she had discovered the kittens. In that time, no answers had been found concerning the suspicious start of the wildfire, and the kittens were thriving under Jennifer's committed care. A smile touched her lips at the thought of Katie and Jake. Jake's eyes had opened that day, just as Emmett Lafferty had predicted, and now the two little black fluff balls followed her about as if she were their mother. Attempts to wean them from the bottle had so far been unsuccessful, but everything else was going well. The kittens would survive.

Oliver had sent her a telegram; after two weeks in San Francisco, he had finally set out for Portland by sea. She wondered why he had tarried so long in San Francisco. With a shrug, she realized she did not care. The longer he was gone, the more time she had to refine her plans for remaining in California. She had also received a wire from Elias Craig acknowledging receipt of her request for an accounting of her financial assets and assuring her that he would gather the information immediately.

Jennifer shifted on the hard seat. As uncomfortable as the settee was, she enjoyed lingering in the shade and letting her mind roam where it would. More and more often lately, her thoughts turned to John, as they did now.

She searched for his tall figure in the crowd and finally found him. He was no longer speaking to Preston, but rather stood alone, nonchalantly resting his lean, black-clothed body against the adobe wall of the courtyard. His casual stance was in sharp contrast to the intensity with which he stared at something, or someone. Jennifer followed the direction of his gaze and stiffened when she realized he was staring at Constanza. A dull pain wrapped itself around her heart. She looked down at the tasteful striped bronze day dress she wore and knew she could not compete with the stunning Constanza in that turquoise satin dress. Few women could.

For the first time in her life, Jennifer felt jealous. She was shocked by the intensity of the feeling, and very uncomfortable with it. Why should she care who John Cantrell stared at? But she did, she admitted miserably to herself, and it especially stung that he seemed so taken with Constanza. The knowledge that John and Constanza had known each other for a long time did not help. Did he hope to renew or deepen his relationship with Constanza? For some reason, Jennifer had assumed that John was wise enough to see through Constanza's machinations, as Bill did. "I also thought he had better taste," Jennifer muttered disgustedly. But she saw, with a sinking heart, that he continued to stare at the black-haired woman in the turquoise dress.

John focused on Constanza. As usual, her hair fell free down her back, covered with a black lace mantilla. The mantilla was decorated with silk flowers that exactly matched the eye-catching shade of her gown. He shook his head in bemusement. How did the woman get away with it?

Constanza's gowns were always of the latest style in terms

of design, but, in a dramatic departure from the dictates of fashion, she had each one made in a single, bright, unrelieved color, with the neckline plunging just a little lower than was truly acceptable. And to wear her hair down! No respectable woman did so in public, yet it was Constanza's trademark. True, she covered the luxuriant locks with the lace mantilla, perhaps at her father's insistence, just as she always wore the heavy gold crucifix that hung exactly to the spot where her deep cleavage disappeared into her bodice. Constanza exuded a curious mixture of flamboyance and pious respectability, a combination John had once found fascinating. They had been lovers; now she held no interest for him at all, and he found that odd. Had he changed so much? If so, what had changed him?

Jennifer.

Would he have been interested in accepting Constanza's invitation to renew their affair if Jennifer had not been at the Santa Maria? John watched Constanza as she flirted with a young man. She was an expert with that black lace fan, covering the lower half of her face so that only her huge eyes showed coyly over the edge. John pushed away from the wall. Constanza was a master of intrigue, and he had grown weary of the games. Since coming to the Santa Maria, he had been treated with refreshing honesty by the people there. Even when a few—Gabe, Jennifer, Rosa, Bill—had warned him not to harm Preston, had even threatened him, their reasons had been clear and, he had to admit, justified. John respected that. He doubted that Constanza, with her scheming games and subtle manipulations, would have held any appeal for him whether Jennifer had been there or not.

He turned in the direction of the olive tree, where he had left Jennifer resting in the shade. She waited there still, watching him, her lovely face wearing a vaguely troubled expression. With a twinge of guilt for being away from her for so long, John started toward her, pausing only at the refreshment table to grab a dainty glass cup filled with lemonade.

"I bet you thought I would never return," he said teasingly as he sat down at her side. "I've brought a peace offering." He held the cup out to her.

"Thank you." Jennifer accepted the cup, but did not take a drink. She stared out at the crowd. "Constanza is very beautiful, isn't she?"

Surprised at the question, John regarded Jennifer closely. Her brows were drawn together in a puzzled frown. "In some ways," he answered cautiously.

At that, Jennifer faced him. "Only in some ways?"

"In the obvious ways. Anyone who gets to know Constanza soon learns that, in her case, beauty truly *is* only skin deep." John was not sure, but he thought he saw relief flash across Jennifer's face. Certainly her expression relaxed. Had she been jealous? Something inside him warmed at the thought, but he did not want Jennifer to worry about Constanza as far as he was concerned. "Others have a beauty that goes to their soul." He gently took her chin in his grasp. "Like you." He placed a soft kiss on her lips.

Jennifer's eyes widened with surprise, and a blush reddened her cheeks. She pulled away from his hold. "John, you'll make me spill this lemonade," she scolded as she snatched her fan from her lap with one hand and furiously fanned her heated face. "And I cannot believe you had the audacity to kiss me in public." Her voice had dropped to an agitated whisper.

John leaned against the wrought iron, draping one arm casually along the back of the settee, behind Jennifer. His hand was within easy reach of the ringlets that cascaded down the back of her neck, and he could not stop himself from touching those soft curls. "You should know by now that I am very audacious, Jennie. Isn't that one of the many things you like about me?"

Jennifer's fan stopped in front of her face, but it did not hide her smile. She kept her gaze averted from him as she spoke in a soft tone. "Yes, you insufferable man, your audacity is one of the things I like about you." She glanced at him from the corner of her eye. "One of the *few* things."

John worked his hand under her curls to the warm skin of her neck, where he began to stroke her. Jennifer went very still.

"Oh, I think you like more than a few things about me, Jennifer Mainwaring. Just as I like more than a few things about you."

"Like what?" Jennifer asked with an endearing note of vulnerability in her voice.

"Well, to begin with, I like your hair." John shifted his hand to tug lightly on one of the ringlets.

Now Jennifer faced him fully, not caring that her astonishment showed. "My plain brown hair?"

"Your hair is a deep, rich brown, Jennie, with red and golden highlights that shine in sun or candlelight. I have often dreamed of what it would look like falling free around your shoulders and down your back."

She pulled away a little. "Like Constanza's?" she demanded, unable to keep the note of bitterness out of her voice.

John shook his head. "No, Jennie. Your hair would fall free for my eyes only, for my hands only. I would not share that beauty with anyone."

There was a curious possessiveness to his tone that sent a shiver of excitement racing through Jennifer's stomach. After a moment's hesitation, she asked, "What else do you like?"

"Your eyes. I like your eyes." John moved his hand from her neck to her cheek. "It is said that the eyes are the mirror of the soul, and in your green eyes I see all of your beauty, your fire, your passion, even when they flash in anger at me."

Jennifer's breath caught at the intensity of his expression. "I like your eyes, too," she whispered. Uncomfortable with the magnitude of the emotions sweeping through her, she added, "And you will definitely make me spill this lemonade, John Cantrell."

John glanced down at the unsteady cup and took it from

her hand. He set it on the ground under the bench, then continued as if she had not spoken, briefly eyeing her dress.

"I like your tasteful style of dress, your spirit, and your loyalty." His gaze travelled up to her face. "I like to kiss you, so much so that I am tempted to kiss you again, right on the mouth, right now."

"John!" Jennifer moved to fan her face again, but he stilled her hand.

He leaned closer and took her other hand as well, his voice dropping to a whisper. "And there are other places I would very much like to kiss you besides your tempting mouth, other things I would very much like to do to your lovely body, and someday, Jennie, someday soon, I promise you, I will."

Jennifer's heart pounded against her ribs. Her lips parted and her breath quickened as a bolt of lightning shot through her abdomen, igniting a fierce fire of desire. She could not pull her gaze from his captivating blue eyes, nor could she speak. Not for one second did she doubt John's words. Once more, the wolf was circling, but this time . . . this time she welcomed his nearness. Jennifer trembled. *El Lobo* was a man of honor. He would keep his promise.

John again gently kissed her lips. "For now, though," he whispered, "we'll . . . dance!" He jumped up and pulled Jennifer to her feet.

She stared at him, stunned by the sudden change in his manner. "What?"

"We don't have enough privacy for what I would really like to do, Jen," John said over his shoulder as he led her in the direction of the music that had just started. "But another thing I really like about you is your grace, especially when you dance with me."

A wide smile covered Jennifer's face as she gladly followed him and was swept into his arms.

Constanza watched them from her position near the opened doors leading to Alejandro's grand *sala*. Her mouth tightened into a thin line while her eyes flashed with a dangerous fury. Without a word to those who stood with her, she whirled about and stormed into the house.

An hour later, Jennifer once again sat alone on the iron settee, trying to catch her breath from the exertion of dancing. John had not been content to let her rest before now, and with the exception of allowing her one dance with Preston, he had insisted on keeping her all to himself, much to her delight. As it was unladylike to have a sheen of perspiration covering her forehead, she vigorously fanned herself in the hope she would be more presentable when John joined her with the promised lemonade. Then she caught sight of him dancing with the stout wife of Gilroy's mayor. Knowing he likely had been pressed into service, and probably by his father, Jennifer smiled, relieved that she had more time to collect herself.

God knew she needed to collect herself. Even after an hour, she had been reluctant to leave John's arms. Again and again, her mind returned to his promise. Besides her mouth, where did he intend to kiss her? What did he have in mind beyond kissing? A shiver ran through her at the wild speculations she came up with on her own. Lord have mercy, she needed the fan again!

"Miss Mainwaring?"

Jennifer blinked, and gradually her eyes focused on a young woman wearing a black dress covered with a neatly ironed white apron. Her red hair was pulled up under a white cap. The maid bobbed a quick curtsey.

Jennifer slowed the frantic motion of her fan. "Yes?"

"My mistress wishes to speak with you. She asks that you join her in *Señor* Noriega's study, if you please." The maid spoke with a lyrical Irish lilt. She curtseyed again, keeping her gaze to the ground.

"I assume your mistress is Constanza Noriega?" Jennifer asked.

"Aye, miss."

"Please convey my regrets to Miss Noriega. I do not wish to speak with her." Jennifer kept her tone emotionless and polite.

The maid raised her head and stared at Jennifer, her brown eyes large and stricken. Jennifer noticed that one side of the girl's face seemed swollen.

"Please, miss," the maid whispered. Then she caught herself. "As you wish, miss," she said dejectedly, and turned to go.

"Wait." Jennifer stood up.

The girl turned back to her, her eyes now filled with hope. "Aye, miss?"

Jennifer studied the girl's face, pale except where redness covered the swelling on her cheekbone. With a sudden flash of insight, Jennifer guessed the cause of the swelling. A surge of anger rushed through her, but she schooled her features to disguise her feelings. "What is your name?" she asked kindly.

"Brigit, miss."

"Why did your mistress strike you, Brigit?"

Brigit dropped her chin, refusing to meet Jennifer's eyes. She did not respond.

"Miss Noriega is no friend of mine, Brigit. You may trust me." At Brigit's continued silence, Jennifer reached out and gently lifted the girl's chin. "Please tell me."

After a long hesitation, Brigit swallowed hard. When she spoke, her voice was barely above a whisper. "The gentleman refused to meet with her, just as you did, miss. When I gave Miss Constanza his reply, she was displeased."

"So she struck you."

"Aye, miss." Brigit looked at her, her expression one of genuine dread. "Please don't tell her I told you," she begged.

"I will not, I promise." Jennifer fought the urge to put a reassuring arm around the girl's shoulder, but she feared

Brigit would be uncomfortable with such a gesture. Her next impulse was to slap Constanza. Her hand closed into a fist. That course of action was not entirely out of the question. A sudden suspicion entered her mind. "Which gentleman refused to meet with her?"

"The handsome one with blue eyes, dressed all in black."

"I know him," Jennifer said softly. "Had Mr. Cantrell been aware of what Constanza would do to you, he would have agreed to meet with her."

"Oh, I don't blame him, miss. He was very kind to me, just as you are."

"Well, I shall meet with your mistress. Please take me to her at once."

Brigit's thin face broke into a grateful smile. "Aye, miss. Thank you, miss." She bobbed a couple of curtseys, then led Jennifer into the main house. They moved quietly down a wide, carpeted hallway. Brigit came to a stop before double doors carved of oak set above two steps. She hesitated with her hands on the brass latches. "Watch yourself, Miss Mainwaring," she whispered in a troubled tone. "The mistress is in one of her states."

"Thank you, Brigit. I shall exercise extreme caution." Jennifer smiled encouragingly at the maid.

Brigit turned the latches and pushed both doors open. "Miss Mainwaring to see you, Miss Noriega," she announced formally.

Jennifer lifted her skirts to negotiate the two steps up into the room, and Brigit closed the doors silently behind her. For a long moment, the maid stared at the solid wood. Then, with a sudden, determined lift of her chin, she hurried away.

Constanza stood behind the carved mahogany desk that formed the focal point of the room, her arms crossed over her breasts, her face set in a stony mask. She stared at Jennifer in malevolent silence.

Jennifer refused to be intimidated. She took her time looking about the tastefully decorated study, noting with appreciation the walls lined with full bookcases; the comfortable-looking, tufted leather sofa off to one side; the thick carpet under her feet; the heavy velvet curtains at the windows, now half-drawn against the heat of the afternoon. Her gaze eventually settled on the hostile woman behind the desk. In a deliberate and exaggerated mimic of Constanza's pose, Jennifer crossed her own arms. "Well?" she demanded.

Constanza only glared at her.

"Your pathetic games of intimidation will not work with me, Constanza," Jennifer snapped. "I will not play." She turned to the doors and grasped one of the brass latches, fully prepared to leave.

"I summoned you here to warn you, Jennifer."

Jennifer whirled to face Constanza. "How kind of you." Her voice was deliberately heavy with sarcasm.

Constanza flushed. "I mean it," she snarled. "I warn you to stay away from Juan Novales."

"Who are you to tell me anything about John?" Jennifer advanced farther into the room, her hands at her hips. "Whatever is between him and me is none of your concern."

"Ha!" Constanza dramatically threw her head back, then leveled her hate-filled gaze on Jennifer. "You know nothing of him, little Jennifer, whereas I know him well. Very well. He was my lover in Mexico, and since we have again found each other, he is once more. Surely he has not crawled into your bed, although I would not put that past him."

Jennifer stiffened, her hands now clenched in fists at her sides. Constanza moved to the end of the desk as she continued.

"During the Revolution, *El Lobo* seduced many French and English *gringas* for what they could give him—information, money. Why not a rich American one now? After all, there is much at stake." She came around the desk and leaned against the edge, again crossing her arms. A malicious glee lit her expression as her gaze swept Jennifer up and down. "Surely you do not believe Juan is drawn to you for yourself.

You are not woman enough to interest a man like him, let alone keep him."

"I'll not listen to this." Jennifer spoke through gritted teeth as she turned again to the door.

Constanza ran across the room to slam the door closed just as Jennifer opened it. "Yes, you will listen." She jerked Jennifer's hand from the latch and shoved her back with enough force to cause her to stagger. "You *will* listen to me."

Jennifer caught herself and stared at Constanza in shock. How familiar was that expression of cruel hatred in Constanza's eyes! Jennifer remembered it well from childhood and knew Constanza was not above violence. She took another step back.

"Do not set your sights on Juan Novales, little Jennifer." Constanza's tone was ominously calm. "He is a dangerous man, too dangerous for you. I am a far more suitable partner for him, and besides, your loving uncle would never allow you to marry Preston Cantrell's bastard son."

"I am past the age of emancipation," Jennifer retorted. "Oliver has no control over me whatsoever, legal or otherwise. My relationship with John is no more his business than it is yours."

"But it *is* my business! I have made plans, important plans, and you are an impediment. I do not appreciate it!"

Jennifer gaped at her. "*I* am an impediment to your plans? Constanza, where do John's wishes fit in with your precious plans? If you think he is a man who can be manipulated or coerced, you are a fool."

"It is you who are the fool!" Constanza spat. "There are things you don't know about him—dark and horrible things that a woman like you could never accept. He was not merely an agent in Mexico. Ask him about the assassin known as *La Serpiente.*"

Jennifer could think of nothing to say. John, an assassin? The very idea was inconceivable.

Constanza advanced on her. "Remember that he intended

to kill his own father. He has not returned to his father's ranch out of the goodness of his heart. He seeks what is rightfully his, what Preston Cantrell denied him even before he was born. One day Juan will have the Santa Maria, which is his birthright. And I shall be at his side." She stood tall and triumphant.

"I think not." Jennifer again headed toward the door, but Constanza stepped into her path.

"Juan is a Mexican patriot," she hissed. "He would never marry a *gringa,* although he would gladly seduce one."

"You do not know John as well as you think you do," Jennifer said firmly.

"Stay away from him, Jennifer. I warn you." She backed against the door in a determined effort to block Jennifer's exit.

The absurdity of the situation hit Jennifer and she stopped. "Stay away from him or what?" she demanded. "What will you do?"

Suddenly, the doors against which Constanza leaned were pushed open from the outside, causing the woman to stumble into the room. She swore in outrage and whirled to face the intruder. When her furious gaze landed on John, her next words died on her lips.

Jennifer was almost overwhelmed with relief, although the dark expression on John's face gave her pause. He stepped up into the study.

"Yes, Constanza, tell us what you will do if Jennifer does not stay away from me." The deadly tone of John's voice caused even Constanza to step backward until she bumped into the desk.

Then she straightened, flinging the lace mantilla back over her shoulder. "I am Constanza Noriega y Gonzalez," she announced imperiously. "You will not speak to me in such a manner in my father's house."

"Jennifer." John held out his hand to her, and she took it. He stabbed his free hand in Constanza's direction. "It is you who will leave us alone, Miss Noriega. Years ago in Mexico, I warned you about interfering in my affairs. Now I warn you for the last time: Do not interfere again. You would not wish to see me truly angry." He turned his back on her and pulled Jennifer toward the open doors.

At Constanza's scream of outrage, Jennifer looked over her shoulder just in time to see the woman heave a carved stone bookend at John. With a cry of warning, she jerked away from John's grasp and pushed him. Jennifer threw her hand up in a desperate attempt to protect herself, but the bookend glanced off the side of her head. Knocked off balance by the blow, she stumbled on the steps at the door. Her ankle wrenched painfully and she pitched forward into the hall, landing hard, the breath knocked out of her.

"Jennie!" John was instantly at her side, cradling her in his arms. He was horrified to see a thin stream of blood coursing down the side of her pale face. She did not answer him, nor did she open her eyes. For one terrible, panicked moment, he feared she was dead. His hand moved to her breast, where he felt the rise and fall caused by her breathing, felt the beating of her heart. The relief that rushed through him was staggering; had he been standing, he surely would have collapsed. He held her to his chest, mindless of the blood that dampened his shirt. She moaned and stirred against him.

John raised his gaze to Constanza, who stood inside the doors. "Get out," he ordered through clenched teeth.

Her eyes widened, but she did not move.

"Get out of my sight, Constanza, quickly, for your own sake."

Constanza hesitated only a moment, then gathered her skirts and passed by them, holding her head high. She continued down the hall to the stairs and disappeared.

"Oh, blessed Mary." Brigit came running and fell to her knees beside John, her eyes filled with tears. "I feared she would hurt the miss."

"You did well to warn me, Brigit." John carefully got to his feet with Jennifer in his arms. "Please bring *Señor* Cantrell to me. Do you know who he is?"

"Aye, sir." Brigit stood and wiped her eyes with a corner of her apron. "I'll hurry." She set off at a run.

"Bring water and a cloth," he called after her.

"Aye, sir!"

Jennifer shifted, clutching at his shirt.

"Shh," John soothed. "I have you, Jen." He carried her back up into the study and laid her on the leather sofa. As he knelt on the floor beside her, he was relieved to see her eyes flutter open.

"Did she hurt you?" she whispered.

His heart grabbed. Injured though she was, her first thought was of him. "No. You protected me well." He pulled a handkerchief from his pocket.

"Good." The word came out on a sigh, and her eyes closed again.

John studied her pale face. Head injuries could be serious—what if she was badly hurt? With a shaking hand, he carefully dabbed at the blood smeared on her cheek, knowing that he was responsible for the whole incident.

He should have set Constanza straight long ago, when they first saw each other again. Rather than pulling Jennifer behind him, he should have pushed her through the doors first. He, better than anyone, should have known not to turn his back on Constanza Noriega. He bowed his head, and for the first time since his grandmother's burial, John Cantrell whispered a sincere, heartfelt prayer, just in case God was listening.

Thirteen

"What in the hell happened?" Preston demanded as he hurried into Alejandro's study.

John looked over his shoulder and saw that Alejandro was right behind Preston, followed by Bill, Barbara, and Gabriel. Arturo stood near the open double doors.

"Jennie got in the way of a missile intended for me," John said grimly. He waved in the direction of the bookend, where it still lay upon the carpet. Bill scooped up the object and examined it for a moment, then set it on Alejandro's desk.

"I do not understand." Alejandro came to John's side. "Are you saying someone threw the bookend at you?"

"Yes, sir."

Preston leaned over Jennifer and brushed the hair off her forehead. She opened her eyes at his touch.

"The maid is bringing water and a cloth," John told him.

"Who did this?" Alejandro demanded.

"Your daughter, sir."

Alejandro stiffened. "Constanza?" he asked, his disbelief evident in his tone. "Why would she do such a thing?"

As upset as he was, John was reluctant to speak ill of Constanza in her father's house. "She was angry," he said simply.

Jennifer tried to sit up, but Preston held her down.

"Lie still, Jennie," he ordered gently.

Brigit came to John's side carrying a china bowl filled with water, a clean cloth draped over her forearm. She set the bowl on the floor and dipped the cloth into it, then handed the wet material to John. He removed his blood-stained handkerchief from the swelling bump on Jennifer's head and replaced it with the wet cloth. She winced and turned her head away.

"Bill, see that our surrey is brought around," Preston snapped. "We're leaving at once. Gabe, go into town and get Doc Meade out to the Santa Maria; we'll be travelling slow and careful, so you may beat us home."

Both men hastened to do his bidding.

"Arturo." Alejandro glanced over his shoulder. "Bring up our farm wagon and see that a soft bed is prepared in the back. *Rápido!*" Arturo hurried away. "Jennifer will be more comfortable lying down than trying to sit in the surrey," Alejandro explained to Preston.

"Thank you, my friend." Preston fixed his fierce gaze on Alejandro. "I don't understand why your children are attacking my family. First Arturo at the dam, and now this."

"They are attacking me, Preston," John said quietly. "That bookend was meant for me."

"And you are part of my family," Preston insisted.

"I am as baffled as you are, Preston." Alejandro spoke through gritted teeth. "But I assure you, I will learn the reason. Please accept my sincere apologies for this unfortunate incident. I pray Jennifer will be all right."

Jennifer tried to raise a hand to her head, but John caught it.

"Shh," he whispered. "Do not move, Jen."

"It's only a bump," she protested. She shifted on the sofa and grimaced.

"What is it?" John asked urgently.

"My ankle." She drew up her left leg. "I think I twisted it when I fell on the steps."

John pulled her skirts back and ran a gentle hand over her stocking-covered ankle. "No swelling yet, but we'll watch it."

Bill came to the double doors. "The wagons are ready."

"One of my men will drive your surrey and bring my wagon back," Alejandro said.

Preston nodded his agreement. "Thank you. Let's go, John. I'll help you carry her out."

John shook his head. "I can get her." He spoke to Jennifer. "Put your arms around my neck, Jen. Hold onto me."

She did as he instructed and John easily lifted her into his arms. Disturbed by how light and frail she seemed, he stood and made his way out the door.

Barbara was already seated on the hard bench of the farm wagon; Bill waited in the wagon bed. He helped John get Jennifer settled on the thick pile of blankets, then clambered over the back of the seat and took up the reins.

"Let me know when you're ready," he said quietly.

John moved into position at Jennifer's side. Again, he dabbed at the seeping blood on her head.

Jennifer looked up at him. "Bring the maid," she whispered.

"I did not hear you." John leaned forward.

"Brigit. Bring Brigit, or Constanza will hurt her."

John furrowed his brow. "What are you talking about, Jennie?"

She grabbed the front of his shirt. "Bring her," she begged.

Preston came to the side of the wagon. "What's the matter?" he asked in a low tone.

"She is worried that Constanza will hurt the maid and wants us to bring the girl along." John nodded in the direction of the house. "The young one with red hair, by the door there, who brought the water."

"Please, Preston," Jennifer pleaded in a whisper. "Do not leave the girl here. I fear for her well-being."

Preston stared at her for a moment, then turned around. The maid in question stood at one side of the group of curious guests, twisting her apron in her hands.

"Alejandro, I have a favor to ask."

"Anything, my friend." Alejandro stepped to Preston's side.

"I'd like to borrow the services of your maid for a few days. Jennie will need nursing, and it'll be of great help to Barbara and Rosa if the girl could come along." He pointed at the maid.

Although he appeared puzzled, Alejandro agreed to the request. "Brigit is Constanza's personal maid, but since my daughter is responsible for this entire situation, she will have to manage on her own for a few days." He turned to the girl. "Collect your things, Brigit. You will go with the Cantrells."

"Aye, sir." Brigit dropped a quick curtsey and disappeared into the house.

"Do not wait for her," Alejandro urged. "I will send her with my man in your surrey. Get Jennie home."

Preston nodded and climbed up on John's horse. The stallion tossed his head and fought the bit, ready to run. Preston kept the animal at a trot and led the way out of Alejandro's yard.

Alejandro watched the small party leave. A moment later, Brigit hurried out of the house with a small bundle clutched in her arms. Alejandro helped her up into the forward seat of the doubled-seated surrey. "Obey *Señor* Cantrell as you would me," he admonished.

"I will, sir. I'll not shame you, *Señor* Noriega."

"I'm sure you won't, Brigit. I wish I could say the same about my own children." Alejandro nodded curtly at the man seated next to Brigit. "Go now. Be certain there is nothing more you can do for *Señor* Cantrell before you return."

"Sí, señor." The man picked up the reins and slapped the horses lightly with them. The surrey moved away.

Alejandro faced the crowd. "Please forgive me, my friends. An unfortunate accident has happened, and I fear it would be in poor taste to continue our celebration. Allow my people to help you prepare for your journey home." Ignoring the curious murmurs of his friends, Alejandro snapped his fingers at the ranch hands who waited off to one side. The men hastened to bring around buggies and horses.

When the last of the guests had departed, Alejandro moved dejectedly into his study. He picked up the bookend and stared at it, shocked to see that it bore signs of dried blood. His jaw clenched.

"Arturo!" he bellowed.

"*Sí*, I am here." Arturo spoke quietly from the doorway.

"Bring your sister to me at once. She owes me an explanation for her reprehensible behavior."

"*Sí*, Papa." Arturo hurried away.

"Both of my children have much to answer for," Alejandro muttered. With the slow, disheartened steps of a much older man, he moved around the desk and sank into his chair.

It seemed to John that the quiet trip to the Santa Maria took forever. He kept a close watch on the oozing bump on the side of Jennifer's head, and because no one had thought to search for her parasol, he protected her face from the late afternoon sun with his own hat. She seemed to have drifted into sleep.

After a few miles of silence, Preston dropped back to ride beside the wagon. "What actually happened?" he asked.

In a dull voice, John explained how he had refused to meet Constanza, how Brigit had warned him that Jennie had gone to the study and that Constanza was in a rage. "When I got there, I could hear Constanza through the door, threatening Jennie, warning her to stay away from me. I went in and told Constanza to leave us both alone. Then I made a critical error." His mouth tightened into a grim line.

"What was that?" Preston gently prodded.

"I turned my back on Constanza before I got Jennie safely out of the room."

The fierce anger in John's voice surprised Preston. It was an anger he knew his son directed at himself. Barbara and Bill glanced at each other.

"John, you couldn't have known Constanza would throw something," Barbara said kindly.

"Yes, I could have," John snapped. "I should have, because I know what she is capable of. I know Constanza better than any of you. Jennie is hurt, perhaps badly, because of my carelessness."

A heavy silence once more settled over the small group.

When they reached the Santa Maria, Gabe was waiting with Dr. Meade. John again insisted on carrying Jennifer up to her bed himself. The physician allowed only Barbara and Rosa to remain in the room while he conducted his examination. Later, he joined the men waiting in the *sala*.

"Miss Mainwaring is resting comfortably," he announced. "She is not in any danger."

"You are certain?" John asked tersely.

Dr. Meade eyed him over the rim of his spectacles. "Yes, young man, I am certain. She has a nice bump on her head, which will go down over the course of the next few days, and her head aches rather fiercely now."

"Has the bleeding stopped?" Preston asked.

"Yes. Head wounds usually bleed profusely, and because of that, often appear to be more serious than they actually are. In this case, Miss Mainwaring's skin was not broken enough to even warrant stitches." The doctor accepted the glass of sherry Preston had poured for him and nodded his thanks, then continued. "She also has a badly sprained ankle, so I would like her to remain in bed for a few days. The ankle is already swelling, and do not be surprised if it swells dramatically. There will be some bruising, as there will be on her head. I have instructed Rosa and Mrs. Cantrell on her care." He took a sip of the sherry.

"I appreciate your coming so quickly, Henry," Preston said. "It will be dark soon; why don't you join us for supper and stay the night?"

"Thank you, Preston. I'll take you up on that."

John stayed to hear no more. He climbed the stairs two at

a time and hurried down the hall to Jennifer's room. When he entered, Barbara looked up from a chair that had been pulled next to the bed. A lamp on the small bedside table glowed softly as dusk gathered in the room.

"She's fine, John," Barbara assured him. "She's asleep."

John moved to the bedside and stared down at Jennifer. Her long braid lay forward over her breast and she now wore a nightdress with a high neck and long sleeves, like the one she had worn the first night they met. A light blanket had been pulled up to her chest, and her arms lay along her sides on top of the covering. A cooling breeze wafted in from the open French doors.

He studied her face. She was still very pale, and a slight bruise showed high on her left temple, but she appeared to be resting peacefully.

"The doctor is staying for supper, and Rosa may need your help," he said to Barbara, his tone more gruff than he intended. "I'll sit with her."

With an understanding nod, Barbara stood. "The Noriega's maid arrived a short time ago; I'll send her up with some fresh water." She looked at John for a moment, then laid a gentle hand on his forearm. "She'll be all right, John. This was not your fault, and no lasting harm has been done."

John tore his gaze from Jennifer to look at Barbara. He was astounded by the depth of compassion he found in her eyes. Deeply moved, he covered her hand with his own. "It *is* my fault, but thank you for your words of comfort."

Barbara smiled at him, a sad smile, and left the room.

John sat on the edge of the bed and took Jennifer's hand in his. She turned her head a little more to one side, but did not awaken. Her fingers tightened slightly on his and relaxed.

"I am so sorry, Jennie," John whispered. He brought her small, soft hand to his lips for a gentle kiss, then continued to stroke her fingers.

A knock sounded at the door, and at John's curt invitation to come in, Brigit entered the room, carrying a crystal carafe of water and a matching glass. She set the items next to the lamp, then stood quietly for a moment.

"How is she, sir?" she asked timidly.

John shrugged. "The doctor said she will recover." He glanced at the maid and, seeing the distress on her young face, softened his tone. "She's sleeping now."

Tears welled in Brigit's eyes. " 'Tis my fault she's hurt, sir. It was I who took her to Miss Constanza."

"No, Brigit, you did nothing wrong. It is my fault. I did not protect her."

"But she went because of me!" Brigit cried. The tears slipped down her cheeks.

John's brow furrowed in a puzzled frown. "She went because Constanza asked her to."

"At first she refused, as you did, sir, but she changed her mind because of me." Brigit's voice had taken on a frantic note.

"What made her change her mind?" John asked quietly.

Brigit looked down at the floor and did not answer him.

"Tell me," he coaxed.

"She feared Miss Constanza would strike me again if she did not go." Brigit refused to look up at him.

Constanza would strike her? Again? John stared at the maid, horrified as the realization dawned on him. He leaned forward and lifted Brigit's chin with a gentle hand so he could see her face. A faint bruise darkened one cheekbone, curling up toward Brigit's eye.

"Did Constanza strike you when you told her I refused to see her?" He dreaded Brigit's answer, but he had to know.

Brigit did not respond. She tried to pull her face from John's grasp.

He released her. "She did," he whispered. He looked from Brigit to Jennifer and back again. Two innocent women hurt because of him. A hot rage rushed through him. Suddenly, he very much wanted to see Constanza. Very much, indeed.

"I am sorry, Brigit. Had I known she would punish you, I would have gone."

"That's what Miss Mainwaring said you would have done." Brigit wiped a hand across her eyes.

"Now I understand why Jennie insisted we bring you with us."

Brigit gaped at him. "She asked for me, sir?"

"Yes. She was afraid Constanza would harm you."

For a long moment, Brigit stared at Jennifer with something akin to adoration. "Oh, sir, will she truly be all right?"

John nodded. "Truly. I will tell her of your concern when she awakens."

"Thank you, sir." Brigit wiped her eyes again. "Miss Rosa said that since the miss is sleeping, she will bring up a tray after she has served *Señor* Cantrell and the doctor their supper."

"Please tell Miss Rosa that will be fine. Thank you for the water." John smiled at her.

"Aye, sir, I was happy to bring it." She dropped a curtsey and left the room, closing the door quietly behind her.

For over an hour John watched Jennifer, thinking. He could not get over the fact that although she had been badly hurt, her immediate thoughts had been for him and Brigit. Darkness filled the sky outside the French doors, and the breeze was now strong enough to stir the filmy curtains. The sound of thunder echoed in the distance.

Rosa brought a tray and insisted Jennifer be awakened to eat. "She must keep up her strength," she said firmly.

John reluctantly woke Jennifer. He helped her move into a sitting position, arranging the pillows behind her. "How do you feel?" he asked.

"I'm fine," she answered quickly.

John looked at her in disbelief.

"My head hurts," she admitted as she leaned back against the pillows with a grimace. "And my ankle." She eyed the food tray doubtfully. "And my stomach is a little queasy."

"Is all right, Jennie." Rosa spread a cotton napkin across Jennifer's lap. "I bring food that is easy on the stomach. Broth, bread, and tea. You will feel better after you eat." She looked at John. "Francisca took a tray and some warm water to your room. You go now, eat and freshen up."

John stubbornly shook his head. "I will stay."

Rosa drew herself up to her full height, her lips tightened in a determined line. She pointed toward the door. "You will go. You do Jennie no good if you faint from hunger or, worse yet, eat her food. You come back later."

John glared at her.

"Where are the kittens?" Jennifer interjected.

"They are with Francisca. She will care for them while you recover. You do not need to be awakened in the night." Rosa spoke to Jennifer, but she did not take her gaze from John.

"No, I think they should be here, Rosa. They are my responsibility."

At that, Rosa swung around to face Jennifer, her hands at her hips. She did not have to say a word.

Jennifer managed a small smile. "John, both of us should know better than to argue with Rosa."

John gave in. "I'll be back soon," he warned.

"I know you will." Rosa seemed very satisfied. *"Señor* Preston and the children will also come to visit. It could get crowded."

John rolled his eyes and left the room.

The clock struck two, then quieted, and still John sat in a chair at the side of Jennifer's bed. Except for the approaching storm, all was silent. He had trimmed the lamp until it gave off only the faintest of light. He did not want to disturb Jennifer, yet he wanted to be able to see her, wanted her to be able to see him should she awaken and need something. The soft light touched her face, enhancing her beauty to an almost ethereal quality. He could not take his eyes from her.

His thoughts travelled back to the first night they met. She had carried her stiff, too-slender body with imperious pride, wearing a gown of the latest fashion, her lovely neck encircled with jewels worth enough to feed an entire Mexican village for a year. Her hair had been perfectly coiffed, not a strand out of place; her green eyes, cold and brilliant. She had defied him that night, stood up to him, threatened him, not fearful in the least, although he had come to kill Preston. He had thought her a petty, arrogant woman, one who assumed that her every wish would be honored, as those raised with a great deal of money were wont to do. How wrong he had been—how very wrong.

She was beautiful, even more so now that she had blossomed within the sheltering arms of Preston's family. Like a wild rose, she had bloomed. Like a wild rose, she was lovely to look at on the outside, tenacious and strong on the inside. Jennifer Mainwaring was honorable and honest, willing to defend those she loved, just as she had defended Preston against him, with no thought of her own safety.

John started. Just as she had defended him against Constanza, again with no concern for her own safety. Aside from his mother and grandmother, no other woman had ever defended him.

Jennie was an amazing woman, with a deep capacity for love that extended even to orphaned kittens. She was a woman who would stand beside her man, facing with him all that life had to offer. Was there room in her heart for him?

Jennifer stirred, feeling very uncomfortable. Her head hurt, and even the light weight of the bedclothes brought painful pressure to her ankle. She raised her left hand and gingerly touched the sore spot on her head. A good-sized bump had formed.

She opened her eyes, only to be momentarily blinded by the soft light of the lamp. Someone took her hand and gently stroked it. She blinked several times, and when her eyes finally focused, she was surprised to see John.

"You are still here?" she asked.

"I told you I would stay through the night." Without releasing her hand, he moved to sit beside her on the bed.

Jennifer tried to sit up. "Are the kittens all right? Did someone feed them?"

John gently pushed her back against the pillows. "Francisca and Brigit tended to them. One was a little fussy about eating, but eventually was persuaded. They will be fine."

Her brow wrinkled with worry. "Who was fussy? Katie or Jake?"

"I don't know, Jen. They look a lot alike." John winked at her. "I did not bother to check between its legs."

Jennifer stared at him, mildly embarrassed at his frank language, then smiled. "I guess I know them better than anyone else," she admitted. "I can tell them apart without such close examination." She sighed and relaxed a little.

"Would you like some water?"

"Yes, please." Now she did sit up, with John's help.

She drained the glass he filled for her, then lay back against the pillows.

"I'm so sorry, Jen." John's voice was no more than a whisper, heavy with remorse. "That bookend was meant for me. Why did you step in the way?"

"It was instinctive, I guess. You didn't see it coming. I tried to get my hand up, but she was faster than I thought." Her lips curved in a rueful smile. "Her aim is accurate, too."

John did not smile in return. Instead, rage flashed across his features before he composed himself. He took her hand again. "I hate to see you in pain."

"I know." She squeezed his fingers. "I would hate to see you in pain, too." They were both silent for a moment. Finally, she asked calmly, "What is she to you, John?"

"What do you mean?"

"You are obviously very important to her, and I think Constanza is accustomed to getting what she wants. I am curious if you feel anything special for her, because she told me that you two have renewed whatever your relationship was in Mexico."

"She lied."

The quiet force in his voice assured Jennifer he was telling the truth, but she would have believed him no matter his tone. John did not lie. She sighed. "This is really none of my business, but even I can see that an alliance between the Cantrell family and the Noriegas could be advantageous—two large land grants joined into one. Are you certain Preston and *Don* Alejandro do not wish for just such an alliance?"

"Preston has never mentioned it, Jennie, and I'm sure he does not feel that way. Perhaps it would be different if neither Constanza nor I had siblings, but Bill and Arturo must be considered. Who would inherit? Joining the two grants would greatly complicate things. Besides, as close as Preston's friendship with Alejandro is, I have always had the feeling my father only tolerates Arturo and Constanza." He toyed with her fingers.

"You are right." She shifted, trying to find a more comfortable position for her foot.

"Jennie, I want to tell you about my past relationship with Constanza."

"You do not have to," she said softly. "It does not matter."

"It does to me. It is important that you understand." John shifted on the bed, turning his body so he could look directly at her. "We met eight years ago. She had come to *Ciudad de Mexico* to stay with her aunt. Maximilian was in power, and I was already working for Benito Juarez. It was a crazy time, Jennie. The city was filled with the glory of the French court and the danger of the revolution. Constanza was eighteen, and lovely. I was drawn to her, as many men were." He paused.

Jennifer nodded in encouragement. "Go on."

"Constanza is very . . . passionate about whatever she desires. Clothes, carriages, money, power, men. For a while, that passion was focused on me. She became very possessive and demanding, which, I am sure, you do not find difficult to believe."

"No," Jennifer answered with a smile. "Do you think she still loves you?"

John shook his head, his lips twisted in wry amusement. "She never loved me. She does not know the meaning of the word. With Constanza, it is all a question of power. She became bored with me soon enough, when she thought she was in control."

Jennifer's eyes widened in amazement. "How could she have been bored with you?" she demanded.

For a long moment, John stared at her. "You are sincere," he said wonderingly.

"Of course I am sincere," Jennifer retorted. "There are many names I could put to you, John Cantrell, but 'boring' is not one of them."

He smiled and tipped his head. "Thank you for the compliment." He paused, his blue eyes sparkling devilishly in the pale lamplight. "It *was* a compliment?"

A faint blush heated Jennifer's cheeks. "It was a compliment," she admitted grudgingly.

Again, he tipped his head. "You must understand, Jennie, that Constanza is one of those people who wants that which she cannot have and disdains that which is within her reach. Even as she allowed me to call on her, she was taking other lovers." He waved his free hand philosophically. "She and I—it never would have worked. Not then, not now."

"Other lovers?" Jennifer repeated in a shocked whisper. "While she was seeing you?" At John's silent nod, she raised her eyes to the ceiling. "Then what was her tirade this afternoon all about? I doubt very much that Constanza has changed her ways."

"You doubt her devotion to me?" John questioned teasingly.

Jennifer rolled her eyes at him.

John sobered. "It is about the Santa Maria; I am certain of it. Even when I knew her years ago, Constanza felt that the Americans had stolen California from Mexico, just as the French stole the Mexican government for a time. My guess is that she wants the Santa Maria, feels somehow it belongs to the Noriega family, that Preston has no right to the land. She probably hoped that through me, she would get it."

Jennifer nodded, remembering Constanza's words. "That fits. She said that you had come to claim it, that she would be at your side when you did."

"And you did not believe her?" John watched her, seeming to hold his breath. Jennifer somehow knew that her answer was very important to him.

"Of course not," she said softly.

An expression of relief flashed across his face and was gone. "Good. But now, no more talk. You must sleep." He released her hand and stood up.

"I *am* tired," she admitted. "But surely you are tired as well." She looked up at him, feeling a twinge of guilt that she had not noticed sooner the fatigue in his eyes, the shadow of stubble on his cheeks and chin. "It's late. Go on to bed, John. I will be fine."

"I'll not leave you tonight. Head wounds can be dangerous." His voice was firm as he pulled the blanket around her shoulders. "I will be here if you need me." He kissed her forehead, then settled back in the chair.

"Don't be ridiculous. I am not that badly injured. Besides, you cannot sleep in that chair." Jennifer ignored the stubborn look that descended over John's face. An idea came to her. "You will sleep right here." One hand snaked out from under the blanket to pat the far side of the bed.

"Jennie, don't *you* be ridiculous. We have stretched respectability too far as it is, just by my being here through the night." John crossed his arms over his chest. "Now go to sleep."

"I am too tired to argue with you, John." Jennifer struggled to keep her eyes open. "Lie on top of the blanket. There is an extra coverlet over the back of the chair if you need it. Thankfully, Oliver is not here. No one need know outside of your family, and they will understand."

Jennifer's suggestion made sense. In a few minutes he lay beside her, his gunbelt draped over the headboard, his boots on the floor, the coverlet over his legs. He sighed in contentment. "Good night, Jennie. Wake me if you need anything."

To his surprise, Jennifer rolled on her side and reached across the bed to take his hand. "Good night, John." She was quiet for a moment, then spoke again. "Those years ago in Mexico—were you her lover?"

John turned and searched her face in the dim light. She was calmly looking at him. "Yes," he answered quietly.

"I envy her that."

John's breath caught in his throat. With her free hand she touched his cheek, her fingers feather-soft against him, then she closed her eyes.

"She told me you are her lover again, but I did not believe her."

John stiffened. "It is not true."

"I know." Jennifer's voice was no more than a whisper. "Kiss me, John."

He raised up on one elbow, staring at her. Had he heard her correctly? Her eyes drifted open; she seemed to wait expectantly. He leaned over to place a gentle kiss on her slightly parted lips.

"Thank you." A smile curved her mouth and she closed her eyes. "When I am feeling better, I will expect you to keep your promise about kissing other places." She squeezed his hand and nestled into the pillow, her breathing relaxed and even.

A wildfire of desire roared through John's veins. Only by severely scolding himself for wanting Jennie so desperately when she was in such pain was he able to bring his stubborn body under control. He stared at her wonderingly, then rolled onto his back, his gaze on the strange pattern of light on the ceiling. A curious warmth filled him.

Jennie played no false games of intrigue and seduction, and never had. From the first night they met, John had always known exactly how she felt about him, whether good or bad. Now he knew she cared; she cared a great deal. Did her feelings for him go as far as love?

He hoped so, for he suddenly knew, without a doubt, that he loved her, deeply and completely. His life would be empty without her.

John shivered from the force of his emotions; then came the fear. How had such a thing happened? He had meant to be so careful, so guarded—against his father, against all of Preston's family. He had failed, for they had all wormed their way into his heart. Especially Jennie.

What did he have to offer her, except his unhappy past and his uncertain future? Yet he knew he could no more leave her now than he could stop the beating of his heart, and the knowledge caused the fear to strike him even deeper. In desperation he faced her again. The expression of peace on her lovely face gave peace to his soul. He loved her.

He brought her fingers to his mouth and kissed them. Although she slept, Jennie snuggled closer in response, the small smile again touching her lips.

God help him, he loved her. For now, that was enough.

Fourteen

Jennifer awakened as early dawn light filled the room. She lay still for several minutes, her eyes closed, listening to the soothing sound of the rain against the French doors. The air felt cool, and she snuggled closer to a beckoning warmth. Then she remembered.

Her eyes flew open. John lay on his back, peacefully asleep, holding her hand to his chest. She was nestled close to his body, warmed by him, although the blankets separated them. So this was what it was like to wake up next to a man, next to John. A thrill of desire raced through her. If not for the aching of her head and her bruised body, Jennifer knew she would give in to the powerful temptation to pull her captured hand free and allow it to roam over his chest. She would slip her hand inside his unbuttoned shirt, touch the dark, soft-looking hair that covered his warm skin, search for the intriguing scar on his ribs.

But her head did hurt and, even more severely, so did her ankle. For now, she had to be content with John's warmth and nearness. The day would come when she would be free to indulge her desire to touch him, when he would touch her; a day when she was not distracted by pain. He had made her a promise, and she intended to see that he kept it. She drifted off to sleep again.

When Jennifer awakened later, she found John's gaze on her. She managed a smile. "Good morning," she whispered.

"Good morning. How are you?"

The warmth in his voice warmed her heart. She rolled onto her back. "My head hurts," she admitted. "And my ankle."

John brushed the hair away from her forehead and inspected the bump. "The scrape has scabbed over, and there is some bruising, but it looks to be healing—no sign of infection." He paused. "I bet it hurts, though."

She smiled. "I told you that." The corners of John's mouth curved up, but she could see the distress in his eyes. She raised a hand to his stubble-covered cheek, taking secret delight in the feel of the unfamiliar masculine roughness. "Please, John, don't worry so. It was not your fault.'

"Yes, it was," he said grimly. He threw back the coverlet, leaving it rumpled at the end of the bed, and swung his feet to the floor. After pushing into his boots, he stood up and moved to tie back the curtains on the French doors. A light rain fell, causing little rivulets to run down the paned glass.

Jennifer followed his actions with her eyes. "I like the rain," she commented.

John nodded. "It is a refreshing change." Without asking her permission, he pulled the blankets back from the end of the bed to expose her feet.

"John!" Jennifer sat up and reached for the blankets, then stopped, shocked when she saw her left foot. The area from just above her ankle to the tips of her toes was grossly swollen. He took her injured foot in his hand and examined it.

"I guess I wasn't very graceful yesterday, was I?" Jennifer asked ruefully.

"It is difficult to be graceful when one is dodging thrown objects." John's expression was one of concern. "There is a little bruising here." He drew a gentle finger under her ankle bone. Jennifer flinched at even that light touch. "Sorry," he said.

"I am amazed at how much it hurts, considering I only twisted it," Jennifer commented with no hint of complaint in her tone. "Dr. Meade assured me no bones are broken."

John set her foot down and pulled the blankets back into

position. "Unfortunately, not much can be done for sprains. They take a long time to heal." He faced her as he buttoned his shirt. "I'll get cleaned up and see what Rosa has planned for breakfast. Is there anything I can bring you?"

"Some tea would be nice." She pushed up on her elbows, wanting to sit back against the pillows.

As if he read her mind, John came around to her side and helped her to a sitting position. He arranged the pillows behind her, then guided her shoulders back.

"Thank you," she murmured.

John reached over her and pulled his gunbelt from the bedpost. He hung the belt over his shoulder as he straightened. His eyes, filled with some deep emotion Jennifer could not name, did not leave her. She stared up at him, puzzled at his intensity.

"I will return soon." John leaned forward and brushed her forehead with his lips. *"Mi amada."*

The last words were spoken so softly that Jennifer was not certain she heard him correctly. He crossed the room, then paused to look back at her one more time before he let himself out the door.

Deep in thought, she turned her gaze to the French doors and the sight of the comforting rain. A low rumble of thunder echoed over the house.

Mi amada. My beloved.

A swell of wondering happiness filled her heart, easing the worst of her physical pain.

It took John longer to get back to Jennifer than he planned. He hurried to bathe and shave, but when he presented himself in the kitchen to take her tray up, Rosa informed him that Brigit had already done so and that she herself would soon go up to help Jennifer wash. John was not welcome to join her.

He opened his mouth to protest, then closed it without

saying a word. The forbidding look on Rosa's face told him that her mind was made up. Of course the women would not allow him in the room while Jennie bathed.

"Do you know where Preston is?" he asked as he poured himself a cup of coffee.

"I think he is still in his study." Rosa dumped a kettle of steaming water over a stack of dishes in the washbasin. "He was having coffee with the doctor."

At that moment, a rain-splattered David barrelled in the side door, skidding to a stop when he saw John. "Unca' John!" he shouted delightedly. He hurried to John's side and clutched his pants leg. "The kitties stayed with Rosa and 'Cisca last night 'cause Jennie has a bump on her head!" His wide, earnest blue eyes revealed the importance of the news he shared.

John set the coffee cup on the table and bent down to swing David up into his arms, struggling to keep a smile from his face. He was determined to treat David's announcement with the respect it deserved. "Did you brave the rain to check on them?" he asked. David nodded solemnly. John looked over David's head and smiled a greeting to Barbara, who had followed her son into the room. She carried Molly on her hip.

"Good morning," she said warmly in response to his smile.

John sat on one end of the bench and settled David on his lap. "So tell me: How did Katie and Jake fare through the night?"

"Fine. 'Cisca took good care of them. I want them to sleep in the nursery tonight, but Mama said no 'cause me and Molly are too little, and so are the kitties." He looked up at John, clearly expecting a comment.

"Well, your mother is right, David. Maybe when the kittens get bigger they can stay with you sometimes."

Francisca came in the kitchen door carrying the wooden fruit box that made up the kittens' bed. David immediately squirmed from John's lap and ran to Francisca's side as she carefully set the box on the floor near the wall. Molly fussed to get down from her mother's arms, and when Barbara released her, she joined her brother at the box. Barbara moved closer to keep a cautious eye on them.

John watched the two small children as they kneeled over the box, cooing at the kittens. There was something deeply touching about their innocent fascination and joy with the tiny creatures. How he loved those two children! Fleetingly, the thought crossed his mind that perhaps one day he would have children of his own, with Jennie as their mother. The idea pleased him. John reached again for his cup and left the kitchen.

He found his father alone in the study. Preston looked up at John's light knock on the open door.

"Come in, John." Preston waved at a chair in front of the desk. "Have you seen Jennie this morning?"

"Yes, but it was some time ago." Unless someone specifically asked, John saw no reason to explain that he had not left her all night. He settled into the chair and stretched his legs out in front of him. "She is bruised and sore. Her ankle is very swollen, but she's doing well."

Preston leaned back in his tall chair. "Henry will check on her one last time before he leaves, which will be fairly soon." He sighed. "This whole situation is disturbing and infuriating. That Jennie should be attacked while a guest in Alejandro's house . . ." He held up a hand when John started to speak. "I know; Constanza was aiming for you. I would be just as upset if she had hit you, for you could have been injured as badly as Jennie was."

"I doubt it," John said wryly. "I have a very hard head." He sipped from his cup.

"It runs in the family," Preston informed him with a brief smile. Then he shook his head. "I don't understand why Alejandro's children have such animosity toward you. Arturo encouraged Baxter Lewis that day at the dam, backed him up, was ready to take you on himself. And now this incident with

Constanza." He met John's gaze squarely. "Can you shed any light on this?"

John sighed. He set his cup on the edge of Preston's desk, then pushed out of the chair to pace the floor. "I knew them both in Mexico. The problems go back that far, at least with Arturo."

Preston frowned. "I didn't think Arturo went to Mexico with Constanza."

"He didn't, not at first. When Constanza's aunt decided she could no longer manage her uncontrollable niece, she asked Alejandro to come and get his daughter. Alejandro sent Arturo in his place to escort Constanza home. Arturo was with her the last few weeks Constanza was in Mexico."

"But you knew Constanza before then."

"Yes."

Preston eyed him. "My friendship with Alejandro, a friendship that has lasted over thirty years, is now threatened because of trouble between our children. Your relationship with Constanza is none of my business, John, but if what happened in the past is going to cause more trouble between the Cantrells and the Noriegas, I'd like to know about it."

John remained silent for a moment. His first impulse was to refuse to tell Preston any more. Whether out of a gentleman's reluctance to discuss his intimate affairs or out of plain obstinacy, he did not know. Perhaps it was a combination of the two. But if Constanza and Arturo continued their attacks on him, others in the Cantrell household could get hurt, just as Jennie had been. For that reason alone, Preston had a right to know everything. "Very well," John said. He moved to close the door just as Bill presented himself in the doorway.

"Good morning." Bill paused, looking from John to Preston. "Am I interrupting?"

"No. You should hear this, too." John waved him into the room and closed the door. The two brothers took the two chairs in front of Preston's desk, and after a moment, John began to speak.

"You already know I worked as an agent for the *Juaristas* when Maximilian was in control of Mexico. My job was to learn military secrets and get the information to Benito Juarez. I lived what some might call an exciting life in *Ciudad de Mexico* as a member of the French court." He glanced at Preston. "For a long time I resented the fact that my mother insisted I learn English, the language of my father. I wanted nothing of his."

Preston did not look away from him. "Your mother could be very strong-willed."

John smiled. "Yes, she could. But eventually, my knowledge of English proved valuable; it even saved my life on one occasion when I heard an English officer discussing plans to capture the agent they called *El Lobo,* who, of course, was I. Father Michel had taught me French, and my fluency in the three languages made me indispensable to Juarez." He looked at his father, then his brother, mildly surprised to find no disapproval on either of their faces.

"It sounds dangerous," Bill commented.

"At times it was." John shrugged. "But the risks were worth it to me. I believed in my cause, as naive as that may sound." He leaned forward. "Benito Juarez was elected president of Mexico in 1861, and in a desperate attempt to give his bankrupt government some breathing room, he suspended government payments for two years on loans to foreign powers."

"I'll bet that angered some people," Bill commented.

"It did. Great Britain, Spain, and France entered into an alliance of intervention, threatening invasion. They went as far as to take Vera Cruz. Juarez backed down, and the English and the Spanish immediately withdrew, but not the French. They continued their march on the capital. Juarez was forced out, and Mexico was handed to the French by her own Assembly. They *invited* Maximilian to take the crown." John's jaw tightened at the memories. "I went north to offer my services to Juarez. In the end, he sent me back to *Ciudad de Mexico*. That is when I met Constanza."

"I remember when she went to Mexico," Preston said. "Alejandro sent her to his sister in the hope that *Doña* Ynez could teach Constanza to be a lady. He always felt inadequate in raising her; he believed she needed a mother figure."

"Have you ever met *Doña* Ynez?" John asked him.

"No. I'm not sure that she ever visited Alejandro here."

"I got to know her when I called on Constanza. *Doña* Ynez was a very sweet woman, charming and polite, if somewhat timid. She was unable to defend herself against Constanza, who ran roughshod over her."

Preston steepled his fingers. "So you called on Constanza."

"Yes."

"How serious was your relationship?"

"In the beginning, I was very taken with her." He glanced at Bill, noticed his brother's raised eyebrows. "You must remember that I was young," John said lamely. "Constanza was lovely, vivacious, outrageous. She was like a passionate breath of fresh air, the darling of the court. And for a while, of all the men in *Ciudad de Mexico,* she chose to be with me." He spread his hands, then allowed them to drop to his lap. "I entertained the idea of formally courting her, but I soon realized it would never work. Then Constanza broke it off."

"She ended it?" Preston asked, clearly surprised.

"Yes, but I would have if she hadn't. The final straw was when she came at me with a knife. I still wear the scar."

Preston and Bill stared at him.

"Now your comment that you should have known not to turn your back on Constanza makes sense," Bill remarked.

John looked at him, an eyebrow raised in curiosity. "You grew up with her; did you never find her attractive?"

Bill shrugged. "We were kids. Rosa was like my sister, Jennie, too, later. All I knew was that Constanza was cruel to them. You know the old proverb—familiarity breeds contempt. Constanza is a beautiful woman, and at one time, she made her interest in me very clear. But I already knew her too well. I could not forget how she tormented Rosa and Jennie." He paused, then continued in a quieter tone. "She was angry when I brought Barbara home, furious when I married her. She swore that one day I'd regret it."

Preston stared at him. "You never told me that, Bill."

"Why would I trouble you with the rantings of that conniving witch?"

"How do you *really* feel about her?" John asked dryly.

Bill flashed him a brief, rueful smile. "Pretty evident, huh?" He was quiet for a moment. "A few years ago, not long before David was born, Constanza invited me to her bed. I was outraged, and told her so, turned her down in vehement terms. Barbara heard the whole thing."

"My God, Bill," Preston breathed.

"It shook Barbara deeply, although she has nothing to fear from Constanza on my account, and never did."

"What did that woman do to Rosa?" Preston wondered in a thoughtful tone.

"I don't know," Bill said. "But it was serious, and it was terrible. It had to have been."

Preston fixed his gaze on John. "Did you compromise Constanza in Mexico? Is that why Arturo harbors such a grudge against you?"

John faced him squarely. "I did not compromise her." He hesitated. "But I was her lover."

Preston slammed his hand on the desk. "You say in the same breath you did not compromise her, yet you were her lover? If Arturo knows, it's no wonder he wants to kill you! I pray Alejandro does not find out!" His eyes blazed with anger. "Constanza was young and innocent, barely out of the schoolroom. You lay with her and did not offer her marriage? What kind of man are you?"

John stiffened. "I am your son, sir. Blood will tell. You lay with my mother and did not offer her marriage."

Bill audibly drew in his breath.

After a long, tension-filled minute of silence, Preston spoke. "Ana Maria did not give me the opportunity."

Suddenly ashamed of himself, John sagged back in his chair. "I know," he said quietly. "My apologies."

"I also apologize, son."

John met Preston's eyes. "There was a world of difference between my mother and Constanza," he explained gently. "Yes, Constanza was young, but she was far from innocent. I was not her first lover, and even while she was seeing me, she took other men. I did not compromise her, Preston. Had I offered her marriage, she would have laughed in my face. Constanza was very free with her favors, and she enjoyed that freedom, revelled in it. Arturo was only a boy at the time, not even shaving yet, and I am sure he knew nothing of his sister's true nature. Perhaps he feels I sullied his family's honor."

"If he does, that would account for his actions," Bill said thoughtfully. "But if Constanza threw you over years ago, why her sudden, fierce display of devotion now? Why would she warn Jennie to stay away from you?"

"Because of the Santa Maria." John told them the same theory he had shared with Jennifer the night before. "It has nothing to do with me," he said in conclusion. "It has everything to do with my name."

Preston stared at him. "Could she be behind the attacks against the Santa Maria?"

"The thought has crossed my mind," John admitted.

"But she was in San Francisco when the wildfire was started," Bill pointed out.

"Arturo wasn't," said John.

Preston slumped in his chair, a stricken look on his face. "Alejandro is my friend."

John felt a twinge of sympathy for his father. He leaned forward in his chair. "Preston, *Don* Alejandro may know nothing about this. You know he has a blind spot when it comes to his children."

"Like any man," Bill added.

Preston nodded. "What are we going to do?"

John stood up. "Let me check into it. For now, we must be very careful. We must draw together, as a wolf pack does, for mutual protection. Warn all the hands to be on the alert. Anything the least bit suspicious or out of the ordinary must be immediately reported to one of us, or to Gabe. And under no circumstances are any of the women and children to be left alone with Constanza or Arturo should they come calling."

"Do you think they will?" Preston asked doubtfully.

"Not by their own choice. But *Don* Alejandro may insist that Constanza apologize to Jennie, as he insisted Arturo apologize to me. In fact, I will be surprised if he doesn't."

Preston nodded. "You're right."

Bill looked up at John. "I don't like the idea of your digging into this alone. You're the one they're after. You are in the most danger."

John shook his head. "Not as long as I can offer Constanza the Santa Maria. I suspect she controls Arturo, so I'll be all right. You have a wife and children, Bill. If it is the Santa Maria she wants, you are a more serious threat to her plans than I am."

"All the same, I don't like it," Bill said stubbornly. "You're no longer the lone wolf. If you need help, ask."

John placed his hand on Bill's shoulder. "Thank you, little brother. I will." He headed toward the door.

"Where are you going?" Preston queried.

"I promised Pedro I would help him with that broken stock gate. It should not take long to repair, even in the rain." John opened the door. "Then, if Rosa is finished with Jennie, I intend to visit her."

"You like her, don't you?" There was a teasing note in Bill's tone. He pulled himself out of his chair.

John paused with his hand on the door latch. He looked back at his father and his brother. "Yes," he admitted softly. "Very much."

With a broad grin on his face, Bill sauntered across the room to join John at the door. He casually draped an arm around John's shoulders. "Guess what, big brother? She likes you, too."

"I know that," John retorted.

"Cocky, aren't you?" Bill pushed John out the door. Their good-natured bantering continued as they crossed the foyer.

Preston watched them go, his heart gladdened at the obvious camaraderie between his two sons. But his joyous feelings were overshadowed with grave concern. He turned in his swivel chair to stare out the window that overlooked the yard. Could it be true? Could Constanza and Arturo Noriega, two people he had known since they were infants, be deliberately attacking all he held dear?

He considered Alejandro Noriega his closest friend, and yet this was something he could not discuss with him. John was right. It was time for the family to draw close, to look out for each other. How strange that the suggestion had come from John. With a start, Preston realized John had not protested when he called him "son." A wild hope flared in his breast. Perhaps at last John felt at home. Perhaps he would stay.

"Oh, Ana," he whispered. "You gave me a fine son." He paused. "As did you, Eliza. I am a fortunate man."

John met Dr. Meade on the stairs. "How is she?" he asked.

"She's doing well," the doctor assured him. "As long as she stays quiet for the next several days, there should be no problems. But she cannot do too much too soon, especially with that ankle. Bad sprains take weeks to heal."

"We will all make sure she rests, Doctor." John grabbed the older man's hand and pumped it vigorously. "Thank you, sir." He sprinted up the remaining stairs and down the hall.

He knocked on Jennifer's door, and after a moment, Brigit, dressed neatly in her uniform, let him in. The faint, pleasing scent of orange flower water filled the air. John's gaze locked on the bed, and the sight there took his breath away.

Jennifer sat up against the pillows, wearing a lace-trimmed bed sacque, a light blanket pulled up to her waist. She watched him with those big green eyes, welcoming him with a happy smile. Her evident pleasure in seeing him warmed his heart, but it was the sight of her hair that made his mouth suddenly go dry. The long shining locks lay unbound, just as he had envisioned, spread out on the pillows. Teasing strands curled over her shoulders, and one lay nestled against her breast.

"Leave us," John said hoarsely, not even looking at Brigit as he spoke.

Jennifer's eyes widened in surprise, but she did not protest his order. "Brigit, Mr. Cantrell and I would like to speak privately. Please see if Rosa needs help in the kitchen."

"Aye, miss." Brigit stared at John for a moment. "If I may be so bold, sir, I'd like to remind you that this is a sickroom. Don't you be tiring the miss."

Surprised at the determination in Brigit's voice, John looked over his shoulder at the young maid. "You've been taking lessons from Rosa, I see," he said dryly.

Jennifer giggled, a sound John found endearing.

Brigit did not move except to cross her arms over her chest.

"Go on." John waved her away. "I promise I'll not tire her. I would never harm her, not in any way."

Brigit's fierce expression softened. "I know that, sir." She looked around him. "I'll check on you later, miss."

"Thank you, Brigit."

The door closed. John turned back to Jennifer. Thanks to the continuing rain, the room was filled with muted light, which had the effect of making her look like an angel. He had not dreamed it. Her glorious hair was free, free to his touch, if he could only make his feet work well enough to take him to her side. He started moving slowly toward the bed.

Wish You Were Here?

You can be, every month, with Zebra Historical Romance Novels.

YOU'RE GOING TO LOVE GETTING

4 FREE BOOKS

These books worth almost $20, are yours without cost or obligation
when you fill out and mail this certificate.
*(If the certificate is missing below, write to: Zebra Home Subscription Service, Inc.,
120 Brighton Road, P.O. Box 5214, Clifton, New Jersey 07015-5214*

4 FREE BOOKS!

Yes! Please send me 4 Zebra Historical Romances without cost or obligation. I understand that each month thereafter I will be able to preview 4 new Zebra Historical Romances FREE for 10 days. Then, if I should decide to keep them, I will pay the money-saving preferred publisher's price of just $4.00 each...a total of $16. That's almost $4 less than the publisher's price, and there is no additional charge for shipping and handling. I may return any shipment within 10 days and owe nothing, and I may cancel this subscription at any time. The 4 FREE books will be mine to keep in any case.

Name _____

Address _____ Apt. _____

City _____ State _____ Zip _____

Telephone ( ) _____

Signature _____ LF1095
(If under 18, parent or guardian must sign.)

Terms, offer and prices subject to change without notice. Subscription subject to acceptance by Zebra Books.

TREAT YOURSELF TO 4 FREE BOOKS.

A $19.96
value.
FREE!

*No obligation
to buy
anything, ever.*

ZEBRA HOME SUBSCRIPTION SERVICE, INC.

120 BRIGHTON ROAD

P.O. BOX 5214

CLIFTON, NEW JERSEY 07015-5214

"The doctor was just here," Jennifer brightly informed him. "He thinks I am doing well."

John stopped at the side of the bed. He could not take his eyes from her.

Her brows drew together in a puzzled frown. "What is it, John? You look as if you've seen a ghost."

"I've seen heaven," he whispered. He sank down to sit on the edge of the bed, reaching out with a trembling hand toward the sweetly scented curls sprawled on the pillow. "I told you that one day I would see your hair down." An ironic smile curved his lips. "I just didn't think it would happen when you were so injured that I would be a brute to even consider touching you."

A warm heat started in Jennifer's stomach and climbed until it felt like her cheeks were on fire. She watched as John took a strand of her hair to his lips. "Rosa helped me wash my hair," she explained self-consciously. "It's not quite dry."

"Your hair is beautiful." John's hand touched her cheek. He leaned forward and pressed a kiss to her lips.

She sighed against his mouth. "I wish I felt better," she murmured.

"You will." John shifted closer, taking her face between his hands. He placed feather-soft kisses on her nose, her cheeks, her chin, her eyelids, her forehead. His fingers moved through her hair, stroking the long strands.

Jennifer forgot about her bothersome aches because she was suddenly having trouble catching her breath. John's firm yet gentle lips returned to her mouth one last time, then he pulled himself away with obvious effort.

"Let's check that ankle." He stood up and moved to the end of the bed.

"Wait." As she sat up, Jennifer slipped her hands under the bedclothes to ensure that her nightdress was pulled down to her ankles before she pulled the untucked corner of the blanket away.

John perched on the edge of the bed, taking her swollen

foot in his hands. He massaged her toes and foot with strong, soothing fingers, taking care to avoid the painful area around her ankle. Jennifer lay back again, giving herself up to the comfort of his touch. After a few minutes, though, one of his hands climbed farther up her leg to stroke the muscles of her calf.

"You are all knotted up here, Jen," he said softly.

Suddenly, her stomach was also knotted, from the familiar, quivering excitement John could inspire in her. She shifted, no longer entirely comfortable, for thrilling sparks shot up her leg as his hand wandered closer to her knee. His fingers felt hot against her skin, and she pulled her leg away.

"Thank you," she said. "I feel better now." Actually, it was her foot that felt better; the rest of her felt as heated as his touch had been.

John put the blankets in order and leaned over her. "Heal quickly, *mi amada,*" he whispered, smoothing her hair back from her face. "There are things I want to tell you, experiences I want to share with you." He rested his forehead lightly against hers.

Jennifer was gratified to realize that John's breath came a little fast, too. She clutched his forearm and closed her eyes. "I know. There are things I would tell you, also."

"Then rest." John again pulled away from her, his reluctance to do so evident in his expression. "Would you like something to read?"

"No, thank you. It seems reading makes my head ache worse." Jennifer leaned back against the pillows. "I think I will try to sleep for a while."

"That's a good idea." John stood up. "I will come back later and read to you."

Jennifer smiled up at him. "Which book?"

"I don't know yet. I will find something."

"That would be nice." Jennifer stifled a yawn.

John smoothed the neat coverlet at the foot of the bed. "Did you fold this?"

"No. Rosa did, and not without question." Jennifer arched an eyebrow at him. "She knew you stayed here all night, because evidently you insisted upon doing so. She asked if I got chilled."

"What did you tell her?"

"The truth." A sleepy smile touched Jennifer's mouth. "I told her I kept very warm. She did not push further, nor did I volunteer further."

John laughed. "I'll bet she is burning with curiosity."

"Of course she is."

"Sleep well, Jennie." John kissed her cheek one last time. "And heal." The last two words came out as a whispered plea. He quietly left the room.

Over the next two days, Jennifer was rarely left alone, and the constant hovering of her friends began to annoy her. Although her ankle continued to bother her, the other aches and bruises receded, including that on her head, yet the entire Cantrell household insisted on treating her as an invalid.

John was not again allowed the opportunity to stay with her through the night. Much to both his and Jennifer's disappointment, Rosa insisted upon moving a cot into Jennifer's room for Brigit, and that was done. Rosa also put her foot down about allowing the return of the kittens, despite Jennifer's pleas to the contrary.

"You need your rest," she said firmly in that tone of hers that caused grown men to quake in their boots. "Kittens are not restful." That was the end of the discussion, but Rosa did relent and allow the kittens to visit during the day.

David made it his personal responsibility to supervise the "kitty visits," and was very thorough in relating to Jennifer all that Katie and Jake—and Molly, for that matter—did throughout the course of the day. Jennifer delighted in the visits, where for the space of an hour or two she shared her bed with two small children and two tiny cats.

On the third day, Jennifer awakened early. After a light breakfast, she insisted that Brigit help her dress. She was determined to leave her bedroom, even if only for a while.

"Very well, miss," Brigit agreed with reluctance as she carefully brushed Jennifer's hair. "If you insist, you may go down to the *sala,* and perhaps even out to the courtyard, but only if you allow *Señor* John to carry you down the stairs."

Jennifer eyed the maid in the dressing table mirror, struggling to suppress a smile. "How old are you, Brigit?"

"Fifteen, miss, sixteen come Christmas."

"John was right. You are taking after Rosa."

Brigit paused in her brushing and met Jennifer's eyes in the mirror, a stricken expression on her face. "I spoke out of turn again, didn't I? I'm sorry, miss." The brush clattered to the floor as she dropped to her knees at Jennifer's side. "It's just that I care so much about you."

Jennifer was astonished to see tears in Brigit's eyes. "Dear girl, I was teasing." She took the maid's hand. "I know it is because you care, Brigit. You should have seen me talk to John when he first came here. I thought he meant to harm *Señor* Preston, and I was ready to battle him."

"He meant to harm *Señor* Preston?"

"I thought he did, but I was mistaken. Still, I was ready to defend my godfather." Jennifer lifted Brigit's chin. "Now, why the tears?"

Brigit hesitated only a moment. "I thought you were angry with me, miss, like Miss Constanza used to be."

"You thought I would strike you?"

"Oh, no, miss, you'd never!" Brigit scrambled to her feet. "I fear you will send me back to the Buena Ventura."

Jennifer looked up at her. "You never have to go back there again, Brigit, not if you do not want to."

"I don't want to, but I need the work, miss. I am alone in the world and must make my own way."

"I understand. I would like you to work for me, if that will fit in with your plans. If not, I will give you references and help you find another situation. You need not face Constanza Noriega again."

Disbelieving joy filled Brigit's young face. She bent down and threw her arms around Jennifer's shoulders. "Oh, thank you, miss!" she cried. "I would *love* to work for you. I promise I'll not disappoint you."

Jennifer smiled and patted the girl's arm. "Good. It is settled then."

Brigit straightened suddenly and stepped back, very self-conscious. "I'm sorry, miss. It was presumptuous of me to touch you in such a manner. Please forgive me."

"Do not worry yourself, I wanted to hug you that day in *Señor* Noriega's courtyard when I realized Constanza had abused you, but I thought it would make you uncomfortable if I did." Jennifer squeezed Brigit's hand, relieved to see a smile return to the maid's face. "Now let us decide what to do with my hair. I am anxious to escape this room for a while."

All business again, Brigit snatched up the brush. "I don't want to pin it up, miss, because it will pull on your poor head. How about if I just tie it back with a ribbon?"

"That will be fine."

After a long minute of silence, Brigit spoke with obvious reluctance. "Miss Constanza must be notified that I'll not be returning."

Jennifer glanced in the mirror. Brigit's reflected expression was filled with fear.

"I will see to that," Jennifer assured her.

"And this uniform must be returned. It belongs to the Noriega household."

Jennifer nodded. "I will take care of it. You won't have to go back, Brigit. We'll send for your things."

"I have all my things." A happy smile again curved Brigit's mouth. "Does *Señor* Cantrell have uniforms for his people? I haven't seen anyone wearing one." She tied the ribbon at Jennifer's neck.

"You will not have to wear a uniform at the Santa Maria. If you wish, you may change immediately."

"I will, miss, as soon as I see you settled downstairs. I'll get *Señor* John." She hurried from the room.

Jennifer stared at her reflection in the dressing table mirror, truly seeing herself for the first time since she had been injured. What she saw shocked her. Her face seemed very pale, with the exception of a faint bruise that covered the far left side of her forehead from hairline to eyebrow. She felt a twinge of regret that John had seen her like this, that anyone had. Suddenly, the idea of leaving the sanctuary of her room did not seem as appealing.

She stood on frustratingly weak legs and limped painfully to the high-backed chair in front of the empty fireplace. As she sank into the chair, regret was replaced with a flash of anger. How dare Constanza accost her in such a manner, accost anyone with such violence?

A moment later the door opened. "So, you think you are ready for an excursion downstairs?" John asked.

"I thought I was, until I looked in the mirror." Jennifer refused to face him. "Why did you not tell me how ghastly I look?"

John circled around the chair and squatted in front of her. "You don't look ghastly, Jen. If you think this is bad, you should have seen it the first day."

Now Jennifer did face him, with a withering glare. "Thank you so much."

John shrugged apologetically. "Sorry. But you should be proud of your battle marks, Jennie. They are a testament to your courage." He stood and swept her into his arms.

"I no longer wish to go downstairs," Jennifer said crossly, even as she wrapped her arms around his neck.

"Yes, you do." John headed for the door. "It will do you good to sit outside for a while. The day is lovely."

Since he held her so close, there was no point in arguing with John, and besides, Jennifer wasn't sure she wanted to.

She liked being in his arms, liked the feel of his body, liked his strength. He made her feel safe, protected, cherished. She found herself wishing the courtyard was farther away, for the trip ended all too soon.

"Thank you," she murmured as he lowered her to a chair set in the shade. She was startled to realize that she rested on one of the comfortable tufted chairs from the *sala,* and a padded footstool had been brought for her feet. When John was satisfied with her position, he spread a light coverlet over her legs.

"Just rest for now," he instructed. "I have a few chores to finish up, then I'll come and sit with you."

Jennifer nodded. "Thank you. I guess a little bruise doesn't matter."

John kissed her forehead. "Not at all, my brave woman, although I wish I could have spared you the pain."

She smiled up at him. "I know." She waved him away. "Go finish your chores."

John raised an eyebrow. "Are you so anxious to be rid of me?"

"No." Jennifer's smile softened with affection. "The sooner you go, the sooner you finish, the sooner you return."

"Well, in that case, I'll go." John sauntered off, looking extraordinarily pleased with himself.

Jennifer leaned back in the comfortable chair and watched him go, unable to ignore how good he looked in his tight denim pants, how hypnotizing his unconsciously graceful walk was. Her heart beat a little faster, and she took a deep breath. She was definitely feeling better. Soon they would tell each other the things they had to say.

She looked around the lovely courtyard, glad to be there. Had it been only three days since Constanza's attack? Somehow it seemed much longer.

"Jennie?"

"Hello, Barbara," she said with a smile. "I did not hear you approach."

Barbara did not smile in return. "You have a visitor." Suddenly her mouth tightened and her voice grew fierce. "I'll send her away if you want me to."

Jennifer did not need to ask who it was. "Her father brought her, did he not?"

Barbara's eyebrows raised in surprise. "How did you know?"

"It is the only way she would have come." Jennifer straightened in the chair. "Bring her out, Barbara."

"Are you sure you are up to it?"

"I can handle Constanza." Jennifer gazed at her concerned friend with understanding. "I will be fine, truly. Bring her to me. I want to get this over with."

Barbara nodded and went back into the house. Jennifer squared her shoulders and raised her chin, preparing herself. Suddenly she was glad for the evident bruise, not that Constanza would feel any remorse. John was right. The bruise was a battle mark, and in successfully protecting John, Jennifer had won the battle. She delighted in knowing that Constanza must have been infuriated at her interference. Although not too infuriated, she admitted. Constanza had shed no tears over the injury she caused, of that Jennifer was certain. She folded her hands in her lap.

Alejandro had forced Constanza to come, without a doubt. But even he could not control his daughter's tongue. It would be interesting to hear what Constanza had to say.

Fifteen

Constanza crossed the courtyard, her heels tapping on the smooth, flat flagstones. As always, her hair hung free, covered with a black lace mantilla, and she wore a fashionable dress, the material a single brilliant color, this time a golden yellow. Her mouth was pressed into a thin line, and her dark eyes fairly flashed with fury. She came to an abrupt halt in front of Jennifer's chair.

Jennifer calmly met the woman's gaze. Although etiquette dictated that she greet her guest, she did not say anything. Constanza was apparently aware of the snub, for her eyes narrowed, and she crossed her arms over her chest. Jennifer noticed that other people were present in the background: Alejandro, Preston, Barbara, and Brigit. No one spoke. The silence grew long.

"Constanza!" Alejandro finally snapped.

Constanza stiffened. "I regret striking you with the bookend, Jennifer." She spat the words out, her tone as full of hatred as her eyes were.

After a moment, Jennifer spoke quietly. "I do not believe you. You do not regret it at all, and you would not be here if not for your father."

"You are right!" Constanza hissed in a low tone. She leaned forward. "I wanted to hit Juan, but I was not too disappointed that you got in the way. I only wish I had thrown the bookend harder." She turned to leave.

Jennifer called her back. "Constanza."

Constanza stopped, but did not turn around.

"Things would be no different even if I were to leave," Jennifer said. "You cannot have John, and you cannot have the Santa Maria."

Constanza whirled with enough force to send the mantilla and her hair flying out around her shoulders. "You will not tell me what I can and cannot have, Jennifer Mainwaring. You cannot stop me."

Jennifer saw Brigit, with a look of fierce protectiveness on her young face, take a few steps forward. Barbara had also come closer, as had Preston. Their determination to defend her was easily read on their faces, and Jennifer was touched by their concern. But Constanza's rage no longer intimidated her.

"You are right," she agreed. "I cannot stop you. However, John can, and he will. So will Preston. If you think otherwise, you underestimate them."

For the first time, Jennifer saw a flicker of doubt in Constanza's eyes.

"No man can stand against me when I set my mind to something," Constanza retorted.

Across the courtyard, the iron gate swung open and John hurried into Jennifer's view, his handsome face twisted with worry. He moved toward her, but Preston grabbed his arm with a slight shake of his head. John stopped, not taking his eyes off her. A surge of warm confidence filled Jennifer.

"John can stand against you," she said proudly. "As can Preston. And your father was able to get you here, much against your will, I am certain. Perhaps your power over some men is not as strong as you would like to think."

Constanza stared at her with blazing eyes, her hands closing into fists and opening again. Jennifer knew without a doubt that Constanza ached to use those hands on her.

"Give up, Constanza," she said softly.

Constanza blinked in confusion. "What did you say?" she demanded.

"Give up," Jennifer repeated. "You have started a battle you cannot win. John will never have you; surely you know that, just as you surely know his decision has nothing to do with me. And Preston will never relinquish the Santa Maria—not to anyone, not for any reason. Besides, you have no right to either the man or the land. Go home. Let us live in peace."

"Imbécil!" Constanza jeered, finally speaking loud enough for the others to hear. "You know nothing of my plans, of my power, nor will you be around long enough to learn of them. Your uncle will soon return and take you back to Philadelphia, where you belong. I told you he will not allow you to throw yourself away on a half-caste bastard."

"Constanza!" Alejandro gasped.

Jennifer's eyes narrowed. "That is enough, Constanza." Her voice was tight with anger. "I told you once that my uncle has nothing to say in my decisions. And I will not allow you to speak of John in such a manner in my presence. I want you to leave now."

"You will not tell me what to do!"

"But I will." Alejandro strode forward to close his hand on his daughter's arm. "As Jennifer requested, you will leave. Again you have shamed me." He yanked her toward the gate.

Constanza went willingly until she saw Brigit. She paused, pulling against her father's hand. "Why are you out of uniform?" she snarled, then shook her head. "No matter. Get your things. I can no longer spare you."

Brigit bravely raised her chin. "No, miss."

Constanza sputtered in outrage, unable to get a word out.

"What is this, Brigit?" Alejandro demanded with a frown. "You speak to your mistress in such a manner?"

"Forgive me, *Señor* Noriega." Trembling, Brigit made her way to Jennifer's side.

"I am now her mistress, *Don* Alejandro," Jennifer explained. "Brigit no longer wishes to serve Constanza."

"I do not understand." Alejandro faced Preston. "I only loaned her to you."

Preston spread his hands. "Brigit is not a slave, nor is she under contract. She is free to leave your employ if she wishes."

Alejandro shifted his gaze to Constanza, suspicion drawing his brows together. "You have a difficult time keeping maids, daughter."

Constanza started to speak, but Jennifer cut her off.

"That is because she abuses her maids, *Don* Alejandro."

"What?" Alejandro turned to her, not releasing his hold on Constanza's arm. "She abuses them? How?"

Jennifer shrugged. "Physically, for certain, for I have seen her handiwork, and I would guess verbally as well."

Alejandro looked at Brigit. "This is true?"

"Aye, *señor,*" she said in a scared voice. "Miss Jennifer speaks the truth. You were always kind to me, but I have no wish to serve your daughter."

"Then you shall not," Alejandro said grimly as he glared at Constanza. "No one shall." He looked back at Brigit. "I apologize for her mistreatment of you, girl; had I been aware of it, I would have put a stop to it."

"Thank you, *señor.*" Brigit dropped a small curtsey.

"We will send Brigit's uniform when it has been cleaned," Jennifer said.

"Gracias." Alejandro pushed Constanza toward the gate. "It seems lately that each time I see you I must apologize for one of my children," he said to Preston. "Perhaps it would be best if we stayed away from each other for a while."

"Alejandro, that isn't necessary," Preston protested.

"I think it is." Alejandro guided Constanza out of the courtyard. A few moments later, the sound of a departing buggy could be heard.

Jennifer heaved a sigh of relief. She looked up and found herself surrounded by Preston, Barbara, Brigit, and John.

John leaned over her chair. "Are you all right?" he questioned, his blue eyes dark with concern.

"I'm fine," she assured him with a smile.

"What was that all about? What did she say to you?"

"As I suspected, her father forced her to apologize. I told her to leave us alone, and she became upset. She said some nasty things, and I asked her to leave."

"And that's all?" Preston asked. "We couldn't hear most of what she said."

Jennifer nodded. "That was all." She looked up at the circle of troubled faces. "Truly," she insisted.

"She didn't threaten you?" John asked.

"No. She only said Oliver would take me back to Philadelphia." She smiled wryly. "I guess you could call that a threat."

"You won't go anywhere you don't want to, Jennie," Preston said firmly.

"Except you are going back to bed right now, whether you want to or not." John picked her up. "You've had enough excitement for today." He started across the courtyard. Brigit followed close on his heels, clutching the coverlet.

"Do you see how he orders me about, Preston?" Jennifer called over John's shoulder. Despite her words, the tone of her voice indicated no displeasure.

"He can be overbearing," Preston acknowledged. "It's a Cantrell trait." With a satisfied smile, he watched his son carry his goddaughter into the house.

With the exception of her ankle, which was taking a frustratingly long time to heal, Jennifer's condition rapidly improved. Only the faintest trace of the bruise on her forehead remained, and her headache disappeared completely. Brigit moved back to her own room.

Each morning, John came to carry Jennifer downstairs, where she now spent most of the day. She joined the family for meals in the comfortable kitchen and was pleased to see how easily Brigit had been assimilated into the clan.

She was also pleased that John seemed especially attentive. Jennifer wondered where he found the time to get his chores done, for he spent a great deal of the day with her. He made certain the children and the kittens visited her in the late morning, he read to her each afternoon, and he sat with her in the courtyard in the early evenings.

Finally he decided her ankle had healed enough to allow a stroll in the orchard. It felt wonderful to be moving about outside again, and Jennifer insisted on a lengthy walk. Back at the house, she asked John if he would mind carrying her up the stairs. He was immediately concerned.

"I knew we went too far," he said as he lifted her into his arms. "Does your ankle hurt terribly?"

Jennifer wrapped her arms around his neck with a pleased smile. "No."

He came to an abrupt halt halfway up the stairs, one eyebrow raised in suspicion. "Miss Mainwaring, are you flirting with me?"

"Yes, Mr. Cantrell, I believe I am."

John nodded in satisfaction. "Good." He continued up the stairs, and Jennifer wondered if he would have kissed her again had Brigit not been waiting in her room.

The next morning at breakfast, Bill offered to take her on a buggy ride. John insisted, quite strongly, that he would take her instead. Bill gave in with only minimal argument, and Jennifer did not miss the triumphant smile he flashed at Barbara. Jennifer narrowed her eyes suspiciously at him, but Bill only shrugged in exaggerated innocence.

John did take her for a ride. He stopped the buggy under a sprawling evergreen oak that crowned a rise from which they could see the *hacienda* compound and beyond to the river and the Diablo Mountains. They rested there, their arms around each other, sharing the stories, disappointments, and dreams of their lives. John used the opportunity to again cover her face with soft kisses, but he held himself in check, promising Jennifer that she would soon be completely recovered.

When she asked him what would happen then, John only smiled, in a way that caused her heart to pound with excitement. After he lightly kissed her lips, he took up the reins, signalling the end to a ride that Jennifer thought was over much too soon. On the pretext that John teach her to drive, she insisted that the buggy rides become a daily occurrence.

Throughout those golden days, Jennifer could not keep her mind, or her eyes, off John. Her heart gladdened at the sight of him, her eyes seemed to drink him in. She thrilled to the sound of his deep, smooth voice when he read to her, when he coached her in Spanish, when he simply talked with her. She delighted in the spirited conversations and debates they shared after reading a book or a poem. One night after supper, when the family was gathered in the *sala,* they argued good-naturedly, in French, over the meaning of a French poem, much to the amazement and amusement of everyone else.

Jennifer held those magic days close to her heart, knowing she would remember them for the rest of her life, for it was during that time that she realized she loved John Cantrell with all her heart and soul.

Ten days had passed since the incident at the Noriega *fiesta,* and in that time, nothing had happened to threaten the Santa Maria or her people. Preston ordered the watches removed, except at night, and everyone relaxed.

Late that morning, Jennifer sat on a blanket spread on the flagstones in the courtyard, keeping an eye on Molly, who was a little too interested in Katie the Kitten. Katie's brother Jake wandered over Jennifer's skirt, his tiny nails periodically catching in the sprigged calico. He would work his little paw free and shake it with great dignity, seemingly affronted that the material would be so rude as to ensnare him. Jennifer laughed with delight at his antics.

John looked up from his cross-legged sitting position on the opposite side of the blanket. He was whittling a boat for

David, who sat close by his side, excited and clearly ready to offer instruction and encouragement. "It is good to hear you laugh," John said, his tone soft with affection.

She smiled at him. "It is good to feel better. Except for an occasional ache in this ankle, I am recovered." She spoke casually, then remembered that John had said he would wait for her to heal. From the sudden flash of fierce joy in his eyes, Jennifer realized that she had just told him that she *was* healed, that she was ready for whatever he meant to share with her.

His expression sobered, became intense. He stared at her, into her eyes, into her very soul, it seemed. Jennifer felt the current of emotion pass between them, communicating their thoughts without the need for words, linking their hearts. She longed to reach out to him, to allow her body the same connection with him her mind enjoyed.

The spell was broken by a distressed mew.

Jennifer tore her gaze away from the bewitching hold of John's blue, blue eyes and saw that Molly had Katie in an innocent death grip. "Don't hold her so tightly, sweetheart," she murmured as she pried the child's fingers loose from the kitten's rib cage. "You will hurt her." With Katie in one hand, Jennifer pulled Molly onto her lap, careful to avoid the roaming Jake. The relieved Katie settled down into the folds of Molly's dress and began to purr, much to the giggling little girl's delight.

"You are good with children," John said approvingly.

"Thank you." For some reason, his words greatly pleased Jennifer. She nodded in David's direction. "So are you."

John glanced down at the boy with a smile, then turned his attention again to the wood he was carving. He moved the knife quickly, sending small, curled chips flying all over the blanket.

Jennifer loved watching him work, for John had beautiful, graceful hands. Over the past ten days she had often found her gaze drawn to his hands as he held Molly, a kitten, a book, or the buggy reins. She yearned to have him again place his long, strong fingers on her face, her neck, her waist. She also imagined them on other parts of her body, as he had once promised.

The familiar heat rose inside her. Jennifer realized that John had a knack for making her feel hot, even without speaking, sometimes even without being there. Perhaps that delicious, intriguing, devastating heat was part of being in love.

Her mind flashed back to the day on the bench in Alejandro Noriega's courtyard, to the shocking, erotic words John had spoken. Since making her that exhilarating promise, John had behaved as a perfect gentleman, waiting for her to heal. Well, her recovery was complete. She loved him. She wanted what he offered, wanted *him*. It was time for John to keep his promise.

David, his brow wrinkled in doubt and concern, pulled on John's shirt sleeve. "Unca' John, that doesn't look like a boat."

With great seriousness, John examined the smooth, nondescript piece of wood in his hand. "No," he finally admitted. "I guess it doesn't." He glanced at David. "But it will, if your Aunt Jennie will quit distracting me."

Jennifer raised her eyebrows in mock indignation.

"It will?" David did not sound convinced.

"I promise." John put an arm around David's small shoulders and hugged him, but he kept his eyes on Jennifer. "And I always keep my promises."

The pounding of her heart started again, the shortness of breath, the heat spreading from her belly, up and down. Jennifer stared boldly at him, knowing her heart was in her eyes. "I suggest you finish that boat in a hurry, John Cantrell. You've made me a few promises, too, and I am growing impatient."

John gaped at her.

"What promises, Aunt Jennie?" David asked.

"Well, for one, he promised to take me on a buggy ride."

Jennifer scooted Molly from her lap onto the blanket and rose to her feet, careful of kittens and kids.

"Can me and Molly go, too? Can we?" David looked up at her, his big blue eyes wide with hope.

She smiled at him. "Not this time, sweetie. Today Uncle John and I need to go alone." She hurried to continue at David's crestfallen expression. "But you'll get to go for a ride tomorrow."

David perked up. "I will?"

Jennifer nodded. "Remember? Your mother is taking you to town with Rosa and Francisca."

"That's right!" David beamed.

Relieved that a potential crisis had been averted, Jennifer looked at John, who had not taken his eyes from her. "I am going to prepare a basket for this afternoon. Would you like me to take Molly or the kittens in with me?"

John eyed the group with which he shared the blanket. He shook his head. "I can handle it. You just hurry with that basket."

David pulled on John's sleeve again. "Why does she hafta hurry?"

"Because I am a hungry man." The passion in John's eyes as he stared at her caused Jennifer's mouth to open. She slid her tongue over suddenly dry lips.

"I will hurry," she promised. She picked up her skirts and ran for the kitchen.

From their vantage point on a blanket spread under the old oak, the Santa Maria lay before them in all her glory, kissed by the soft September sun. A cooling breeze whispered through the surrounding grasses and the leaves above them, and played with the curls that escaped Jennifer's hat.

"I love this view." She sat with her knees drawn up, her skirt discreetly arranged, her arms wrapped around her calves.

"So do I."

Something in John's tone made her look at him. He was lying on his side, his head propped on one bent arm, staring at her. He had removed his hat and his gunbelt; both lay close to his head. Jennifer pulled her own wide-brimmed hat off and affectionately swatted him with it. "I was talking about the ranch."

"I wasn't."

Jennifer laid the hat on the grass next to her hip. "I know," she said softly. "But do you not love this view as well?" With a sweep of her arm, she encompassed the ranch and all that it represented.

John sat up and followed Jennifer's gaze. "Yes," he admitted. "I do love it. All of it."

They were content to sit in silence for a while. Behind them, the horse waited patiently in the buggy traces, blowing softly every now and then, occasionally stamping his feet. Finally, Jennifer spoke.

"When did things begin to change for you?"

"What do you mean?"

"You came here fully prepared to kill Preston. When did you decide not to?"

"That first night." John shrugged. "I was so surprised that Preston denied nothing, except knowing my mother was pregnant. I carried a letter she had written to him just before she died, a letter I had not read until that night. In it, she verified that she had left him, that Preston hadn't known about me." He faced Jennifer. "I can be a stubborn fool sometimes, but I'm not afraid to admit when I am wrong. I was wrong about Preston."

Jennifer nodded in satisfaction. A sense of wondrous well-being filled her. John had found some measure of peace.

"I was wrong about you, too." His words startled her.

"Wrong about me? How so?"

John laughed. "We did not exactly get along that first night, Jen. You threatened me."

"You insulted me," Jennifer retorted teasingly.

John instantly sobered. "I truly do regret that. I was very rude."

"You've already apologized, John. And besides, you were right. I was skinny, and I was rich." She smiled at him.

"And I thought you were arrogant, spoiled, and cold-hearted. That's where I was wrong." John pounced on her, knocking her back on the blanket, playfully nuzzling her neck.

Jennifer shrieked with laughter. "I thought you were arrogant, obnoxious, and deadly," she said breathlessly.

"And you were right." John was half on top of her, his chest covering her stomach, pressing against her breasts. "Do you still find me arrogant, obnoxious, and deadly?"

Jennifer pretended to ponder his question.

"Jennie," he said warningly.

"Sometimes," she blurted with a smile.

"You will pay for that, woman," John growled. He again attacked her neck with his mouth, drawing forth from her a giggle that quickly changed to a sigh, then a moan.

"Oh, John." Her arms tightened around him, pulling him closer. "I have dreamed of holding you like this."

John captured her lips with his, his touch gentle and demanding at the same time, his tongue teasing for entry into her mouth. His fingers worked through her hair, loosening the pins, freeing the long, scented strands. He lifted his head for a moment, looking down at her with passion-filled eyes.

"As I have dreamed of you, *mi amada*." He positioned his body more intimately against her, draped one of his legs over hers. His mouth found hers again, while his hand slowly, firmly, caressed her from neck to hip and returned to her breast.

Jennifer gasped against his lips. Tremors wracked her body as his fingers teased her nipple to hardness through the material of her calico dress. He opened the button at her throat, and the next, and the next, then moved his arm under her to press her closer to his seeking mouth. He planted his lips against her revealed skin, kissing, licking, nibbling.

"I promised you," he whispered against her breast.

"You did, John." Her words escaped on a sigh as he opened yet another button. She clutched his shoulders, his arms, plucking with irritation at the barrier of his shirt.

At last he had access to the treasures he sought, although the enticing tips of her breasts were still covered by her thin cotton chemise. John moaned and ran his hand down her leg as far as he could reach; then, resisting the temptation to slip his hand under her skirt, he slowly travelled back upward, his hand coming to rest over her woman's mound. Jennifer lightly bucked against him, her eyes widening in excited surprise.

John stared at her as his hand moved in a slow circular motion over the layers of petticoats and skirt. "Jennie." He whispered her name, prayed her name. "Dear woman, I want you so."

"You have me, my love. You may have anything I have to give."

John stared into her eyes—her green, lovely, honest eyes—and saw her love there. "Do you know what you are saying?" he asked.

"Yes, John Novales Cantrell. I know exactly what I am saying." Her arms tightened around him as she shifted her legs a little farther apart.

John knew she did not understand the fire she so innocently played with. He moaned and buried his face against her breast. Her heart beat under his ear; her softness rose and fell with the accelerated rhythm of her breathing. Powerful feelings warred within him. More than anything, he wanted to strip Jennie of her clothes, those cruel clothes that hid her beauty from him. He wanted to see her in naked splendor, to worship her perfection with his eyes and hands and tongue. Right here, in full sunlight, he wanted to bury himself within her welcoming warmth. He knew she would allow him to fulfill his wishes.

He also knew he wanted better for her, for them. Aside from his mother, Jennie was the most noble, honorable woman he had ever known. Although the question of a woman's virginity, or lack thereof, had never been an important issue to him, John was certain that Jennie had never offered another man the gift she offered him, and he was deeply moved. He would not accept her gift lightly.

The decision was made. John felt relief, and a pang of regret. His hand travelled farther upward to tarry at her breast, then on to her face and into her hair. The faint scent of orange water reached his nose, a clean scent he would always associate with his beloved Jennie. He kissed her mouth softly, reverently.

"You have offered me a precious gift," he whispered.

Jennifer stiffened. "One you will not accept?" she asked anxiously.

"No, it is not what you are thinking, *mi amada.*" John held her chin in his hand, forcing her to look up at him. "We will be lovers, Jennie, I promise you. But not here, not now. When we come together for the first time, I want it to be in the comfort of a bed, in the privacy of a room with a door that locks, so we can love each other all night if we wish, so we can fall asleep in each other's arms. I want no guilt or shame to be associated with our mating, for either of us."

Her magnificent eyes filled with tears. "Oh, John," she whispered. Her hand moved up to stroke his cheek. "There could never be any shame with you."

Disappointment coursed through her, as well as a powerful feeling of joy. He cared for her, deeply. She could feel it. And his words proved it. "I'll not wait long, John Cantrell. As I told you, I am an impatient woman."

"And as I told *you,* I am a hungry man," John said, again nibbling on her neck. "If you don't feed me, and soon, all my fine intentions will fly away on the wind, and I will have you here and now."

Jennifer pursed her lips as if giving his words careful consideration, then giggled when he tickled her ribs.

"Ah, Jennie, sweet Jennie," John breathed happily. "I always knew that under that too-tight corset was a woman of astounding passion."

"Is that why you cut it off me?" she demanded. She pushed his hand away and sat up. John rolled onto his back and smiled smugly up at her.

Suddenly, the horse tossed his head and whinnied. John immediately tensed. He jerked to a sitting position, his eyes narrowed and alert.

"What is it?"

"Someone is coming." John scrambled to his feet, securing his gunbelt as he rose. The sound of an approaching horse reached their ears.

Jennifer closed the buttons of her bodice with trembling fingers. John reached down to help her to her feet. She stood beside him and smoothed her wild hair, her eyes straining as she attempted to identify the coming rider. Her shoulders slumped with relief when she saw that it was Bill. He pulled his horse to a halt before them.

"I'm sorry to intrude on you two. I wouldn't have come if I didn't think this was important." He took off his hat and ran a gloved hand over his sweat-covered forehead. "It's getting late, and I thought you might want to get home before dark."

"Why?" John demanded.

Bill settled his hat back on his head. "Oliver Mainwaring has returned."

Sixteen

John lifted her down from the buggy, his hands lingering at her waist longer than was necessary. Jennifer noticed, wishing she could throw herself into the haven of his arms, but instead, she smiled at him, then turned to Rosa, who stood on the veranda.

"Where is he?" There was no need for Jennifer to name her uncle.

"In the *sala*. He is waiting for you."

Jennifer nodded and started for the front door.

"Do you want me to come with you?" John asked.

She looked over her shoulder at him. The troubled, protective expression on his handsome face endeared him all the more to her. "No, but thank you. Let me ascertain his mood."

"It won't be pleasant," Rosa muttered. "That one is never pleasant." She sniffed with disgust and went back inside. Jennifer followed, trying unsuccessfully to hide a smile. Rosa headed toward the kitchen, while Jennifer continued across the foyer to the open double doors of the *sala*. She stood there and watched Oliver silently for a moment.

He sat alone on one of the matching sofas, sipping a glass of sherry. Her uncle's journey seemed to have agreed with him; he looked well, and more relaxed than she had seen him in a long time. He had evidently visited a tailor, for his perfectly fitted frock coat was new, as was the azure brocade vest he wore. Oliver looked up and saw her. He leaned forward to set his glass on the low table, his lips curved in what passed for a smile.

"There you are, Jennifer. Preston told me of your injuries; I have been worried." He stood up as she came into the room.

"As you can see, I am quite recovered." Jennifer sat on the opposite sofa, wondering why she felt so nervous. She knew Oliver would disapprove of her simple calico dress, and he was probably horrified by her wide-brimmed felt hat. But she did not dare remove it. Even with John's help, she had not been able to find all of the pins he had pulled from her hair; many were lost forever in the California grasses. Again with John's help, she had pulled up her hair and secured it as best she could with the few pins left to her, and had covered the untidy result with her hat. Now she wished she had taken a few minutes to freshen up before meeting with her uncle.

Oliver settled back on his sofa, crossing one leg over the other. The look he gave Jennifer carried detectable traces of disapproval and hostility. "Knowing her as I do, I find it difficult to believe that the charming Miss Noriega was moved to such violence toward you. What did you do to provoke her?"

Jennifer stared at him, scarcely able to believe her ears. "Evidently you do not know her at all if you can even ask such a ridiculous question. Really, Oliver."

"I am well aware of your animosity toward Miss Noriega, Jennifer. It is nothing more than childhood jealousy, carried on far too long." He reached for his sherry glass.

"On the contrary, jealousy is not an issue between her and me, at least not on my part. Constanza has nothing I want," Jennifer ground out, trying to clamp down on her growing irritation.

Oliver continued as if she had not spoken. "Obviously, you are not aware of the fact that I am well acquainted with the lady. I will admit that she is possessed of a somewhat, shall we say, passionate nature, but I cannot believe she would lift her hand to you without justification."

"She lifted more than her hand," Jennifer snapped, giving up any attempt to control her tongue. "She lifted a stone bookend, and her intended victim was John. Believe it, uncle. She assaulted us without justification."

"Ah. All becomes clear to me." Oliver's eyebrows rose; his lip curled in derision. "The bastard insulted her, and you were foolish enough to get in the way of her appropriate retaliation."

Jennifer shot to her feet. "John did not insult her, and do not refer to him with that term again, *ever.*" She trembled with the force of her rage. "I shall not bore you with the truth, as you obviously have no interest in it. Just remember that whenever you enjoy the *charming* Miss Noriega's company, be certain to watch your back." She stormed toward the door.

Oliver laughed scornfully. "Do you not wish to hear of my trip, dear niece?"

Jennifer did not pause. "I will speak with you later," she said over her shoulder.

"You will dress properly for supper, Jennifer."

Her hands clenched at the imperious sound of his command. She continued up the stairs, ripping her hat off as she climbed. It had taken less than five minutes for the conversation with Oliver to escalate into another of their verbal battles. Jennifer shook her head in frustration. There was no possible way she would ever consider living under the same roof with her uncle again. They were no longer compatible, if, indeed, they ever had been. Oliver was her only living blood relative, but she would not grieve if she were to never see him again. It surprised her that she felt no sense of loss. All she felt was anger.

Jennifer stomped into her room, unbuttoning her bodice as she pushed the door closed with her hip. Perhaps a hot bath would soothe her frayed nerves and make her fit company for the rest of the family. She needed help from somewhere, or she feared she would explode.

* * *

Deep in thought, Jennifer stared at her reflection in the mirror as Brigit fixed her hair. In deference to Oliver's expectations, Preston had decided to serve a formal supper tonight, and Jennifer was dressed accordingly. The bath had calmed her mind, as had the glass of sherry she had sipped while luxuriating in the warm, comforting water.

She hoped she could find the strength to keep a tight rein on her temper tonight. It was imperative that she find out what Oliver's plans were. Since she had not yet heard further from Elias Craig, she had not been able to finalize her own plans. Jennifer had spoken to no one of her intention to ask Preston if she could make the Santa Maria her home. Until she had some idea of her financial affairs, she did not feel comfortable broaching the subject. It was important to her that she not appear as a homeless waif thrown on Preston's doorstep.

For some reason, Jennifer found herself viewing Oliver's return as a portent of bad things to come. She had the uneasy feeling that she was standing in the path of an oncoming flood that would sweep her away if she was not very careful.

In addition, a persistent warning bell had been ringing in her head ever since her earlier discussion with Oliver. First, Constanza had insisted, more than once, that Oliver would never allow her to marry John, indicating that the woman knew Oliver well enough to guess—correctly—how he would feel about such a liaison. Now, Oliver insisted that he also knew Constanza well. When had the two had an opportunity to develop a friendship? As far as Jennifer knew, the only time Oliver and Constanza had spent together was the night they first met at Preston's *fiesta*. Oliver had left for San Francisco two days later. There had been no time for them to become well acquainted.

"You look lovely, Miss Jennie."

"I beg your pardon?" Jennifer forced her attention to Brigit, who stood back with a satisfied smile.

"You look lovely," Brigit repeated. "I did a fine job, if I do say so myself. I love working with your hair; it is so pretty. And you let me do things with it. Miss Noriega always wore hers the same way—down." Her expression announced her disapproval.

Hiding a smile, Jennifer examined her hair in the mirror. Brigit had pulled it up and back into an arrangement of rolls and curls crossed with thin braids and decorated with a few tiny satin flowers that exactly matched the color of her burgundy gown. She had to agree with Brigit, although she would not go as far as to say she looked lovely; but she looked good. Very good.

"You are absolutely right, Brigit," Jennifer announced as she hooked the ruby earrings in her ears. She decided to forego the matching necklace and stood up. "You did a fine job."

Brigit fairly glowed with pride.

Jennifer smoothed the skirt of her satin gown. She had deliberately chosen this gown, for it was the one she had worn the night she first met John. Her life had changed that night. Jennifer suspected that her life would change again this night, and because the gown reminded her of John, it gave her courage and confidence. She would need both in the forthcoming battle with Oliver.

"Are you all right, miss?" Brigit's brows were drawn together in concern. She held out a lace fan.

With a smile, Jennifer accepted the fan. "I'm fine, thank you. It is just that I have a great deal on my mind, and I fear I am somewhat preoccupied."

"Francisca said the gentleman is your uncle," Brigit said in a troubled tone. "Does that mean we'll leave for Philadelphia soon?"

"No," Jennifer said emphatically as she moved to the door. "I've no wish to return to Philadelphia. I plan to stay right here." She looked back at Brigit. "Would that please you?"

"Oh, yes, miss," Brigit exclaimed. "I *love* living here! But I would follow you anywhere," she hastened to add.

"There will be no need, Brigit. This is our home."

"Yes, miss." Brigit scurried to open the door for Jennifer.
"That suits me fine."

"And me." Jennifer smiled at Brigit, then gathered her
skirts and walked down the hall, her head held high, her heart
pounding with a strange combination of dread and elation.
Oliver waited downstairs, but so did John.

Supper was an interminable affair. Oliver shared the stories
of his travels in mind-numbing detail, testing the patience and
courtesy of all present. If the fact that John sat at Jennifer's
side bothered Oliver, he gave no sign of it. On the contrary,
he seemed to go out of his way to include John in the conversation—when he allowed someone else to speak. His mo-
nopoly of the evening continued even into the after-supper
gathering in the *sala*. And much to Jennifer's growing frustration, he gave no hint as to what his plans were or how
soon he intended to leave for Philadelphia.

Although it was still early, Barbara and Bill used the excuse
of checking on the children to make their escape. Barbara
shot Jennifer an apologetic smile as she passed through the
doors. Jennifer nodded in understanding.

"Kiss the children for me," she called after them.

She and John shared one of the sofas, while Preston and
Oliver occupied two chairs. A moment of silence ensued, then
Jennifer could bear the suspense no longer.

"Have you made plans for returning to Philadelphia,
Oliver?"

Oliver looked at her over the rim of his brandy snifter, his
expression bland except for the devious gleam in his eyes.
He sipped of the amber liquid before answering her. "Nothing
definite yet. I made the acquaintance of two gentlemen while
in San Francisco who have expressed an interest in joining
us on our return trip, and I must take their wishes into consideration." He rolled the snifter between his hands. "Have

you at last tired of life in the wild West, Jennifer? Are you anxious to return to Philadelphia?"

"No, I am not." She calmly met his gaze. It did not sound as if he intended to leave soon.

Oliver's lips tightened in irritation, and anger flashed in his eyes, but Jennifer suspected she was the only one who saw the signs of his displeasure, so swiftly did they pass. "We shall discuss it another time," he said tightly. He leaned forward and set the snifter on the table. "My travels have wearied me; I shall retire for the night." He stood up.

"Good night, Oliver," Jennifer said.

"Good night, Jennifer. Preston. John." Oliver nodded at each person in turn, then left the room.

Jennifer sighed with relief. "I thought this evening would never end," she murmured.

"It was tedious," John agreed. He reached for her hand, evidently not caring that Preston was still in the room.

She tightened her fingers on his with a smile, then looked at Preston. "I apologize for Oliver's boring discourses. He is acting strangely tonight."

Preston smiled. "He was no more rude than usual, Jennie."

"This was a different kind of rudeness." Jennifer frowned. "He was a bore tonight, not arrogant."

"Oh, I don't know," Preston mused. "It's pretty arrogant for him to assume everyone wants to listen to every detail of his life over the last month."

Jennifer smiled. "You are right."

"Still, you have a point, Jennie." John's expression was thoughtful. "He was different. Do you think he is planning something?"

"I don't know. What could he be planning, other than his return to Philadelphia? There should be no secrecy associated with that." Her gaze travelled from John to Preston. "When we spoke earlier, he said some things that have been troubling me all evening."

Preston set his snifter on the table. "What is it, honey?"

She shrugged. "I just get the feeling from both Oliver and Constanza that they are much better acquainted than we realize. In light of your concerns about the Santa Maria, is it possible he is plotting something with her?"

Preston leaned back in his chair, his thick brows drawn together in thought. "How could they know each other so well? When did they have time?"

"I don't know," Jennifer answered. "I asked myself the same questions. As far as I know, they only saw each other the night they met, at the *fiesta*. Oliver left two days later."

"Wait a minute." John leaned forward. "Didn't Bill say something about Constanza being in San Francisco when the wildfire was started?"

Preston nodded. "Alejandro mentioned it at supper here the night we beat the fire. She had gone to shop, or something."

"Then Oliver and Constanza were in San Francisco at the same time," said Jennifer. "Do you think they ran into each other?"

John hesitated, meeting Preston's eyes. Jennifer saw the look.

"What?" she asked. "What are you thinking?"

"Knowing Constanza as I do, Jennie, I think they may have deliberately arranged to meet there," John said gently.

Jennifer stared at him, a blush heating her cheeks as she caught his meaning. "Oh." She looked down at her lap for a minute. It was difficult to imagine her uncle in such a situation, especially with Constanza. But if it were true, many things would be explained. "Perhaps that is why he tarried so long in San Francisco, why he defended Constanza to me earlier this evening."

"He defended her to you?" John asked.

"Yes, when I told him how I came to be injured. He could not believe that the 'charming Miss Noriega' would be moved to violence without provocation." She shook her head. "He was infuriating."

"He blamed you for your own injuries?" Preston demanded.

Jennifer nodded. "He blamed John as well. His position on the matter was puzzling, but if he and Constanza know each other . . . intimately," she fought another blush, "it clears things up somewhat." She smiled ruefully. "In a way, they deserve each other."

Preston frowned. "Why would Oliver join forces with Constanza in an attempt to gain the Santa Maria? He despises this place."

"Perhaps he hasn't," John said. "Perhaps their brief union was only that. We may be dealing with two unrelated situations."

"Brigit might know something," Jennifer suggested. "She was Constanza's maid at the time. Surely Constanza would have taken her along to San Francisco."

"That is a good idea, Jennie." John looked at her approvingly. "Ask her."

"We'll meet tomorrow and discuss what we've learned," Preston said. He rose. "And we'll add Oliver Mainwaring to our list of people to watch." He patted Jennifer's shoulder as he passed behind the sofa. "I'm off to bed. Remember that all of the men are leaving early tomorrow morning to move the herd to the north pasture, Jennie. You two probably have plenty to talk about, but don't keep John up too late." He paused at the door long enough to wink and flash a knowing smile over his shoulder at her, then he was gone.

Jennifer blushed again. She placed a hand on her hot cheek. "I think he likes to tease me," she complained.

"He was teasing me, too, Jen." John stood and pulled her to her feet. "But I think he is pleased to see us together."

"I agree." Then she realized he was staring at her. His blazing blue eyes roamed over her from head to foot and back again, igniting an answering blaze within her.

"I remember that dress," he said. "You wore it the first

night I met you. I've been wanting to tell you all evening how much I like it."

Once more, Jennifer's face warmed, but this time with pleasure. "Thank you, John."

He drew her arm through his and led her out to the moonlit courtyard. She was silent until John showed her to a carved wooden settee placed under a lemon tree, and when she did speak, there was a soft, dreamy quality to her tone. "I love this place."

John settled an arm around her shoulders. "So do I."

She peered up at his face in the dim light. "Have you decided to stay?"

"I'd like to. Preston has invited me to make the Santa Maria my home."

"What would make you leave?"

"I would leave only if someone I love left."

Jennifer's heart skipped a beat, then rapped out a tattoo of hope. "I think you love many people here, John Cantrell."

"I suppose that is true." He paused. "But I love one above all others." He turned to face her, and before she could say anything further, he kissed her. He caressed her mouth with his lips and tongue while his hands moved over her neck and shoulders, where her skin was bared to his gentle, arousing touch by her low-necked evening gown. Liquid fire filled her veins. She moaned against his mouth and tangled her fingers in his hair, meeting his passion. When he finally released her, she was gasping for breath.

"Oh, John." She could say no more.

He pressed a kiss to the exposed swell of her left breast. "I can feel your heart," he murmured against her skin. "Does it beat so swiftly for me?"

"Yes," she whispered, fighting the urge to pull her bodice down far enough to bare all of her tingling breast to his hot mouth. Instead, she ran her fingers through his thick hair. "Only for you."

"Good." John kissed her again, then straightened. He

grabbed her hand and laid it against his chest, holding it there. "My heart beats for you, also, Jennifer Mainwaring." He placed his free hand over her breast. "Our hearts beat as one."

It was true, Jennifer realized as she covered his hand to hold it against her breast. Their hearts beat in rhythm with each other, in rhythm with the night, in rhythm with life. The warm, scented air of the courtyard swirled around them, enveloped them in a world where nothing existed except the two of them.

"I never want to leave this place, or you," she whispered.

"You don't have to."

"Oliver will try to make me."

"He will fail."

Jennifer was sorry she had mentioned her uncle, for something of the spell faded away. John's hand lightly tightened on her breast, then he released her.

"If you don't go up to your room, and soon, I will lose all control and take you here." His voice sounded hoarse.

"I wouldn't mind," Jennifer said softly, cupping his cheek in her hand.

"I know." He turned his head to kiss her palm. "But I told you how I want it to be for us. The wait will be worth it."

"Do you promise?"

"I promise."

Jennifer marvelled that those two simple words could send such a rush of delicious desire through her. "I will hold you to your promise."

John only smiled, in a way that intensified her longing for him. He stood and held out a hand, pulling her to her feet. She put her arm around his waist and held onto him as he walked her to the doors of the *sala*.

There he turned to her, taking her face between his hands. "Good night, sweet woman," he whispered.

"Good night, sweet man."

She thought he was about to kiss her, but he hesitated. "Sweet?" he repeated doubtfully. "You think I'm sweet?"

"Among other things." Jennifer lost the battle to keep from smiling.

"What other things?"

"When you keep your promise, *El Lobo,* I will tell you, and not before."

John groaned. "Tormentor." He finally kissed her. "Sweet, sweet tormentor." He kissed her again, then set her away from him. "Off with you, woman. I can bear no more torment tonight."

Jennifer stared at him, feeling that she almost floated with happiness. "Good night, John."

He reached out and lightly touched her cheek. His blue eyes seemed to shine. "Good night, Jen."

With great reluctance, she turned into the *sala* and extinguished the lamps, hearing John's footsteps fade across the courtyard. The smile on her face widened, and Jennifer knew she was grinning like an idiot. She gathered her skirts and ran lightly up the stairs, wanting to dance. But all was quiet in the long, dimly lit hallway, and she held herself in check. She was almost to her room when she was startled by the sound of a door opening. Even before she turned, she knew it was Oliver.

His door stood partly open. He stared at her, his face impassive except for the furious, burning suspicion in his eyes.

She raised her chin and met his gaze, waiting for him to speak. A long minute passed. His eyes did not leave hers, nor did he say anything. Finally, he quietly closed his door.

Jennifer released a breath she had not realized she was holding. She clasped her shaking hands together. What had that been about? she wondered as she continued on to her room. She closed the door and leaned against it, her earlier feelings of euphoria dashed on a rock of disturbing fear.

"Is that you, miss?" Brigit's sleepy voice came from the direction of the chair. A moment later she stood.

"Why are you here so late?" Jennifer asked in astonishment.

Brigit glanced at the mantel clock. "It's not that late, Miss Jennie, only just past ten. I stayed to help you undress. That gown would be difficult to get out of by yourself."

"Thank you, Brigit. I've had to get out of it alone before, and it is difficult." She removed her earrings while she walked to the dressing table. Brigit followed her, and when Jennifer halted, the maid began to unlace the gown.

Jennifer slipped her shoes off. "Brigit, did you travel with Constanza to San Francisco about a month ago?"

Brigit's hands paused. "Yes, miss."

"Did Constanza meet my uncle while she was there?"

The gown loosened. Jennifer clutched the bodice to keep it from falling to her waist and turned to face Brigit. The girl stared miserably at the floor, her face almost as red as her hair.

"Brigit?"

"I've no wish to carry tales about your uncle, Miss Jennie."

"I know, and your discretion is commendable. But we fear he may be planning something with Constanza, something that might harm the Santa Maria, or those living here. Did you ever hear them discuss *Señor* Preston, or John, or the Santa Maria?"

Brigit finally looked up. She shook her head. "No, miss. Of course, Miss Constanza always sent me away when she and Mr. Mainwaring were together in her room. But I was only behind the door, in the adjoining maid's room." Brigit's face flamed again. "I heard enough to know what was going on, if you understand my meaning. It seems to me they didn't do much talking." She motioned to Jennifer to turn around. Jennifer obeyed, and Brigit freed her from the gown.

"Did they ever leave the room together?" Jennifer asked.

"Oh, yes. He squired her all over the city. Took her shopping, he did, and to amusements, and for meals. I usually went along, to carry her purchases and such, and I never heard them discuss the Santa Maria. They mostly talked about, well, silly things. Flirty things. Sometimes downright filthy things, when they thought no one could hear." She accepted the bustle Jennifer had untied from her waist, then held her hand out for the petticoats. "Truth to tell, miss, it was rather sickening. Now sit down and let me get those flowers and pins out of your hair."

Wearing only her chemise, drawers, and stockings, Jennifer obediently sank down onto the dressing table stool. She was not surprised by Brigit's news, but relieved, because it explained many things. She also felt disturbed by the idea of Oliver and Constanza together, and did not doubt that they had lapsed into displays of offensive vulgarity. "Oh, Brigit," she said sadly. "What an education you have had, for all you are so young."

"Yes, miss, but it's been helpful in some ways. No smooth-talking man will take advantage of me." With massaging, expert fingers, Brigit found and removed the pins and flowers. She took up the brush and stroked the long locks until Jennifer was practically purring with contentment, which reminded her of the kittens.

"Did you check on Katie and Jake tonight?"

"Yes, Miss Jennie. They're just fine. Since you're recovered now, it won't matter if they wake you in the night. I'll bet Miss Rosa will let you have them back."

Jennifer nodded. "I will get them tomorrow. It's time they learned to drink from a saucer. I will work with them on that." She turned on the stool and took the brush from Brigit's hand. "And you should get to bed. Thank you for waiting for me."

"My pleasure, miss. Good night." With a tired smile, Brigit left the room, also leaving her new mistress with many troubling, unanswered questions, and not a few well-grounded fears.

Seventeen

Jennifer stared down at the brush she held in her hand. So Oliver and Constanza did know each other well. A chill of dread ran down her back. The combination of the calculating, manipulative Constanza and the spoiled, selfish Oliver was a potentially dangerous one. Both were accustomed to having every little whim satisfied. God only knew what they had set their sights on now.

Of course, there was the possibility that John was right, that their meeting in San Francisco had been for carnal reasons alone. Jennifer tossed the brush on the dressing table and stood up, resolutely pushing Oliver and Constanza from her mind. For tonight, there were no answers. She did not want to think about them any longer.

Jennifer slipped out of her undergarments and into the sleeping shift Brigit had laid out on the bed. One hand reached out to caress the pillow where John had laid his head the night he had stayed with her. A fresh torrent of longing filled her, so intense that it was almost painful, and she closed her eyes against it. How curious that the feelings brought by love so often conflicted with each other. Pleasure and pain, euphoria and despair, anticipation and impatience, contentment and longing. She welcomed them all, for they were part of the same blissful package. She loved John, needed him, wanted his arms around her, wanted the full knowledge of his beautiful body. The familiar heat rose through her again, causing her breasts to tingle and her womanhood to ache.

She could not wait much longer for what he had promised her.

Shaken by the depth of her desire, almost frightened by it, Jennifer turned from the lonely bed, pulling the mass of her hair forward over one shoulder. She was about to weave the thick length into its customary braid when her eyes fell on her reflection in the mirror. How different she looked with her hair down!

Impulsively, Jennifer shook her head, sending the long strands flying. The faint scent of orange blossom water filled the air. Her hair finally came to rest, covering her shoulders, her arms, her breasts. She stared in the mirror, stunned. Could that be her? That woman with her hair set free, wearing only a cotton shift made of material too thin to hide the outline of her body from the lamplight behind her? That woman with her breath coming too fast between sensuously parted lips? The woman in the mirror was ready for love, in all its glorious forms. The woman in the mirror was ready for John.

A tremor rocked through Jennifer. Did she dare to throw away the conventions and dictates of society as easily as she had thrown away her ruined corset? John had made no mention of marriage, had made no promises for the future beyond that to make love to her—did she dare to follow her heart, even if it led to his bed? Did she dare not to? In the mirror she met her own eyes, and could not deny the honest answer she found there.

Without another thought, she blew out the lamp on the dressing table, snatched up her wrapper and threw it around her shoulders, then slipped out of her room.

The joy in her heart lent speed to her bare, silent feet as she hurried along the quiet hall, down the stairs, through the *sala,* across the courtyard. She stood before his door, breathless and trembling. Pale, inviting light made its way through the curtains at his window. He was still awake.

She raised her arm to knock, then realized someone might hear the noise. Before her fear-tinged nervousness overwhelmed her courage, she grabbed the latch and threw the door open.

John's bed stood directly in front of her. He was sitting up, the sheet covering him to his hips, his gun pointed straight at her.

"My, God, Jennie," he said, his tone low and concerned. He eased the hammer back into place. A book that had been precariously balanced on the edge of the bedside table fell to the floor with a soft thud. "What is wrong?"

"Nothing." Without taking her eyes from him, she stepped into the room and closed the door, tossing her wrapper aside. With a soft rustle, it landed on the floor. Jennifer did not care. She drank in John's near nakedness, allowed her gaze to roam over his black hair, his blue eyes, his beloved face. Her gaze continued down his muscled chest, over his flat stomach, both kissed with more black hair that narrowed to an intriguing arrow pointing beneath the sheet. His covered legs seemed incredibly long. How she wanted to strip the hateful sheet away!

She turned momentarily to slide the lock bar home, then faced him again. "You said you wanted a bed for us." She waved a shaking hand toward his bed. "A door that locks. All night to love each other. We have those things now."

John's heart slammed in his chest. He blindly set his gun on the bedside table, unable to look away from her. Her bewitching eyes were shining with love, and hope, and desire, emotions that exactly matched his own. She wore only a simple, sleeveless shift, trimmed with delicate lace at the rounded neckline, decorated with tiny buttons down the front to her waist. Her glorious hair fell free, flowing over her shoulders and breasts, streaked with gold from the lamplight. John swallowed, hard. A flame shot through him, stirring him, stiffening him. His fingers fumbled with the lamp, turning it low, then, without a word, he held his hand out to her.

She stepped toward him, reached for him, a tremulous smile on her lips. Their fingers touched, held, and he pulled

her closer and closer, until she stood right next to the bed.
With his free hand, he fingered the soft material of her shift.

"Take it off." The words came out in a whisper, firm yet
pleading.

Jennifer blinked, hesitated.

"Please, *mi amada.*"

She released his hand and worked on the row of buttons
with unsteady fingers. His breath caught as the twin swells
of her breasts were revealed, then the inviting skin of her
stomach. When the last button came free, her hands fell to
her sides and she waited. John raised his gaze from her exposed skin to her eyes. He was moved by the nervous vulnerability he read in those green depths.

"You are so lovely, Jennie," he breathed, and was gratified
to see some of the fear leave her eyes. He leaned forward,
touching the long soft tresses that shielded her breasts, pushing the strands out of the way, running his finger down the
length of skin exposed from neckline to stomach. She gasped,
a sound that pleased him to no end. He reached up with both
hands and guided the shift off her shoulders. She shivered as
the material whispered down the length of her body and
pooled on the floor. Now it was John who caught his breath.

How often he had imagined this moment, yet his dreams
had not come close to the reality of it. His eyes and hands
wonderingly explored her beauty, from her long, lovely neck,
to her enchanting breasts that were just the right size to fit
perfectly in his hands, to the taut, rose-colored peaks he
longed to taste. He caressed her narrow waist and gently flar-
ing hips, brushed his hand over the dark triangle of curls that
held so much promise, and stroked her shapely thighs. He
could feel the vitality of her lean, strong body, her glowing
health evident in her firm, supple muscles and her incredibly
silky, smooth skin. She clutched at his shoulders, her breath
escaping in a soft moan of his name.

John pulled the sheet back and moved over. "Come here,"
he whispered. She placed one knee on the edge of the bed

and leaned forward, her arms closing around his neck, her breasts pressing to his chest. He fell back against the pillows, carrying her with him. She gasped as the lengths of their bodies met, as their legs entwined. He took her mouth, plunging his hands into her fragrant hair.

"Oh, Jennie," John moaned between kisses. "How I have longed for you."

"I know," she whispered. "I have longed for you as well. I could wait no longer."

John shifted his body, guiding her to a more comfortable position beside him. Their hands roamed over each other while their mouths and tongues met in a loving duel. Eventually, John pulled his mouth from hers and kissed her neck, brushing aside the long strands of hair. He gently pushed her shoulder, easing her from her side to her back. His mouth continued its wet, teasing journey down her neck, eliciting shivers of delight from her. Jennifer closed her eyes and ran her fingers through his hair as she gave herself up to the new, incredible sensations his hands and mouth gave to her.

When his lips latched onto her nipple, she cried out in surprise and pleasure, now understanding what the aching bud had been longing for. John's hand wandered down the length of her body, stroking her ribs, her stomach, her hip, her thigh. Then, while his mouth continued its exquisite teasing of her breasts, his hand began the return journey, upward along the inside of her thigh, very slowly. Jennifer moved her leg, giving him easier access as he approached her most secret place. She held her breath as his gentle fingers touched her, parted her.

He moaned against her breast. "Ah, Jennie. You are so warm and wet for me. My beautiful woman."

His words sent another shiver through her, and she cried out again when his searching fingers found the most sensitive place of all. He began to stroke her there, over and over, murmuring soft words of endearment and encouragement.

"Come to me, *mi amada*. Give yourself up to my touch."

Jennifer pulled at his hair, tossing her head, overcome with the marvelous, unfamiliar feelings his relentless fingers brought forth. His words confused her. *Come to me.* "But I'm right here, John." His name ended on a sigh. He was leading her closer and closer to the edge of a precipice of ecstasy.

"That's right, Jen. Let the waves come. Ride them."

Waves? But suddenly waves did come, waves of pleasure, one after another, causing her body to quiver. Jennifer whispered his name in astonishment and wonder. She had not known, had not dreamed that such rapture existed. She relaxed against the pillows, holding him close, aware that her breathing and her heartbeat seemed very fast.

John placed his hand over her breast. "I knew you were a woman of great passion, Jennifer Mainwaring." His voice held a note of satisfaction, as well as something akin to awe.

She smiled weakly, now mildly embarrassed at the way she had opened herself to the magic of his fingers. "What did you do to me?"

"I kept a promise." John smiled down at her, then kissed her softly.

Jennifer ran one hand down his side, from rib cage to thigh, and back up to his hip. "And what of your pleasure?" Her hand moved over his stomach and abdomen.

John's breath caught. Her hand traveled lower, brushing against his hardened length, then she carefully closed her fingers around him.

"Jennie!"

Jennifer was amazed at the contrast of that fascinating part of him—the incredible strength and heat, the unbelievable softness of his skin there. "I want to give you the same gift you gave me, John." Her hand moved to his hip, pulled him closer.

He needed no further encouragement. He settled between her thighs. She felt his hardness pressing against her and widened her legs.

"I'll try not to hurt you," he whispered.

"You could not hurt me, John Cantrell." Jennifer closed her arms around him, holding him tightly to her.

"I love you, Jennie." John's voice was filled with a curious combination of tenderness and passion. In one smooth thrust, he buried himself in her, then lay still for a moment.

The pain was sharp, but of short duration. Jennifer shifted, concentrating on the sensation of her body adjusting to his presence. "And I love you," she breathed. Instinctively she raised her hips and tightened her muscles around him.

John gasped. He began to move with her, and to Jennifer, the action was as easy as dancing. She gave herself up to his rhythm, following his lead, knowing he would again take her to the heights of ecstasy. He led her on and on, until she bucked under him, whimpering with pleasure, and at last she cried out as he sent her over the edge. With one final thrust, he joined her over that edge, moaning her name. She felt the vibrations as his seed pumped into her, felt the answering quivers of her own body where she enclosed him.

They were quiet for a long time. Jennifer was content to lie under him; she welcomed his weight, just as she welcomed him in her body. Never had she felt so close to another human being, so connected to someone else's soul. She felt loved, and treasured, and wanted to return those gifts to John ten-fold.

"You were right," she finally murmured.

"Of course I was." He nuzzled her neck. After a moment, he raised up on his elbows to look at her. "About what?"

"Arrogant man!" Jennifer slapped his bare flank, smiling, and again tightened her arm around him. "About the wait being worth it."

His expression softened. "Yes, it was worth it." Gently he kissed her mouth, then eased out of her and onto his side. She felt bereft for a moment, somehow empty without him. He drew her close, pulled the sheet up over them. She nestled against his length, feeling warm, safe, and loved within the shelter of his arms.

"You realize, of course, that now we must marry." Although John said the words almost flippantly, Jennifer caught the note of vulnerability in his tone. Her heart swelled with love and happiness.

"We *must* marry?" she repeated. She felt John nod against the top of her head.

"I fear I have compromised you, Miss Mainwaring. There is nothing else to be done. We must marry, and soon, in case there is a child."

"A child." Jennifer breathed the words, the thought of carrying John's child causing a thrill of excitement to course through her stomach.

When she said no more, John again raised up on his elbow. He met her eyes, held her with his intense gaze. "Will you marry me, Jennifer Mainwaring?"

She stared up at him, then placed her hand on his chest, over the place where his heart beat. "Yes, John, I will marry you, gladly, with all my heart."

Something flared in his eyes; joy, relief, pride, satisfaction—perhaps a combination of all those things. She did not know for sure. He kissed her again, then lay back beside her, his hand roaming through her hair. Her fingers wandered over from his chest to his ribs, and encountered the scar there.

"How did you get this?" she asked.

"It is a war wound." He sat up suddenly. "Come. We have plans to make." He piled the pillows against the headboard, including the one that Jennifer's head had been resting on only a moment ago, and leaned back.

Jennifer raised up on one elbow, pulling the sheet over her breasts. Obviously, John did not want to talk about how he had gotten that scar. She would not press him now. "Come where?" she asked.

"Here." John patted the pillows next to him.

With a smile, she scooted up to the place he indicated. He wrapped one arm around her shoulders and held her close.

Her cheek rested on his shoulder, while her arm lay across his belly. "What plans must we make tonight?"

"Plans for our future." John caught her hand with his free one. "You know Preston has invited me to live here. How would you feel about making the Santa Maria our home?"

"I would love it," Jennifer said simply.

"You won't miss the East, your home and friends in Philadelphia?"

"No." She raised her eyes to his face. "Preston mentioned once that I could stay here as long as I wished, John. I had already decided to ask him if I could stay forever."

"Good." John's arm tightened on her shoulders. "That is settled then. Now, about my finances. I have quite a sum set aside in banks in *Ciudad de Mexico* and San Francisco, enough to support us comfortably, to build our own house if we wish, to invest in the Santa Maria."

Jennifer nodded eagerly. "So do I. My father split his estate between Oliver and me, and in addition, my mother left me a respectable sum when she died. I have wired my solicitor, and any day I expect an accounting of my financial assets. I was waiting for that report before I brought up the subject of staying here." She snuggled against him. "When it comes, we'll go over it together and decide what to do."

"It wouldn't matter if you had nothing, Jen. I can support you and our children."

"I know," she said, remembering that day at the dam when she had realized that John Cantrell would be a good husband, a good provider, a good father. Now he was to be hers.

"What of your house in Philadelphia?" he asked.

"Oliver can have it. I have no attachment to it."

"Your family home? Where you lived for years?"

Jennifer sighed. "It was never my family home. My father bought that house when he married my stepmother. She and I did not get along; in fact, she sent me away to boarding schools for most of the year. And my father let her." She could not keep the note of hurt out of her voice. "I did not really live there until I finished my schooling, which was a few years after they died. By then, of course, Oliver was there."

"I'm sorry, Jennie." Again, John's arm tightened around her.

She nuzzled her face against his shoulder in response. "After my mother died, my father was lost to me, it seemed. The only time since then that I have felt like part of a family is when I have been here, with Preston and his clan at the Santa Maria. I don't want to leave, John, especially now that I have found you."

"Then we will not leave. I think Preston will be pleased."

"He will be. But Oliver will not. He may try to prevent our marriage." She sat up and faced him.

John's jaw tightened. "Because of my Mexican heritage or because of my illegitimacy?"

Jennifer placed a hand on his cheek. "Perhaps because of both. Perhaps because of neither."

"What do you mean?"

"Oliver has been hinting that he wishes to see me married to a particular young man in Philadelphia. It would be quite a social coup, in Oliver's mind, if he could arrange that."

"A social coup?" John's brow furrowed in confusion.

"Because my father made his initial fortune during the Gold Rush, my family was and is considered *nouveau riche*, as opposed to 'Old Money,' and as a consequence, certain doors have always been closed to us," Jennifer explained. "I have never been concerned about it, but it bothers Oliver terribly. He is socially ambitious, almost to the point of obsession. If I were to marry Bradley Ames, Oliver's elevation in the ranks of Society would be assured. My marriage to you will ruin his plans, and I fear he will not take it lightly."

"I don't give a damn about Oliver's plans." John reached out to push a strand of hair behind her ear. "His plans never seem to take your wishes or feelings into consideration." He frowned. "But this is the first I have heard of another suitor, Jennie. Why did you not tell me of him?"

"There is nothing to tell," Jennifer said firmly. "I said *Oliver* is hopeful of the match, not I. Bradley and I have done nothing more than dance." Her eyebrows raised. "Do not tell me you are jealous, John Cantrell."

"I am not jealous." John folded his arms over his chest. "But once we are wed, I will not allow you to dance with Mr. Ames again."

"Not ever?" Jennifer trailed her finger over his folded arms and down his stomach. She delighted in the feel of his warm skin, of the soft dark hairs covering that skin. His muscles quivered under her touch, giving her a heady sense of feminine power.

"Never."

"You *are* jealous." Her errant finger toyed with the folds of the sheet that covered his hips.

"Why would I be jealous of some Eastern dandy I will never meet?" His eyes followed the stealthy movement of her hand.

"But you will surely meet him when I take you to Philadelphia." Her hand slipped under the sheet to caress his hip.

"Why will you take me to Philadelphia?" John's voice was not as firm now.

"To introduce you to my friends, to finalize my business affairs, to collect my things. We must go back at least once." Jennifer allowed the part of the sheet she had been holding to her chest to fall. John stared at her breasts, the heat in his eyes alone causing her nipples to harden.

"We will go to Philadelphia once." He reached out to touch one pink tip.

Jennifer caught her breath. "And I cannot dance with Bradley?" she whispered.

John merely shook his head as he cupped the fullness of her breast in his hand, brushing his thumb across the taut nipple.

Suddenly very impatient, Jennifer jerked the sheet back

from his hips and watched in wonder as his manhood rose to greet her.

"You will dance only with me from now on, Jennifer Mainwaring." John grabbed her waist, guiding her until she straddled his legs. He pulled her forward so that she rested against him, her breasts pressed to his chest, his hardened length pressed to her stomach. His hands stroked her hair and back and hips as his mouth claimed hers with a possessive passion that took her breath away. His wandering fingers explored her waiting female warmth from behind, fondling and teasing until she moaned against his chest, thinking she would go mad with wanting him. At last, he ended the sweet torment by again grabbing her hips and lifting her. As he slowly lowered her, she was astonished to feel him fill her. She gazed into his burning blue eyes.

"You will dance only with me," he repeated.

"Only with you," she sighed, and gladly surrendered to the wonder he again showed her.

Jennifer awakened early the next morning. She lay on her side with John beside her, his arm around her middle, one leg thrown possessively over hers. The bedside lamp still gave off a faint glow, dimmed even more now by the sunlight touching the curtains at the window. She nestled against his warmth, revelling in the feeling of his naked body so intimately entwined with hers. A contented sigh escaped her slightly swollen lips; she could stay in his arms forever.

He stirred against her. Although she was loath to move, she rolled over to face him, brushing strands of her hair away from his face.

"Good morning," she whispered, and pressed a soft kiss to his lips.

"Good morning." He wrapped his arms around her and held her close.

"I should go." Jennifer had to force the words out.

John tightened his hold on her and mumbled something in dissent.

"You have to leave early to help with the herd, John. Preston will come looking for you." She kissed his stubble-roughened cheek. "As overjoyed as he may be to learn of our feelings for each other, I doubt he will approve of our putting the cart of passion before the horse of marriage."

At that, John raised an eyebrow and opened one eye. "The cart of passion before the horse of marriage?"

Jennifer shrugged apologetically.

He laughed then. "You are a delight, Jennifer Mainwaring." He kissed her mouth, exuberantly at first, then more tenderly. "And you are right. Off with you, woman, before I once more lose control of myself."

Even as he spoke the words, Jennifer could feel his manhood stirring against her thigh. A shiver of longing raced down her body. She reluctantly sat up. "When will we tell everyone?"

John sat up as well. He leaned across her legs to retrieve her shift from the floor. "I will talk to Preston this morning, while we are moving the herd." He shook out the wrinkled shift and helped Jennifer pull it over her head. "I will tell him of our plans, make sure we are truly welcome here, although I know we are, and ask for his help with Oliver. Can you wait until tonight to make the announcement to the rest of the family?"

Jennifer nodded. "I want everyone around me when we break the news to Oliver." She pulled her hair from between her back and the shift and began to close the row of buttons.

"I hate to see you cover yourself," John said mournfully.

With a smile, Jennifer slipped from the bed, pushing the garment down over her hips. "I cannot very well run around naked, John Cantrell." She crossed the small room to collect her wrapper from the floor, grateful now that she had brought it with her. As she tied the belt at her waist, she faced him, and her breath caught. His dark, tousled hair and stubble-covered cheeks combined to make his blue, love-filled eyes all the more striking in the early morning light. The wonder of the knowledge that this beautiful man was hers, that he wanted her, loved her, filled Jennifer's heart. Tears of happiness gathered in her eyes.

"What is it?" John asked, suddenly concerned.

Shaking her head, she hurried to his side. "Nothing." She placed her hands on his shoulders. "My two dearest friends in the world live in Wyoming; on our way to Philadelphia, we must stop there. You must meet Susannah and Alina."

John wrapped his arms around her waist and looked up at her, a quizzical expression on his face. "That is what brought tears to your eyes?"

"No," she said softly. "I visited them in July, on the way out here, and attended Susannah's marriage to Conor O'Rourke. Both she and Alina advised me not to marry until I found a man who could make me glow." She cupped her hands on his cheeks and stared into his eyes. "I have found him."

John was silent for a moment, then he pressed his face to her breasts. She held him to her, her fingers stroking his hair.

"Te amo," he said quietly. He raised his head.

"I love you, too."

With sweet longing, with reverence, with love, their lips met, held, caressed. Finally, she pulled away from him, breathless again. "I must go," she whispered.

"I know." He took her hand.

She backed up until their arms were stretched between them, connected only by grasping fingers.

"Do not worry about Oliver, Jennie. He cannot hurt you, or force you to leave. We will face him together."

Jennifer nodded. With one final squeeze of her fingers, she released him. "I will see you at breakfast." She unbolted and opened the door, glanced quickly about the courtyard, and slipped outside.

John watched as she blew him a kiss just before she closed

the door. It seemed some of the light had gone out of the room with her departure, and not because the closed door blocked the sunlight. He looked down at the pillow where her head had rested, at the sheets where her sweet body had lain, had opened to him. He saw the small stain of her virgin's blood, and was struck with the magnitude and value of the gift she had given him. Like her body, her heart had opened to him, and he treasured her beyond all else in his life. His hand absent-mindedly caressed the rumpled sheets. He hoped they could marry soon; he did not relish the idea of sleeping without her.

Jennifer bathed quickly. She hoped to be back in her own room before anyone knew she was gone, but the bath would offer her an excuse if Brigit or Oliver found her missing. The unfamiliar soreness between her legs both surprised and thrilled her. John had truly claimed her; she was his woman now, and proud of it. A thrill ran through her at the memory of the pleasures they had shared throughout the long, wonderful night. She had left his bed not twenty minutes earlier, and already she hungered for his touch.

A knock sounded on the bathing room door. "Yes?" she called.

"I'm glad I knocked rather than just bounded in." Preston's muffled voice came through the door.

Jennifer smiled. "I am nearly finished, Preston. I will be right out." She pulled the cork in the bottom of the tub, stepped out of the comforting warmth of the water, and quickly toweled herself off. As she again donned the wrinkled shift and robe, she hoped no one would notice the curious condition of the garments. She opened the door to find Preston waiting.

"You're up early," he commented with an affectionate smile.

"Yes, I am." Jennifer spoke softly, but she could not keep a happy grin from her face.

Preston stared at her. "What is it, honey? What's happened?"

Was it that obvious? Jennifer wondered. Did she truly glow, as Susannah had before her marriage to Conor? "What do you mean?" she asked evasively.

"I don't think I've ever seen you so happy."

Jennifer hesitated, then said, "Perhaps because I have never been this happy."

"Will you tell me about it?"

She shyly shook her head. "But John will, and soon."

A great joy flared in Preston's eyes, blue eyes so like his son's. He nodded in satisfaction and held his arms out. Jennifer went to him. They held each other tightly.

"I have always loved you as a daughter, Jennie."

"I know." For the second time that morning, Jennifer's eyes teared. "And I love you as a father." She stood on tiptoe and kissed his cheek, then hurried away.

A short time later, Jennifer stood at the huge cast-iron stove, deftly flipping pieces of sizzling side pork. She had dressed quickly and simply in a black skirt and a white cotton waist with long sleeves and a slightly scooped neckline. Her hair was pulled back into a plain chignon, and a clean white apron was tied at her waist. The happy chatter of the Cantrell clan flowed around her, seeming even more special this morning because she knew she would never have to leave. Her cheeks had begun to ache from smiling so much.

She glanced over at the wooden box on the floor. As she watched, Katie succeeded in scrambling over the top. The kitten plopped to the floor, picked herself up, and began to explore while her brother mewed loudly, demanding his release from the box. Jennifer bent down and scooped Katie up.

"Back you go for now, little one," Jennifer said affectionately as she returned the fluffy kitten to the box. "I'll take you out later for some playtime and a lesson with the saucer."

She turned back to the stove just as John came in the outside door with a look of sated contentment on his handsome, freshly shaved face. His eyes lit up when he saw her. He came straight to her, snaking an arm around her waist from behind, and bent to nuzzle her neck. His hair was damp, and he smelled of soap. She leaned against him with a happy sigh.

"Good morning again," he whispered for her ears only. The feel of his breath on her sensitive skin caused her to shiver in delight.

Jennifer was suddenly aware that the noise level in the big kitchen had dropped dramatically. She glanced back over her shoulder, and John turned in the same direction, not taking his hand from her waist.

With the exception of Preston, David, and Molly, everyone seated at the table gaped at them. Only the two children continued eating, chattering quietly to each other. Preston wore a small, knowing smile.

"What are you all staring at?" John demanded good-naturedly. "Can't a man get a cup of coffee without causing a scene?" He reached around Jennifer to snatch the big, blackened coffeepot off the back burner. As he pulled away from her, his hand slid down from her waist to give her bottom an affectionate pat. Jennifer blushed, although she knew no one could have seen what he'd done, and returned her attention to the sizzling pan. John grabbed a cup on his way to the table. He filled it, then held up the pot with a questioning look.

Bill lifted his cup in response. As John circled the table to fill it, Bill asked, "Is there anything you and Jennie want to tell us, big brother?"

"Not until I talk to Preston," John answered. He refused to say another word, although the room was suddenly ringing with questions.

Jennifer kept quiet as well. She brought a plate heaped with crispy pork to the table and took her seat next to John. Finally they were successful in turning the conversation to more neutral topics.

The meal was finished and the children, their faces and hands freshly washed, played with the kittens. The adults were lingering over their coffee when Oliver pushed through the swinging door from the dining room. The irritated look on his face quieted everyone.

"Good morning, Oliver," Jennifer said quickly.

"No one brought my tray," Oliver snapped.

"The family has a habit of eating breakfast together, here," Preston said. His voice was calm, but his tone held an underlying edge of steel. "You are welcome to join us, or I will send Brigit up with a tray when we are finished."

Oliver stiffened. "A tray would be nice," he said frostily. "With coffee, bread, and fruit." He hesitated, then continued with heavy sarcasm. "When it is convenient, of course."

"When it is convenient," Preston agreed.

With an affronted toss of his head, Oliver pushed back through the door.

The easy mood of the morning was gone. When the door stopped swinging, Bill stood up. "We've got a herd to move. We'd best get at it." He drained his cup, then headed toward the back door.

"I'll meet you on the veranda with your noon meal," Barbara called after him.

He smiled at her over his shoulder. "Give us a few minutes to get saddled up."

"In a few minutes, then."

"Me and Molly will meet you on the v'randa, too, Papa," David announced.

"All right, son." Bill grinned at David, then left, followed closely by Gabe and Preston. John swung his legs over the bench and stood, offering his hand to Jennifer. When she stood up, he pulled her close.

"Will you fix me a meal to take?"

She smiled shyly up at him. "I'd be happy to."

"Thank you."

He winked at her, then trailed the rest of the men out the

door. Jennifer watched him go, a wild happiness singing in her heart. As she began to clear the table, Barbara, Rosa, and Brigit eyed her curiously, but no one said anything.

A short time later, the women and children gathered on the front veranda to see the men off. Most of the cowhands were already on their way out of the yard. Rosa and Francisca waved to Gabe as he left. Bill pulled up in the surrey, then nimbly jumped down and came to where Barbara stood with Molly astride her hip.

"Thank you for hitching the team for us," she said as Bill kissed their daughter's cheek. Molly cooed happily.

"How long do you think you'll be in town?" Bill asked. He accepted the cloth-wrapped bundle of food David held up to him and packed it in his saddlebag, then scooped his son up into his arms.

"Most of the day, I think. We'll be back by supper."

"We should be back about the same time. Will that be all right with you, Pard?" he asked David.

"Sure." David nodded vigorously. "Me and Molly is goin' to town with Mama and Aunt Rosa and 'Cisca and Br'git. Aunt Jennie won't come 'cause she hasta take care of the kitties."

Both Bill and Barbara smiled at David's informative discourse. Barbara turned to Jennifer. "Are you sure you won't come with us, Jennie?"

Jennifer shook her head. "Thank you, but I have things to do here—letters to write and, as David pointed out, kittens to watch."

"Well, I'd best be going." Bill planted a noisy kiss on David's cheek, which sent the little boy into fits of laughter. "Papa!"

Bill lowered David until the boy stood on the veranda. He kissed Barbara tenderly, stroked Molly's cheek, then vaulted into the saddle without using the stirrup.

"See you tonight, Jennie." He turned to Preston. "Where is John?"

Preston shrugged. "He'll be along."

At that moment, John cantered across the yard from the corral to the veranda. Jennifer watched him approach. His long legs were encased in his work denims and covered with protective leather chaps, and he wore a clean white shirt with a black vest and a blue neckerchief that brought out the already incredible blue of his eyes. His black hat and his gunbelt completed his ensemble. When he pulled back on the reins, the excited stallion danced to a reluctant stop not far from her.

"Let's go," Preston said.

"I'll be along directly," John answered. He had eyes only for Jennifer.

Bill winked at Preston and jerked his head in the direction of the gate.

"Catch up to us," Preston ordered with a smile. He and Bill guided their horses out of the yard.

Jennifer stepped up to the edge of the veranda, clutching John's dinner in her hands.

"Rosa, I think we'd best go in," Barbara said as she gently pushed David toward the door. "We have our own day to prepare for."

With a broad smile, Rosa herded Francisca and Brigit after Barbara.

Jennie stared up into John's eyes. "I made your dinner," she said shyly. "It's not fancy, but it will fill you." She held the bundle out to him.

"Thank you." John took the bundle from her and stuffed it into his saddlebag. His eyes never left her face.

"I shall count the hours until you return," she blurted out.

At that, John urged Diamante alongside the veranda. He leaned out of the saddle and reached for her, catching her around the waist with one strong arm, pulling her up against him.

Jennifer gasped in surprise and wrapped her arms around his neck.

"As shall I," he whispered before he took her mouth in a hot, urgent kiss.

Her blood drumming through her body, Jennifer slanted her lips across his to give him easier access. When they finally separated, she was again breathless. It pleased her to notice that John's breathing was not exactly calm.

"Talk to Preston," she instructed. "I shall expect a very short betrothal period."

"I promise." John's eyes burned into her. After one final, quick kiss, he carefully set her back down.

He turned Diamante's head and urged him to a gallop. When John passed under the gate arch, he looked back at her and lifted his hat in a gesture of farewell.

Jennifer waved in return and watched until the dust from Diamante's hooves settled back to the earth. Only then did she turn into the house, with a secret, happy smile on her lips.

Oliver stood at the window of Preston's study, peering around the edge of the curtain. His brows were drawn together in an angry, worried frown. At first, his displeasure had been caused by the lukewarm coffee that Irish twit of a maid had brought him, and he had marched to the kitchen, filled with righteous indignation. But he had found no one there. In his search of the lower floor, he had ended up in Preston's study and heard the commotion on the veranda. He had watched the leave-taking of the men, down to the bitter end.

Oliver turned from the window, deep in thought. He had obviously stayed away from the Santa Maria far too long. Never would he have imagined that Jennifer might form an attachment for John Cantrell. Once, she had despised the man! But she obviously no longer did. How far had things gone between them?

He paced the room. Jennifer had grown much too independent, if not downright belligerent, over the past two months. No doubt she would refuse to answer any questions about her relationship with the Mexican bastard. But he had to know the depth of her feelings! Too much was at risk. Where could he get the answers he needed? No one at the Santa Maria would help him, of that he was certain.

Oliver halted, a sly smile twisting his lips. *Constanza.* Surely she would know something, and surely she could be persuaded to tell him. He would leave for the Buena Ventura immediately, providing someone was left at the Santa Maria who could saddle a horse for him.

Eighteen

"How dare you keep me waiting?" Oliver demanded when Constanza finally entered Alejandro's study. He was not in a good mood. As he had feared, all of the men at the Santa Maria were out with the herd. He had been forced to saddle his own horse, and the sorry nag had made the job difficult indeed. Then, for a half an hour, Constanza had left him cooling his heels in her father's study, of all places, rather than the formal parlor, as was proper for guests. Nor had she provided him with any refreshment. Now she had the temerity to waltz up the two steps into the room as if nothing were amiss. He fought the urge to cross the room and shake the irritating smile from her face.

"My dear Oliver, how impatient you are!" Constanza scolded him, pointing her folded fan at him. She wore a more simple gown than usual today, one of pale blue muslin, and no bustle. The lace mantilla was conspicuously absent from her free-falling hair.

"I have important things to discuss with you, and you abandon me here in the study for an odious length of time! You are very rude, Constanza."

"Yes, I am. I am also very selfish. You should know that by now." She nonchalantly waved her hand. "I had you shown here because my father and brother are away, and this room offers the most privacy, especially when the doors are closed." She demonstrated by pushing the double doors until they latched shut. "Unless you wish the servants to hear what you have to say." She turned and leaned against the wood, eyeing him.

"Well, no—" Oliver began somewhat sheepishly.

"However, I kept you waiting because it pleased me to do so." Constanza arched an arrogant eyebrow and stared at him, a haughty challenge in her brown eyes. "It pleased me to know you were waiting, because I knew it would infuriate you."

"You bitch! By God, you will not start these games again, not with me." Oliver strode toward her. "I warned you in San Francisco that I would not tolerate your ill-treatment." He grabbed her arm in a tight hold and pulled her around the desk.

Constanza screeched in outrage and swatted at his head with her fan. Oliver wrenched the fan from her grasp, tossing it to the floor.

"I will teach you some manners, Miss Noriega." He dropped into Alejandro's large chair and jerked the struggling Constanza across his knees, face down.

"Bestia! Bastardo!" she shrieked. Her long hair fell forward to the floor, covering her face.

"I may be a beast on occasion, but John Cantrell is the bastard," Oliver ground out. He worked through layers of skirt and petticoats, shoving the material up over her back. When nothing but her silk drawers covered her rounded buttocks, his hand landed on her with a loud, resounding slap.

He ignored her cry of pain and outrage. Constanza struggled violently against him, to no avail. Again and again his hand descended, eliciting an enraged response from Constanza each time.

"You will not treat me as you do your other lackeys," Oliver said through clenched teeth. "Do you understand?"

Constanza's answer was a foul word.

Oliver slapped her again. She moaned this time. "Do you understand?" he repeated.

She ceased her struggles. "Yes," she whispered as she wiggled her hips suggestively against his thighs. One of her hands caressed his calf.

He looked down at her for a moment, disgust twisting his features, then jerked her skirts back into place. He stood and lifted her from his lap to sit her on the edge of the desk so that she faced him.

Constanza threw her wild hair back over her shoulders and stared at him with passion-glazed eyes. The pink tip of her tongue ran over her lips in blatant invitation.

"There is no time for that," Oliver snapped. "Apparently my foolish niece has developed an affection for John Cantrell. I need to know how serious it is."

Suddenly all business, Constanza narrowed her eyes. "What has happened?" she demanded.

He described the scene he had witnessed from Preston's study that morning.

"Maldición!" Constanza jumped off the desk to pace the floor. "I knew it! I warned her to stay away from him!"

"It was serious enough that you warned her away from him?" Oliver asked in alarm. "Is that why you struck her with the bookend?"

Constanza waved impatiently. "I meant to hit Juan. She got in the way. That is not important now."

"But how far has it gone?" Oliver repeated. "Are they speaking of marriage?"

With an unladylike snort, Constanza whirled to face him. "Juan Novales will never marry a *gringa!* But he will seduce her, if he has not already."

Oliver paled. "No."

"Sí! If you want her precious virginity intact so you can marry her off to the highest bidder, you'd best get her away from here. But I tell you, it could already be too late."

"Surely he would not seduce her under his father's roof. Preston would not allow it." Oliver ran a hand through his hair.

Constanza gave a harsh laugh and crossed her arms over her chest. *"Imbécil!* Preston would never know! But if Juan did seduce Jennifer, it will comfort you to know he will not seek out her thin, stiff body again. He was merely taking his revenge against the *gringos* who have cheated him of his rightful heritage. Years ago when he and I were in *Ciudad de Mexico,* I saw him do just that many times over."

Oliver stared at her. "What do you mean?"

She began to circle him. "Juan Novales was not just an ordinary agent for the *Juaristas,* as he would have everyone believe. Juarez gave him the mission of learning military secrets and bestowed upon him the code name of *El Lobo.* Juan gave himself another mission, just as the French and Mexican officials in power at the time bestowed upon him another name. They called him *La Serpiente,* the Serpent. And do you know why?"

Constanza's eyes glittered. Oliver waited with morbid fascination for her to continue, fearing he would not like what she had to say.

"The French invaders took our country from the traitorous Assembly, who handed Mexico over to them. Juan could not tolerate that. They had to be punished, traitor and invader alike. If it helped the Revolution, so much the better." She shrugged dramatically. *"La Serpiente* could penetrate any bastion, be it a guarded villa, a locked bedchamber, or a lady's undergarments. Like a serpent, he eased his way into the beds of the wives and daughters of those he sought to punish. He took their women for his own pleasure."

"He raped them?" Oliver gasped.

"Oh, no. That was the beauty of it. It was not necessary for him to rape." Constanza's mouth twisted in a strange smile. "They gave themselves to him, gladly."

Oliver eyed her with suspicion. "How do you know so much of this?"

"I gave myself to him, gladly."

"Wh-what?" Oliver choked out. "You could have been no more than a girl!"

She nodded. "I was young, and innocent. He was handsome, and so intriguing. I could not resist his charm." Her expression softened with regret.

"The bastard! If he tried the same thing with Jennifer—"

"If he did seduce her, Oliver, she went willingly."

"Never." Oliver shook his head. "Jennifer would never compromise herself in such a manner."

"Believe what you like." Constanza shrugged and turned away. "If he has had her, you will, of course, have to insist that they marry."

"Never!" Oliver repeated, with more vehemence.

Constanza continued as if he had not spoken. "But how will you feel with your dear niece married to an assassin?"

Oliver gaped at her. "An assassin?"

"La Serpiente took the women first." Constanza faced him again, moving closer. "Then he killed the men, those traitors and invaders, all in the same manner—a knife wound where the neck joins the skull." She was close enough to reach out and touch the back of his neck. Her fingers played in his hair. "Right here," she whispered. "Death came quickly."

Oliver shivered and stepped away from her.

"The officials searched for the assassin for years, but they never discovered the true identity of *La Serpiente*. While the Mexicans now regard him as something of a hero, the French still have a price on his head."

"How do you know all this?" Oliver demanded.

Constanza settled herself on the sofa. "Like Juan, I am a fervent Mexican patriot, and I also worked as an agent for the *Juaristas*. And I was his lover—it was not difficult to learn of his other . . . duties." She looked up at him, her eyebrows lifted in mockery. "Men are very boastful in bed."

"I must get Jennifer away from him, away from the Santa Maria, before she and that bastard ruin everything." Oliver bolted for the double doors.

"When? How?"

"Today. By force if necessary." He paused with his hand on the latch and turned to her. "Jennifer is alone. The women and children have gone to town, and the men are out all day herding cattle." His lip curled in derision at the last two words. "You must come with me, Constanza. I want you there when I tell her this tale, for Jennifer will never believe me. Also, bring me a rider at once— it is imperative that I get a message to my companions at the Gilroy Hotel."

Constanza merely looked at him.

"Well? Why do you tarry? I must have Jennifer on the afternoon train to San José!" Without waiting for her response, he jerked one of the doors open and stormed down the steps to the hall, shouting for his horse.

A cruel, triumphant smile twisted Constanza's lips. *"Sí, Oliver dear,"* she whispered as she stood. "Whatever you say."

John guided Diamante up a small rise. Preston, astride his horse, was at the top, overlooking the roundup.

"May I speak with you?" John asked as he pulled Diamante to a stop at Preston's side.

"I've been waiting for you," Preston answered. He crossed his arms over the saddle horn and leaned forward, his sharp gaze on John's face. "What's on your mind?"

"Jennie."

"I suspected as much. She told me you would be talking to me."

"Did she tell you why?"

"No. She said she couldn't, that you would. But I have my suspicions. I've never seen her so happy." He squinted against the bright sunlight as he studied John. "In fact, you look pretty damn happy yourself."

John smiled. "I've asked her to marry me, Preston. We'd like your blessing, and we'd like to make our home with you, here on the Santa Maria."

Preston straightened, and his mouth widened into a broad grin. "Nothing could make me happier, son." He held out his hand, which John gladly took. A wealth of emotion passed between the two men, with no need for words. When they dropped hands, Preston said, "Your brother will be pleased, John. Everyone will."

"Everyone except Oliver." John lifted his hat and wiped the sweat from his forehead. "Jennie is worried about him."

"He can't do anything," Preston said flatly.

John adjusted his hat. "I told her that. Still, she wants us with her when she tells him."

"We'll be there."

"I have some money, and I'd like to invest it in the Santa Maria." He held up his hand to keep Preston from protesting. "I know, I know. You're going to say it isn't necessary. You and Bill have already offered to give me full partnership, but I'd like to buy in. Jennie and I have discussed it. She wants to contribute, too. There is much we could do with an influx of cash—purchase some new equipment, buy more breeding stock, replace some of the fence, maybe even get gas piped out to the house."

Preston nodded thoughtfully. "It would be nice to do some of that." He started his horse down the rise.

John rode at his side. "Jennie is expecting a statement of her financial assets from her solicitor any day now and would like us to go over it with her when it comes. She requested it weeks ago, when she decided that she didn't want to return to Philadelphia. She was going to ask you if she could make the Santa Maria her home."

A satisfied smile curved Preston's lips. "I told her I love her like a daughter, John. I would have hated to see her leave, just as I hated to see her leave when Albert took her back East all those years ago. And that the two of you have come to love each other—it's more than I should have hoped for, but I did." He looked at John. "Let's tell your brother."

"All right," John agreed. "I'd like him to stand up with me."

They urged their mounts to a gallop.

* * *

"No, Jake, don't walk in it!" Jennifer laughed as she plucked the kitten from the saucer of cream and set him on the floor. He shook his little paw, then licked it. "That's the idea," she said encouragingly. "Lick it." Katie had learned the lesson quicker than her brother. She was cautiously lapping at the cream, her legs neatly folded under her.

The house seemed very quiet to Jennifer. The men were out with the herd, Barbara, Rosa, Brigit, and the children had left for town over an hour ago, and Oliver had gone for a ride. It felt strange to be completely alone.

Even as she thought the words, the sound of an approaching horse reached her ears. At first, she assumed it was Oliver returning from his ride, but after a moment, someone pounded on the front door.

Jennifer plopped the kittens into their box and hurried through the dining room to open the door. An unfamiliar young man stood there with a tied bundle in his hand. He whipped his hat off when he saw her.

"Howdy, ma'am. I'm Gus Howard from the Henderson ranch up north. I just come from town and figured I'd drop off the mail for the Santa Maria." He held out the bundle.

"Why, thank you, Mr. Howard. How thoughtful." Jennifer accepted the bundle. "Would you like some refreshment before you continue your journey?"

"No, but thanks, ma'am. I'd best be on my way. Mr. Henderson is waiting for his mail." He put his hat back on and tugged at the brim, then climbed into the saddle. "Good day to you."

"Thank you again!" Jennifer waved as he rode under the archway. He held up a hand in response and was gone.

Jennifer turned back into the house and took the bundle to Preston's study. After cutting the string with a letter knife, she sifted through the collection of letters, newspapers and packets, dividing them into appropriate piles. Most were for Preston, but one was for Bill, and one letter was labeled to Juan Novales, with a return address of *Ciudad de Mexico*. At the very bottom of the bundle was a thick packet addressed to Jennifer, bearing the name of Elias Craig in the upper left-hand corner.

"At last," she whispered excitedly. She used the letter knife to open the packet, then sat in Preston's chair, smoothing the folded sheets of paper flat. As she read the letter on top, the smile faded from her face, and her heart began to pound.

"Sept. 14, 1873

"My dear Miss Mainwaring,

"With personal shock and deepest regret, I must inform you that your financial situation is dire. For the last year, Mr. Lawrence Atwater, your uncle's solicitor, and Mr. Harold Smythe, your uncle's accountant, have been assuring me all is well, and I, having had no reason in the past to doubt either man, took each at his word. Your request for a full report of your situation is all that prompted me to insist that Mr. Smythe turn over the account ledgers for my study.

"I was horrified to discover that over the last few years, Mr. Oliver Mainwaring has evidently made several ill-advised investments, many on the West Coast, that have resulted in huge losses. As he has power of attorney to act on your behalf in financial matters, he has been free to deplete your share of your father's estate. He has gone as far as to put up your Philadelphia home as collateral against loans he took in an attempt to cover some of those losses. Debts are mounting, creditors are demanding payment, the loans are being called in, and I fear your uncle, and possibly you, may be facing bankruptcy. I have enclosed supporting documentation for your inspection.

"Happily, the trust left to you by your dear mother has been kept safe from Mr. Mainwaring's grasping fingers, and those funds remain available to you. I urge you

and Mr. Mainwaring to return to Philadelphia with all
possible speed. The situation is grave.

"As I did not insist upon more periodic and detailed
reports from Messrs. Atwater and Smythe, I fear I bear
some of the responsibility for this situation. Please accept my sincere apologies, Miss Mainwaring.

"Upon your return to Philadelphia, notify me at once.
I place myself at your disposal to assist you in any manner I can. I remain, truly yours,

"Elias Craig, Esq."

Jennifer fell against the back of the chair, her eyes wide
with shock. What had Oliver done to her, to himself? Elias
Craig's letter made it sound as if her father's entire fortune
were gone, as if *her* entire fortune were gone, with the exception of her mother's trust. How could that be? Surely there
had to be some mistake. John would go with her to Philadelphia, and together they would get to the bottom of the matter.

They had to marry immediately, for they could not travel
together unmarried, and leave at once for the East. Then a
terrifying thought occurred to Jennifer. If John married her,
and it turned out that she was indeed bankrupt, he, as her
husband, would be liable for any debts the court determined
were her responsibility. She could not do that to him.

She leaned forward and buried her face in her propped
hands. Why had she not insisted Oliver relinquish power of
attorney the day she reached her majority? Why had she not
asked for a financial report years ago? *Because young women
are not meant to worry their pretty little heads about such
matters.* Even now, she could hear Oliver's condescending
tone when he had refused to answer her questions. And she,
fool that she was, had let the matter drop, time and again. A
moan of despair escaped her dry lips.

The clamor of approaching horses reached her ears. Her
heart leapt with hope; perhaps John had come home early.

She rose from the chair. A moment later, the front door was flung open with enough force to slam it against the wall.

"Jennifer!"

At the sound of Oliver's angry voice, Jennifer quickly folded the pages from Elias Craig and slipped them into Preston's stack of mail. She saw her uncle stride past the open door of the study, heard him start up the stairs.

"Jennifer, where the hell are you?"

She came around the desk and moved to the door, reaching the portal just as Constanza did. Jennifer stopped in surprise. The smirking smile on Constanza's face caused her stomach to knot.

"She is here, Oliver!" Constanza called without taking her eyes from Jennifer.

Oliver appeared at the top of the stairs. "Come up here at once, Jennifer. You must pack, and quickly. The carriage will be here any moment."

Jennifer pushed past Constanza. "What are you talking about?" she demanded as she moved into the foyer.

"We have a train to catch!" Oliver shouted impatiently.

"I am not going anywhere with you." Jennifer's voice rang with defiance.

"I will pack her things." Constanza shoved past her and hurried up the stairs.

"The last room on the right," Oliver instructed as he pointed Constanza down the hall.

"You will not touch my things!" Jennifer shouted, and raced after Constanza, holding her skirts high. Oliver grabbed her arm in a painful grip when she topped the stairs, jerking her to a halt.

"If you will not pack yourself, Constanza will do it for you. You will not hinder her."

The fury in Oliver's eyes gave Jennifer her first tremor of fear. She tried to pull away from him. "You're hurting me, Oliver."

Rather than loosening his hold on her, he started down the hall, dragging her with him.

"Why are you so desperate to leave?" she pleaded.

Oliver shoved her into her room, where Constanza had pulled garments from the wardrobe and was stuffing them into the trunk that already held most of the clothes Jennifer had brought from Philadelphia.

"This will not take long," Constanza said cheerfully. "Many of her things were in the trunk. It is mostly these peasant clothes that remain to be packed."

"Leave them," Oliver growled. "She will not wear them again." Finally he released Jennifer, pushing her away.

She rounded on him. "What has happened?" she demanded, rubbing her arm. "Why are you determined to leave in such a hurry?"

"You tell me what has happened." Oliver glared at her. "You tell me, dear niece, how far things have gone between you and that Mexican bastard."

Without conscious thought, Jennifer slapped Oliver full across the face. "I told you never to refer to him in that term again. I won't have it. Nor will I tolerate any more of your bullying and manhandling."

Oliver stared at her, shocked into silence, his hand coming up to his reddening cheek. Constanza straightened from her task and watched with undisguised glee.

Jennifer shook with anger; her hands were clenched in fists at her sides. "Go wherever you wish, uncle. I'll not go with you. And in answer to your question regarding my relationship with John, that is none of your business." She looked at Constanza and pointed a finger. "You get away from my things. Get out of my room. Both of you!"

With a furious roar, Oliver grabbed her arm with one hand and viciously struck her across the face with the other. The force of the blow knocked Jennifer against the bed. She crumpled to the floor, stunned, as pain exploded along her jaw and through her head. Her vision blurred for a moment, and she tasted blood. Her disbelieving mind whirled with the realization that her uncle had actually assaulted her.

Oliver seized Jennifer, jerking her to her feet. "I'll not allow you to ruin everything by throwing yourself away on a bastard like John Cantrell," he warned, his voice fairly crackling with anger. "The man is a seducer, a spy, an assassin."

Jennifer pulled away from his grasp and sank onto the edge of the bed. "You are wrong," she spat, touching her tender lip. She glanced at her fingertip, not surprised to see blood. "Constanza has filled your head with her vicious lies, and you are too stupid to see through her. She is evil. I warned you to watch your back."

"Ask her about *La Serpiente,* Jennifer. Ask her about the assassin still sought by the French government for the murder of their officials in Mexico City during Maximilian's reign." Oliver imperiously crossed his arms over his chest.

Fresh anger surged through Jennifer. "Constanza would lie about the color of the sky if it suited her," she snapped, ignoring Constanza's gasp of outrage. "John has told me all about his life in *Ciudad de Mexico.* He was an agent known as *El Lobo,* and his mission was to seek military information. He was not an assassin."

Oliver nodded in satisfaction. "Constanza told me John would tell you that. Of course he did not reveal that he also coldly and deliberately seduced the wives and daughters of the men he later killed. Nor would he tell you that he intends to seduce you in order to get even with Preston for robbing him of his birthright, if the bastard hasn't done so already."

Jennifer stood up. "I will listen to no more of this," she said firmly.

"Hello? Hello!" An unfamiliar male voice called from down the hall.

"Ah, good. The carriage has arrived." Oliver went to the door. "In here, gentlemen." He stood back to allow two men to enter.

One was tall and heavyset, wearing ill-fitting clothes, his

narrow eyes almost hidden in the puffy flesh above an unkempt beard. The other was of average height and build, well-dressed, his dark hair slicked down with an abundance of cloyingly scented hair oil. Even though the tall one was clearly a brute, Jennifer sensed that the other man was more dangerous. She could see the cruel intelligence in his black eyes. With a shudder, she took a small, involuntary step backward.

Oliver pointed first to the shorter man, then to the tall one. "Mr. Hayward Creed and Mr. Otto Rutherford." He waved at Jennifer and Constanza. "My niece Jennifer and my dear friend Miss Noriega."

Both men nodded once. Neither woman said anything.

Oliver pointed at Rutherford. "My room is across the hall. Start packing my things." Rutherford nodded and left. Oliver looked at Creed. "Did you bring what I asked?"

At the man's silent nod, Oliver faced Jennifer with a pleased smile. "You will do as I instruct, Jennifer."

"I will not." Jennifer marched to Constanza's side and ripped her hairbrush from the woman's grasp. "I told you not to touch my things. Now get out of here." She pushed Constanza away from the trunk and toward Oliver.

With a snarl, Constanza whirled back toward Jennifer, her face flushed with fury, her hands up in position to strike. "You will not push me, Jennifer Mainwaring."

Oliver grabbed Constanza's arm, shaking his head at her. He motioned her back.

"For the last time, Jennifer, I am telling you to finish packing. We must be on the afternoon train to San José."

"For the last time, Oliver," Jennifer said in sarcastic mimicry, "I'll not go anywhere with you." She bent down to pull a skirt from the trunk.

"Yes, you will."

Jennifer glared at him as she shook out the skirt. "You cannot force me. Now please leave my room and take your friends with you." She turned to the wardrobe, speaking over her shoulder. "Have a safe journey. John and I will no doubt see you in Philadelphia before too long, for we have certain business matters there that require our attention."

Keeping his eyes on Jennifer, Oliver motioned Creed forward with two fingers. Creed came to his side, a small glass bottle in one hand and a cloth in the other. Oliver nodded. Creed pulled the cork from the bottle and saturated a section of the cloth, then replaced the cork and handed Oliver the bottle.

"I can force you, Jennifer."

Something in Oliver's tone sent a chill down Jennifer's back. As she turned toward him, a strong arm wrapped around her throat and the reek of Hayward Creed's hair oil filled her nostrils. She cried out and struggled against her attacker, grabbing at his arm, trying to kick him. A damp cloth was pressed to her nose and mouth. Clawing at the hand that held the cloth, Jennifer jerked her head, desperate to escape the new, nauseating smell, but she could not get away. She held her breath as long as she could, then was forced to breathe. The strength drained from her limbs.

"John," she whispered against the cloth. The darkness closed in and claimed her.

Oliver watched dispassionately as Hayward Creed lowered Jennifer's limp form to the floor. "How long will she remain unconscious?" he asked as he returned the bottle to Creed.

Creed placed the bottle in his inside coat pocket and shrugged. "Hard to say. As slender as she is, maybe thirty minutes, maybe a little more. Chloroform don't last all that long. You have to keep giving it."

"Well, keep it handy. She has forced us to resort to abduction, and we can't afford any public scenes that may draw the attention of the authorities."

"You have to be careful with chloroform, Mr. Mainwaring. Too much will kill her."

"*You* have to be careful, Mr. Creed. If you kill her, I will see you hanged. Now help Rutherford finish packing my things."

"Yes, sir." Creed carefully wrapped the cloth in a piece of oilskin and put it in his hip pocket, then, after pausing briefly at the door to glare back at Oliver, made his way from the room.

"Somewhere she has a black mantle that will match this skirt, Constanza. Find it and help me get her into it. She cannot appear to have been pulled from her housework." Oliver's face twisted into a disgusted expression as he untied the apron at Jennifer's waist.

Constanza found the wrap, and together they maneuvered Jennifer's arms into the sleeves. Constanza closed the clasps down the front while Oliver pulled a black hat with a face veil from the top shelf of the wardrobe.

"This will help," he murmured. "And these." He tossed a pair of black gloves in Constanza's direction. "Get them on her while I go check on those two dolts." He left the room without a backward glance.

Swearing under her breath, Constanza did as he instructed.

A few minutes later, Rutherford carried the unconscious Jennifer down to the depot wagon they had borrowed from the hotel and deposited her in the enclosed rear seat, leaning her against the corner of the interior. One trunk was lashed to the boot, the other forced inside under Jennifer's legs. Her satchel was placed on her lap.

Creed took the reins, and Rutherford finally clambered up next to him, clutching Oliver's satchel.

From his position near the wagon, Oliver turned to Constanza, who waited on the veranda. "Straighten Jennifer's room so there is no evidence she was forced to leave," he ordered, ignoring Costanza's sudden scowl. "What explanation will you give for our disappearance?"

"I will tell Juan Novales how Jennifer danced with joy when you informed her that it was time to return to Philadelphia," she said petulantly. "I will tell him how she begged to leave today so that she would not have to tolerate this place and his unwelcome attentions one more day." Her scowl changed to a smile of smug confidence. "I will tell him she is the cold-hearted *ramera* I always knew her to be."

Oliver frowned. "He will not believe you. I saw their impassioned farewell this morning. He will never believe her feelings changed so quickly."

Her eyes narrowed in anger. "I will *make* him believe me."

"You'd better. I don't want John Cantrell coming after us."

"I will give him reason to stay." Constanza's angry expression faded to one of sultry invitation. "Do not doubt me in that, Oliver. You yourself know how good I can be. Juan will soon forget your skinny little niece."

"I hope so," he snapped, "for all our sakes."

Constanza stepped closer to him, reaching out to run her finger along his lapel. "Trust me," she whispered, then launched herself into his arms. "It is a shame Philadelphia is so far away. I would enjoy more time with you, like that we shared in San Francisco." She opened her mouth for him as he lowered his lips to hers. The kiss was long and deep, then Oliver pulled her arms from his neck.

"I must go." He turned and climbed into the wagon. As he reached for the door, he said, "Buy me some time, Constanza. Keep Cantrell off my trail for a while. When we reach San José, I will notify the authorities that *La Serpiente* can be found here. I am certain the French Embassy in San Francisco will be very interested to learn of his whereabouts."

In a flash, Constanza was at his side, jerking the door from his grasp. She clutched at his coat. "You will not," she hissed. Her eyes blazed with rage. "Juan Novales belongs to me. If you turn him in, I will find you, and I will kill you. Juan is essential to my plans, and you will not interfere."

Oliver's lips tightened. Her words infuriated him, but he did not doubt that she would try to make good on her threats if he turned Cantrell in to the authorities. Constanza was one complication he did not need now. There would be plenty of time later to exact revenge on John Cantrell.

"Very well," he said coldly as he plucked her fingers from his coat. "I will keep quiet. But if he is to remain free, your story of Jennifer leaving him will not work. No matter how convincing you are, he will not believe you."

"He will," Constanza insisted.

Oliver shook his head, then, after a moment of thought, said, "Tell him one of her friends in Wyoming suffered a terrible accident, was thrown from a horse or something, and is near death. We had to leave at once and will wire him soon. When we are safely in Philadelphia, you will tell him Jennifer has had a change of heart and intends to marry another man."

Constanza merely glared at him.

"Her friend's name is Susannah," Oliver said, his jaw tight with irritation. He leaned forward on the seat. "It is imperative that you tell the tale well, Constanza."

"I will make them believe me." She backed away from him and closed the wagon's door. "Go now. Get Jennifer Mainwaring from my sight."

At the mention of Jennifer's name, Oliver glanced at his niece. Her head leaned against the wall, and her face was very pale, but she seemed to be sleeping peacefully. He looked back at Constanza. "I will be in touch."

She nodded with imperious pride, crossing her arms over her breasts. Oliver appreciated that the action pushed those generous mounds further above the low neckline of Constanza's dress. Her ever-present gold crucifix glittered in the noon sun, and a breeze caused a few shining black tendrils of her free-falling hair to brush against her cheek. She made an arresting picture.

Constanza Noriega was a beautiful, fascinating woman, but she was also a disturbing one. Oliver would not miss her.

He knocked on the front wall of the compartment. "Let us go, Mr. Creed. It is critical that we make the three-forty train from San José to Sacramento, and to do that, we must make the one o'clock train from Gilroy. The success of our plan depends upon it."

"Yes, sir, Mr. Mainwaring."

Constanza watched through narrowed eyes as the depot wagon rolled away. "Wyoming!" she snarled softly. "You will not order me about, Oliver Mainwaring. I will tell my own tale." The wagon disappeared from sight, leaving the dust it raised to slowly settle back to the earth. A fierce sense of triumph roared through Constanza, and she almost jumped in the air from sheer exhilaration. Then her eyes fell on the two horses still tied to the rail. Oliver had ridden one, and the other was her own mare, carrying her sidesaddle.

With a snort of disgust, Constanza marched over to lead them to the corral. She knew Juan well enough to know that he would be furious if he came home to find the two animals still saddled, with no access to water. Juan would be angry anyway; she would see to it. But Constanza did not want his anger directed at her for any reason. She wanted him angry with Jennifer. She wanted him to hate Jennifer. And she would do all in her power to ensure that he did.

Nineteen

John led the group of racing cowboys into the yard, all of them whooping and hollering. He was out of the saddle before Diamante came to a complete stop in front of the veranda.

"Jennie!" he called joyously as he pulled the reins over Diamante's head.

Barbara came out onto the veranda, closing the door behind her. Her eyes were rimmed with red, her expression sober. "John."

Something in her tone gave him pause. Preston came up on his horse, while Bill jumped from his saddle. The three men stared at her. The rest of the group gradually quieted.

"What is it?" John asked, his voice harsh with fear.

Barbara took a deep, steadying breath. "She's gone. Jennie left."

John shook his head in disbelief. "She can't be gone."

Bill moved to his wife's side and placed a comforting arm around her shoulders. "What do you mean, honey?"

"She and Oliver left for Philadelphia late this morning." Barbara brushed a hand across her watering eyes. "I'm so sorry, John."

Without a word, John stalked past them and threw the door open. His footsteps could be heard pounding up the stairs, his voice calling her name.

"How do you know she went back to Philadelphia?" Preston asked.

"Constanza was here when they left. She waited for John."

Preston's eyes narrowed in suspicion. "Where is she?"

"In the *sala*."

"Keep her there." Preston hurried into the house and up the stairs. He found John in Jennifer's tidy bedroom. Everything was neat and orderly, and with the exception of a few of Jennifer's new clothes in the wardrobe, not a trace of her remained. Even the lingering scent of her orange blossom water was gone.

John stood deathly still, his anguish and confusion evident in his eyes. Preston's stomach grabbed, as did his heart. How well he knew what John was feeling! Even now, thirty years later, the remembered agony of Ana Maria's disappearance caused him deep pain. It tore him apart to see that same agony on his beloved son's face. He placed a gentle hand on John's shoulder.

"Something is wrong." There was a harsh certainty in John's voice. "There is no note. She would not leave without explanation, Preston, no matter the reason."

"I don't believe she would, either. Constanza is downstairs, claiming she was here when they left."

John's jaw tightened. Without another word, he spun around and stormed down to the *sala*.

"What did you do with her?"

At John's curt words, Constanza looked up at him from her seat on one of the sofas, her eyes wide with sympathy.

"What did you do with her?" John repeated. His voice had risen to a roar. Preston followed him into the room, and Bill came in a moment later.

"I did nothing, Juan." She affected a hurt look. "I knew you would be upset. That is why I waited for you." She rose to her feet.

"Why were you here in the first place?"

"I came to call. Neighbors do that, you know." Constanza tossed her head, sending her long hair dancing about her hips.

"You don't," John stated. "Your relations with my family are strained, to say the least."

Constanza shrugged. "I was trying to make amends. *Señor* Preston's friendship is very important to my father. It was for Papa's sake I came today."

"Did Oliver force Jennie to leave?" Preston demanded.

"No!" she cried. "He said he needed to return to Philadelphia, that pressing business matters awaited him. Jennifer was only too eager to go. She said she was sick to death of this ranch, of Juan's attentions, that he was pressuring her. Even under those circumstances, I could not believe Jennifer would be so cold-blooded as to leave with no explanation, but she did. When I begged her to at least write a note, she refused." Constanza spread her arms in a helpless gesture.

"You lie," John said coldly.

"Juan!" Constanza stared at him in disbelief. "I would not lie to you about this!"

"I agree with my son," Preston cut in angrily. "It is certain you are lying, Constanza. What I don't understand is why you think we are stupid enough to believe you."

"*Señor* Preston, you must believe me," Constanza pleaded, her large eyes filling with tears. "You are my father's dearest friend. I could not lie to you. Jennifer has poisoned your mind against me. Her sweet act is just that: an act. She is a conniving fortune hunter who hoped to tie herself to your family to save herself from financial ruin."

A gasp of outrage sounded from the door. The three men turned to see Brigit advance into the room bearing a tea tray. The young girl's face was red with anger, causing her freckles to blend in almost completely with the tone of her skin.

"Ye lyin' witch!" Brigit hissed, her Irish accent amazingly strong. She set the tray down on the table, causing the china cups to rattle against each other. "Miss Jennie is the kindest, most good-hearted person I have ever met. She would never run off without a word to any of us, without saying good-bye to *Señor* Preston, or *Señor* John, or those sweet children, not for any reason. And ye know why?" Brigit's eyes filled with tears. "Because she loves us. I'll not stand by while the likes o' you say such hateful, untrue things about her."

Constanza flushed with fury. She advanced on the maid with her hand raised. "I will not be spoken to in such a manner by a servant!"

Bill put a protective arm around Brigit's shoulders and frowned at Constanza. "You will not lay a hand on anyone in this house." He guided Brigit to the door. "Go find Barbara," he said kindly. "Help her with the children."

"Yes, sir." She shot a parting glare at Constanza and left.

"I cannot believe you let her speak to me like that!" Constanza turned accusing eyes on Preston.

"She merely spoke the truth." Preston crossed his arms over his chest. "Which is something I would like you to do."

Constanza whirled away in frustration. "How deep Jennifer's hooks go! Are none of you able to see her for the lying, manipulative *ramera* she is?"

John strode across the room to grab her arm and turn her to face him.

"I have never struck a woman, Constanza, but I swear to you, I will today if you say anything more against Jennie. Either tell us the truth or get out of here."

Constanza stiffened. "I will leave." She pulled away from him and crossed the room, pausing to look back at him. Her expression appeared sad and sincere. "You will learn that I am telling the truth. I know Jennifer Mainwaring for the selfish, cold-hearted woman she is."

"Constanza—" John warned. He took a few steps toward her.

Preston jerked his head in the direction of the door. "Bill, have her horse saddled and see that someone escorts her home." He said nothing more as Bill ushered Constanza from the room. After a few minutes of troubled silence, Preston spoke again. "What do you think happened?"

John raked a hand through his hair. "I don't know. I cannot

believe Jennie left of her own free will, but how could Oliver and Constanza get her out of here without any help? Or without hurting her? There is no sign of a struggle."

"This might shed some light on the subject." Bill spoke from the door. He pulled a wad of papers out of his shirt pocket as he came into the room. "I checked your desk, Pa, to see if she left a note there. There was no note, but these were hidden in a stack of your mail, already opened, as if she were hiding them." He handed Preston the papers.

Preston held the pages out so John could also read the letter from Elias Craig. When they finished, the two men stared at each other in consternation.

"Now Constanza's remark about Jennie's impending financial ruin makes sense, but how did she know about it?" John asked. "I swear, Jennie did not know herself until she read that letter today."

"Remember that Constanza and Oliver are close," Preston commented. "Perhaps he hinted at something. Surely he knows how close he is to ruin. He's not a stupid man."

"It would explain why Jennie may have felt she had to leave in such a hurry, but she still would have left a note." Bill dropped wearily onto one of the sofas.

"Perhaps she did," Preston mused. "Perhaps Constanza destroyed it."

"I'm going after Jennie." John started for the door.

Preston grabbed his arm. "It's too late to go tonight. You won't be able to catch a train to San José until one o'clock tomorrow afternoon. I think we should explore the possibility that Jennie left of her own free will."

"You can't be serious!" John exploded.

"Think of her pride, John. You have asked her to marry you. You and she made plans to invest in the Santa Maria. Suddenly, she is threatened with bankruptcy. It would be very difficult for her to come to you destitute."

"I don't give a damn about her money," John growled.

"Of course you don't. But think how you felt when Bill

and I offered you equal partnership. We don't give a damn about your money either, yet you insisted on buying in. Jennie may feel the same."

John slumped onto the sofa opposite Bill. "I would have gone with her. We could have faced this together."

"If you are married to her, you are legally responsible for her debts," Preston said gently. "She may wish to save you from that."

"I think we have to consider the strong possibility that Constanza destroyed any note Jennie may have left," Bill said. "She would do something like that. And I agree with Preston. We'll go into Gilroy tomorrow and check with the stationmaster. If there is any indication that Jennie was being forced to accompany Oliver, we'll set out after her immediately. If not, we have to assume that Preston is right, that she wants to deal with her financial problems herself."

"In that case, we'll wire her," Preston said. "Assure her that we are willing to help her in any way she needs."

"I'll not wait long," John warned. "If I do not hear from her soon, I'm going after her."

Preston nodded sadly. "As well you should, son. Don't lose her as I lost your mother."

"I do not intend to." John's determined tone belied the desolation in his heart. He pulled himself up from the sofa and left the room through the doors that opened onto the courtyard.

Was it only last night she had been here with him, swearing she never wanted to leave this place? She had come to him in the night, offering her body and her heart, promising to be his bride. How could she leave him the very next day, with no word of explanation? Why couldn't she have delayed her departure for a few more hours so she could talk to him in person, tell him what her plans were, allow him to help her?

For the first time, John had some understanding of what Preston must have felt when Ana Maria left all those years ago. His own feelings were a strange mixture of disbelief, devastation, anger, and betrayal. He fought the urge to saddle

Diamante and go after her immediately, to chase her across the country if he had to, to take her in his arms and assure her that she was not alone.

John sank down onto the bench he had shared with Jennifer the night before. It would be difficult to wait until tomorrow to learn if she had gone with Oliver willingly, but Preston's suggestion made sense. Jennie had the right to try and solve her problems herself.

With his elbows propped on his knees, John buried his face in his hands. Tonight he should have been celebrating his betrothal to the woman of his dreams; instead, he feared the hours ahead would be among the most anxious and lonely of his life.

"They did not believe me!" Constanza paced the length of her room, her hair flying each time she whirled to retrace her steps in the opposite direction. "Not one of them believed me!"

Arturo watched her from his position near the door. "You *were* lying, sister," he said cautiously. "I've warned you again and again not to underestimate the Cantrells."

She pointed a finger at Arturo. "Do not goad me, *brother*. I have no patience for it this night."

Arturo dropped his gaze to the floor, grateful that he had only been reprimanded.

Constanza continued. "We must be very careful. Juan did not react as I expected him to. Are you certain there was nothing in the mail from Mexico?"

"Nothing."

"*Maldición!* I expected to hear from my compatriots in Mexico long before now." She stopped, chewing on her lip. "I hope nothing is wrong." Her eyes found the ceiling, and her voice dropped to a whisper. "So much is at stake."

Arturo watched her nervously. This was a different Constanza tonight. As always, her unpredictable temper simmered just beneath the surface, with the constant and very real threat of boiling over, but her mood was unusually contemplative. Something was genuinely bothering her, on a very deep level.

"Oliver has removed Jennifer from our way, but we must be patient," Constanza remarked. "Juan's feelings for the *gringa* run much deeper than I expected. I must give him time."

"Will she not try to contact him?"

"Oliver has assured me that no communication will be allowed between them. Juan will come to believe that she has betrayed him, especially when Oliver notifies Preston of Jennifer's betrothal to a man in Philadelphia. Then Juan will turn to me, and we will be able to proceed with our plans."

"Do you want me to scatter the Santa Maria cattle tomorrow, as we planned?" Arturo asked hesitantly.

"No!" Constanza glared at him. *"Imbécil!* We must lie low. I know *El Lobo*. He will search for any evidence that Jennifer was taken to Philadelphia against her will. God help Oliver Mainwaring if Juan ever discovers the truth." She tapped her lip thoughtfully. "We must be patient, Arturo, as *La Serpiente* was patient. In time, we will triumph, as *La Serpiente* did."

Hearing the quiet confidence in her voice, Arturo believed her.

Bill shoved his hat back on his head. "The stationmaster remembers them—a man fitting Oliver's description, a tall, slender woman dressed all in black, two other men, perhaps those companions Oliver mentioned. They caught the train to San José with only minutes to spare. The woman seemed dejected and weary, but she did not resist."

"I do not believe him." John attempted to push by Bill. "He will tell me the truth, or regret it."

Preston and Bill each grabbed one of John's arms.

"That is precisely why I would not let you question him,"

Preston snapped. "Get a hold of yourself, John. Intimidating the stationmaster won't change what he saw."

John struggled against them, but only briefly. He turned despairing eyes on Preston. "She would not willingly have left me like this. I know her."

Preston's shoulders sagged with a weariness that ran deeper than the purely physical. "I know, John. I knew Ana Maria, too. She was a proud, strong, determined woman, just as Jennie is. And as well as I thought I knew her, there was a side to her she kept hidden from me. I never dreamed she was capable of leaving as she did. How well do any of us really know another person?" He moved his hand from John's arm to his shoulder in a comforting gesture. "Let's send a wire to Philadelphia. It will be there when Jennie arrives. Then we must wait for her to tell us what she needs from us."

John straightened, staring out at the dusty street with unseeing eyes. "I'll wait," he finally agreed. "But not for long."

From a sitting position on the edge of the bed, Jennifer slowly looked about her old, familiar room. The rich burgundy bed hangings and curtains complemented the costly, floral-patterned carpet and the tiny flowers that decorated the wallpaper. Her bedroom occupied a corner at the back of the house on the second floor and offered her the luxury of windows on two walls. It did not offer her an avenue of escape.

The ache in her head had receded, as had the nausea that had plagued her since she had first awakened from the effects of the chloroform at the Gilroy train station. Oliver had been merciless in his use of the drug. Only after her desperate, failed attempt to flee during the layover in Laramie City had Jennifer given up.

She had been within a city block of the Satin Slipper Saloon, owned by Katie Davenport, who was a dear friend of Alina Parker, when Hayward Creed and Otto Rutherford found her. The hated cloth had again come over her nose, and that time she had not awakened until the train was close to Omaha.

Too weary and too ill from the effects of the drug to fight any more, she had surrendered, at least outwardly, determined to recover and guard her strength. When she reached Philadelphia, she would see Elias Craig and get a message to John. He would come for her, and Oliver would pay dearly for his crimes.

Things had not turned out that way.

Since she and Oliver arrived in Philadelphia three days ago, she had been kept a virtual prisoner, locked in her room, her meals brought by a maid she did not know, forced to use a chamber pot, let out only to bathe once a day. Desperately she had searched her room for some way to escape, either through the windows or by forcing the door, all to no avail. She had been prepared to form a rope by tying blankets together, but her windows were nailed shut. Oliver had thought of everything.

Once Jennifer accepted that escape was not possible for the time being, she renewed her determination to rebuild her strength and spent her days resting, reading, and writing letters. Oliver could not be trusted to send her letters to John and Preston, so she wrote to Alina and Susannah, explaining what had happened and begging her friends to forward the letters she enclosed for the Cantrells. Mrs. Eugenia Nelson, the housekeeper, checked on her periodically, taking the letters and assuring her each day that no wires and no mail had come for her. Jennifer had not heard from Elias Craig, nor had she seen her uncle since the afternoon they had returned to the house. Today, for some reason, Oliver was going to allow visitors.

The key grated in the lock. Mary Anne, the maid, bobbed a curtsey. "Mrs. Hawthorne and Miss Arabella are here to see you, miss," she said politely.

Jennifer had to stop herself from rushing out of the room. She stood and smoothed the skirt of her striped bronze day dress, the same dress she had worn to Alejandro's *barbacoa,* when John had danced with her all afternoon. She momentarily closed her eyes against the searing pain that gripped her heart. How she missed him!

"Are you well, miss?" Mary Anne asked in alarm.

"Yes." Jennifer walked toward the door. "The drug my uncle used on me has caused a lingering malaise, that is all." She shot an accusing glare at the maid, who lowered her head in embarrassment.

Jennifer found Mrs. Hawthorne and Arabella waiting for her in the parlor. She had never been close to the portly woman, nor to her vapid, pretty daughter. Why Oliver had allowed them, of all her acquaintances, to call, she could not imagine. True, the formidable Mrs. Hawthorne was a force to be reckoned with in Philadelphia society, if for no other reason than the fact she was an incorrigible and very knowledgeable gossip. Because of that, Jennifer was surprised that Oliver was nowhere to be seen. Did he not fear she would tell all?

"Mrs. Hawthorne, Arabella, how nice to see you. It is kind of you to call." Jennifer settled onto a chair and reached for the teapot that rested on the low table in front of her.

"When Mr. Mainwaring mentioned that you had been feeling somewhat under the weather, we simply had to visit. Friends can do so much to cheer each other. One's duty, you know. Do you not agree, Arabella?" With a condescending smile, Mrs. Hawthorne accepted the cup Jennifer held out to her, inclining her head in thanks.

"Oh, yes, Mother." Arabella nodded with such vigor that it set her perfect blonde ringlets dancing against her shoulder. She stared at Jennifer, her blue eyes wide with undisguised curiosity. "Mr. Mainwaring is most concerned about you, Jennifer. He said you've not been yourself since your return from California."

The cup Jennifer held out shook on its saucer. Arabella quickly accepted it.

"How interesting," Jennifer said tightly. "Did my concerned uncle also tell you that he returned me to Philadelphia by force, and completely against my will?"

Mrs. Hawthorne glanced at Arabella, then turned back to Jennifer. She set her cup on the table. "Yes, my dear, he did."

"He did?" Jennifer stared at her, amazed.

"Jennifer, you may remember that Mr. Mainwaring's mother—your grandmother—and I were very close friends. Because of that friendship, and because there is no other woman in your family, your uncle has asked me to speak with you about the unfortunate situation you seem to have gotten yourself into. Please forgive me if I mention some topics you may find delicate." Mrs. Hawthorne affected a sorrowful expression. "He told us you had become enamored of a very dangerous man, and he feared for your well-being as well as your virtue. When you refused to accompany him home, he did what he felt was necessary. Mr. Mainwaring acted in your best interests, as any devoted uncle would. In time, you will come to realize that."

A hot anger rushed through Jennifer. "My uncle left out pertinent information, Mrs. Hawthorne. I am not merely enamored of Mr. Cantrell; I love him dearly, and he returns my feelings. In fact, he and I are betrothed." She ignored Arabella's gasp of shock. "I am past the age of emancipation, and am free to marry whomever I choose. The one person to whom John presents any danger is my uncle, and then only because of Oliver's cruel and outrageous conduct toward me."

Mrs. Hawthorne leaned forward and placed a commanding hand on Jennifer's forearm. "Is it not true that your Mr. Cantrell is illegitimate, that his mother was a Mexican servant in his father's house, that he was a spy and assassin for the Juarez revolution? Does he not have a reputation as a seducer of innocent young girls and married women alike? Did he not seek out his own father with the intention of killing him? For heaven's sake, Jennifer, the man is a barbarian!"

Jennifer's heart began to pound, and the ache in her head

returned. A myriad of emotions washed over her: protectiveness toward John, shock that Mrs. Hawthorne knew so much,
anger that Oliver would tell only the worst. She looked from
Mrs. Hawthorne's concerned, plump face to Arabella's slightly
flushed one. The girl's eyes glittered with titillated excitement.

"He was never an assassin, or a seducer. He is a good,
kind man, possessed of a great deal more honor and decency
than my uncle," Jennifer said heatedly, although she knew her
defense of John was in vain. Oliver had told his tale well,
with just enough of the truth in it to invalidate any protest
she might make.

Mrs. Hawthorne shook her head in genuine sympathy. "You
poor dear. Our traitorous hearts can lead us down dark and
dangerous paths. Thank the Lord your uncle was there to
keep you from throwing away your virtue and your life."

Jennifer was about to make a proud and sarcastic remark
about her lost virtue when Oliver appeared at the parlor door.

"Mrs. Hawthorne, Miss Hawthorne. How lovely to see you
both." He stepped into the room and bent over each lady's
hand in turn, bringing a blush to Arabella's cheeks. "I appreciate the time you took to call upon Jennifer." He settled into
a wing-backed chair next to Arabella.

"One must stand by one's friends in times of difficulty,"
Mrs. Hawthorne explained self-righteously.

"My only difficulties are caused by my uncle, Mrs. Hawthorne." Jennifer kept her eyes on Oliver as she spoke, taking
perverse delight in the way his mouth tightened in anger at
her words.

Mrs. Hawthorne patted Jennifer's hand. "My dear, you
must trust me. You are young, and your passions are engaged.
You will one day thank Mr. Mainwaring for saving you from
yourself. In times of emotional turmoil, one must depend
upon the advice and wisdom of one's elders."

Jennifer crossed her arms. "Oliver is only six years my
senior, Mrs. Hawthorne. That hardly qualifies him as my

elder. Nor is he my guardian. He had no right to force me to leave California. He abducted me!"

Mrs. Hawthorne fixed her with a disapproving eye. "I realize you are overset, Jennifer, but that does not give you license to be impudent. Mr. Mainwaring acted in your best interests. Men are not such sentimental creatures as women are; they are far more capable of making sound, logical decisions. It distresses you to do so now, but you must honor your uncle's wishes. He knows what is best for you."

Jennifer flushed with anger. "No more, Mrs. Hawthorne, I beg you. My uncle has lied to you about his intentions and his concerns, and I am not able to convince you of that. I fear my head has begun to ache. Please excuse me." She stood and turned to the door.

Mrs. Hawthorne stiffened, and once again, Arabella gasped.

"Jennifer!" Oliver's very tone was a reprimand.

"Good day, ladies." Jennifer left the room without looking back.

"Perhaps we should go." With a little difficulty, Mrs. Hawthorne pulled herself up from the sofa. "Come, Arabella."

"I will show you out," Oliver said.

"The problem is quite serious, Mr. Mainwaring." Mrs. Hawthorne took Oliver's offered arm, leaving Arabella to follow them. "At first, I thought you had perhaps exaggerated the gravity of Jennifer's sad situation, but I am now convinced that you are entirely right. She must be protected from the force of her passions, by any means necessary, or she will be lost."

"I knew I could count on your support, Mrs. Hawthorne." He led the two women to the front door.

Jennifer stopped halfway up the stairs, watching in silence as the women prepared to take their leave. When the butler held her cloak for her, Arabella looked up and met Jennifer's gaze. Her expression momentarily softened with a curious sympathy, then she and her mother were turned over to the capable hands of their driver.

After the Hawthornes left, Jennifer was surprised to see Oliver enter his study and close the door. She had expected him to come to her room and angrily scold her for her behavior, but instead, judging from the expression on his face as he walked to his study, he was pleased by the scene she had made. His irritating, triumphant smile gave her the uncomfortable feeling that she had played into his hands. Although Mrs. Nelson waited on the landing for her, Jennifer marched back down the stairs and thrust open the study door without knocking.

Oliver looked up in surprise.

"Well done, uncle." She folded her arms and glared at him.

He raised a nonchalant eyebrow and leaned back in his chair. "Thank you."

"You planned that whole scenario!"

"Yes, Jennifer, I did. And you fell into the trap, just as that pompous Mrs. Hawthorne did. By the end of the day, all of Philadelphia will know the story of your unfortunate affection for John Cantrell, and you will receive no sympathy from anyone. I have even admitted to your abduction, and my actions will be applauded." He laced his fingers across his stomach in satisfaction.

Jennifer's heart sank, for she knew he was right. She dropped into one of the two chairs that faced his desk. "I do not understand. What do you hope to gain by this, Oliver? What will you do when John comes for me?"

"He will not come for you. Constanza will make certain that he soon forgets you."

"You are wrong." Jennifer shook her head. "He despises Constanza, and he loves me. You cannot change that."

Oliver's lip curled in derision. "A man like John Cantrell would never be satisfied with a woman like you. You are too much of a lady, too refined, too boring. It is the Mexican blood—they are all peasants at heart. There is a certain wildness, a passion Constanza possesses that makes her irresistible. They were lovers once, you know. They will be again."

His words did not even bother her, so sure she was of John. "Again, you are wrong." She rose out of the chair to brace her hands on his desk. "Let me send for him, Oliver. It is only a matter of time before he comes anyway, and I promise you, you do not want him to come angry. Let us all meet with our solicitors, work out a solution to our financial difficulties, and you and I can bid each other farewell. Surely you can see that things will never be the same between us. I have changed too much."

"No!" Oliver slammed a hand down on the desk, his eyes flashing with anger. "You will not send for him. If you wish to ever escape your room, you will forget him!"

"Forget him? How can I forget my heart? My soul? You may as well ask me to forget to breathe!"

"You will never see him again, or hear from him, nor he from you. Never! Do you understand?"

Jennifer took a step back, startled and a little frightened by his vehemence. Did he truly believe her feelings for John, and John's for her, were so shallow that they would never communicate with each other again?

"And what do you know of our financial difficulties? Who told you?" Oliver stood and leaned over the desk. "Who?"

"Mr. Craig told me. He is quite concerned, as am I. The situation must be dealt with, Oliver." Jennifer sat back down.

"Craig had no right to tell you anything!"

Jennifer stared at him. "Of course he had the right; he is my solicitor. In fact, he had a responsibility, once I asked him for a detailed report of my financial assets."

"Why would you ask him for a report?" Oliver's voice took on a dangerous tone.

"Because I had decided to make my home in California," Jennifer explained patiently. "You were on your business trip, and I needed the information to make my plans. I certainly did not expect to learn we are facing bankruptcy." She settled an accusing glare on her uncle. "But that is another issue. I insist that you allow me to contact John. This whole sorry affair has gone on long enough. I will tolerate no more."

"You will not contact him, and that is final."

Jennifer's anger boiled over again. "This is ridiculous! You cannot keep me a prisoner for the rest of my life! Someone will come for me, Oliver."

Oliver settled back in his chair. "Why? Because you have written to your friends, asking for their help?" He removed a small bundle of letters from a desk drawer.

Her eyes widened in horror.

"How clever of you to write to the Cantrells by way of your Wyoming friends, Jennifer. I also intercepted the wires John sent. I burned those, as I will burn these." True to his word, Oliver jumped up and strode over to the fireplace, tossing the bundle on the flames.

"No!" Jennifer cried. She hurried to grab the poker, but Oliver stayed her hand before she could save the letters. Her eyes filled with tears as the papers were quickly devoured.

"I do not understand," she whispered. Jennifer released the poker and returned to her chair, turning pleading eyes on him. "We are each other's sole remaining blood relation, Oliver. We have shared this house for thirteen years. Surely you have not hated me for all that time. If you ever felt even the slightest affection for me, please explain your actions. I cannot bear not knowing."

Oliver folded his arms over his chest, a look of scorn twisting his attractive face. "Yes, I have lived here, brought in when my mother died, treated as a poor relation by my brother and his witch of a wife."

Jennifer frowned. "I did not care for my stepmother either, but surely my father did not treat you so poorly."

"He always took her side, always believed the lies she told about me. I never did well enough to please him. In school, in business—it was never enough."

"He was demanding of both of us," Jennifer admitted. She watched Oliver closely. Albert had considered Oliver a lazy

and spoiled boy, and had driven him to excel. The horrendous
arguments in which the two had engaged were still vivid in
Jennifer's memory. But Albert had been dead for almost ten
years. She had never suspected Oliver harbored such resentment toward her father even now.

Oliver continued. "I am just as clever as he was. I can
make just as much money as he did."

"But there is one major difference between you and my
father," Jennifer said sadly. "You are not willing to work. My
father got his start by wresting gold from the streambeds of
California with his own hands. I cannot see you doing the
same. He scrimped and saved and invested wisely. He sup-
ported you and your mother in luxury after your father died.
You owe him your gratitude, and instead, you despise him."

"Silence!" Oliver roared. "I owe him nothing! He never
treated me with respect. But I'll show him, just as I'll show
you. Once our financial difficulties are reversed, I shall build
the Mainwaring fortune to even greater heights than he did."

"With what?" Jennifer demanded. "If I understand Mr.
Craig's report, all the money is gone, except for the trust my
mother left me, and you shall not have a penny of that."

Oliver eyed her coldly. "I don't need your precious trust.
Certain arrangements have been made. Upon your marriage
to Bradley Ames, our troubles will come to an end."

"You must be mad," she snapped. "I have no intention of
marrying Mr. Ames, nor has he shown any interest in me. I
am betrothed to John Cantrell, and there is nothing you can
do about it. You cannot keep us apart." She watched warily
as Oliver advanced to rest his hands on the arms of her chair.
He leaned forward until his face was only inches from hers.

"Hear me well, Jennifer." His voice was ominously calm.
"I have ways of bending you to my will, as I did when I
brought you from California, and I will not be thwarted. The
situation is too desperate. You will not interfere with my
plans. You will marry Bradley Ames if I have to drag you
kicking and screaming to the altar."

"This is preposterous." Jennifer pushed at Oliver's arms, fighting the morbid urge to laugh, although the situation was far from humorous. She feared her uncle truly believed his own absurd words. "You remind me of a villain in one of those exaggerated melodramas that are all the rage. This may come as a surprise to you, but the days of captive brides and forced marriages are long gone."

He stepped back and she slipped out of the chair.

"You will marry Bradley Ames."

Jennifer walked toward the door. "No, I will not. You may as well return me to John, as I doubt Mr. Ames will want me when he learns I am no longer innocent."

"*What?*" Oliver shrieked.

With her hand on the latch, Jennifer looked back at him, not surprised to see his face white with shock. "You heard me, uncle. I may even carry John's child. All your precious plans, plans you had no right to make in the first place, will come to naught."

Oliver crossed the distance between them and grabbed her arms, shaking her violently. "You *slut!*" he snarled as he slammed her against the door. "Constanza warned me that bastard would seduce you, but I did not believe her. I told her you would never compromise yourself. I guess it takes a slut to know one, doesn't it?" He threw Jennifer to the floor, then began to pace.

She pulled herself to a sitting position against the wall. Her head reeled and her stomach clenched. She glanced up at the door, wondering if she could escape before he assaulted her again. *And where would I go?* she asked herself despairingly. Creed and Rutherford would see that she never got out of the house.

Oliver faced her, his hands on his hips, his face twisted with disgust. "You had better pray you don't carry the bastard's bastard, Jennifer. If you do, I will see that you lose it. Constanza told me there are ways. While the absence of your virginity is unfortunate, Ames will accept you anyway, because he has no choice. But there will be no black-haired brats making an untimely entrance into the world."

Genuine terror snaked around Jennifer's heart as she unconsciously wrapped her arms over her stomach in a protective gesture. For the first time, she fully realized that Oliver meant everything he said. His words were not the rantings of a foolish man, or even a madman, but those of a desperate man, a frightened man. And a desperate, frightened man could not be trusted to act rationally. She was finally convinced that Oliver would take whatever steps were necessary to avoid the humiliation of financial ruin. He truly had no concern for her. Then she remembered something he had said.

"Why will Bradley Ames have no choice but to accept me?" she asked. "Are you forcing him into this charade as well?"

"Very good, Jennifer. Yes, I am privy to a little secret he would prefer never be revealed. In order to ensure my continued discretion, he has agreed to marry you, and to invest a substantial amount in my business ventures."

"You are blackmailing him into marriage with me?" Jennifer demanded, aghast.

"Blackmail is such an ugly word." Oliver straightened his cuffs. "I prefer to think of it as a business arrangement." He stared at her as he pulled the servant's bell cord. "But now we must decide what to do about your potential problem. How soon will you know for certain whether the bastard's seed took root?"

Jennifer flushed with embarrassment. She bit her tongue to keep from shouting the angry, bitter words that came to mind, reminding herself that Oliver was not above using violence. If she were indeed pregnant, she had to protect the babe at all costs. A cold determination filled her; under no circumstances would she allow Oliver to harm her child. She could not afford to anger him further. The best plan for now was to act as if she reluctantly accepted his plans. In answer to his question about the pregnancy, how much time could she give herself and not make him suspicious? She calculated quickly. "Probably within ten days," she said, hoping she would know sooner.

"Then we will wait."

A discreet knock sounded at the door.

"That will be Mrs. Nelson," Oliver said. "She will escort you to your room. Now get out."

Almost faint with relief that Oliver had not raised his hand to her again, Jennifer pulled herself up and opened the door.

"Do keep me informed of any interesting developments, dear niece," Oliver sneered.

Jennifer looked back at him. "You may go to hell, Oliver," she said quietly, and left the room.

Twenty

Jennifer dejectedly climbed the stairs, followed by Mrs. Nelson. She made her way to her room and, once inside, surveyed the elegant furnishings. *A gilded cage,* she thought sadly.

"Will there be anything else, Miss Jennifer?" Mrs. Nelson asked politely. "Any letters to send?"

Jennifer turned to glare at the woman. "So that you may hand them over to my uncle?"

Mrs. Nelson paled.

"There will be no more letters," Jennifer snapped. "You betrayed me, Mrs. Nelson, and I would like to know why. What have I done to deserve such treatment?"

"You haven't done anything, miss." Mrs. Nelson lifted her chin. "It's just that my loyalties lie with Mr. Mainwaring. He asked me to bring him the letters; I could not refuse."

"You could have warned me."

"Mr. Mainwaring is my employer, Miss Jennifer."

"So am I."

"Yes, miss." Mrs. Nelson looked away. A faint blush tinged her pale cheeks.

Her curiosity piqued, Jennifer studied the housekeeper. The long-widowed Mrs. Nelson was in her mid-thirties, with dark hair she kept hidden under a prim muslin cap. The severity of her uniform went a long way to disguise her pleasing fig-ure, just as her reluctance to smile detracted from her attractive features. Suddenly, Jennifer understood the reason for Mrs. Nelson's blush.

"He is more than your employer, is he not, Mrs. Nelson?"

There was nothing faint about Mrs. Nelson's blush now. "I-I don't know wh-what you mean, miss," she stammered.

Jennifer eyed the woman with sympathy. "Guard your back and your heart, Mrs. Nelson. My uncle is not to be trusted."

Mrs. Nelson looked at her, startled.

"That will be all."

"Yes, miss." The housekeeper backed out of the room and locked the door behind her.

Jennifer sank down on the edge of the bed and covered her face with her hands. None of her letters had been sent. She had received none of John's wires, and even if she had, she would not have been allowed to wire him in return. He would think she deserted him, just as his mother deserted Preston.

She could not stop the despairing sob that worked its way up from her aching heart. Her hands moved over her flat belly as she fell back on the bed. A part of her prayed that John's babe grew there, even while she feared for the tiny being's life if it did. The tears came then. Jennifer curled on her side and cried until she could cry no more.

Alejandro Noriega drew the buggy to a halt in front of the Cantrell *hacienda.* As she waited for her father to help her down, Constanza smoothed the skirt of her new violet-colored gown, then fingered the matching silk blossoms that decorated her mantilla. She had taken special care with her appearance this afternoon. If all went according to plan, Juan Novales would be hers. The thrill of the hunt was upon her.

Rosa showed Constanza and Alejandro into the *sala,* where Preston waited for them, and left without a word. A moment later, John came in from the courtyard. He stopped when he saw Constanza.

"What do you want?" he demanded.

"Juan, please do not speak to me so," she begged, dabbing at her eyes.

"You may dispense with the theatrics, Constanza," John said coldly.

"*Señor* Cantrell, I do not appreciate your attitude toward my daughter," Alejandro protested.

"I mean no disrespect to you, *Don* Alejandro. It is just that I know your daughter very well."

Constanza's lips tightened in anger, and her tears miraculously disappeared. Juan's attitude presented a problem; she would have to tread lightly and with caution. She glanced at Preston, then her father, forcing her expression to soften. "I received a rather long wire from Mr. Mainwaring," she said demurely. "He asked me to speak with you, to explain the situation in the hope that the news will be easier to hear from a friend." She settled onto one of the sofas and pulled a few sheets of paper from her beaded reticule. "I am sorry to tell you this, Juan, but Jennifer will soon announce her betrothal to a young man from one of the wealthiest families in Philadelphia."

The only outward indication that John had heard her was a tightening of his mouth. He said nothing.

Constanza hesitated, then continued. "Evidently there was some understanding between them before she came to California, one that Oliver, uh, Mr. Mainwaring, was unaware of until they returned to Philadelphia. He has begged Jennifer to write to you, and to *Señor* Preston, to explain her feelings, but she refuses. She does not want the past to interfere with her happiness." Constanza took a deep breath. "That is why she asks that you make no further attempt to contact her."

John still made no comment, nor did he move. He continued to impale Constanza with his hostile gaze.

He was not reacting at all as she had expected. Suddenly unsure of herself, Constanza held the pages up with an irritatingly shaky hand. "You may read Mr. Mainwaring's wire if you wish." Her voice faltered at the end.

Preston stepped forward and grabbed the papers. The room settled into awkward silence as he read. Without a word, he handed the papers back to Constanza. He looked at John and nodded.

Constanza cleared her throat. "I know you cared for her, Juan. I deeply regret the pain my words must cause you. Only the hope that the blow would be softened by hearing the sad news from a close friend rather than from cold written words could have persuaded me to come here today. I hate to see you hurt."

When John still made no response, Constanza continued with more confidence, struggling to keep her voice soft and soothing. "I tried to warn you about her. It grieves me that my fears were well-founded." She deliberately widened her eyes in an expression of sympathy. "If there is anything I can—"

"His name."

Constanza blinked. "I beg your pardon?"

"What is the man's name?" John demanded in a dangerous tone.

Again disconcerted, Constanza fumbled with the papers.

"Bradley Ames," Preston provided.

John did not move for a moment, then nodded in Alejandro's direction. *"Buenas tardes, Don* Alejandro."

Constanza watched in disbelief as John crossed the room without so much as a glance in her direction and exited into the foyer. A moment later, his footsteps could be heard climbing the stairs. She flushed with embarrassment and stuffed the papers in her reticule, then jumped up from her seat. "Please take me home at once, Papa," she snapped.

Alejandro drew himself up, his eyes flashing in anger. "Preston, I must protest your son's rudeness. Constanza came here out of genuine concern for an old friend's feelings, and I do not care to see her treated so shabbily."

"My apologies, Alejandro. John is very upset." Preston raised an eyebrow at Constanza. "At least he didn't throw anything."

Constanza gasped. She picked up her skirts and marched from the room, holding her head high, clenching her jaw. Preston and Alejandro looked at one another, each recognizing the stubborn protectiveness the other felt for his child.

"*Adiós,* Alejandro," Preston said formally.

"*Adiós,* Preston," Alejandro answered. He followed his daughter from the room.

Constanza waited for her father on the veranda, slapping her folded fan against the palm of her hand. The meeting had not gone well. Damn him! Juan was as unpredictable as he had been in Mexico. One would begin to suspect that he actually cared for Jennifer! Constanza waved her fan as if to wave the ludicrous idea away, then used it to thoughtfully tap her bottom lip.

His reaction had been all wrong, no matter what his feelings were. If Juan truly cared for Jennifer, he should have exploded with anger at the news of the betrothal. If he did not care, he should have been more receptive to her own kind overtures.

At the sound of Alejandro's approach, Constanza stamped her foot in frustration. If she could not control Juan Novales, her plans were doomed.

As he suspected, Preston found John pacing the floor in Jennifer's room.

John looked up as his father came through the door. "I apologize if my rudeness to Constanza caused additional friction between you and *Don* Alejandro."

Preston shrugged. "You have a long way to go to match Constanza's rudeness." He leaned against the wall and folded his arms. "What do you think of Oliver's message?"

"It's a lie," John stated flatly. "The minute she spoke, I

knew the tale was false, but I did not want to tip her off. She would warn Oliver. That is why I did not argue."

"What makes you so certain it's a lie?"

"Jennie told me about Bradley Ames, that Oliver entertained hopes of a match between them because of the societal status of the Ames family. Knowing what we now know about Oliver's disastrous investments, I would bet that the family's wealth plays an important role in his sudden determination to see them wed. I know Jennie has no feelings for Ames." He faced his father. "She loves me, Preston. She would not willingly marry another."

"Is that why you keep coming back here, to her room?" Preston queried gently. "To remind yourself of that?"

John shook his head. "It is my room that will not let me forget. We made wonderful memories there." His words carried no trace of shyness or embarrassment. He strode over to the wardrobe and jerked the door open, then removed the few articles of clothing stored there. "I came here now to get these. Jennie may want them."

Preston nodded in understanding. "When will you leave for Philadelphia?"

"Tomorrow."

"Do you need help?"

"I don't think so. Jennie's solicitor has not yet responded to my wire, but I think I can count on his help. He seemed genuinely concerned about her in that letter he sent her." John moved to the door and out into the hall, where Preston joined him. "It is imperative that Constanza not learn I have gone, for she will warn Oliver. I don't want him doing something rash if he finds out I am on my way."

Preston nodded his agreement. "Don't catch the train in Gilroy. Ride further north to the Tennant station. We'll send Bill or Gabe along to bring your horse back." He placed a hand on John's shoulder. "Bring Jennie home, son."

"I will," John said solemnly. "I promise." His face darkened. "And I also promise that Oliver Mainwaring will come to regret the day he took her."

Several days later, early in the morning, Jennifer rolled over and lay on her back, staring up at the burgundy bed hangings. One hand rested on her stomach. A deep sadness washed over her as she recognized the mild cramps for what they were. Her monthly flow had started, right on time. She did not carry John's baby.

A sob caught in her throat, and she fought the urge to cry. Yet, she also felt a sense of relief. If there was no baby, there was nothing for Oliver to try to kill.

Over two weeks had passed since the awful day she had been taken from California. Somehow it seemed like a lifetime ago. Since her arrival in Philadelphia, her days had been long, lonely, and frightening. A few more ladies had called to visit, all eyeing her with the same condescending sympathy Mrs. Hawthorne had shown, all very vocal in their approval of Oliver's actions.

It sickened Jennifer to watch him charm those foolish matrons. With his good looks and flawless manners, Oliver blinded them to the truth and led them to believe as he wished. She no longer bothered to defend her position, knowing she only strengthened Oliver's when she did. However, if anyone dared ask her about John, or said a word against him, she immediately exited the room, leaving her visitors to self-righteously shake their heads and commend Oliver for his wisdom.

Jennifer sighed. She still had trouble accepting the lengths to which Oliver was evidently prepared to go in order to save his reputation, and at the same time, she could not afford to disregard any of his threats. But surely he did not believe that she would go meekly to the altar, like a lamb to the slaughter. The only man she would accompany to the altar was John Cantrell.

She saw him in her mind's eye, standing tall and handsome in his black clothes, his blue eyes warming her blood with their fire. A familiar, aching despair closed around Jennifer's heart, causing her eyes to tear again. Surely John trusted her enough to know she would never desert him. Surely he could feel the power of her love, even across the continent. Surely he would come for her.

A knock sounded on the door, and a moment later Mrs. Nelson let herself into the room, clutching the handle of a steaming bucket of water in one hand, balancing a breakfast tray on the other. "That stupid Mary Anne caught the stomach gripe, or some such thing," she muttered as she set the bucket down and quickly righted the sloping tray. "Which leaves me to do everything." She set the tray on Jennifer's writing table, then turned to one window, drawing the floor-length curtains open. "Forgive my grumbling, miss. Good morning to you. I trust you slept well."

"No, Mrs. Nelson, I did not sleep well, nor will I again until I am freed from this abominable situation."

"Yes, miss." Mrs. Nelson kept her eyes averted as she opened the curtains at the other window. "Have you any news for your uncle?"

Jennifer could find no good reason to delay sending Oliver the message. Mrs. Nelson would recognize the signs soon enough. "Tell my uncle there is no child," she said quietly. "He need not drug me or beat me senseless or drag me to an abortionist or follow through with whatever diabolical plot he had devised."

"Yes, miss." Mrs. Nelson's face was impassive. "Will you be needing my help to dress?"

"No. I need nothing from you, Mrs. Nelson."

The housekeeper marched to the door. Just before she closed it, she said, "Mr. Mainwaring wishes you to be informed that Mr. Elias Craig will call upon you at ten o'clock this morning." With that, she was gone, the key grating in the lock.

Jennifer sat up and stared at the door, her heart pounding in excitement.

"Mr. Craig!" Jennifer hurried across the small, panelled library to take the solicitor's outstretched hands. "I cannot believe my eyes! How did you persuade my uncle to allow us to meet, and alone, at that?"

"I warned him that I would have the law on him if he did not. Client-solicitor privilege, you know." Elias Craig was a dignified man in his mid-fifties, of medium height and slender build. The passing of the years had cost him a great deal of his hair, and that which remained to encircle his head was kept neatly trimmed. His kindly, clean-shaven face served to emphasize his intelligent brown eyes. Jennifer felt a surge of affection for her father's old friend.

"How good it is to see you," she said softly. "I have been so alone."

His sharp gaze travelled over her. "Are you well, my dear? You seem pale, and nervous."

"I am much better now that you are here, sir. Would you care for some refreshment?"

"Thank you, no." Elias patted her hand as he led her to a pair of matching chairs positioned in front of the fireplace. A cheery fire crackled on the hearth, keeping the chill of the October day at bay.

"Before we discuss what your uncle has done regarding your finances, I must again apologize, Miss Mainwaring. As I explained in my letter to you, I fear I was remiss in my duties." Only when Jennifer was situated in her chair did Elias settle into his, heaving a remorseful sigh as he did.

"Mr. Craig, I do not hold you at fault," Jennifer assured him. "Evidently my uncle has been very clever, with the exception of his recent investment decisions, of course, and from the sound of your letter, he has been aided in his duplicity by his accountant and his solicitor."

"I fear so. What I do not understand is why Mr. Mainwaring chose to make his move now, after so many years of honesty. As I explained to you, I have had no cause in the past to question the word of either Mr. Atwater or Mr. Smythe."

Jennifer shrugged. "We may never know the full truth. I doubt Oliver will be anxious to explain in detail the reasons for his disastrous investments."

"I was able to learn that one of his unsuccessful investments was actually a case of fraud. Last year, your uncle, along with a surprising number of influential people, was duped into investing a large sum of money in a phony diamond venture in Wyoming Territory."

Her eyes widened with surprise. "I know of it. I have friends in Wyoming. One of them, Mr. Beauregard Parker, was instrumental in the exposure of the fraud." She shook her head. "To think that some of my money was lost in that swindle."

Elias leveled his sober gaze on her. "Miss Mainwaring, as urgent as your financial situation is, I find the rumors I hear of your personal circumstances far more disturbing. Your uncle may cut our visit short at any moment, and I must be satisfied of your safety." He raised an eyebrow. "My dear wife has carried fantastic tales from her Ladies Relief Society meetings, tales I am hard put to believe. Am I to understand that your uncle forcibly removed you from California, utilizing drugs and brutal henchmen? Are you actually being held prisoner in this house?"

Jennifer nodded. "All is true, Mr. Craig. My uncle has been very shrewd in how he explained his actions to his acquaintances, and mine. All believe he acted in my best interests; none will help me."

"Help you what?"

She leaned forward and placed a hand on his forearm. "Escape. I am being held here against my will. I must escape or, at the very least, get a message to my dear friend and his family in California. Oliver has fiendish plans for me that go as far as to force me to marry against my wishes. My friend and his family will help me escape my uncle's clutches." Jennifer strove to keep her voice from cracking with desperation. "Please help me, Mr. Craig, I beg you. Take me with you when you leave."

"Is this friend's name John Cantrell, by any chance?"

"Y-Yes." Jennifer stared at him. "How did you know?" Then, with a sinking heart, she answered her own question. "Oliver. He told you I would try to enlist your aid, did he not?" When Elias did not respond, she tightened her fingers on his arm. "Mr. Craig, you must believe me. The picture my uncle paints of John is a false one. John is a wonderful man, one who would never harm me. We plan to marry, with my godfather's blessing. Surely you remember how highly my father spoke of Preston Cantrell. John is his son."

"His illegitimate son, who threatened to kill him, I am told."

"Well, yes, at first he did, thinking he had cause. But when John realized he had been misled, he—" Jennifer released him and slumped back in her chair. "It is no use," she whispered despairingly. "Even to my ear, my defense of him rings hollow, like that of a foolish woman defending her scoundrel of a lover."

"Calm yourself, Miss Mainwaring," Elias said kindly. "Your young man has contacted me. He is most concerned for your well-being."

"You have heard from John?" Jennifer cried, then clapped a hand over her mouth, casting a worried glance in the direction of the closed door. Her eyes filled with joyous tears as she spoke in a lower tone. "Is he well? Does he know I was taken from him by force?"

"He suspects as much."

Her shoulders sagged with relief. "Thank God. I so feared he would believe I deserted him. Oliver has intercepted all communication between us." Jennifer reached for Elias's arm again. "Please, sir, wire him at once, as soon as you leave here. Tell him what happened, and that I will rejoin him as quickly as I can." She looked down, suddenly shy. "Tell him I love him with all my heart," she whispered.

Elias remained quiet.

Jennifer looked up at him, her eyes wide with fear. "You do believe me, do you not, sir? You must believe me! All hope is lost if you do not."

The door suddenly opened. "Your time is up, Mr. Craig," Oliver said coldly. "Jennifer has not been feeling well; we must take care not to weary her."

Elias Craig stood, while Jennifer struggled to compose her features. She rose from her chair and faced Oliver. "I am fine, uncle. Mr. Craig and I have not finished our discussion."

"Yes, you have." Oliver advanced on her and took her upper arm in a tight grip, pulling her toward the door.

Elias followed them, frowning. "Mr. Mainwaring, I shall insist upon speaking with my client again in the very near future, and I suggest you attend that meeting, with your solicitor and accountant at your side. Certain pressing financial matters must be dealt with."

"I shall send Mr. Atwater to you, Mr. Craig. Discuss those matters with him."

Upon reaching the foyer, Jennifer was finally able to shake Oliver's hand off. She turned to Elias with a bright smile and held out her hand as Oliver bellowed for the butler to bring Mr. Craig's coat and hat.

"Thank you for coming, Mr. Craig. It was a pleasure to see you, even under such trying circumstances."

Elias took her hand and bowed over it. "I believe you," he said for her ears alone, "and I shall do as you requested." He cleared his throat and spoke louder. "I am certain we will find a way out of this muddle, Miss Mainwaring. Do not fear. I will communicate with you in a day or two."

A flash of wild hope caused Jennifer's fingers to tighten

on his, then she released him. "Good day, sir. Thank you again."

"Good day, Miss Mainwaring. Be well."

Jennifer watched as the butler closed the door behind him, then turned to the stairs.

"Jennifer!" Oliver barked. "What did you discuss?"

"We discussed the unfortunate financial predicament you have apparently gotten us into," she snapped over her shoulder as she continued up the stairs.

"You did not discuss Cantrell?"

"Why would I bother? You have done a masterful job of weaving your web of half-truths and lies, Oliver. No one believes me." Her answer seemed to satisfy Oliver, for he did not question her further.

At the top of the stairs, Jennifer paused and looked back. Mrs. Nelson had stopped halfway up the stairs, her eyes on Oliver.

"Well?" Jennifer demanded, her hands at her hips. "Am I to be returned to my cell or not?"

At Oliver's curt nod, Mrs. Nelson continued up the stairs. Jennifer fought to keep from smiling, and she succeeded, until Mrs. Nelson locked the bedroom door. Then she sank to her knees and sat back on her heels, her hands clasped in prayerful thanksgiving, and finally allowed her lips to curve in hopeful joy.

Two days later, Oliver himself came to Jennifer's room, followed by Mrs. Nelson and an unknown woman carrying bolts of cloth. Jennifer, seated near the window in a chair that was angled to catch the best of the light, looked up from the book she was reading.

"I am hosting a ball this coming Friday," Oliver announced without preamble. "Mrs. Wright will create a gown of the latest fashion for you."

Although her heart leapt with sudden hope, Jennifer calmly

met Oliver's gaze. "As you wish, uncle." She was gratified to see a look of surprise flash over his face; perhaps he had expected her to argue with him.

Oliver's expression turned to one of unease. For a moment, he seemed at a loss for words. "Very well, then," he said stiffly. "Our guests will arrive at nine o'clock in the evening. Mrs. Nelson will help you dress."

"As you wish."

With a flick of his wrist, Oliver motioned the two waiting women forward. He backed toward the door, his brow furrowed with wariness. But he said no more and left the room, slamming the door behind him.

With a tranquil smile, Jennifer watched him go. "As you wish, uncle dear," she repeated in a soft whisper, trying to hide her elation. Oliver had just given her the diversion she needed to effect her escape. With Mr. Craig's help, she should be able to disappear in the crowd attending a ball. *Four more days.*

Mrs. Nelson eyed her with suspicion. Jennifer merely stared at the woman until she looked away.

Twenty-one

Jennifer gazed at herself in the mirror as Mrs. Nelson put the finishing touches to her hair. Memories of watching herself in the mirror while Brigit fixed her hair rushed painfully over her. That night she had worn her burgundy gown, the one John liked so much. Later she had gone to his bed, had promised to be his bride. She closed her eyes, seeking relief from the tormenting pictures that paraded through her mind.

"Miss Jennifer, are you all right?" Mrs. Nelson asked in concern.

Jennifer opened her eyes. "I am fine," she lied. In truth, she felt almost ill with anxiety. Elias Craig had called upon her early in the week and they had finalized their plans for her escape tonight. Even now, her packed carpetbag was hidden under the far side of the bed. Her satchel waited in the wardrobe for the last of her personal effects, such as the brush Mrs. Nelson was using, for those items could not have been packed without arousing suspicion. There had been no word from John.

"I'm finished with your hair. You may stand up now." Mrs. Nelson stood back.

With a final glance in the mirror, Jennifer obeyed. She smoothed the white gauze overskirt of her elaborate pale yellow gown while Mrs. Nelson adjusted the bustle and straightened the train.

"Mrs. Wright truly outdid herself with this gown, Miss Jennifer," Mrs. Nelson said admiringly. "You look lovely."

"No, I do not." Jennifer faced her. "Once again, I have grown too thin. My complexion is far too pale, and the color of this ridiculously lavish gown only emphasizes it. The bustle is so large as to be absurd, and I cannot breathe in this accursed corset Oliver insists I wear."

Mrs. Nelson was genuinely shocked. "Miss Jennifer, you will be the envy of every woman here tonight," she protested. "Mrs. Wright's creation will start a new rage. You are fashionably pale; a lady cannot take the sun, you know, and of course you must wear a corset. It wouldn't be proper not to." She eyed Jennifer critically. "Perhaps you are a trifle thin, but that will change once you are feeling better. Your appetite will return."

"I doubt it, Mrs. Nelson," Jennifer said quietly. "Food does not hold much appeal when I am locked away like a common criminal or an insane relative, when I feel lonely, betrayed, and frightened."

Mrs. Nelson had the grace to blush. She awkwardly patted Jennifer's arm. "I know this has been difficult, Miss Jennifer, but you'll come to see that your uncle is right. You will soon forget about that terrible man, that assassin who seduced you. You have nothing to fear. Mr. Mainwaring has only your best interests at heart."

"John is not an assassin, nor did he seduce me," Jennifer snapped. "And my uncle's plan to marry me to Bradley Ames is in his own best interests, not mine."

"Mr. Ames?" Mrs. Nelson blanched. "He intends to see you wed to Bradley Ames?"

"Yes. I thought you were privy to all of his plans."

"No, not all. How well do you know Mr. Ames, miss?"

"Not that well. We have danced a few times, sat at supper together one night several months ago. He is more my uncle's friend than mine." Jennifer frowned. "Mrs. Nelson, what is it? This is more concern than you have exhibited throughout this whole ordeal. Please tell me what is troubling you."

Mrs. Nelson bit her bottom lip. "Miss, I know things about that man. He—"

A single knock sounded at the door, and before the house-keeper could continue, the door was thrown open. Oliver stood there, dressed in formal attire.

The worried expression on Mrs. Nelson's face vanished. "You look very fine tonight, Mr. Mainwaring," she said stiffly.

"Thank you, Mrs. Nelson. Jennifer, are you ready? Our guests are beginning to arrive."

"I am ready."

Oliver crossed the room to take her gloved hand and pull it through his arm. He cruelly squeezed her fingers. "Remember, dear niece. You will be charming and gracious. To everyone." Jennifer gasped with pain, and he eased his hold on her. "Should you entertain any ideas of escape, know that I have hired guards surrounding the entire property on the pretext of protecting our guests. And of course, the charming Mr. Creed and Mr. Rutherford shall be watching you."

"You may rest easy, uncle. I shall not be a burden to you." *For much longer,* she added silently.

Oliver appeared pleased with her answer, for he said nothing more, but led her to the door.

"Your fan, Miss Jennifer." Mrs. Nelson held out a white lace fan, which Jennifer accepted with a nod of thanks. She and Oliver left the room.

Neither spoke as they walked the length of the hall and descended the stairs. The sound of many voices reached her ears, and it was all Jennifer could do to disguise the rising sense of excitement and hope she felt. The plan was in motion.

"Is he really an assassin?" Arabella Hawthorne's high-pitched voice grated on Jennifer's nerves. Arabella and two of her friends had trapped Jennifer in a relatively quiet corner

of the ballroom. For some reason, the three young women
found the subject of Jennifer's dangerous paramour enthrall-
ing, and all of her polite attempts to steer the conversation
to another subject had failed. Although Jennifer guessed that
the women surrounding her were only a year or two her jun-
ior, she felt much older.

"He is not an assassin," she explained somewhat shortly.
"He was an agent whose responsibility was to learn military
secrets."

"A spy!" Arabella breathed in delight. "How romantic!"

Rebecca Wentworth laid a gloved hand on Jennifer's forearm, causing Jennifer to look at her. Rebecca was tall and
slender and elegantly dressed, but even the most doting of
parents would be challenged to describe her mud-brown hair
and plain features as anything but what they were. However,
she was possessed of a witty, intelligent spirit and the most
arresting pair of long-lashed, violet eyes ever seen in Philadelphia. "Is he handsome?" she asked in an excited whisper.

At Rebecca's question, Jennifer smiled, a gentle, sad smile.
She realized there was no malice behind the woman's inter-
rogation, but rather a fascination for the forbidden. "Yes,"
she said softly. "He is very handsome. He is tall, with black
hair and the bluest eyes I have ever seen."

"Bluer than mine?" Arabella questioned doubtfully.

Jennifer eyed Arabella, giving the question fair consideration. The young woman was a vision in a pale blue gown
that highlighted her huge eyes and golden hair. "I think it's
a tie," Jennifer decided.

"Do you pine for him?" Henrietta Duke asked with a melo-
dramatic sigh. A tangerine-colored feather waved from her
auburn hair as she fanned herself. Her gown matched the
color of the feather, and with her rotund figure and huge
bustle, one could not help but be reminded of a rather large,
round fruit. But Henrietta was a kind soul, and Jennifer knew
she asked the question in all sincerity.

"Yes, I do," she admitted, unable to keep the tears from

forming in her eyes. Aside from Mr. Craig, no one had shown her the least bit of compassion since her return to Philadelphia, and the sympathetic interest of the three women moved her. "I miss him terribly. We are betrothed, you know. My uncle took me from his side by force."

Henrietta blinked her own watering eyes. "How sad," she said mournfully.

Rebecca patted Jennifer's shoulder in an attempt to comfort her. "Feeling as you do, you must find Bradley's attentions annoying." Her voice had dropped again to a whisper.

"Exceedingly so," Jennifer said through clenched teeth. She dabbed at her eyes and hurriedly glanced about, searching the room for the man in question, relieved when she did not find him. "My uncle has been throwing him at me all evening."

"I've heard that he has a problem with demon rum," Henrietta announced in a low, conspiratorial tone.

"Really?" Arabella's eyes widened with shock. "How dreadful." She shuddered.

Jennifer wondered if that was the secret which had provoked Mrs. Nelson's interrupted warning. She doubted, however, that a threat to reveal such a problem was serious enough for Bradley to succumb to her uncle's demands. Although frowned upon, it was not uncommon for a gentleman to sink into his cups on occasion.

Rebecca turned her perceptive violet gaze on Jennifer. "Your uncle hopes to dim the memories of your California gentleman by forcing you into Bradley's company, doesn't he?"

Jennifer nodded. "It will not work."

"I should hope not." Henrietta sniffed with disdain. "Mr. Ames is a boor. One can always tell when he has too freely imbibed, for he becomes brash and loud. Most unattractive." She waved her fan in righteous judgment.

"Well, he certainly holds no attraction for me." Jennifer spotted the man in question across the room, standing with her uncle. Bradley was of average height, with wavy, light brown hair and a solid build. Both he and Oliver appeared to be searching for someone in the crowd. Jennifer ducked behind Henrietta's generous figure. "I fear he is seeking me," she whispered desperately in answer to Rebecca's questioning gaze.

"I see him," Arabella said behind her fan. "He is with your uncle."

"I shall go speak with him for a while," Rebecca volunteered. "Arabella, you and Henrietta take Jennifer outside. She looks as if she could use a breath of air."

Jennifer grabbed her hand. "Thank you, more than I can say."

Rebecca smiled and hurried away. Arabella and Henrietta hooked arms with Jennifer, then walked her toward the French doors that led out onto the terrace.

"Arabella!" Mrs. Hawthorne's strident voice reached them.

"Oh, fiddle!" Arabella rolled her eyes. "There's no use ignoring my mother when she uses that tone." She planted an impulsive kiss on Jennifer's cheek. "We will help you avoid Mr. Ames tonight, Jennifer. You must save yourself for your one True Love."

Jennifer stared at her in surprise and gratitude.

"Arabella!"

"I will join you later," Arabella promised, and hurried away.

Henrietta tugged on Jennifer's arm. "Let us make our escape while we can," she urged, pulling her toward the French doors. Amazed by the sudden display of loyalty from the three young women, Jennifer allowed herself to be led outside.

Although she seethed in silent frustration, Rebecca Wentworth smiled graciously as Oliver Mainwaring, Bradley Ames, and Bradley's friend, Donald Tenley, left her. The three men were headed toward the smoking parlor, where she knew they would find stronger drink than the champagne punch offered to the ladies. Bradley did not need more to drink, but short of causing a scene, she could not prevent his leaving. It was only a matter of time before he went looking for Jennifer.

She caught Arabella's eye, who was dancing with her own father, and raised her hands in a helpless gesture. Arabella shrugged in response and was lost to Rebecca's sight among the swirling dancers. Rebecca sighed. The only thing to do now was to find Jennifer and stay close by her side. She started to ease through the crush of guests circling the dance floor, realizing that the sense of intrigue surrounding Jennifer had made this the most enjoyable evening she had spent in a long time. Near the main entryway she paused, recognizing a newly arrived guest as her father's, and Jennifer's, solicitor.

"Mr. Craig," she said warmly, holding out her hand.

"Miss Wentworth. How nice to see you." Elias Craig bent over her hand. "Did your dear parents accompany you this evening?"

"Yes, indeed. You know Mother would not miss a gathering such as this. But where is your charming wife?" She eyed Elias's tall, exceedingly handsome companion with unabashed curiosity. The gentleman wore the same formal evening attire as every other man in the room, but Rebecca found him especially striking, in a way that went beyond his dark good looks and remarkably intense blue eyes.

"Sadly, Mrs. Craig is suffering from the headache and sends her regrets." He glanced at John, then back at Rebecca. "Miss Wentworth, allow me to introduce my friend, Mr. John Cantrell. Mr. Cantrell, Miss Rebecca Wentworth."

John bowed over Rebecca's extended hand, relieved that his name apparently meant nothing to her. "Miss Wentworth."

"Mr. Cantrell," she responded.

"We were hoping to offer our solicitations to Miss Mainwaring," Elias said casually. "She was not feeling well when I visited her earlier in the week. Might you know where she can be found?"

Rebecca stared at John. Her extraordinary violet eyes widened and she sucked in her breath. "It is *you*," she breathed. "You have come for her."

Alarmed, John took her arm and led her over to the wall. "I beg you, Miss Wentworth, do not draw attention to us," he said in a low tone. "Serious and possibly dangerous events may occur if Oliver Mainwaring discovers my presence."

"I will not betray you," Rebecca vowed. "But you must also concern yourself with Mr. Bradley Ames. He is in his cups, and only a step away from becoming obnoxious." She glanced at Elias, then back at John. "Does anyone here besides Jennifer and Mr. Mainwaring know your face?"

John thought for a moment, then shook his head.

"Not even Mr. Creed and Mr. Rutherford, Mr. Mainwaring's associates from California?" She nodded discreetly in the direction of two men who loitered near the front door.

John glanced at the pair, wondering if they were the two men mentioned by the stationmaster in Gilroy. His lips tightened. If they had aided Oliver in Jennifer's abduction, he wanted very much to meet them, but now was not the time. He again shook his head. "We have not met."

Rebecca nodded in satisfaction. "Mr. Craig, I suggest you find Mr. Mainwaring and keep him occupied. I saw him last entering the smoking parlor with Mr. Ames. I shall take Mr. Cantrell to Jennifer. My friend, Miss Henrietta Duke, has smuggled her out onto the terrace in the hope of giving her a much needed respite from Mr. Ames's unwelcome attentions." She hooked her arm with John's. "Well, gentlemen, what are we waiting for?" she asked with a bright smile.

Elias and John looked at each other.

John shrugged. "I do not have a better plan."

"Nor do I," Elias remarked.

"Then you keep Oliver out of the way and I will find Jennie," John said. "We will meet back here in a few minutes."

With a nod of agreement, Elias took himself off in the direction of the smoking parlor.

Rebecca pointed with her fan. "The terrace is reached through those doors on the opposite side of the room. I shall trust you to guide me through the crush, Mr. Cantrell."

"With pleasure, Miss Wentworth," John said, smiling. He started forward, leading her with care through the throng of guests. "I must ask you, is my lady well?" he asked over his shoulder, almost fearing the answer.

"She is well, Mr. Cantrell, although she longs for you."

John's heart rate increased with joy and anticipation. Soon he would see Jennifer. He wanted to hurry, but did not wish to attract attention, and the press of the crowd forced him to go slowly. He glanced back at Rebecca. "Forgive me, but Mr. Craig led me to believe Jennifer was without allies."

"She was, until this evening." Rebecca fanned her face. "My friends and I had no earlier opportunity to speak with her privately; her uncle or our mothers were always present. Of course, we have heard the worst of the gossip about your situation, but now we are all convinced Jennifer's feelings for you run very deep indeed." A fleeting sadness raced across her face and was gone. "Perhaps it takes a young, hopeful woman to understand another. Our parents have forgotten what it is like to love, if indeed they ever knew."

"We both appreciate your help," John said as he took another step.

"There is my friend, Miss Arabella Hawthorne," Rebecca said, waving her fan at a young blonde woman on the dance floor. "She is another of Jennifer's allies."

John was amused to see Rebecca incline her head toward him and wink at her friend. Arabella's eyes widened in comprehension and astonishment, and she nodded when Rebecca pointed toward the terrace doors.

"She will meet us outside," Rebecca said with satisfaction.

"Good. I should like to thank her for her assistance in person."

"Jennifer told the truth about one thing for certain." Rebecca's eyes sparkled with mischief.

"And what is that, pray tell?"

"You are very handsome, Mr. Cantrell."

Now John smiled outright. "Thank you, Miss Wentworth."

"You are welcome, sir," she said primly.

Neither said any more as they maneuvered through the crowd.

Henrietta and Jennifer shared a low stone bench next to the ornate balustrade that overlooked the gardens, each content to rest quietly for a few minutes.

The cool October air was refreshing compared to the stuffy ballroom. After a week of chilling rain and high winds, Philadelphia had been blessed with a few days of glorious Indian summer. Although just past eleven, the night remained comfortable.

A large fountain in the center of the terrace spilled its water into the receiving basin with a soft continuous rush of sound that painfully reminded Jennifer of the smaller one in Preston's courtyard. Would she ever enjoy that fountain again?

"I agree with what Arabella said about True Love," Henrietta said suddenly. "It is clear that you love your gentleman—what is his name?"

"John Novales Cantrell," Jennifer said proudly.

"You must wait for your Mr. Cantrell, Jennifer. Few of us are lucky enough to find genuine love. We are merely pawns in the social and financial games our parents play." There was a note of bitterness in Henrietta's usually sweet voice.

Jennifer glanced at her new friend's plump, sober profile. "Have your parents decided whom they wish you to wed?" she asked gently.

"Yes," Henrietta answered with a sigh. "But I do not agree with their choice. I may elope." Her lips suddenly clamped shut.

Even in the pale light of the lanterns, Jennifer could see Henrietta's blush.

"I am the third daughter," Henrietta hastened to explain. "Both of my sisters married well; it's not as if I must, too."

"You must follow your heart, just as you have advised me to do," Jennifer said.

Henrietta turned hopeful eyes on her. "Do you really think so? Even though my gentleman is a professor from a middle class family?"

Thinking of her own reduced financial circumstances, Jennifer nodded. "Happiness is much more important than money. Have you spoken to your parents about him?"

"No."

"Before you do something as drastic as elope, speak to them, Henrietta," Jennifer urged. "I truly believe most parents want their children to be happy. They may surprise you."

"Perhaps they will." Henrietta briefly squeezed Jennifer's hand. "Thank you. Now, what can we do to help—"

The French doors were thrown open and Bradley Ames came outside, followed by one of his friends, a man Jennifer recognized as Donald Tenley.

"Jennifer!" Bradley called in a falsely sweet voice.

"Oh, dear," Henrietta whispered. "Do not fear, Jennifer. I shall not leave your side."

Jennifer was genuinely grateful for Henrietta's presence, for Bradley's voice held a note of meanness.

"There you are." Bradley came toward her, stopping in front of her. He swayed slightly. "One would almost think you were avoiding me."

"You are aware that I have been unwell," Jennifer retorted. "I am weary and in need of a rest. If you don't mind, Henrietta and I would like to continue our conversation."

"Your uncle warned me you would be difficult." Bradley leaned forward and grabbed Jennifer's hand, yanking her to her feet. "I want to dance." He pulled her roughly into his arms. "Remember, little Miss Jennifer, that we are to be married. The least you can do is be polite." He drunkenly whirled her around.

Jennifer struggled to escape his hold. "I will never marry you," she vowed.

"Yes, you will," Bradley sneered. "I'll make you forget all about your Mexican lover." He placed a wet, sloppy kiss on her neck.

"Unhand me!" Jennifer cried, striking him with her fist.

"Mr. Ames, you go too far!" Henrietta hit him over the head with her fan. "Let her go! Mr. Tenley, do something!"

Tenley backed off, holding his hands up. "It is none of my affair," he said firmly. "I'll not interfere."

Jennifer ground her heel into the top of Bradley's foot and finally succeeded in breaking away from him. She stood back from him, panting, and pulled a handkerchief from her reticule, while Henrietta moved loyally to her side.

"How dare you?" Jennifer demanded through clenched teeth as she wiped her neck. "You will never touch me again, no matter what my uncle says, no matter the agreement between you."

Bradley lurched toward her, limping, his florid face twisted with rage. "You welcomed the attention of a Mexican bastard and refuse me?"

Jennifer glanced back over her shoulder and saw Rebecca arrive at the opened French doors, accompanied by a tall man whose face was hidden by shadows. "I believe Rebecca is waiting for us," she said calmly to Henrietta. "Shall we go?"

Henrietta nodded, glaring at Bradley. "Perhaps I will suggest to Mr. Mainwaring that his drunken guest be invited to leave, before he causes a scene."

"Oliver won't ask me to leave." Bradley pushed the two women apart, knocking Henrietta against the balustrade. Jennifer would have fallen had he not grabbed her arm and pulled her against him. "Let's go see the gardens, little Jennifer," he suggested in a lewd tone. Jennifer fought him as he propelled her toward the stairs.

"I think not." A masculine voice came from behind them, a voice that was so angry it came out as a low growl. Suddenly, Jennifer was free of Bradley's bruising grip. Rebecca and Henrietta hurried to her side.

"Are you all right?" Rebecca asked anxiously as she guided Jennifer toward the French doors.

"Much better now." Jennifer rubbed her aching arm. "I must thank your friend. And how are you, Henrietta?"

"This big bustle of mine protected me nicely," Henrietta answered cheerfully. "I never even touched the wall."

From behind her, Jennifer heard a muffled protest, then a strange sound resembling a slap, but much stronger. A loud groan followed, and a big splash. She glanced over her shoulder to see Donald Tenley rush to the fountain and pull Bradley's face out of the water. She could not suppress a grim smile. "Most fitting," she murmured as she faced forward again. Arabella came to the French doors, a gleeful look of anticipation on her pretty face. Before Jennifer could call to her, Rebecca spoke.

"Jennifer, you wanted to speak to my gentleman friend. He wishes to speak with you as well, and has travelled a long way to do just that." With a wide smile, she turned Jennifer around to face John, who stood in the light from the open doors. "I believe you are already acquainted."

To Jennifer, Rebecca's last words seemed to come from far away, over the roar of wild joy that raced through her. She took a few steps toward John and reached up with a shaking hand to caress his cheek. "Oh, my love," she whispered in wonder, her eyes filling with tears. "Is it truly you?"

John nodded, holding her hand to his face so that he could place a kiss on her palm. He prayed he was successful at hiding the shock he felt at her appearance. Her elaborate gown could not disguise how pale and thin she had become in the weeks since he had last seen her. But her sparkling green eyes were the same, as was her glorious hair, now piled into an intricate mass of curls and ringlets. He reached for her and crushed her to his chest.

"Jennie." Her name came out as a deep sigh.

Jennifer's arms went around him, holding him tightly. "John, he forced me away," she said, her voice low and frantic. "He drugged me, and has imprisoned me here. You must believe that I would never leave you."

"I know, I know. Do not upset yourself, *mi amada.*" He cradled the back of her head with one hand and placed a gentle kiss on her lips. "We are together now."

A soft feminine sob, then another, was heard behind them.

Jennifer looked up at him. "Did Mr. Craig wire you?"

"Yes, but I was already gone. I left the Santa Maria right after Constanza came to tell me that Oliver had sent her a wire, telling of your betrothal to Mr. Ames."

"It is a lie!"

"I know. The minute she told the tale, I knew it to be a lie." He slipped an arm around her shoulders and turned until they both faced Bradley, who sat on the edge of the fountain, dripping water and coughing. "I assume that is the famous Mr. Ames?" John asked dryly.

"Yes," said Jennifer, her voice heavy with disgust.

John locked his deadly gaze on Bradley. "If you ever touch her again, Ames, I will hunt you down like the snake you are and kill you. You cannot hide from *El Lobo.*"

Fear flashed in Bradley's eyes, although his expression remained belligerent. "You can have the slut," he snarled, fingering his swollen lip.

In one smooth movement, John stepped away from Jennifer and landed his fist squarely on Bradley's jaw. Bradley toppled backward into the fountain and came up a moment later, sputtering.

"You will never refer to my future wife in any but the most respectful of terms," John said coldly. He glanced at Donald Tenley. "Do you have anything to say?"

"N-no, sir." Tenley held his hands up and backed away.

"I thought not." John returned to Jennifer's side, again wrapping an arm around her shoulders. He led her to the open doors, where her three friends waited. "Ladies, Jennie and I are most grateful for your assistance." He smiled at Arabella, then Henrietta, then Rebecca. Each woman in turn blushed under the full force of his intense gaze.

Henrietta dabbed at the corner of one eye. "I was delighted to see Mr. Ames receive his just desserts, Mr. Cantrell," she declared.

"Thank you, Miss Henrietta. I was delighted to serve him his just desserts. Unfortunately, Jennie and I must now take our leave, in the hope that we can spirit her away before Oliver discovers what we are about."

"What is your plan?" Arabella asked excitedly.

"Mr. Craig is to meet us at the main door. His carriage awaits." He looked down at Jennifer, who nestled contentedly against his side. "He said you would be packed."

Jennifer nodded. "All is ready. I have only two bags."

"Good. Let us get them at once; haste is of the essence."

"Not you, Mr. Cantrell," Rebecca warned. "You cannot be seen near Jennifer's room. You and I will keep watch near the front door."

John frowned. "Now that I have found you, Jen, I don't want you out of my sight."

"I shall help her," Henrietta announced.

"And I," Arabella breathlessly added. "We can say we are off to freshen up."

"We won't be but a few minutes," Jennifer promised. "I cannot wait to be free of this place."

John took her face in his hands and looked into her eyes. "I will not leave without you, no matter what happens. You have spent your last night under Oliver's roof. If you need help, send one of the ladies for me. If none of you shows within twenty minutes, I will assume something has gone wrong and I will come for you."

Jennifer nodded. "My room is on the second floor, the last door on the right."

"I will find you." John kissed her, hot and deep, expressing all his pent-up worry and love. Jennifer was gasping when he pulled away from her. Arabella sighed wistfully.

John glanced over his shoulder at Bradley, causing the ladies to look in the same direction. Tenley was attempting to pull Bradley's struggling form out of the fountain, with little success.

"He will not drown," Rebecca said, raising her eyebrows in mock disappointment.

"He is very fortunate," John said darkly. "Now, let us be off." He pulled a watch from his vest pocket. "It is eleven-thirty. We shall meet in twenty minutes at the main door. You ladies go first."

Jennifer glanced back at him with love-filled eyes, then followed Arabella and Henrietta through the doors.

John held his arm out to Rebecca. "Miss Wentworth, would you care for something to drink?"

"Thank you, Mr. Cantrell. I believe I would." With a smile, she took his arm and they, too, passed through the doors, leaving a dazed and furious Bradley Ames to stare after them.

"I am almost ready," Jennifer said excitedly. She pulled a nightdress from the wardrobe and tossed it to Henrietta, who unceremoniously stuffed the garment into the satchel. "I packed everything except those items Mrs. Nelson might notice were missing." Next came her underclothes. The large carpetbag, already filled with her few treasured books on veterinary medicine and two of her favorite gowns, waited behind the slightly opened door.

"Someone is coming," Arabella squeaked from her guard position. She eased the door closed, then hurried to the dressing table, snatching up a hand mirror as she sat on the little bench.

Jennifer stuffed her cloak back in the wardrobe and slammed the door shut, while Henrietta dropped the satchel to the floor and sat on the edge of the bed, covering the bag with her voluminous skirts.

"Do you really think my hair looks all right?" Arabella asked in an unnaturally loud voice.

A moment later, the door opened to reveal a very suspicious Mrs. Nelson.

"What are you about?" she demanded.

"We are merely freshening up," Jennifer said, struggling to keep her voice calm. She glanced down and was horrified to see part of her wool cloak protruding from between the wardrobe doors. She stepped forward in a desperate attempt to hide the telltale patch of material.

Mrs. Nelson closed the door and advanced into the room until she stood directly in front of Jennifer. Without a word, she gently pushed her aside and opened the wardrobe. She pulled out the wadded up cloak.

Arabella gasped. Henrietta jumped off the bed and moved to stand protectively in front of the door.

Jennifer stared at the housekeeper. "What will you do?" she whispered.

Mrs. Nelson raised tormented eyes to Jennifer's face. "You cannot marry Mr. Ames, Miss Jennifer. Your uncle is wrong to plot such a thing, for Mr. Ames is a cruel man. He enjoys hurting women . . . in the bedroom . . . if you catch my meaning." She stopped, her face red. At Jennifer's amazed look, she shrugged. "Those of us who work as servants in the big houses, we talk. We warn each other. Mr. Ames, he doesn't care if a woman is willing or not. Many a maidservant left his family's employ after being severely abused and violated."

Arabella gasped in horror. Even Henrietta seemed speechless for once.

"Do you think my uncle knows this?" Jennifer asked, fearful of the answer. Was the brutal rape of a maidservant grounds enough for blackmail? Jennifer suspected that a family as wealthy and as powerful as the Ames family could cover up such a scandal. Who would take the word of a servant over that of Bradley Ames?

"Surely he cannot know, miss," Mrs. Nelson protested. "Mr. Mainwaring would never bind you to that man if he knew."

"Whether he knows or not, Mrs. Nelson, he binds me against my will," Jennifer responded. "My uncle tore me from the arms of my betrothed, drugged me, abducted me, imprisoned me in my own house. Who can say how far he will go?"

Mrs. Nelson handed Jennifer her cloak. "What can I do to help you?"

Jennifer's shoulders sagged in relief as she accepted the cloak. "God bless you, Mrs. Nelson." She hesitated, thinking. She had to assume she would never come back to this house. What was truly important to her? "The silver tea set on the sideboard in the dining room was a wedding gift to my parents from my godfather, and it rightly belongs to me."

"Yes, miss." Mrs. Nelson hurried to the door. "Shall I bring the set back here?"

"Please meet us at the main door. And take care."

"Yes, miss." She was gone, closing the door behind her.

"Can she be trusted?" Henrietta demanded.

"This morning I would have said no, but tonight, I think she can be." Jennifer again opened the wardrobe. "We will know soon enough. Arabella, there are a few jewel boxes in the top drawers of the highboy. Please give them to Henrietta to pack. And the small paintings of my parents on the bedside table."

Arabella scurried to do as she asked, and in a matter of minutes, all was ready.

The three women hurried down the hall, pausing at the top of the stairs. Besides John, Rebecca, and Elias Craig, the foyer was empty except for the impassive butler who stood at the door. Jennifer led the way, dragging the heavy carpet-bag behind her. It bumped down each step. Henrietta followed with the satchel, and Arabella brought up the rear, carrying Jennifer's cloak.

John looked up and saw them. He hurried up the stairs to take the carpetbag from Jennifer and the satchel from Henrietta and escorted the ladies down to the foyer.

"I shall see the bags loaded in my carriage," Elias said, taking the carpetbag and the satchel from John. He hurried past the butler, who held the door open with an inscrutable expression on his face.

Mrs. Nelson came down the hall from the direction of the dining room with a burlap bag in her arms. "I could find nothing else to pack the set in," she said apologetically, glancing down at the unwieldy bundle she carried. "But I took care to wrap each piece in cloth."

"Thank you, Mrs. Nelson." Jennifer smiled at her as John accepted the bag. He took it to the butler with a low-voiced request that the man take it out to Mr. Craig.

"Very good, sir," the butler calmly replied, as if being asked to carry out a burlap bag containing the family silver was an everyday occurrence.

Jennifer grabbed one of Mrs. Nelson's hands. "For your own sake, leave this house," she said urgently. "My uncle will only bring you grief. Call upon Mr. Craig in his offices tomorrow afternoon. I will leave a letter of reference for you. You are an efficient and loyal housekeeper; you shall have no trouble finding another position."

"I will think on it, Miss Jennifer. Thank you for your concern." Mrs. Nelson nodded at John. "Is that your young man?"

"Yes. He has come for me."

John stepped over to Jennifer's side, and the housekeeper stared at him for a moment. "You do not look, or act, at all as Mr. Mainwaring depicted you, sir," she said in a troubled tone.

"I should hope not, madam," John said with a smile.

Mrs. Nelson straightened her shoulders, as if she had just reached an important decision. Her voice was again brisk and businesslike when she spoke. "I have taken the liberty of asking Mr. Creed and Mr. Rutherford to explore the gardens, for I am certain I heard an unusual noise out there."

"I was wondering what had happened to those two fine gentlemen," Elias commented as he joined them.

Mrs. Nelson looked at Jennifer. "Please forgive my role in your unhappy time here, for I was wrong to do as I did. I truly wish you well, miss, both you and your gentleman."

"Thank you, Mrs. Nelson."

The housekeeper nodded, then hurried away down the hall.

"Are you off, then?" Rebecca asked. Her face was becomingly flushed with excitement.

Jennifer turned to John with a happy smile. "I guess we are."

He took Jennifer's cloak from Arabella and settled it around her shoulders. "You are sure you have everything?"

"Yes—no! Preston's sword is in the library." Jennifer hurried down the hall, with John on her heels. Henrietta trotted after them.

"Preston's sword?" John asked.

Jennifer hurried into the room. "There, on the wall over that chair. He gave it to my father as a parting gift when we left California the second time."

John reached up and carefully lifted the encased sword down from its mounting. The silver scabbard was beautifully engraved, the handle of the sword itself made of intricately wrought steel.

"Where did he get it?" John asked in wonder.

"I'm not sure; it may have been his father's. I was only a child when he presented it to my father, and I do not remember the entire story. But I am sure Preston would like to have it back."

"Hurry!" Henrietta hissed from the door, just as a sudden

commotion was heard from down the hall. "Oh, dear. I fear we are found out." She backed away from the door to take a protective stand at Jennifer's side.

John positioned himself on her other side, and they waited. A minute later, Oliver burst into the room, followed by a wet, angry, bruised, and curiously sober Bradley Ames. Creed and Rutherford also crowded into the room.

"You." Oliver's eyes blazed with fury as he stared at John. "You dare to come into my house?"

"I have come for my betrothed, Mainwaring. Get out of our way or I will take you apart with my bare hands." John's quiet tone held a distinct note of menace.

"You shall not have her," Oliver vowed.

"Yes, he shall," Jennifer interjected angrily. "I warned you that your plan would fail, uncle. I am leaving with John, and you cannot stop me."

"I can and I will!"

"No, you will not." Elias Craig spoke from the door. He pushed past Creed and Rutherford, as did Arabella and Rebecca, while Mrs. Nelson waited in the doorway. "You have overstepped your legal and moral bounds, Mr. Mainwaring. Jennifer is free to leave this house, just as she is free to choose her husband. I will see that she is allowed to exercise those freedoms."

"As will I," John added. "By whatever means necessary."

"We all will, Mr. Mainwaring," Rebecca stated. "Surely you do not intend to forcibly detain her in front of us."

Oliver glared at Elias and John, then at the women. He finally focused on Jennifer. "If you leave, I will notify the French Ambassador in Washington that your lover is the dreaded *La Serpiente.* He will be tried and shot as the assassin he is!"

John stared at him, shocked. How did Oliver Mainwaring know of *La Serpiente?*

"Do your worst, uncle," Jennifer snapped. "John is not an assassin."

"No, I am not," John asserted. He looked down at Jennifer. "Are you ready to leave?"

"Yes." Jennifer started toward the door, but Oliver refused to move out of her way. He crossed his arms and belligerently stared at her.

"Do not tempt me when I am holding a sword, Mainwaring," John warned softly.

After a long, tense moment, Oliver stepped aside and allowed Jennifer to pass. John approached him and stopped. He stared at Oliver Mainwaring's flushed and angry face as fleeting memories of all Oliver had done rushed through his mind. Something inside him snapped, sending waves of hot rage pounding through his veins.

"Mr. Craig, would you hold this for a moment?" John spoke in a deceptively calm voice as he held out the sword.

Elias took the weapon from him.

John pulled back his right arm and smashed his fist into Oliver's face, knocking him backward to the floor. "You are lucky there are ladies present, Mainwaring. You got off easy." He glared down at the stunned man, then left the room, followed by the three women and Elias Craig.

"Do you want us to go after them, Mr. Mainwaring?" Hayward Creed asked as Rutherford helped Oliver to his feet.

"Not yet," Oliver ground out. He dug in his pocket for a handkerchief and wiped his bleeding nose. "I must think." He snapped his fingers at Mrs. Nelson, who still stood in the doorway. "Have my valet pack my things, Mrs. Nelson. I am off to Washington in the morning."

She nodded and disappeared.

"I shall see John Cantrell hanged for the murderer he is," Oliver vowed as he dabbed at his rapidly swelling lip. "You two," he indicated Creed and Rutherford, "will wait here for the next few days, until I send you further instructions. Now go help with the guests' carriages." The two men left the room.

"Well done, Mainwaring," Bradley sneered. "Things certainly went smoothly, didn't they?" He stomped toward the door.

"Where are you going?" Oliver demanded.

"Wherever I choose. The deal's off. No marriage, no investment money."

"Oh, no, you don't." Oliver advanced on him and grabbed his arm. "I only threw Jennifer in to sweeten the pot, because you wanted her. She has nothing to do with the original agreement, which stands or I go to the authorities with what I know."

Bradley shook off his hand. "So I got a little rough with one of the maids. So what? No one will take the word of a loose-moralled serving wench over mine."

"You got rough with several maids, and one died as a result of your ill-treatment."

"Shut up, you fool!" Bradley cast a wild glance at the open door.

"I swear, Ames, if you do not keep your end of the bargain, I will go to the authorities. Be reasonable, man. I am asking you to invest, not pay me off. You will see a handsome return on your money."

Bradley eyed him suspiciously. "Are you saying that if I stick to the agreement, you'll not turn me in?"

"I do not care about the death of some stupid maidservant, nor am I concerned with how you find your pleasure. I need your investment funds, and that is all I need. But I assure you, I will have those funds."

Bradley glowered at him. "All right."

Just outside the door, Eugenia Nelson leaned against the wall, trembling. So Oliver Mainwaring had known all along about Bradley Ames's cruelty, and still he would have given his niece to the man. She crept silently away, determined that Oliver's bag would not be the only one packed tonight. Hers would be as well. And she would check with her sister, who was one of the unfortunate women who had suffered horribly at the hands of Mr. Ames. Perhaps her sister knew which of his victims had died. And perhaps, when she called upon Mr. Craig the next day for her references, he would be able to advise her. She would see to it that Bradley Ames did not escape the legal consequences of his actions, no matter what Oliver Mainwaring promised.

At the main door, Henrietta straightened the tie of Jennifer's cloak. "Be happy," she whispered. "And I promise I shall speak to my parents."

Jennifer hugged her. "Good. Write to me at the Santa Maria Ranch, Gilroy, California. Let me know what happens."

Henrietta nodded and stepped back. Jennifer took Arabella's hands next. "Thank you for everything."

Arabella's big eyes filled with tears. "I am so happy for you, Jennifer. Treasure him."

"Oh, I will," Jennifer promised.

"This has all been very exciting," Rebecca said, "but there is something I must ask you, Mr. Cantrell."

"By all means, Miss Wentworth."

"You *do* have honorable intentions toward our friend? You do intend marriage?"

John smiled and took Jennifer's hand. "Oh, yes, if she will still have me."

"You know I will, John," Jennifer said softly.

"When?" Henrietta demanded.

"Tomorrow," John said without hesitation.

"Where?" Arabella queried.

John looked at Elias.

The solicitor smiled. "My office, ten o'clock. I have already made arrangements with the justice of the peace."

Arabella clasped her hands together. "Do you need witnesses?" she asked, her eyes wide with hope.

Jennifer looked up at John and laughed. "I think we do."

"Absolutely," he agreed.

"We shall be there," Rebecca said. "Now go, before Mr. Mainwaring comes up with some other plan to stop you."

"Yes, Miss Wentworth." John took her hand and kissed it, then Henrietta's, then Arabella's. "Thank you, ladies, from the bottom of my heart." Finally, with great pleasure, he turned to Jennifer, taking her hand securely in his, and led her safely from Oliver Mainwaring's house.

Twenty-two

"Are you sure it would not have been wiser to stay with the Craigs?" Jennifer asked, looking around John's luxuriously appointed hotel suite. Several lighted gas lamps cast a pleasing glow over the furnishings.

John shook his head as he set her bags on the floor near the wardrobe. "I doubt Oliver will try to find you tonight, but we can't be sure. I do not want the Craigs endangered because of us. Besides, I have no intention of letting you out of my sight until we are wed and you are safely out of Oliver's legal reach. I doubt very much that the noble Mr. Craig and his gracious wife would have understood my insistence upon sharing your bedroom."

Jennifer blushed. "Well, this is very nice," she commented as she untied her cloak. "You were clever to mention that your wife would be joining you when you checked in. Thank you for protecting my reputation." Now that she was alone with him in such intimate surroundings, she felt surprisingly shy.

He came up behind her and lifted the cloak from her shoulders. "Tomorrow you *will* be my wife." He placed a kiss on her neck.

With a sigh, Jennifer turned into his arms. "Oh, John," she whispered. "These weeks have passed so slowly. I have longed for you so."

He held her tightly. "I cannot describe my feelings when I came home that day and found you gone. It was as if the sun had left the sky. And then to have to listen to Constanza's lies—"

"She waited for you that day?" Jennifer looked up at him, appalled. "Oh, my darling, I am so sorry. I shudder to think what she said. Oliver told me she would make sure you despised me, that you would turn to her."

"Never," John vowed. "Even if you left me, I would never turn to her."

"I know." She placed her gloved fingers on his lips. "I did not, for one moment, consider that you would." She replaced her fingers with her lips.

With a deep groan, John latched onto her mouth like a starving man, forcing her lips apart, plundering her sweetness until they were both breathless. When their mouths separated at last, he cradled the back of her head as she rested her cheek against his shoulder.

"It has been a long, anxious night," he said. "Are you hungry? Would you like something to drink?"

"No, but thank you." Jennifer's voice was muffled against his coat. "More than anything, I want to get out of this costume."

John set her back from him and examined her from head to foot. "The gown is unique," he said cautiously. "I've never seen anything quite like it."

Jennifer bubbled with laughter. "It is ridiculous, John. Everything about the gown is so exaggerated. Look at the size of this bustle." She walked away from him, swaying her hips from side to side, sending the back of the skirt into drunken undulations. "Oliver chose it," she explained over one shoulder as she peeled an elbow-length glove from one arm. "He was determined that I would be the envy of all Philadelphia."

"Well, it is eye-catching," John said with a wide grin. He pulled his own white gloves off and tossed them onto the dressing table, then loosened his white silk tie and removed it.

Jennifer set her gloves next to his, pausing to touch one of his. "I like to see our things side by side," she said softly.

"I like to see us side by side." After shrugging off his coat, John came up behind her, as close as her bustle would allow, careful not to step on her train, and put his arms around her waist. They both stared at their reflection in the mirror. He held her for a moment, then frowned as he moved his hands over her corsetted stomach. "They have you all trussed up, don't they?"

"Yes. And I am most uncomfortable."

"We shall see about that." With deft fingers, he unlaced the back of her pearl-embellished bodice. Jennifer held the loosened garment to her breast as he went to work on the skirt. "This is no time for modesty," he said briskly when he had the skirt opened. "Give me the blasted thing."

Jennifer obediently pulled the bodice off her shoulders and down her arms and handed it to him. He tossed it on the floor in the corner, then held his hand out to her.

"Off with the skirt now. Step out of it."

Again she obeyed, taking his hand for balance, and the heavy underskirt with its filmy gauze overskirt landed in an ignoble heap on top of the discarded bodice. John removed his vest, then together they went to work on the many petticoats and the huge bustle, all of which joined the skirt.

"Damn these corsets," John muttered as he fought with the laces. At last he succeeded in freeing Jennifer from the contraption and threw it down with disgust.

"Thank you," Jennifer sighed. She rubbed her hands over her ribs, delighting in the sense of relief, wondering if her skin was as wrinkled as her chemise. Then, in the mirror, she saw that he was staring at her with a look of deep concern on his face. "What is it?" she asked.

"These bruises." He took her elbow, examining the purplish marks on her upper arm. "How did you come by them?" His tone was not nearly as gentle as his touch.

Jennifer pulled away and covered the bruises with her hand.

"Neither Oliver nor Bradley are known for their kindness, John. It is over. Can we not just forget it?"

John's hands clenched, as did his jaw. "They both man-handled you, and I will not forget it. They had better pray they never see me again." He tore at the buttons of his shirt and pulled the garment off.

She sat on the dressing table stool, deliberately hiding her face from him as she removed her high-heeled, white kid shoes and gartered stockings. Although she had dreamed of their being together like this again, Jennifer felt strange about their mutual, gradual disrobing. She found John as breathtakingly beautiful as she always had, but now that she wore only her chemise and drawers, she was painfully aware of how thin she had become. Suddenly self-conscious, she swivelled on the stool to face the mirror and began to pull the flowers and pins from her hair.

"Let me," John said quietly. "Please." He stood behind her again, wearing nothing but his black trousers. Jennifer dropped her hands to her lap and closed her eyes. Neither of them said anything for several minutes while John searched out each pin. When her hair finally fell free down her back, he massaged her scalp with his strong fingers. She sighed in contentment.

"Where is your brush?" John's voice was a mere whisper against her ear.

A delightful shiver ran down her body. "In the satchel," she said, waving a languid hand in the general direction of her two bags. "My nightdress is there as well."

John searched through the bag and pulled out the brush. "You won't be needing the nightdress."

His sultry words ignited the familiar fire in her, and Jennifer bit her bottom lip. She closed her eyes again as he worked the brush through her long hair with gentle expertise.

"I love your hair," he whispered. "I love the scent of your orange blossom water. I love your neck." He lifted her hair to place a kiss at the back of her neck. "I love everything about you, *mi amada.*" His hand caressed her shoulder, pushing the strap of her chemise down.

She caught his hand and turned sideways on the stool. "I'm sorry, John," she whispered miserably, pressing a kiss to his palm. "I wanted to be beautiful for you, but instead I am pale and thin and bruised. I was ill and frightened, and I had no appetite, and I just could not force myself to eat. I tried, but—"

"Jennie, no. No." John dropped to his knees in front of her, setting the brush on the table. "Please don't." He took her face between his hands and stared into her eyes. "You are beautiful tonight, you will be beautiful when you have recovered from this ordeal, you will be beautiful when you are heavy with my child. However you come to me, I will find you beautiful, because I love you." He kissed her reverently. "I love you."

With a sob, Jennifer threw her arms around his shoulders. He held her while she softly cried; he stroked her hair; he swore silently to kill Oliver Mainwaring.

After a few minutes, she sighed and straightened, wiping her eyes. "I don't know what came over me."

"You have been through an ordeal, sweetheart." John pushed her hair back over her shoulders and trailed his hands down her arms. "You should sleep." There were other things he wanted to do before they slept, but he would not pressure her. He could read the weariness in her tear-bright eyes, see the fatigue in her slumped shoulders.

"I will," she said with a watery smile. "But not yet. I have not found you again only to sleep. I love you, John." Her fingers wandered through the hair that covered his chest, and her voice dropped to whisper. "I need you." She moved her hands over his shoulders and pulled him close, pressing her mouth to his, pushing her tongue between his lips.

John moaned and opened his mouth to her. His hands worked their way under her hair to stroke her back from shoulder to hip. She scooted closer to him, wrapping her legs around his thighs in sweet invitation. He moaned again and moved his hands under her arms to cup her breasts, then he fought with the tiny buttons down the front of her chemise, pulling the thin material out of the way. She threw back her head as he trailed hot kisses from her mouth along her jaw, down her throat, across her chest, until his lips found her taut, tingling nipple. She released her breath in a joyous sigh and grabbed at his hair, holding his head against her breast as he teased and suckled her.

John pulled away from her and stood, sweeping her up into his arms. He carried her to the bed and with one hand jerked the bedclothes back before he laid her on the sheet. Without taking his eyes from her, he stripped out of his pants.

Jennifer's heart pounded in anticipation when he stood before her naked. She sat up and slipped the chemise from her arms, allowing it to drop over the side of the bed. When she fumbled with the ties of her drawers, John leaned forward to lend his assistance, and soon that garment, too, lay on the floor.

They stared at each other for a moment, then Jennifer held her arms out to him, and he fell on top of her, pushing her back against the pillows. Feverishly they explored each other with lips and fingers. When John's hand moved between Jennifer's legs, he was surprised to find her deliciously slick.

"You are ready for me so quickly?" he asked in wonder.

"I have always been ready for you," she whispered, searching for his hardened length, guiding him to her wet warmth. He pushed into her with one smooth thrust. She sighed and arched her back, drawing him deeper, and their movements became a dance of love. He led her, then she led him, always dancing closer to the beckoning flames, until they were both consumed in the fires of ecstasy.

Afterwards, they lay together for a long time without moving, still intimately joined, contented to hold each other. Jennifer stroked John's back down to his smooth, muscled flank, pulling him in a little more, wiggling against him.

"Careful, woman," he growled as he nipped her shoulder. "If you start something else, you'll have to finish it."

"I'll finish anything I start with you, John Cantrell." She wiggled again.

"Will you live out your life with me?"

Jennifer stared up into his eyes. "I will be yours until the day I draw my last breath, and beyond, throughout eternity."

"As I will be yours." John kissed her again, then eased out of her onto his side. He pulled the blankets up over them and they snuggled together.

"When did you arrive?" Jennifer asked, stifling a yawn.

"Two days ago."

Jennifer frowned. "And you did not come for me immediately? What were you doing?"

His arms tightened around her. "Believe me, Jen, it was torture to be so near and not go to you. But I met with Mr. Craig, and we decided to follow the plan you and he had devised. The ball was still the perfect opportunity to make our move, when so many people would be about. We also discussed your financial situation. He would not divulge everything without your permission, but since I had the letter he had written to you, he knew I was aware of the situation. It was very wise of you to leave his letter where we could find it."

"I acted out of panic, John, not wisdom. Oliver came home with Constanza just after I received the letter, and I did not want him see it. There was no time to do anything but shove it into Preston's stack of mail. Later, when they drugged me and carried me off without allowing me to write a note, or wire you along the route, I prayed you would find the letter."

"Mr. Craig will meet with us tomorrow immediately following the marriage ceremony, and we will learn the full truth of your financial situation. Then we will face it together."

"I'd rather we met with Mr. Craig first," Jennifer insisted in a troubled voice. "He and I had no time to discuss finances in our two brief meetings. I would know the full extent of the damage before we are wed, so that you enter our marriage completely informed."

John stroked her shoulder. "If you wish, sweetheart. But nothing Craig can say will change my mind."

"Thank you." She kissed his jaw. "Now tell me, how is everyone at home?"

"Aside from missing you terribly, everyone is fine and they all send their best. I think Rosa and Gabe will be announcing their engagement soon. It was as if your disappearance made them realize how fragile life can be. Things have definitely accelerated between them."

"How wonderful!" Jennifer exclaimed. "They will be good for each other, and Francisca will have a father again. I know Gabe already loves her as his own."

"Brigit desperately wanted to come with me, insisted that you would need your maid. Not until Barbara pointed out that it would not be proper for a young lady to travel alone with a gentleman did she accept our decision." John chuckled. "She sure is a fiery little thing, and deeply devoted to you." He kissed her forehead. "As am I."

Jennifer smiled. "Brigit will be surprised to learn that you served as my maid quite well tonight. You even managed to free me from my corset without using your knife."

"Only just," John grumbled.

"How are the kittens?"

"Growing like weeds. They are all over the house now."

"Did Jake learn to drink from the saucer? I was working with him when the mail came, and then Oliver . . ." Her voice trailed off.

John's hold on her tightened again. "Yes, he learned. I'm sorry you weren't there to see it." He was quiet for a moment, then commented, "Those kittens mean a lot to you, don't they?"

She sighed. "I am not sure I can explain it, John." Her fingers moved in an idle caress through the soft hair on his chest. "For most of my life, I felt that my own life was out of my control. My parents, my stepmother, then my uncle, made the decisions that governed where I lived, what I did, even what I would become. I experienced my first taste of freedom at the Santa Maria, and *I* decided I would live there. Then, just a few minutes after making that decision, I found Katie and Jake."

She rose up on one elbow and looked down at him, desperate to make him understand. "I had the power to determine whether those kittens lived or died. That sounds arrogant, I know, but I resolved to exercise that new, unfamiliar power; I had so little power over anything in my life before that. Those kittens *had* to live, John, even if it meant defying Preston. There was more at stake than just their lives. They helped me find the courage to insist that I be allowed to live my own life. Can you understand that?"

John reached up to take a strand of her hair in his hand. "I understand perfectly, Jennie. I am proud and honored that you decided to live your life with me."

"We will make a good life together, John," she said earnestly. "For us and for our children."

"I am certain of it." John held her even more closely. With Jennie at his side, offering him her undying love, he felt he could accomplish anything, even find the inner peace that had eluded him for years. With Jennie at his side, he could learn to live in peace.

At nine o'clock the next morning, John and Jennifer presented themselves at the doors to Elias Craig's offices on Front Street. Jennifer pushed the hood of her cloak back off her head, self-consciously patting her simple chignon. In her haste to leave Oliver's house, she had neglected to bring any of her hats, and she felt naked without one.

"You look lovely," John assured her, his eyes roaming over her bronze-striped day dress. "The color of that gown highlights your hair, and I do not wish you to cover it."

Jennifer gave him a sweet smile. "Yes, my lord," she teased, just as Mrs. Craig opened the door.

They were ushered into the office, and after Mrs. Craig poured them fresh coffee, they sat down to discuss the state of Jennifer's finances.

She was relieved to learn that although the situation was very serious, it was not as bad as she had feared. She would not be forced into bankruptcy.

"Since Mr. Mainwaring is the one who signed the loan notes, he will be held responsible for them," Elias explained. "However, as long as his power of attorney is in effect, he can legally use your funds towards those loans. You must revoke his power of attorney at once. I have the papers here."

Elias pushed some pages across the desk toward Jennifer, while Mrs. Craig set an ink bottle within reach and handed her a pen. Jennifer read quickly, then signed them.

"We shall get these over to the bank at once," Elias said. "I shall also request a statement of what remains in your accounts. As I said in my letter, the trust your mother left you has been untouched, as it was specifically excluded from the original writ of power of attorney. The last statement showed there was a little over seven thousand dollars in the trust."

Jennifer heaved a sigh of relief and glanced at John. He smiled encouragingly at her.

"Which debts are mine, Mr. Craig?" she asked.

Elias shrugged. "It depends on which debts you wish to accept. We could insist that Mr. Mainwaring be held responsible for all of them, but his solicitors will battle us. How anxious are you to fight your uncle?"

She reached for John's hand, and his fingers closed comfortingly on hers. "No more than is necessary," she said. "I wish to return to California and make a new life there, and I want this behind me. What debts are there?"

"In addition to the loans, there are several outstanding debts to honest creditors, some months old. Dressmakers and tailors, milliners and haberdashers, decorators, the livery, the coach-maker, even the grocer. Some of your help are owed back pay."

Jennifer stared at him. "None of them have said a word," she said, shaking her head. "What a fool I have been." She cast a worried glance at John. "I know these people; they need their wages, and payment for their goods, and they shall be paid." He nodded his agreement. She turned back to Elias. "Does any of my share of my father's estate remain?"

Elias leaned back in his chair. "I will not know for certain until we get a report from the bank."

Again, Jennifer looked at John. "Oliver's loans are his responsibility, as are his debts to his tailor and his haberdasher. I shall make good on any debts incurred for me, including part of the grocer's bill. Perhaps the coach-maker will accept the return of the buggy in lieu of payment." Her brow furrowed. "And the help must be paid what is owed them, as well as severance, for they must be let go, and I will write reference letters for them. Do you agree?"

"Yes," John said. He looked at Elias. "As I explained to you yesterday, my funds are also available."

"No, John, I do not wish to use your funds," Jennifer said with a frown.

"It may not be necessary," Elias interjected. "What do you wish to do with the house? You are listed on the deed as half-owner."

"I do not want it," Jennifer said firmly.

"Is there a mortgage on it?" John asked Elias.

"No. Albert Mainwaring left a debt-free estate. However, Oliver Mainwaring put it up as collateral for one of his loans."

Now John frowned. "Does the amount of the loan exceed the value of Oliver's share of the house?"

Elias shook his head. "I do not believe so."

John turned to Jennifer. "Jennie, my advice is to sell the house as quickly as possible."

"I agree," Jennifer said. "Use my share of the proceeds to

pay our creditors. I feel very strongly that my uncle's debts to his tailors and haberdashers and decorators and grocers be settled before his loans are. The banks will survive if my uncle defaults; the men struggling to make a success of their small businesses will have a more difficult time of it."

Elias nodded. "I will do what I can." He pulled out his pocket watch. "It is nearly ten." He turned his piercing gaze first on John, then on Jennifer. "Do either of you have doubts about the forthcoming wedding ceremony?"

Jennifer faced John with a loving smile on her face. He met her gaze, and at the same time, they both said, "no."

At that moment a knock sounded at the door, and Mrs. Craig rose to admit the justice of the peace. A few minutes later, Arabella Hawthorne, Rebecca Wentworth, and Henrietta Duke arrived, all three resplendent in walking costumes of the latest fashion. Without further ado, the ceremony began, with Mr. and Mrs. Craig standing with John, and Jennifer's new friends standing with her.

Jennifer listened with rapt attention to the solemn words the justice spoke, speaking her part with a joyful heart, meaning every word. That John spoke with equal sincerity was evident in the loving tone of his voice. She was deeply moved when he slipped a plain gold band on her finger. The simple ring shone in the sunlight that poured through the window, representing to Jennifer the start of a new life, as surely as the sunrise signalled the start of a new day.

When the justice announced that they were husband and wife, Jennifer threw her arms around John's neck, while his arms closed around her waist. He lifted her slightly off the floor.

"My wife," he whispered wonderingly.

"My husband," she sighed, and their lips met in a reverent kiss.

As they separated and faced their friends, a soft sniffling sound was heard.

"I beg your pardon," Henrietta said huskily, just before she blew her nose into a lacy handkerchief. "I always cry at weddings."

"Me, too." Arabella daintily dabbed at her eyes.

"Congratulations, Mr. Cantrell." Elias Craig held out his hand. "It pleases me greatly to see Jennifer as your wife, for I know I no longer need worry about her."

Rebecca gave Jennifer a hug. "Well done, Mrs. Cantrell. What are your immediate plans?"

Jennifer looked at John. "What are our plans, husband?"

"I think we should remain here for a few days, in the event Mr. Craig needs to speak with us on certain matters," he said. "And as this is my first visit to Philadelphia, I would not mind seeing some of this fair city. We will leave for home by the end of next week."

"You must come and visit us," Jennifer urged as she looked at the people who surrounded her. "All of you. It takes only a little over a week to travel from Philadelphia to the Santa Maria."

Rebecca laughed. "You may regret that invitation, Jennifer. One day we shall descend upon your ranch *en masse*. I want to see a land that breeds men such as John Cantrell."

Jennifer turned admiring eyes on her husband. "It is a glorious land."

"Apparently," Arabella commented.

"I have arranged a celebratory luncheon at the hotel," John said, taking Jennifer's hand. "We would be honored if all of you would join us."

All present agreed, and the happy gathering trooped out the door.

Jennifer's first week as John's wife passed in a blur of pleasurable days and long, passion-filled nights. The fair weather of Indian summer continued, adding to the enjoyment of their excursions about the city. She delighted in showing him the sights of Philadelphia and discovered in him an interested student, for he was anxious to explore the historical buildings. Their visit to Independence Hall and the Liberty Bell deeply moved him. Having fought for Mexican independence, he appreciated the significance of the American War for Independence and commented how sad it was that so many men throughout the ages had died in pursuit of liberty.

As agreeable and entertaining as her days were, each afternoon Jennifer found herself looking forward to sunset. Sunset meant returning to the hotel and, after a light supper, returning to the bed where their love for each other was celebrated again and again by the glorious sharing of their bodies. It seemed as if she could not get enough of him, nor he of her, and their lovemaking ran the gamut from fierce and needing to tender and reverent. After a few short days in John's loving company, the gaunt look left her face, the fatigue and fear were gone from her eyes, and her cheeks regained their rosy color. Not even the uncertainty of her financial circumstances could mar the joy of that magical time.

Eugenia Nelson called on the newlyweds at the hotel on Wednesday morning. She thanked Jennifer for the funds and the letter of reference left with Elias Craig, and explained all she had learned about Bradley Ames and the death of one of the women he had abused.

Jennifer was horrified, and John furious, to learn that Oliver had intended to marry her to such a man. John promised to pay Mr. Craig's legal fees for Mrs. Nelson and her sister if they decided to pursue the matter. Nearly weeping with gratitude, she accepted his offer and took her leave, wishing them a lifetime of happiness together.

Elias Craig met with them on Thursday, having finally gathered all of the information on her accounts. There was enough of her father's money left to pay a few of her debts, and she made up the difference out of her trust. She was left with a balance of almost four thousand dollars, enough to make a nice contribution to the future of the Santa Maria.

When Elias learned that Oliver had left town for a few days, he and John escorted Jennifer to the house, where she met with the staff and presented them with their back pay, severance payments, and letters of reference. Only Hayward Creed and Otto Rutherford received nothing, and she informed them that they would have to wait for Oliver's return.

They had accomplished all that they could.

Rebecca, Henrietta, and Arabella joined them for a farewell supper at the hotel that night. Early Friday morning, Elias drove John and Jennifer to the train station, where he waited with them on the platform.

"Do not worry about a thing, Mrs. Cantrell. All is well in hand now. Mr. Atwater has been in contact with Mr. Mainwaring, and we shall meet next week. I shall keep you informed."

John held out his hand to Elias. "Thank you, sir. You have been of invaluable help to us. I do not know what we would have done without you."

"You probably would have stormed the Mainwaring house with blazing guns and rescued Mrs. Cantrell by whatever means necessary," Elias said as the two men shook hands.

"I fear my uncle would not have survived such an encounter," Jennifer said with an affectionate smile.

John's face darkened. "Had I known then what I now know about Oliver Mainwaring—and Bradley Ames, for that matter—I would have used Preston's sword on them both that night."

"They will pay for their actions, Mr. Cantrell, have no doubt," Elias assured him. "I regret that the charge of kidnapping against Mr. Mainwaring would have been so difficult to prosecute, but he has plenty of other trouble awaiting him. As for Mr. Ames, even his family's wealth and position will not save him from charges of rape and murder."

The conductor shouted that it was time to board. Jennifer turned to Elias, holding her hand out to him. "Thank you for everything, Mr. Craig. My father's trust in you, and mine, was well placed." She leaned forward and kissed his cheek.

"Just be happy, Mrs. Cantrell." He looked at John. "Both of you be happy."

"We will be," John said with a confident smile. He guided Jennifer onto the train and to their compartment. She waved to Elias as the train began to move. The solicitor's figure was soon lost in the billowing steam put out by the departing train.

She leaned back against the seat with a sigh. "Do you think we will ever return to Philadelphia?"

John settled beside her and took her hand. "Not on my account. But if you wish to visit your friends here, or show our children where you once lived, I will bring you back."

Jennifer turned toward the window and watched as the city of Philadelphia passed by. "I don't know if I will ever feel the need to return, John." She leaned against him. "We are going home."

John wrapped his arms around her. "We are going home," he repeated in a soft voice.

Twenty-three

"I knew you would like these people," Jennifer said to John from her perch on the edge of the bed. He lay back on the pillows with his hands under his head, watching contentedly as she pulled the brush through her hair.

The trip so far had been long but uneventful, with the exception of a surprisingly early Wyoming snowstorm that had forced a two-day stay in Cheyenne. They had finally arrived in Laramie City the day before and had been warmly welcomed by Alina Parker, Susannah O'Rourke, and a jovial gathering of their families and friends. John and Jennifer were staying with the Parkers for a few days, then they would spend a few days with the O'Rourkes at their neighboring ranch before continuing on to California.

"I was last in this house in July," Jennifer said thoughtfully as she looked around the cozy bedroom she and John shared. "Susannah and Conor were married here, in the main room. And now they have their own land and a new home, and they are going to have a baby." She glanced at John. "I know you are anxious to get home. You don't mind the delay, do you?"

"I promised you a visit with your friends, Jennie. And as you said, I like them all. Alina and Susannah are as wonderful as you told me they were, and Beau and Conor seem like good men. Their friend Mr. Pike is a real character, and Lily Carolina and Elizabeth are delightful children. They make me miss David and Molly. Everyone has made me feel very welcome." He reached out to finger the sleeve of her high-necked nightdress. "I only regret that these cool Wyoming nights dic- tate that you wear this."

"At least I'm not wearing a nightcap," she said tartly as she set the brush on the bedside table.

"Thank God for that." John threw back the blankets and opened his arms to her. She blew out the coal-oil lamp, then scooted into his embrace, snuggling against his naked warmth as he arranged the blankets around her shoulders.

"Would you like to ride over to the O'Rourkes with me tomorrow?" he asked. "Beau said that Conor has an impres- sive stock of horses. We may want to buy one or two for the Santa Maria."

"I would love to," Jennifer responded, thrilled that he ob- viously intended to include her in a business discussion.

"Good." When John spoke again, his voice dropped to a sensual whisper. "Do you know what I would love to do?" His hand moved down Jennifer's back to cup her bottom.

"Tomorrow?" Jennifer teased, running her hand down his back to grab him the same way.

"Tonight, woman. Right now." John nibbled on her mouth, then let his lips wander over her cheek to her jaw.

"I think I can guess." She opened the buttons at her throat, and those down the front of her garment. John's greedy mouth followed her fingers, kissing each inch of skin as it was ex- posed. "Why did you not say something before I donned the nightdress?" she asked rather breathlessly.

"Because unwrapping the package is part of the fun," he murmured against her breast. His searching hand found the hem of her nightdress and slipped underneath.

"I will remember that, Mr. Cantrell," Jennifer whispered as a shiver ran through her, a shiver that had nothing to do with the chill in the room.

The late October morning dawned cool and clear, a perfect day for a ride. John invited their hosts to join them, but Beau and Pike claimed they had fence to check. Alina declined because her daughter, Elizabeth, who was only five months old, had spent a restless night and was at last sleeping soundly. She promised to drive over in the buggy and meet them at the O'Rourkes for the noon meal.

After a hearty breakfast, John and Jennifer set out for the O'Rourke ranch. John rode a spirited bay Beau had referred to as Bay, appropriately enough, while Jennifer rode Alina's black mare, a sweet-tempered creature named Lucy.

"This is beautiful land," John commented, waving an arm to encompass the grass-covered, tree-dotted hills through which they rode. Although the weather had warmed substantially after the snowstorm three days earlier, patches of snow still covered the ground in the shady areas. In the far distance, the whitened peaks of the Rocky Mountains proudly rose into the sky.

"It is," Jennifer agreed. "There is a wild freedom about this part of the country that I find very appealing. Alina and Susannah certainly seem to like it."

John eyed her curiously. "Would you rather settle here than in California?"

"No! As much as I love Wyoming, and my friends here, the Santa Maria is my home." She smiled at John. "But thank you for asking."

"I want you to be happy."

"I am," she assured him.

With a satisfied nod, John allowed Bay to break into a trot. Just as Jennifer encouraged Lucy to catch up, the sound of a shot split the air, followed a moment later by the strange whine of a ricocheted bullet.

Lucy whinnied in fear and sidestepped. Jennifer struggled to control the horse, thankful that she was riding astride. At the same time, Bay danced in an excited circle. John kept his seat, looking wildly around. "There, on the hill behind us!" he cried.

Jennifer saw two riders on top of a rise a short distance

away. "Surely they aren't shooting at us." As she spoke, one of the riders stood up in his stirrups and took aim with a rifle. Sunlight glinted off the long barrel.

"They sure as hell are!" John shouted, kicking Bay to a gallop. "Ride, Jennie!"

Instinctively leaning low over the saddle horn, she urged Lucy to run. The rifle sounded a second later, and Jennifer heard the bullet rush by.

John raced to an outcropping of rock a short distance away, with Jennifer right behind him. He jumped from the saddle, then pulled her from hers and hurried her to the dubious cover offered by the rock formation.

"What about the horses?" she fretted. The two animals milled nervously at the foot of the formation.

"They don't want the horses." John's face was set in a grim, determined mask. He pulled his pistol from its holster and checked the loaded chambers. "They want us."

Jennifer stared at him. "Do you think Oliver sent someone after us?"

"No one else has reason to wish us harm." John took a careful look around the edge of the rock and was rewarded by an immediate rifle shot. He jerked his head back. "Until they get within range, my pistol is of no use," he muttered.

"They cannot intend to kill us." Jennifer huddled in a crouched position. The tone of her voice indicated her disbelief.

"My guess is they mean to kill me and return you to your uncle."

Her eyes widened in horror. "John, no," she whispered.

John managed an encouraging smile. "I'll do my best to stop them, Jen. Just stay back against that boulder."

She took a deep breath and nodded. After a moment, she reached for a rock the size of a man's fist. John raised a curious eyebrow.

"I'll not give up without a fight," she said fiercely.

He winked at her. "Neither of us will." Another shot rang

over their heads. "They're getting closer." John's jaw tightened. He had not come this far to die now, not when he had finally found a reason for living. Nor would he allow any further harm to come to his wife. He risked a second look around the rock. The two horsemen had advanced down the rise and were about a hundred yards away. One of them fired again.

John pulled back. "I wonder why they haven't split up," he mused with a frown. He peeked again and saw that they had done just that. "Damn," he muttered.

"What is it?" Jennifer whispered anxiously.

"They've split up, to come at us from two sides. Get more rocks ready, sweetheart."

A cold fury raged through Jennifer as John's words sank in. How dare Oliver send men after them? How dare those men threaten them? She glanced at John; his back was to her, his pistol up and cocked. He was prepared to die for her—and she would not allow it. They would have to kill her as well. She was not leaving this place without John; they would live together, or die together. She gathered several rocks of varying sizes into a pile at her feet. The rocks made pitiful weapons, but they were better than nothing. She clutched one as her lips tightened in a line of fierce determination.

Another shot rang out, then another, and another.

"What the hell—" John looked again, and his eyes widened with surprise. "Jennie, we have help!" He jumped to his feet, waving his pistol over his head. "It's Beau and Pike."

"Thank God," she whispered as she followed John out from behind the boulders. Beau and Pike had their guns trained on the two men, two men she now recognized. "Creed and Rutherford," she said, her voice heavy with disgust.

"Let's go." John hurried to the horses, soothing them with low murmurs as he approached. Both allowed him to gather their reins, and he led the animals to Jennifer. "You can put the rock down, Jen," he said gently.

Jennifer looked down in surprise to see that she still clutched one of the rocks, so tightly that her knuckles had whitened. It took an act of conscious thought to force her fingers to open. The rock dropped to the ground.

John drew her into his arms and held her tightly for a moment, then helped her into the saddle. He swung up on Bay and they rode to join Beau and Pike.

"We sure are glad to see you," John said as they drew up.

"Are ya two lovebirds all right?" Pike asked. A friendly, grizzled man in his early sixties, Pike sported a full, grey beard and a wooden leg, having lost the original limb in the War Between the States. The tip of his peg fit snugly into a special pocket that took the place of one of his stirrups.

"We're fine," Jennifer assured him.

"Thank God." Beau Parker pushed his hat back on his head. He was an attractive man in his early thirties, tall and strong, with long dark hair, a thick, neatly trimmed mustache, and brown eyes that now flashed with anger. "Do you know these two murderous fools?" he asked in his deep, distinctive voice, using his rifle to indicate the disarmed men on the ground.

"Hayward Creed and Otto Rutherford," John supplied. "No doubt sent by Jennifer's uncle, Oliver Mainwaring."

"I never did like that pompous ass," Pike commented dryly, then tipped his hat at Jennifer. "Beg pardon, ma'am, for my language."

Jennifer smiled at him. "No apology is necessary, Mr. Pike. I feel the same about my uncle." She turned her gaze on the two miscreants. Rutherford lay on the ground moaning, clutching his arm, and she could see that blood seeped between his fingers. Creed crouched next to him, staring stonily at the ground.

"What were my uncle's instructions to you, Mr. Creed?" she asked.

Creed looked up at her. "Turn him over to the law and take you back to Philadelphia."

She frowned. "Turn John over to the law? On what charge?"

"The French ambassador in Washington wants to talk to him, thinks he's some assassin who killed a lot of Frenchies in Mexico a few years back."

Beau and Pike looked at John with interest, while Jennifer met his gaze with wide, worried eyes.

"Oliver gave in too easily," she said. "We should have expected trouble."

"I did," John said soberly. "I just didn't know what kind of trouble or where it would come from."

"Well, I don't take kindly to folks shooting at my guests on my own land." Beau adjusted his hat. "Pike and I will take these two into Laramie City and talk to the deputy. John, why don't you take Jennie on over to the O'Rourkes' place? We'll meet you there in a couple of hours."

"Wait a minute," Creed protested. "My friend needs a doctor. And why take us to the law? What have we done?"

"Your friend will receive medical care, Creed. And as for what you have done, we'll start with trespassing, conspiracy, and attempted murder and go from there. Now help Rutherford into the saddle and mount up yourself." Beau kept his rifle pointed in Creed's direction.

"And don't think of tryin' nothing," Pike warned. "This old squirrel gun of mine might just go off."

Creed did as he was instructed. It took a few minutes to maneuver Rutherford into the saddle, for he was a much larger man than Creed and, due to his wounded arm, of little assistance. Finally, both men were ready to go.

"We'll see you at Conor's place," Beau called as they moved out.

John waved after them, then guided Bay along Lucy's side. "Are you truly all right, Jen?" he asked. He reached for her, and she grabbed his hand.

"Yes. But let's get to Conor's house, and quickly. I'll feel safer with four stout walls around me for a while."

He nodded, and they urged their mounts to gallop.

Jennifer sat at the table in Susannah O'Rourke's big, comfortable kitchen, nursing a cup of hot tea. She watched in admiration as Susannah's five-year-old sister fed herself from a bowl of soup. Lily Carolina had been left blind after suffering a terrible fever a year and a half earlier, but one would not know it except for the fact that the child guided the spoon to her mouth with her free hand. Jesse, the O'Rourkes' big black dog, sat on the floor at Lily Carolina's side, clearly interested in the soup.

"I am so relieved no one was hurt this morning," Susannah declared. She opened the oven door on her new, huge, cast-iron stove to check a batch of biscuits. "Land sakes! These are done already." Using a corner of her apron to protect her hand, she snatched the pan of biscuits from the oven, allowing the door to slam shut. "I'm just not used to the efficiency of this stove," she said as she set the steaming pan on the table. "But it sure is nice."

"Rosa has a stove just like it," Jennifer said. "Can you believe we have all learned to cook?"

Susannah sank into a chair next to her little sister, resting her hands on her slightly rounded belly. Jennifer was struck by the resemblance between the woman and the child; both had hair the color of ripened wheat, both had beautiful facial features. While Lily Carolina's unseeing eyes were a lovely shade of blue, Susannah's were grey-green, today appearing even greener than usual thanks to the dark-green calico dress she wore.

"We've all come a long way since our pampered days in England," Susannah said. "I actually like to cook; Alina does, too."

"I do," Alina agreed. She came from the main room, where

she had just settled Elizabeth down on a thick pile of folded quilts. She and the baby, along with Sundance, the Parkers' golden dog, had arrived a few minutes earlier.

"Is she asleep already?" Susannah asked.

Alina nodded as she slipped into a chair. "Like I said, she didn't sleep well last night. Consequently, neither did I, nor Beau, for that matter."

"I still find it hard to think of you as a mother," Jennifer said as she gazed affectionately at her friend. A trace of fatigue was evident in Alina's blue eyes, but it did not detract from her Irish beauty. She wore her glossy black hair in the same simple style as both Susannah and Jennifer, pulled back into a neat chignon. Soft natural curls had escaped to frame her face.

"Sometimes I am still surprised myself," Alina admitted. She smiled at her friends. "But in a few months, Susannah will also be a mother, and now that you have found a man who makes you glow, I'm sure that one day you will be, too."

At the thought, a primal excitement curled around in Jennifer's stomach. "Oh, I hope so," she said fervently. "You both were right when you advised me to wait for a special man."

"John sure seems like a special man," Susannah remarked. "I like him."

"I like him, too, very much," Alina added. "But I especially like how he treats you, how he looks at you. He loves you, Jennie, and all the world can see it."

"I like Uncle John, too," Lily Carolina chimed in.

Jennifer laughed. "Well, I guess it's unanimous, then."

The back door opened suddenly and a panting Sundance barrelled into the room, followed by John and Conor. Sundance ran around the table, his tail wagging furiously, and greeted Jesse with an enthusiastic lick before he settled down on the other side of Lily Carolina's chair.

"I think those dogs have soup on their minds," Conor commented as he hung his hat on a hook by the door.

"I think you're right," Jennifer said with a laugh.

John removed his hat. "Conor has a couple of horses Preston would be impressed with, Jennie," he said. "After we eat, I'll take you out to the corral; I'd like your opinion before I make a decision."

Jennifer smiled up at him, her face alight with pleasure. "All right."

"Hello, cousin," Conor murmured before kissing Alina's cheek. "I didn't properly greet you earlier. Where's that little one?"

"Asleep in the other room," Alina answered. "She has to make up for all the sleep she missed last night."

Conor moved to stand beside Susannah's chair. "That sounds like a portent of things to come, wife." He kissed Susannah's cheek as well. "It sure smells good in here. I might have to test one of those biscuits."

"Keep your hands off those biscuits, Conor O'Rourke," Susannah admonished lovingly. "Our guests come first."

"Yes, dear." Conor squatted down at his wife's side. "How are you feeling?"

"Conor, I'm fine." Susannah pushed his long brown hair back from his handsome, clean-shaven face. "For heaven's sake, I'm not sick; I'm expecting."

Jennifer watched the tender exchange between Susannah and Conor, saw Conor's love for his wife revealed in his expressive blue eyes. Jennifer looked up at John and was startled to realize that his eyes held that same loving expression. A curious warmth enveloped her as she remembered Alina's words. *He loves you, and all the world can see it.* Feeling blessed, she knew it was true.

Suddenly, Jesse jumped to his feet and raced to the door, barking. Sundance was right beside him, eagerly adding to the din.

"Evidently we have company," Conor commented in a loud

voice. He went to the front door and opened it, just as Beau and Pike stepped onto the covered porch, followed by a third man Jennifer recognized as Sam Trudeau, the deputy sheriff from Laramie City. Jesse's barking calmed to joyous whimpers as Pike patted his head, while Sundance wagged his tail in ecstasy when Beau leaned down to scratch his ears.

"Who's here, Susannah?" Lily Carolina asked.

"Uncle Beau, Uncle Pike, and Deputy Trudeau," Susannah answered.

Lily Carolina dropped her spoon onto the table. "Uncle Pike, where are you?" she called out happily as she raised her arms.

Pike crossed the room, his peg leg making a thumping sound on the wooden floor, and lifted the little girl into his arms. "Hello, sweetpea." He planted a deliberately noisy kiss on her cheek.

The child giggled. "Your beard *tickles!*" she said, and wrapped her arms around his neck.

With a wide grin, Pike settled into Lily Carolina's vacated chair and positioned her on his lap.

Beau introduced Sam Trudeau to John, and the two men shook hands.

Sam nodded at Jennifer. "Nice to see you again, ma'am."

"And you, sir," Jennifer responded with a smile. She noticed John's questioning look. "Mr. Trudeau and I met at Susannah and Conor's wedding last summer," she explained as John took the chair next to her.

"We have some things to discuss," Beau said, inclining his head in Lily Carolina's direction.

Conor took the cue. "Lily Carolina, why don't you take Jesse and go up to your room for a few minutes?"

"So the adults can talk?" she asked guilelessly.

Conor smiled. "Yes, honey, so the adults can talk. I'll come and get you when we are finished."

"Then can me and Jesse and Sundance have a biscuit?"

Pike set her on her feet. "I'll see to it that ya get all the biscuits ya want," he promised. "And those dogs, too."

"All right. C'mon, Jesse." Lily Carolina waited until the big dog came obediently to her side, then she placed her small hand on his back. "Let's go upstairs," she said, holding her free hand out in front of her.

As if he understood her words, Jesse slowly walked to the base of the stairs. Lily Carolina searched for the lower of two parallel hand rails, one that Conor had added just for her, and when she found it, grabbed on. The child and the dog climbed the stairs and were soon out of sight. Lily Carolina's young voice floated back down the stairs. "Sundance, come with us."

"Go on, boy," Beau urged. The golden dog ran up the stairs.

Conor, Beau, and Sam joined the others at the big table.

"Sam has some questions for you, John," Beau said. "I hope you don't mind."

John leaned back against his chair. "Not at all."

Jennifer looked from him to the deputy and back again, suddenly fearful. John's hand lay on his thigh; she covered it with hers in a silent display of support. His only reaction was to squeeze her fingers.

Sam cleared his throat and began. "Several days ago, Sheriff Boswell received a wire from a man named Oliver Mainwaring, who I understand is Mrs. Cantrell's uncle."

"He is," John affirmed. "Before you go any further, Deputy, I should inform you that there is no love lost between Oliver Mainwaring and myself."

"I gathered as much from the two men who are now guests in my jail." Sam leaned back in his chair. "In his communication, Mr. Mainwaring told a very interesting tale about an assassin wanted by the French government for crimes committed against their people years ago in Mexico. He believes that assassin is you, Mr. Cantrell, and unfortunately, the

French ambassador apparently agrees with him. They insist that you be returned to Washington for questioning."

Jennifer's fingers tightened on his hand. "Is there a warrant out for my arrest?" John asked calmly.

Sam shook his head. "There is no mention of a warrant."

"Unless there is just cause, you cannot take me into custody without a warrant," John pointed out.

"I am aware of that, Mr. Cantrell. However, before I risk incurring the wrath of the French ambassador and perhaps that of my own government, I would appreciate it if you could shed a little light on this affair."

With a sigh, John pulled his hand from Jennifer's and rested his forearms on the table, his fingers entwined. She focused on her hands, which were now clasped in her lap.

John began speaking in a soft, curiously flat voice. "During the recent revolution in Mexico, I acted as an agent for Benito Juarez, the leader of the revolutionaries."

"You were a spy," Sam observed calmly.

"If you prefer that term." John shrugged. "I was known as *El Lobo,* the Wolf. My mission was to uncover military secrets and report them. That is what I did; that is all I did."

"What did this 'Serpent' do?" Sam asked.

John spread his hands. *"La Serpiente* is the name given to an assassin who preyed upon high-ranking French and Mexican officials. He was so called because he seemed to be able to penetrate any fortress and then escape undetected."

Conor frowned. "Why would a Mexican, assuming *La Serpiente* is a Mexican, assassinate his own people?"

"You must understand the history of the Revolution, Conor." John turned his intense gaze on his new friend, then looked around the table. "Benito Juarez, who was my friend as well as my leader, was duly elected president of Mexico. When, in a desperate attempt to keep his country from bankruptcy, he halted payments on foreign debts for a period of two years, certain foreign countries protested. Matters were eventually resolved with all but the French, who insisted upon invasion." He tried, with little success, to keep a note of fury from his voice. "To the outrage of most Mexicans, our own Assembly turned the reins of power over to Maximilian, proclaiming him Emperor of Mexico. Some viewed the actions of the Assembly as traitorous and worthy of punishment."

"Did you?" Sam demanded.

"Yes, I considered it traitorous," John snapped. "I did not murder my countrymen because of it."

"Did you ever kill?" Sam asked.

John glanced at Jennifer before he answered. "Yes," he said quietly, hating to see her flinch, as she did at that simple word. "It was a time of war. I killed on the battlefield, and twice, while acting undercover, I was forced to kill in defense of my own life. Never did I murder or assassinate, if such a distinction can be made in the taking of a human life."

Silence reigned at the table for a minute. Finally, Beau spoke. "What led Oliver Mainwaring to suspect you as this assassin?"

"I do not know for certain." John shook his head as he leaned against the back of his chair. "To my knowledge, *La Serpiente* was never seen and, therefore, never identified. Even with all my connections, I was not able to learn who he was. As for Oliver, I suspect that Constanza Noriega gave him the idea that I am the assassin."

In answer to everyone's questioning looks, Jennifer explained, "Constanza Noriega y Gonzales is the daughter of Preston Cantrell's closest neighbor and friend. She and John knew each other in the City of Mexico. In addition, she and I could be considered antagonists, if not outright enemies."

John stretched his arm across the back of Jennifer's chair, lightly squeezing her shoulder in a comforting gesture.

Sam looked at her. "Why are you enemies?"

"Many reasons. We knew each other as children and never got along. She assisted my uncle when he abducted me. Now, I have something Constanza desperately wanted for herself, and she will not forget that."

"And what is that, Mrs. Cantrell?"

"I have John. She wanted to marry him in order to combine her father's land with Preston's."

"I see." Sam thoughtfully rubbed his chin. "Is there anything else I should know?"

John and Jennifer glanced at each other. Finally, Jennifer spoke. "Only this, Deputy. I know this whole affair is very strange, and you are forced to choose which side of the story you will believe. Both my uncle and Constanza have a great deal at stake; one is facing financial ruin, the other the destruction of years of careful planning. Both are calculating and unscrupulous, and both have gone to surprising lengths to see their plans through. On the other hand, John and I merely want to live our lives together in peace."

"Fear and greed are indeed powerful motivations, Mrs. Cantrell, but so is love. Heinous crimes have been committed in the name of love." He pushed his chair back. "However, I see no reason to detain you. As you pointed out, Mr. Cantrell, there is no warrant. Without a physical description of the wanted man, I can't take Oliver Mainwaring's word that you are he. I do suggest that you go to the law, or the French consul in San Francisco, when you return to California, though. Mainwaring shows no sign of giving up."

"Thank you, Deputy." John stood and held out his hand. "I had already decided to do that. I don't want this hanging over my head." The two men shook hands.

Jennifer sighed with relief. Another hazard had been successfully avoided, but what else did Oliver have planned? And what would Constanza do when she learned of their marriage? As desperately as she wanted to, Jennifer could not believe their troubles were at an end.

Later that night, she lay again within the sheltering circle of John's arms. He kissed her forehead.

"You seem quiet tonight, Jen. You have been all afternoon."

"A lot happened today." She moved her hand over his chest, coming to rest on his ribs, where she again felt his scar. She was about to ask him how he had come to be wounded when he spoke.

"I should have told you earlier that I was forced to kill during the revolution," he said. "There just never seemed to be a good opportunity to bring it up."

"I think I knew, John. It was a time of war. Men kill each other in the course of a war." She ran a finger along his scar. "And wound each other."

He was silent for a moment. Her voice sounded so sad! For some reason, he was reluctant to tell Jennifer that Constanza had given him that scar. Suddenly, a terrible fear rocked him. "Jennie, you do believe me when I tell you I am not *La Serpiente,* don't you?"

Jennifer sat up, facing him, her features intense in the soft light of the lamp. "Of course I believe you! John, you must never doubt that." She leaned forward to take his face in her hands. "I love you. And I trust you."

With a heartfelt sigh, John pulled her back into his arms. "Thank you, *mi amada.* I have never lied to you."

They were silent for a few minutes, listening to the wind whistle against the window. Then Jennifer spoke.

"Constanza told Oliver about the deaths of those men, John, that *La Serpiente* killed them with a knife. She also told him the assassin was a seducer who first enticed the wives and daughters of the doomed men into his bed."

"The part about the knife is true, but as far as I know, the victims' women were never compromised. *La Serpiente* was too efficient; he would not have taken the time. I wonder why Constanza said that." John sounded genuinely puzzled.

"I don't know. But that was one of the reasons Oliver was so desperate to get me away from you; he wanted my virginity intact. He did not give me a chance to tell him it was already too late until after we had returned to Philadelphia."

John's grip on her tightened. "I can imagine what he said then."

"Oh, he was furious, all right." Jennifer shivered at the memory. "I told him he should return me to you because there was a possibility I carried your child. It turned out I didn't, but for a while, I prayed that I did, even though Oliver threatened to rid me of any babe I carried."

"I would have killed him had he hurt you or my child."

The cold rage in John's voice frightened her. She did not doubt him. "I know. John, there is something I must ask you. Do not answer if you don't wish to, for it is a personal question."

"Go ahead."

"Constanza told me you seduced women to get information or money from them, that you would seduce me in revenge for the Santa Maria being lost to you for so long." She placed her hand on his chest when he started. "I know that is not true about me. But I must know if you used other women in such a way."

John gave a deep sigh. "No, Jennie. A few married women sought my company in their beds, and I had relationships with other willing women, such as Constanza. Sometimes, as a result of such intimate connections, I was able to learn things I otherwise might not have known, but that was never my initial intention. Calculated seduction was not my method of operation. I listened, I intercepted messages and, on occasion, outright stole documents. And I was very good at what I did."

She was quiet for a time, digesting all he had said. "I believe you," she whispered finally. Then, in an attempt to lighten the somber mood that had come over both of them, she continued. "However, just as you once forbade me to dance with anyone but you after we were wed, I must insist that you no longer allow married ladies to entice you to their beds."

John's blue eyes sparkled with relief and humor. "None?"

"Well, with the exception of me, of course."

"Yes, ma'am." John turned on his side to face her, his expression suddenly serious. He reached out to smooth her hair back from her cheek. "Together, we will resolve things with Oliver and the French consul, and together, we will deal with Constanza. Nothing will destroy what we feel for each other, Jennie. And remember, we are not alone. We have Preston and his family, our family, waiting for us in California."

"I know, my love." She smiled at him. "Do you want to leave for California immediately? Cut our visit short?"

"I don't think that is necessary. You have so looked forward to this visit, and now your friends have become my friends. Besides, Alina and Beau are hosting a reception for us on Sunday, and I simply must meet Katie Davenport. I have heard so much about her."

"You will like her. When we go back into town, I'll take you to her saloon. The Satin Slipper is quite an establishment."

John took her hand. "Since I've told you such deep secrets, are there any you wish to tell me?" he asked casually, playing with her fingers.

Jennifer pursed her lips in thought. Finally, she shook her head. "No."

"None?"

"John, my life was very boring, at least until I met you. I have no secrets, unless you count the time, years ago, when Bill, Rosa, and I took a pie from the cooling shelf where her mother had set it. We raced to the barn and ate the whole thing, and were clever enough to share it with one of the shepherd dogs. Because of his sloppy eating habits, the poor creature was blamed for the theft and mildly scolded. We three took a vow of silence, and now I have broken it." Jennifer shook her head in mock remorse and reached over to extinguish the lamp.

John laughed as he welcomed her back into his arms.

"Your secret is safe with me, unless I decide to blackmail Bill. And I promise, your life will never be boring again."

Jennifer sighed happily. "I believe you, John Cantrell."

Twenty-four

"I see Preston!" Jennifer cried joyously as the train pulled into the Gilroy station. "And Bill!"

Her joy must have been contagious, because John felt it, too. He pressed a kiss to the back of her gloved hand.

The rest of their visit in Wyoming had passed without incident, as had the last three days of travel. Now they were very close to the final leg of their journey—the wagon ride out to the Santa Maria. John found it hard to believe he had been across the continent and back in the last five weeks.

A few minutes later, Jennifer threw herself into Preston's arms, while John and Bill shook hands and slapped each other's shoulders.

Preston held Jennifer tightly. "Jennie," he said softly. "How I have missed you. Welcome home, daughter."

She looked up at him with tear-filled eyes. "I truly am your daughter now."

"And I am honored." Preston turned to John, holding out his hand. "Welcome back, son. You did well."

John smiled at his father as he shook his hand, then his eyes travelled over Jennifer. "I think so."

"Now you are an official member of the family." Bill gave Jennifer an enthusiastic hug. "I always wanted a sister."

Jennifer's heart swelled with love. "Just as I always wanted a brother," she said happily.

Preston herded them toward the door. "If I don't get you home in a hurry, Rosa will greet me with her cleaver."

"I can see her doing that," John said in mock seriousness. "We'd best hurry."

To Jennifer, the hour-long wagon ride out to the Santa Maria passed quickly. All four of them kept up a steady stream of conversation, telling each other what had happened in the weeks they had been apart. When the wagon pulled into the yard, people seemed to pour from each building in the compound, all calling joyous greetings and shouting congratulations.

Rosa, Barbara, Brigit, and the children waited on the veranda and fell upon Jennifer with open arms.

"We have missed you so," Barbara said, while David and Molly clutched at Jennifer's skirts. Jennifer scooped Molly up and kissed her as David propelled himself into his "Unca' John's" arms.

After a few minutes of greetings, John, Bill, and Preston grabbed pieces of luggage and trudged up the stairs, with Jennifer following them. Preston explained that Jennifer's old room had been made into *their* room, and he hoped that was all right with them.

Jennifer stepped through the door and looked around in pleased surprise. A second wardrobe for John graced one corner; another chair had been set in front of the fireplace, and a shaving stand now stood next to the dressing table. All in all, it was a welcoming, intimate bedroom, made all the more inviting because she would share it with John.

"If you don't like being in the main house, we can make other arrangements," Preston said. "We all want you here, but you may want to build your own house."

"This is fine, Preston," John assured him.

"Perfect," Jennifer added. "I haven't come back to live in another house."

"Good." Preston grinned. "We'll leave you to get settled, then. Come on down when you're ready." He and Bill left the room, pulling the door closed.

Jennifer stared at John, and he at her, then he opened his arms to her. With a glad cry, she ran to him.

"We are home, John," she said joyously as he turned her in a circle. "We are home."

"Have you read this wire?" Constanza demanded, waving the paper at her brother.

"No." As had become his custom when they carried on their secretive discussions, Arturo was leaning against the wall near her bedroom door, where escape was close at hand.

"It is from Oliver. He says Juan and Jennifer were married in Philadelphia three weeks ago." Constanza's voice had a cold, deadly tone.

"So he was not successful in keeping them apart."

"The fool!" Constanza threw the paper in the fire. "I did not even know Juan had left California until now. Why did Oliver wait so long to notify me?"

Arturo crossed his arms over his chest. "John Cantrell returned today, sister."

Constanza whirled to face him. "How do you know this?"

"I saw him at the train station this afternoon."

"Was he alone?"

"Of course not. Jennifer was with him. They were met by Preston and William."

Constanza's eyes narrowed. "So the happy couple has returned." She sank down into the tall-backed chair, deep in thought. "What can be done to end their marriage?" she mused.

Arturo pushed away from the wall, suddenly worried. "You are not considering murder, I hope."

"If I thought for one minute I could kill Jennifer and get away with it, I would do it instantly, Arturo." Constanza slashed her finger in front of her throat. "Instantly."

Because of the frightening, icy look in her eyes, Arturo

believed her capable of such an act. He drew a shaky breath, grateful she had decided against it of her own accord.

"But it is too great a risk," she continued. "Juan would know it was I. Somehow we must break them up."

"You have already tried that, Constanza," Arturo pointed out somewhat impatiently. "Neither of them will listen to anything you say against the other. I know this is difficult for you to believe, but I think they genuinely love each other. Perhaps we should just give up."

"Give up? *Give up?*" Her voice rose to a shriek as quickly as she rose from the chair. "Never! I will not give up! That would be giving up on Mexico, our homeland."

Arturo stepped back from her fury. "But what else can we do?" he asked, spreading his arms in a helpless gesture.

Constanza paced for a minute, chewing on one finger. Suddenly she stopped. "The marriage will be annulled."

"Annulled? How?"

She faced him, wearing a curious, triumphant smile. "I will tell Papa that Juan promised to marry me before he married Jennifer."

Arturo scoffed. "No one will believe you."

"Yes, they will. I will make them believe me."

"Constanza, you are fooling yourself."

"Trust me, brother." She ran to her wardrobe and flung open the door. "I must find a more demure gown." She yanked a grey garment out. "This will do. Get my rosary from the top drawer." She waved at the dressing table. "Then you must help me change."

Arturo retrieved the rosary and threw it on the bed, then strode to the door. "I will not help you change."

"But I have no maid," Constanza protested.

"I will send up the housekeeper." Arturo opened the door.

"Oh, very well." Constanza glared at him as she struggled with the laces of her gown. "Tell Papa I must speak to him at once, on a very important and delicate matter. Both of you meet me in the parlor."

An uneasy feeling crept over Arturo. "What do you intend?"

"You will not like it, brother, and Papa will be furious, which I need him to be. But this can work. Trust me. And back up my story. Now go, and send that stupid housekeeper. I need help with this." A tearing sound came from the back of her gown. *"Maldición!"*

With no further argument, a very nervous Arturo closed the door and set off to find the housekeeper and, reluctantly, his father.

After supper that night, the extended Cantrell family once again gathered in the *sala,* with the exception of the children, who had gone to bed under protest a few minutes earlier. To Jennifer, the room was filled with a comforting sense of camaraderie as the men enjoyed their brandy and the women sipped from small, stemmed glasses of sherry.

She shared one of the sofas with John. Katie was nestled contentedly in her lap, purring loudly, while Jake explored the room. The kittens had grown dramatically in the weeks she had been gone. They seemed very big to her now.

Bill and Gabe sat at a table near the window, engaged in a game of chess, which Rosa watched. Barbara, on the opposite sofa, stitched on a dress she was making for Molly, and Preston sat in one of the wing-backed chairs.

A powerful sense of well-being surged in Jennifer's heart. "It is so *good* to be home," she said softly.

"It is good to have my family together and with me," Preston responded. "But there is something I want to ask you two." He looked at John and Jennifer.

"Go ahead," John said.

"While we understand that you felt it was important to marry quickly in order to remove Jennie from Oliver's reach, we are all disappointed that we could not be present for the wedding." Preston waved a hand to indicate the others in the room. "We would like to hold a reception for you, a big one, and really do it up right. How do you feel about that?"

John glanced at Jennifer and, at her small nod, faced his father. "Thank you, Preston. We would be honored."

"Good. We'll plan it for two weeks from today."

"I'll start on the invitations tomorrow," Barbara said. She paused in her stitching and held up the little dress.

"That is darling," Jennifer said approvingly. "Molly will be adorable in it."

"It's one of the things I love about having a daughter. I get to make these frilly little—" She stopped at the sound of someone pounding on the main door.

John glanced at the tall clock, which had struck nine only a few minutes earlier. "Rather late for visitors, isn't it?"

"I will see who it is." Rosa hurried from the room. A moment later, angry voices sounded in the foyer, and Alejandro Noriega stormed into the room with Constanza in tow. Arturo followed them in, as did Rosa.

The Cantrell men quickly stood.

"Alejandro, what is it?" Preston asked.

Alejandro glared at him. "Your son John has terribly wronged my daughter, and I am here to see that amends are made."

A bolt of impatience and irritation shot through Jennifer with such force that she could not sit still. She lifted Katie from her lap onto the sofa cushion and jumped up to stand at John's side, noticing that his mouth had tightened into an angry line.

A guarded look came over Preston's face. "Please make yourselves comfortable," he invited. "But I warn you, Alejandro: I will not listen to slander against John or any member of my family." He cast Constanza an accusing glance. "I suggest you instruct your daughter to tell the truth."

Alejandro stiffened. His dark eyes blazed with anger, but he did not say anything. He held up a hand when his son started to protest. Arturo remained silent, fuming.

Bill stepped forward with the ladder-back chair he had been using and set it close to Constanza. Alejandro released her and motioned her to the chair. She sat on the edge, gripping a handkerchief in one hand and a rosary in the other, and kept her gaze on the floor. Alejandro and Arturo remained standing.

Jennifer's eyes narrowed in suspicion. Constanza was curiously subdued tonight, in both manner and dress. While she still wore her heavy golden crucifix, her plain grey gown was high-necked and unadorned, and the ornate Spanish combs and silk flowers that usually decorated her black lace mantilla were conspicuously absent.

"Get on with it, Alejandro." Preston crossed his arms. "I grow weary of these attacks against my son and would be finished with them. What tale has Constanza told now?"

A dull flush stole over Alejandro's face as he drew himself up. "My daughter is with child, and she has named Juan Novales as the father."

Jennifer gasped.

"She lies!" John spat.

"Bastardo!" Arturo started toward him. "You will not insult my sister!"

Gabe stepped in to grab the young man's arm. Arturo struggled against his hold, but only until Alejandro again stilled him with a wave of his hand.

"Silencio!" Alejandro thundered, his voice ringing with outrage. "I will be heard! Juan Novales seduced my daughter with protestations of love and promises of marriage. His marriage to Jennifer must be annulled so he can honor his prior contract with Constanza. If necessary, we will take him to court."

"No!" Jennifer cried.

John started around the sofa in the direction of Constanza's chair. "You liar." His voice was deep with rage and loathing. Preston and Bill each grabbed one of his arms.

"Please, Juan, do not deny our love," Constanza pleaded,

her large eyes filling with tears. She reached a hand toward him, although he was some distance away from her. "I forgive you all if you will but honor your word to marry me. Let our little one be born within the bounds of holy matrimony. Let him know both of his parents, as you could not."

"Jennie, you must believe that she lies!" John called over his shoulder. He lunged against the hands that restrained him. "By God, Constanza, you will tell the truth if I have to beat it out of you!" Preston and Bill struggled to hold him.

"You will not touch my daughter!" Alejandro roared.

Arturo strove to break free from Gabe's grip. "If you touch my sister, you will die!" he shrieked.

As Barbara and Rosa did, Jennifer stared at Constanza, horrified and, on some level, fascinated. The woman's expression was one of agonized sincerity, and pleading, and longing. Tears coursed down Constanza's cheeks, strengthening the impact of her whimpering of John's name. No judge would doubt such an act.

Jennifer felt that John, her marriage, her very future, was slipping away before her eyes. "No more," she whispered. She wildly looked around, seeking a weapon. Barbara's sewing scissors rested on the low table directly in front of her. Jennifer snatched them up, hiding them in the folds of her skirt, and circled the sofa to come up behind Constanza.

Alejandro and Preston shouted at each other. Arturo struggled with Gabe. John demanded that the weeping Constanza admit to her lies.

Suddenly, Constanza screamed. The room fell to instant silence as all eyes turned to her. She sat rigidly in her chair, her hands clenched in fists in her lap, her tears miraculously gone. The lace mantilla lay on the floor at her feet. Jennifer stood behind her, a long lock of Constanza's waist-length, black hair twisted around one of her hands, the opened scissors poised in the other.

"You will tell the truth, Constanza," Jennifer said harshly, jerking on Constanza's hair, "or, with God as my witness,

you will be bald before you leave the Santa Maria this night."
Her words seemed to ring in the quiet room. Preston and Bill
released John, and the three men stood still, waiting, watching.

"Papa," Constanza squeaked, reaching a hand in Alejandro's direction. "Not my hair. Anything but my beautiful
hair."

"I will not tolerate this abuse of my daughter." Alejandro
started toward them.

"One step closer, *Don* Alejandro, and I use the scissors."
Jennifer positioned the weapon near Constanza's scalp. "I
swear I will."

Alejandro stopped.

"Tell the truth, Constanza," Jennifer ordered. "John is not
the father of your child, if you even truly carry one."

"I am telling the truth! I swear it!"

Jennifer closed the scissors with a snap and threw a thick
lock of long black hair to the floor, quickly grabbing another
handful.

A tortured cry escaped Constanza's throat. Arturo struggled
against Gabe in vain.

"The truth!" Jennifer jerked on the hair she held. "John
has not touched you since his arrival here, has he?"

"He has! Just as we were lovers in Mexico years ago, we
were lovers here, before you returned to Philadelphia." Constanza again reached for her father. "Papa, I am telling the
truth!"

Another thick strand of hair landed on the floor. Constanza
screamed.

Jennifer resolutely grabbed yet another handful of Constanza's hair. "Yes, you took a lover here, but it wasn't John.
Tell your father who you met in San Francisco."

"I met no one in San Francisco! I was shopping!" Constanza clawed at Jennifer's hand, and the scissors promptly
snipped again. With a moan, Constanza sagged against the
chair.

"Tell them who your lover was, Constanza, or I will ask Brigit to, although she will be reluctant to reveal your secret." Jennifer grabbed more of Constanza's hair. "It is a shame you treated her so wretchedly, for she is a trustworthy, loyal maid. Only with great reluctance did she confide in me, and only then because she feared you and your lover meant me harm."

Alejandro stared at Constanza. "What is this?" he demanded, his expression both angry and fearful. "God help you, daughter, if you have lied yet again."

"No, Papa, I haven't lied—" Her words ended on a sob when Jennifer dropped another severed lock of hair directly into her lap.

"I am only halfway done, Constanza," Jennifer warned.

"No, no. Stop." Constanza's hands fluttered over her head, finding the short, uneven tufts on one side. She shrieked and her tears started again, this time in earnest. "It was Oliver Mainwaring," she sobbed. "It is his child, not Juan's."

Jennifer released her and stepped back from the chair. She felt no sense of triumph, only weariness.

Constanza slipped to the floor and grabbed the mantilla, covering her head with the piece of black lace. She desperately gathered the lost locks of hair into her lap, then buried her face in her hands. The small crucifix at the end of the rosary swung silently from her fingers.

Gabe loosened his hold on Arturo, who immediately went to his sister's side, glaring at Jennifer as he did.

John hurried to Jennifer and, after taking the scissors from her and laying them on the chess table, gathered her into his arms. She held him tightly, feeling that he, and their future together, had been restored to her. After a moment, they faced the center of the room.

Constanza and Arturo remained huddled together on the floor, while Alejandro seemed to be in a state of shock.

"At least now the truth is out," Preston said quietly. He approached Alejandro. "I am sorry, my friend."

Alejandro looked at Preston with sad, listless eyes. "It is I who must apologize. To you, Preston, and to your son and new daughter." He looked at John and Jennifer. "May your marriage be blessed."

"Thank you, sir," John responded.

After a pause, Alejandro focused on Jennifer. "Where is your uncle, Mrs. Cantrell?" His tone had hardened.

"As far as I know, he remains in Philadelphia," Jennifer answered.

"He will return to face his responsibilities," Alejandro vowed. "Arturo, bring your sister." He marched to the door and into the foyer. Arturo helped Constanza to her feet and guided her out the door.

"Gabe, be sure they have enough lanterns to see their way home," Preston said. "Send some of the men with them if need be." With a nod, Gabe left.

Rosa slowly approached John and Jennifer. Jennifer was surprised to see that tears streaked the woman's face.

"Rosa, what is it?" she asked.

"You did not let her destroy your love." Rosa gripped John's arm and reached for Jennifer's hand. *"Gracias a Dios,* you did not let that evil woman destroy you as she destroyed my Enrique."

Jennifer glanced over Rosa's shoulder at Preston, whose brows had come together in a troubled frown. He shrugged and turned his palms upward, indicating he did not know what she was talking about.

"Rosa, come and sit down." Barbara patted the cushion next to her. Jennifer guided Rosa to the sofa and watched as Barbara took the distraught woman's hand. "Tell us how Constanza destroyed Enrique," Barbara encouraged.

"You all think he died accidentally," Rosa said softly, wiping her eyes with her free hand.

Bill pulled a handkerchief from his pocket and handed it to Barbara over the back of the sofa. She pressed the material into Rosa's hand. "Was it not an accident?" Barbara asked.

Rosa crushed the handkerchief in her fist and shook her head. "He died deliberately, because of her."

Preston stared at Rosa. "Are you saying Constanza killed him?"

"She was responsible for his death as surely as if she had held his face in the river." Rosa patted her cheeks with the handkerchief, then twisted the cloth in her fingers.

"Rosa." Gabe spoke from the door. "The Noriegas are gone. You do not have to tell the story."

When Rosa raised her tear-filled eyes to Gabe, her expression softened with love. "I do not have to, but I feel it would be best." She took a steadying breath and met the gaze of each person in the room. "Shortly after Constanza returned from Mexico, she seduced my Enrique."

Jennifer's eyes filled with tears, just as her heart filled with sadness at Rosa's quiet words.

"He left me a letter the day he died, trying to explain what he felt could not be explained. She had come upon him while he was riding fence, had teased and enticed and lifted her skirts. He swore that he tried to resist her, and I believe that he did." Rosa dabbed at her eyes again. "But he was young, and she was insistent. Afterward, she laughed at him. She told him that the only reason she did it was to hurt me, that she would tell me he had betrayed me. And she did, just after his funeral. But I already knew."

The tears that had filled Jennifer's eyes spilled down her cheeks, and she reached blindly for John's hand. She could not comprehend that one person could act with such evil cruelty toward another, yet she did not doubt Rosa's words.

"My God, Rosa," Preston whispered.

"Enrique went into the river with no intention of coming out, Señor Preston." Rosa began to cry. "If only he had come to me. I knew how evil she was; I would have forgiven him.

We would have faced her together, just as John and Jennie did tonight."

Gabe hurried to sit at Rosa's side, taking her in his arms, holding her while she sobbed. "She never told of Enrique's letter," he explained, "because she feared the priests would not allow him to be buried in consecrated ground if it became known that he committed suicide."

"The knowledge will not leave this room." Preston looked at each person. "We all swear it." Everyone nodded in agreement. "And Constanza Noriega will not be invited to this house again. Had I known this before, she would have been banished long ago. I am so sorry that I expected you to serve her, to treat her as an honored guest."

"Is all right, *Señor* Preston. You did not know." Rosa sniffed and raised her watery gaze to Gabe. "I would like to go now."

"I'll see you to your room." He stood up, drawing her with him, and led her out the door.

Barbara brushed at her eyes. "Poor Rosa," she whispered. Bill stepped behind the sofa and laid comforting hands on his wife's shoulders.

Preston sat down wearily in one of the tall chairs. "I wonder how much I should tell Alejandro. He should know that his daughter's machinations have not been aimed only at John and Jennie, but it is a delicate matter. He may not believe me, and our friendship is already strained to the breaking point."

"I suggest we let it rest for now," John said. He put an arm around Jennifer's shoulders and drew her against his side. "Give *Don* Alejandro time to adjust to the true Constanza. He may surprise us. He may find a way to keep her on a leash from now on."

"I agree with John," Bill said. "Let's hope we have seen the last of Constanza Noriega."

"And Oliver Mainwaring," Jennifer added. But she feared that would not be the case.

* * *

The next week passed in peace. John and Jennifer happily settled back into the routine of life on the Santa Maria with a newfound sense of belonging. Their days were filled with camaraderie and humor as everyone willingly shared the chores and work necessary to run the large ranch, and their nights were filled with private, tender loving.

Jennifer received a letter from Henrietta Duke, bearing the happy news of her betrothal to Mr. Michael Hastings, Professor of Archeology at Lehigh University in nearby Bethlehem. She mentioned that Oliver had reappeared in Philadelphia for a few weeks, then had disappeared again. The Mainwaring house had been sold, and Henrietta feared that Oliver might be headed West.

Elias Craig wrote also, again telling them that the house had been sold and that although most of Oliver's debts had been satisfied, his reputation was severely damaged. Bradley Ames had been charged with several counts of rape and one of murder, causing a city-wide scandal. Elias feared the trial would be difficult, for the Ames family had hired the best defense attorney in the country, but he was confident justice would be served. He, too, warned that he believed Oliver was headed West.

Jennifer was not surprised when, a few days later, both Henrietta and Elias were proven right. So intent was she upon her chore of sweeping the veranda that she did not hear the approach of a buggy until it pulled to a stop in the center of the yard. She looked up, and her heart caught in her throat when she realized one of the two men who had just arrived was her uncle; the other she did not know. With the broom firmly in hand, she moved to stand at the top of the step.

The two men approached. Oliver's gaze flicked disapprovingly over her simple calico dress and apron. "I see you have easily settled into the role of housekeeper and wife," he jeered.

"Yes, I have, Oliver." Jennifer met his hostile stare. "But I doubt you have come to congratulate me on my marriage, so please state your business."

Oliver's mouth tightened. "Will you not even invite us in?"

Jennifer looked at Oliver's companion, a well-dressed, pleasant-looking man in his mid-thirties. "My apologies, sir. Due to his ill-treatment of both my husband and myself, my uncle is not welcome in our house."

"Jennifer, you are speaking to President Grant's personal representative!" Oliver barked. "Surely he is welcome in your precious house."

With an unconcerned shrug of her shoulders, Jennifer said, "Again, sir, my apologies, but I must ask if you are indeed who my uncle claims you are."

The man's lips curved in a slight smile beneath his dark, thick mustache. "Yes, ma'am, I am. Geoffrey Mercer, at your service." Mercer swept his hat off and bowed.

"I am Jennifer Cantrell, Mr. Mercer. How can I help you?"

Before Mercer could answer her, Preston came through the front door. "I thought I heard a buggy; do we have—what are you doing here, Mainwaring?" he demanded.

"Preston, this is Mr. Geoffrey Mercer, President Grant's personal representative," Jennifer hastened to say. "Mr. Mercer, this is my father-in-law, Mr. Preston Cantrell."

Preston nodded at Mercer. "What can we do for you?"

"I would like to speak to your son, John Novales Cantrell, on a matter of some importance." Mercer tilted his head in Oliver's direction. "Mr. Mainwaring led me to believe I could find him here."

"You can." Preston looked at Jennifer. "He's in the orchard with Bill; please go get him."

Without a word, Jennifer leaned the broom against the wall and hurried around the side of the house.

"Please come in, Mr. Mercer." Preston indicated the open door, then looked at Oliver. "You may as well come in, too." He waved at one of the cowhands across the yard and pointed at the horse that waited patiently in the buggy traces. The man nodded in understanding, and Preston led the two men to the *sala*. When Rosa appeared at the door, he asked her to bring some refreshments, and a moment later, Jennifer and John came in from the courtyard. Preston made the introductions.

"Why do you want to see me, Mr. Mercer?" John asked from his standing position near the fireplace.

Mercer settled back on one of the sofas. "President Grant asked me to interview you about a case that may have international repercussions if it is not satisfactorily resolved." He glanced at Oliver, who sat in one of the wing-backed chairs, then back at John. "Mr. Mainwaring has made serious accusations against you, and the French Ambassador is insisting that the charges be investigated."

"This is about *La Serpiente*," John said in a grim voice.

Jennifer looked up at him from her position at the end of the sofa. She could tell from John's tight jaw and clenched hand that he was furious, for all he spoke so calmly. When she glared at her uncle a moment later, he only twisted his lips in a smug, irritating grin.

"Yes," Mercer said. "I know the crimes of this assassin are several years old and took place in another country. I personally have serious doubts about the wisdom of U.S. involvement in the matter, but the president insisted. I'm sure I don't need to tell any of you that the centennial of the United States is only a few years away. As the French were our allies during the revolution, they have been invited to participate in the official centennial celebration, which is already in the planning stages. The president is most anxious to avoid ill feelings between the countries."

"Mr. Mercer, I have already written to the French consul in San Francisco," John said. "I will tell you the same thing I told him, and you may consider this a formal statement. I am not *La Serpiente*. I was an agent for Juarez, but not an assassin. I do not know who *La Serpiente* was, nor does any-

one, to my knowledge, and Mainwaring certainly doesn't."
He pointed at Oliver. "He and I have had serious problems
in the past, so I suggest you carefully examine anything he
may say against me, as the man is on occasion a stranger to
the truth."

Oliver flushed. "Are you calling me a liar, Cantrell?"

"Calm yourself, Mr. Mainwaring," Mercer interjected. "Mr.
Cantrell is merely suggesting that I do something I already
intend to do."

"Well, I suggest you speak with Constanza Noriega if you
want to know the truth about *La Serpiente*," Oliver said huff-
ily. He crossed his arms over his chest.

"Ah, yes, the daughter of the neighboring rancher who
knew Mr. Cantrell in Mexico." Mercer steepled his fingers.
"I will speak with her, Mr. Mainwaring; you may be assured
of that."

Preston fixed his stern gaze on Oliver. "You had best be
speaking to Constanza yourself. It seems you left some un-
finished business, and Alejandro is most anxious to discuss
it with you." He looked back at Mercer. "Miss Noriega is an
accomplished liar, Mr. Mercer. Weigh her words with care."

"How dare you slander her, Cantrell?" Oliver demanded.

"Do not tell us you are prepared to defend Constanza's
honor, Oliver," Jennifer snapped. "You, of all people, know
her for what she is. And I am weary of the both of you. Your
lies and intrigues have interfered in our lives far too long."

Oliver opened his mouth to reply when Rosa spoke from
the door.

"*Señor* Preston, forgive the interruption," she said in a
troubled tone.

"Yes, Rosa, what is it?"

"*Don* Alejandro is here."

"Please show him in."

Rosa hesitated. "He is not alone, sir."

Preston frowned in confusion. "Then invite everyone in.
No, wait. Is Constanza with him?"

"*Sí, Señor,* and—"

Bill rushed in through the opened French doors to the courtyard, breathless and alarmed. "I saw them, Pa, from the orchard. The Noriegas are here, along with a dozen armed men, and none of them look happy."

Twenty-five

"Rosa, see that Brigit and Francisca stay in the kitchen," Preston ordered.

"Jennie, Barbara is upstairs with the children," Bill said. "Please go to her; tell her to wait there." He pulled his pistol from its holster and checked the chambers, then replaced it.

Jennifer did not want to leave John, but he nodded in agreement with his brother.

"Go to Barbara," he said softly. He gave her a quick hug, then urged her toward the door. "Go on, now."

She went, pausing briefly at the door to look back at him, then hurried up the stairs.

"Mr. Mercer, I suggest you and Mainwaring wait here," Preston said as he left the room.

"My thoughts exactly," Mercer murmured. He glanced at Oliver, who had not moved from his chair. Oliver nervously looked away.

Preston strode out onto the veranda. John followed to stand at his one side, Bill at the other. All wore their gunbelts. From the corner of his eye, John saw Gabe come from the bunkhouse to join them, a rifle in his hands.

The group of riders milled about the yard, led by Alejandro and Arturo. Constanza rode a little behind them, sitting a sidesaddle, her face set in an angry, sullen expression. As Bill had stated, many of the accompanying riders were heavily armed, some with their rifles pulled from the cases.

"What is the meaning of this, Alejandro?" Preston demanded.

"I want Oliver Mainwaring," Alejandro said firmly. "My men have been following him since he returned to California, and I know he is here."

"What do you intend to do with him?"

Alejandro grimaced. "I would like to kill him. Unfortunately, I must instead insist that he join my family." He motioned with one hand, and a man rode to the front of the group.

John was startled to realize the man wore the simple robes of a Catholic priest.

"I will see my daughter wed to the man who dishonored her, Preston," Alejandro said. "For the sake of what remains of our friendship, please do not interfere."

"That seems fair, old friend, on one condition. Although I don't much care for him, Mainwaring must be allowed to speak his piece. Your daughter has lied before; I'll not take her word alone that he is the culprit."

Alejandro's mouth tightened, but he nodded. "Agreed."

Preston headed toward the door. "Then please come in. John, go get Jennie. She should be present. Bill, Brigit is in the kitchen. We may need her as a witness. And send Francisca up to watch the children. Barbara will want to be with you."

Everyone did as instructed, and soon all were gathered in the *sala*. For such a large group, they were surprisingly quiet. John led Jennie to stand behind the sofa on which Barbara, Rosa, and Brigit were seated. He stayed at her side, with her hand tucked securely in his.

While Geoffrey Mercer remained in his place on the opposite sofa, watching the proceedings with calm interest, Jennifer saw that Oliver had risen from his chair; he looked pale, and almost ill. An armed man was positioned on either side of him.

Constanza stood stone-faced near the fireplace with her father. She again wore the plain grey gown and the heavy crucifix, but no lace mantilla covered her head, nor did her remaining hair fall free down her back. Rather, a large black scarf was tied under her chin, giving her a severe look that reminded Jennifer of a nun. Constanza as a nun! At the thought, Jennifer fought the urge to laugh, involuntarily squeezing John's hand. He looked down at her in curiosity, but she only shook her head. She would share the thought with him later.

"Oliver Mainwaring, my daughter has named you the father of her unborn child," Alejandro declared. "What have you to say?"

Oliver turned startled eyes on Constanza. "What?" he whispered.

"Speak, man. Are you the father of her child?"

"What is this foolishness, Constanza?" Oliver demanded. He glanced at the priest and suddenly chuckled. "So that's the game. If you are looking for a rich husband, you won't find him in me. I am bankrupt; ask Jennifer."

Constanza only stared at him with hate-filled eyes.

"Did you dishonor my daughter?" Alejandro roared.

Oliver laughed, a short, harsh sound. "Dishonor her? How does one dishonor a slut? If you mean did I lay with her, yes, I did, as have many other men, including John Cantrell."

Jennifer felt John stiffen beside her, and she tightened her hold on his hand.

Alejandro crossed the distance to Oliver in a few short steps, pulling his pistol as he did. He grabbed the front of Oliver's fine shirt and positioned the mouth of the gun barrel directly under the younger man's chin.

"I told Preston I would not kill you, but if you slander my daughter again, I will, even with *Padre* Baptiste present." His eyes seemed to bulge from his red face. "As she has named you, I care to hear only of *your* involvement with my daughter. Did you meet her in San Francisco with the intention of seducing her?"

Oliver seemed incapable of speech. He stared at the enraged Alejandro with wide eyes. His hands hung limply at his sides. For all her dislike of him, at that moment Jennifer pitied him.

"Answer with care, uncle," she cautioned quietly. "There is a witness who saw you together."

"Admit it, Oliver," Constanza said in a voice sharp with anger. "The game is lost."

"It was her idea," Oliver finally gasped. "She is the seducer."

Alejandro released him. "So you fathered her child."

Oliver straightened his shirt, regaining some of his composure. "Perhaps," he sneered. "I have no way to know if she was unfaithful to me."

Alejandro halted in his action of returning his pistol to its holster. "I warned you—"

"The brat is yours!" Constanza shouted at Oliver. "Stop whining and face up to it like a man."

"He will," Alejandro promised grimly. He motioned to the men on either side of Oliver, and they dragged the reluctant man to stand next to Constanza.

The marriage ceremony was over in a matter of minutes. How strange it all was! Jennifer thought. With the uttering of a few short sentences by Father Baptiste, Constanza Noriega became her aunt, just as the unborn child legally became her cousin. She was stunned by the thought and felt a surge of pity for the poor child. What an unhappy lot in life, to have Oliver and Constanza as parents.

Out of courtesy, Preston invited the Noriega party to stay for an informal wedding supper. Alejandro declined, insisting that they leave soon in order to return to the Buena Ventura by nightfall. He sent two of his men into Gilroy to bring Oliver's things from the hotel and was about to usher his daughter and new son-in-law out the door when Constanza begged for a chance to freshen up before the ride home.

"I would also like an opportunity to speak to my *niece* for just a moment," she added, glancing at Jennifer.

"I will show her to the bathing room," Jennifer offered. Perhaps now, Constanza would be willing to make some measure of peace, if only for the sake of the coming child.

Alejandro nodded his permission, and Jennifer led Constanza through the kitchen to the bathing room beyond. She was surprised to see that John followed them.

"John, really—"

"I will wait here," he interrupted in a tone that allowed no argument. He leaned against the wall in the hallway outside the small room and hooked his thumbs in his gunbelt.

Touched by his protective concern, Jennifer followed Constanza into the bathing room and closed the door.

"These water reservoirs on the stove ensure that warm water is almost always available," she said as she set a bucket underneath the spout and turned the handle. Constanza did not reply. When the bucket was half full, Jennifer twisted the handle back into place and turned to place the bucket on a low table next to the chair where Constanza sat. "Here is a clean cloth." Jennifer held out the cloth, and Constanza snatched it from her. Then, for the first time since her arrival that day, Constanza looked directly at her.

So powerful was the hate emanating from the woman that Jennifer took a step back. She was suddenly very grateful that John was near.

"Ramera!" Constanza hissed. "Do you think all is well between us now that we are related?"

"I doubt things will ever be well between us, Constanza, but I hope, for the sake of the child—"

"The child!" she spat. "Do you truly believe I will allow myself to grow fat and ugly with any man's brat? There will be no child, Jennifer; I already made certain of that."

Horrified, Jennifer remembered Oliver telling her that Constanza had assured him there were ways to terminate a pregnancy. A curious grief for the lost child filled her. "I don't understand," she whispered. "If there was to be no child, why did you accuse John?"

Constanza's eyes glittered with rage. "I told you I would have Juan. I *had* to have him, and the Santa Maria, but you thwarted me at every turn. I knew how my father would react to my tale; there is little in this world more frightening than the outrage of a father who believes his innocent daughter was seduced and betrayed. Had we gone to court, it would have worked. But you cut my hair. *You cut my hair!*"

"You left me no choice, Constanza. I would not, could not allow you to ruin my beloved husband with your lies." She moved toward the door.

Constanza jumped up from the chair and grabbed Jennifer's wrist in a vicious grip. "You will not leave yet. Not until you see what you caused." She tore the black scarf from her head with her free hand.

"You yourself are responsible—" Jennifer stared in shock at Constanza's head. Only a short, uneven stubble remained of all that thick, lovely hair. She had indeed been shaved bald; a few scabs indicated where the razor had nicked her. Jennifer twisted free of Constanza's grasp.

"My loving father finished what you started that night," Constanza said in a deadly tone. "He told me it was fair punishment for a whore, that it was a shame my hair would grow back when my virtue could not. And you will pay for it, Jennifer, you and that bastard husband of yours."

Jennifer backed to the door, reaching behind her for the latch, afraid to look away for even a moment as Constanza advanced on her.

"I will have my revenge on the house of Cantrell," Constanza vowed. Her eyes blazed with hatred. "A curse on you, Jennifer, and on your husband, and on—"

"Stop it!" Jennifer cried. She spun around and jerked the door open.

John was instantly there, his arms around her. "What is

it?" he demanded. His eyes briefly widened in astonishment when he caught sight of Constanza.

"I was cursing you and your wife, Juan," Constanza taunted. "As I told her, I will have my revenge on you all."

"Do not try it," John said coldly.

"You cannot stop me."

"Yes, I can. *El Lobo* can. Remember what you knew of me in Mexico. Remember that the wolf will go to any lengths to protect his own."

Jennifer shivered at the depth of menace in his voice. Evidently Constanza heard it as well, for doubt flickered in her eyes.

"I warn you one last time, Constanza, do not challenge me. You will lose, just as you have lost so far. Your father and your husband are waiting for you." With that, John pulled the door closed. A moment later, a furious, frustrated shriek was heard, followed by the sound of something hitting the wall. John walked Jennifer to the kitchen, where they were met by an impatient Alejandro.

"Where is she?" he demanded. "What was that noise?"

"She will be out in a moment, *Don* Alejandro," Jennifer said quietly.

"If she's not, I shall go after her," he warned.

It was not necessary. Constanza emerged a few minutes later with the scarf back in place and an impassive expression on her face. Without a word, she allowed her father to lead her to her horse. Oliver rode one of the Santa Maria's mares, and Ross Latham went along to bring the animal back. The Cantrell clan, along with Geoffrey Mercer, watched the party leave.

"You did not have a chance to speak to Constanza, Mr. Mercer," John commented.

"The time did not seem appropriate," Mercer said wryly. "Besides, after what I witnessed today, I fear her word is no more trustworthy than Mainwaring's, as you warned me, Mr. Cantrell."

"It isn't," Preston assured him. "You are welcome to stay for supper, Mr. Mercer, and the night, if you have need of accommodations."

"Thank you, but no." Mercer set his hat on his head. "I have a room at the Gilroy Hotel; I shall return there tonight, for I am awaiting a wire from Washington. However, if you don't mind, I'll come out tomorrow morning and let you know what I decide regarding *La Serpiente*."

"We will look forward to your visit," Preston said. He motioned to one of the hands to bring Mercer's buggy up.

Mercer looked at John, who stood at Jennifer's side. "You may rest easy tonight, young man. So far there is no firm evidence against you, and I do not expect my wire to contradict that."

"Oh, thank you, sir," Jennifer interjected.

"You're welcome, Mrs. Cantrell. Good day now." He climbed into the buggy and was gone.

Later that evening, Jennifer leaned against the railing of the balcony off the bedroom she now shared with John, watching the November night sky. Since she wore only her nightdress, she had wrapped a light shawl around her shoulders, and her hair fell free as she stared up at the heavens. The half-moon played hide-and-seek with a few wispy clouds that drifted by on the breath of a cool wind.

"There you are," John said from the French doors. A moment later he stood behind her, his arms wrapped around her middle.

She looked down and saw that his arms were encased in the sleeves of his dressing robe. "So, it is finally cool enough that even you will cover yourself at night," she teased.

"Only until I climb between the sheets, woman." He nibbled on her ear. "I want as little as possible between us. It is bad enough that you make me work my way past these infernal nightdresses."

"I seem to remember your saying something about the pleasure of unwrapping the package, sir," Jennifer retorted as she leaned back against his strength.

"True," John admitted. After a moment of easy silence, he asked, "What brought you out here?"

"I don't know. The search for peace, perhaps. This day was very disturbing, in many ways."

"I know, *mi amada.* It was for all of us."

"John, Constanza frightens me," Jennifer confessed. "She is positively twisted with hate. I almost feel sorry for Oliver."

"I fear for the child," John remarked.

"There will be no child."

"What?"

Jennifer sadly shook her head against his chest. "She destroyed it. She told me herself."

"Then why did she stage that scene last week? I don't understand."

"Neither did I, until she explained that she needed you and the Santa Maria and that her plan would have worked had I not cut her hair. That was the one thing she did not anticipate."

"That *was* brilliant, sweetheart." John kissed the top of her covered shoulder.

"I hated to do it, but I could think of nothing else. Her father finished the job as punishment for her 'sins.' "

"I wondered what happened."

"Do you think she will try to hurt us?"

"In all honesty, Jen, I don't know. She knows I am not a man to cross, and yet, as you said, she is filled with rage and hatred. Such a person is not rational. We must all be very careful, and pray that she settles down." His arms tightened around her. "I will protect you. I promise."

"I know you will, John. But she threatened you as well. I will do my best to protect you, but I am not *El Lobo.*"

"You are *El Lobo's* mate. Together, we will prevail."

Jennifer sighed as a measure of peace stole over her. "We will, won't we?"

"Yes," John said firmly. "And now we will go to bed."

"All right." She turned in his arms. "But hold me first. Just hold me."

"I will hold you for the rest of your life, Jen."

She believed him.

"You bitch." Oliver Mainwaring paced the carpet in Constanza's bedroom, now his bedroom as well. "How could you be so stupid as to catch a brat in the first place, and then to name me as the father?"

Constanza's cold eyes followed him in the dressing table mirror before which she sat. "Oh, I assure you, you were the father, Oliver. My selection of bed partners was very limited at the time. If it makes you feel any better, I am just as displeased with this turn of events as you are. And do not blame me; you have your niece to thank for our unfortunate marriage. May she rot in hell."

"Jennifer? What did she have to do with this?"

"I named Juan Novales as the father. My father had every intention of forcing an annulment of John's marriage to Jennifer until she ruined everything." Constanza's fingers tightened spasmodically on the brush she held in one hand.

"Damn it, what did she do?"

Constanza stared at her reflection in the mirror. "She cut my hair."

"She what?"

"I told you; she cut my hair." Constanza's voice took on an ugly tone.

Oliver placed his hands on his hips. "What the hell does your hair have to do with our marriage?"

"She forced me to admit that you had been my lover, not Juan. That is why my father insisted that we marry."

Oliver eyed the black scarf with new suspicion. "Let me see your hair."

With a sneering smile, Constanza slowly untied the knot under her chin. "Would you like to see what you have married, dear husband? Feast your eyes on this!" She tore the scarf away, throwing it to the floor.

"My God." Oliver stared at her in horror. "Jennifer did that?"

"She started the job; my father finished it as punishment for my wanton ways." Constanza stood and faced him. "Come to me, Oliver. Do you not wish to make love to me? This is our wedding night, after all." There was a taunting, sarcastic note to her voice. She came up close to him, pressed her breasts against him. Her hands grabbed his hips, stroked his buttocks, then travelled around to rub his groin. "Run your hands through my hair, husband, what's left of it." A strange laugh, tinged with hysteria, burst from her throat.

"In your delicate condition?" Oliver snarled sarcastically. He pushed her away. "You told me you could prevent a child."

Constanza shrugged and fell into the chair by the fireplace. "Prevention is not always successful; termination is, though."

"Then why didn't you get rid of it?"

After a long moment, she said, "I did, you fool, weeks ago."

Oliver stared at her, stunned. "What?"

"There is no child, Oliver, not any longer." She offered him a smug smile.

"Then why all this?" he cried.

She shrugged again. "Things got out of hand. Because of my lost virtue, my father would have forced us to marry even if he knew there was no child."

"You bitch." He said the words in a strangely calm voice.

Constanza looked up at him, startled.

He descended upon her, jerked her from the chair, slapped her viciously. "You forced me into this farce of a marriage, and you shall pay dearly for it." He raised his hand to strike her again.

"Do you like to hit me, Oliver?" she taunted. "Does it make you feel strong and manly?"

"Now that you mention it, yes." He slapped her again.

She moaned and laid her head against his shoulder. "I rather like it, too," she whispered, fondling his hardening length through his trousers.

"Yes, by God, I will at least have that from you, *wife*." Oliver held her shorn head between his hands and plunged his tongue into her mouth. He tasted the blood from her split lip, felt her mounting excitement in the way she ground her hips against his. His hands dropped to her shoulders, then to her neckline, and he took the material in his hands and tore it to her waist. "I don't want to see you wearing anything but that damned crucifix," he panted.

"As you wish," Constanza breathed. She began to peel off her clothes while Oliver did the same.

Later, he lay on top of her, spent, his head resting on the pillow above her shoulder.

"Do you really want out of this marriage?" Constanza whispered as she stroked his back.

"Of course I do, just as I'm certain you do," Oliver said, his voice heavy with sleepiness.

"There is a way."

"How? Annulment? Divorce?"

"The Catholic Church does not allow divorce, and an annulment is very difficult to obtain. In most cases, the final decree must come from the Pope, and that can take years."

"How then?" he repeated, impatiently.

"One of us will die."

"Constanza, don't be absurd. That, too, could take years."

"Not necessarily."

Something in her tone bothered him. He raised his head to look at her face.

A strange smile curved her lips. "Do you want to know who *La Serpiente* really is?" she whispered.

His eyes widened with horrified comprehension just as Constanza buried the knife blade in his neck at the base of his skull. Encircled by the arms of his smiling bride, Oliver Mainwaring died silently, and within seconds.

The next morning, Geoffrey Mercer presented himself at the Santa Maria shortly after nine o'clock. Rosa showed him into the *sala,* where Jennifer and Barbara waited. The men joined them a few minutes later. Jennifer sat on a sofa opposite Mercer, and John took a position directly behind her.

"I will get right to the point," Mercer said, setting his coffee cup on the table. He rifled through his leather folder and pulled out a piece of paper. "The wire I expected from Washington was in answer to one I had sent." He fixed his gaze on John. "I interviewed Deputy Sam Trudeau in Laramie City when Mr. Mainwaring and I travelled through there. I have also been in communication with the French consul in San Francisco. He confirmed that you contacted him, and he, as well as Deputy Trudeau, share my feelings about the case."

"And what are those feelings, Mr. Mercer?" John asked. He laid a hand on Jennifer's shoulder. She reached up and covered his hand with hers.

"That the accusations against you are without foundation, based solely upon rumor and innuendo. Oliver Mainwaring was either very lucky or very clever to have stirred up so much trouble without any witnesses or hard evidence at his disposal."

Jennifer breathed a sigh of relief. Perhaps *La Serpiente* could finally be laid to rest.

"So what will happen now?" John asked.

"I will suggest to the president that the entire investigation be dropped. This is not a matter for the United States to resolve. The crimes were committed in Mexico, against

French and Mexican citizens." Mercer returned the paper to his folder. "Suppose the true *Serpiente* were apprehended. Suppose he even confessed. Could charges for such acts committed during a time of war hold up in court? If so, where would he be tried? Not in the United States. I doubt even in Mexico, where, my sources inform me, he is regarded as somewhat of a hero, albeit a dark one. Would France go to the trouble to extradite him?" He shook his head. "Doubtful, in spite of the righteous indignation of the French ambassador in Washington."

"So *La Serpiente,* whoever he was, literally got away with murder," Jennifer commented.

"Yes, Mrs. Cantrell, he did." Mercer stood up. "I will stop by the Noriega ranch later today to interview Mrs. Mainwaring for the record, but I seriously doubt she will impart any information that will change my mind. Mr. Cantrell, good luck to you. With this unpleasant episode behind you, may you and your new wife experience only the best of life."

"Thank you, Mr. Mercer." John came around the sofa to extend his hand. "I appreciate all you have done." He glanced back at Jennifer. "We both do."

"My pleasure."

Rosa came to the door. *"Perdón, Señor* Preston, but there is a man from the Buena Ventura to see you. He says it is urgent."

"Thank you, Rosa. Please send him in."

Jennifer and John exchanged a wary glance as Rosa escorted the man in. He was one of Alejandro's *vaqueros,* a young man who twisted his hat nervously in his hands.

"What is it?" Preston asked.

"I bring a message from *Señor* Noriega for Mrs. Jennifer Cantrell, sir. Is she here?"

Jennifer stood up. "I am Mrs. Cantrell."

The *vaquero* faced her. "Yes, ma'am. *Señor* Noriega regrets to inform you that your uncle, Oliver Mainwaring, was found dead this morning."

Jennifer stared at him in disbelief. "I beg your pardon? My uncle is dead?"

"Yes, ma'am."

"How?" John demanded. He came to Jennifer's side and put an arm around her shoulders.

"*Señor* Noriega did not say. He asked that Mrs. Cantrell come as quickly as possible. I'll wait outside for her."

"Her husband will bring her," Preston said firmly. "Please tell Alejandro they'll be there shortly."

"Yes, sir. Thank you, sir." The *vaquero* hurried away.

"I cannot believe it," Jennifer whispered. "What could have happened?"

John held her in a close embrace. "We'll find out." He looked at Preston. "Will you come with us?"

Preston nodded. "Of course."

"I'll come if you think it would help," Bill offered.

"Thank you," John said.

"I would also like to come along," Geoffrey Mercer added.

"Very well. We'll take the surrey." John looked down at Jennifer. "Meet us out front in a few minutes."

She nodded mutely. John kissed her forehead, then followed the other men out of the room.

"Oh, Jennie, I'm sorry." Barbara came up and took her hands. "Even though you and Oliver did not get along, this must be an unpleasant shock for you."

Jennifer's brows drew together in a troubled frown. "It is. I can't even imagine what could have happened."

Barbara nodded in understanding. "Arrangements will have to be made; do you want me to come with you?"

"No, but thank you." Jennifer hugged her. "With the Cantrell men around me, I will be fine."

"All right, if you're sure. What do you need from upstairs? I'll get it for you."

Jennifer smiled gratefully at her. "I think my hooded cloak will be fine. Thank you."

Barbara kissed her cheek and was gone.

Without focusing on anything in particular, Jennifer looked around the *sala*. Only yesterday, her uncle had stood in that very room, very much alive. She could not grasp the idea that he was truly gone, and with him, the Mainwaring name. All of her old family was gone.

Twenty-six

Alejandro himself was waiting at the door when Bill brought the surrey to a halt in front of the Noriega *hacienda.* He ushered them into the parlor, where Constanza sat in a tall-backed chair and Arturo stood at her side.

Constanza's gold crucifix offered the only splash of color against her somber, high-necked, long-sleeved dress made of black muslin. Her head was again covered by the black scarf, now tied at the back of her neck rather than under her chin. Her reddened eyes seemed huge in her pale face, and she dabbed repeatedly at them with a lacy handkerchief. Jennifer could not help but question the sincerity of the woman's grief.

A moment later, two more men came into the room. Alejandro introduced one as Sheriff Watson from Gilroy, and the sheriff introduced the other as Inspector Timothy Todd of the Secret Service, a federal law-enforcement agency not even ten years old. Jennifer noticed that Mr. Mercer and Inspector Todd exchanged glances. She wondered if the two men already knew each other.

"When did Oliver Mainwaring die, and how?" John asked. He stood next to the chair Jennifer occupied.

Constanza started sobbing.

"He died sometime during the night," Alejandro said. "My daughter awakened this morning to find him cold beside her. He had been stabbed."

Jennifer sagged in her chair, stunned. *Murdered.* Oliver had been murdered. John placed a comforting hand on her shoulder.

"I understand Mr. Mainwaring and your daughter were married yesterday," the sheriff said.

"Yes," Alejandro replied.

Constanza let out a soft wail.

The sheriff walked over to stand in front of her. "I know this is a difficult time for you, Mrs. Mainwaring, but I must ask you some questions." He pulled a pencil and a small notebook from his pocket.

Constanza nodded and blew her nose. "I understand," she whispered.

Jennifer's stomach grabbed. Constanza's portrayal of a grieving bride was convincing, but something very subtle rang false.

"When did you and your husband retire for the night?" Sheriff Watson asked.

"Late. It was late, around eleven, I think."

"That is correct, Sheriff," Alejandro put in. "We all retired at that time."

"Did anyone else come into your room, to perhaps visit or offer congratulations?"

"It was our wedding night, Sheriff." Constanza wiped her eyes again. "We were left alone, except for a silent murderer. I cannot believe Oliver died next to me and I did not awaken."

Sheriff Watson wrote in the notebook. "So, you fell asleep and heard nothing. You were not aware that anything was wrong until you awakened this morning."

"That is correct."

"To your knowledge, did anyone have cause to wish your husband harm?"

Constanza turned tear-filled eyes on John. "Yes," she answered in an agonized whisper. "I hate to say this, but Juan Novales Cantrell did. He threatened him."

"Constanza . . ." John said warningly.

Jennifer closed her eyes for a moment as a deep fear rushed

through her. Constanza had promised revenge. Was this how she intended to get it? To see John charged with Oliver's murder? Jennifer blindly reached for his hand and clung to him.

"Mrs. Mainwaring, are you saying you think John Cantrell killed your husband?" the sheriff asked calmly.

"I don't want to even imagine that, because I think highly of Mr. Cantrell." Constanza twisted the handkerchief in her hands. "But I fear it is possible."

Jennifer heard John groan at the same time his fingers tightened on hers.

"What motive would he have?" the sheriff asked.

Constanza shrugged. "Many motives, I think. Oliver was often unkind to his niece, who is now John's wife. Also, with Oliver gone, Jennifer will inherit all of her father's estate."

"There is no estate," Jennifer interjected heatedly, "and I will not listen to this slander of my husband." She looked at the sheriff. "It is Constanza who threatened revenge, against both my husband and me. Besides, John could not have killed Oliver, for he was with me all night."

"What wife would not say the same in defense of her husband?" Constanza demanded, her tears suddenly gone. "I warned Oliver about Juan, about *La Serpiente*. It was he who killed my husband, using the same ploy he used in Mexico all those years ago. It was he who left his wife's bed, as quietly as a snake, and came here. He stole into our room and murdered my husband, then returned to his wife's side with no one the wiser, unless she lies and did in fact know and approve of his plan. It is no secret that Jennifer hated her uncle."

"That is enough, Constanza." John's menacing voice echoed off the walls. "Sheriff, I would like to see Oliver's body. I would also appreciate the opportunity to speak to you in more private circumstances and, if you do not mind, have Mr. Mercer accompany us."

Sheriff Watson nodded. "All right, but only if Inspector Todd comes along. He has an interest in this case."

John nodded in agreement.

"We left the body as we found it," Alejandro said. "I will take you there."

John bent down to give Jennifer a quick hug. "All will be well," he whispered. "I promise."

She clung to him for a moment, then watched as he followed the other men from the room.

"How touching," Constanza sneered.

Jennifer turned away, grateful that Bill pulled up a chair and sat at her side.

"Leave her alone, Constanza," Preston ordered.

Constanza glowered at him, but said nothing further.

Preston looked at Arturo. "Would you please send for coffee? I think we all could use some."

With a nod, Arturo moved to pull the servant's cord, and the room settled into a tense silence.

Upstairs in Constanza's opulent room, John approached the massive, heavily carved mahogany bed. Oliver Mainwaring's body lay on its stomach, covered with a sheet. One exposed arm hung over the edge of the mattress. At the sheriff's nod, John pulled the sheet back to the dead man's hips.

Oliver's head was turned to one side, showing opened eyes that emphasized the horror hinted at by his frozen expression. John frowned. Aside from a few minor scratches, Oliver's bare back was unmarked.

"Where is the stab wound?" he asked.

"At the back of the head," Alejandro answered. "If you have any other questions, I will be downstairs." He left the room, closing the door behind him.

At the back of the head. The words filled John with a deep sense of foreboding. He leaned over the body. At the base of the skull, a small amount of dried, darkened blood matted the

sandy-brown hair and crusted around and over the inch-long
wound. John's heart started pounding. He straightened and
faced the other men.

"What is it, Mr. Cantrell?" Geoffrey Mercer asked. "You
look as if you've seen a ghost."

"I have seen the work of one I had hoped was a ghost,"
John said quietly.

"What do you mean?" Sheriff Watson asked.

John rubbed his eyes. "Constanza mentioned a killer called
La Serpiente. Several years ago, during the Juarez revolution,
an assassin known by that name operated in the *Ciudad de
Mexico.* He killed several high-ranking French and Mexican
officials. That name was all that was known of him. He was
never captured or identified."

"Both the late Mr. Mainwaring and the new Mrs. Mainwaring accused Mr. Cantrell of being that assassin," Mercer
put in.

"Which, of course, is not true," the sheriff commented
dryly.

"No, sir, it is not," John stated. "As I told Mr. Mercer, I
was in Mexico at the time of the murders, but I did not
commit them. Thanks to one of my connections, however, I
was able to examine the bodies of some of the victims. They
were killed in exactly this manner, most of them while in
bed. This may very well be the work of *La Serpiente.*"

Inspector Todd spoke for the first time. "If you are not
the culprit, Mr. Cantrell, who could it be? Do you know of
anyone else in this proximity who was also in Mexico at the
time of the assassinations?"

John shook his head. "Only Constanza." He blinked. *"Constanza."* Her name came out in a whisper. "Of course. I have
been so blind."

Sheriff Watson frowned. "Are you saying that you think
Mrs. Mainwaring is this assassin? That she killed her own
husband?"

John did not answer. Deep in thought, he turned to stare

out the window with unseeing eyes. Constanza had been in *Ciudad de Mexico* at the right time. The mysterious deaths had started a few months after her arrival and, to John's knowledge, ended with her return to California. Of course, Juarez had resumed power just before Constanza left, so there had been no further need for *La Serpiente's* work. The French had been driven out, the traitorous Mexicans ousted and punished.

But he himself had been her lover then. Could the spoiled, vivacious young woman he had known, danced with, made love to, been a cold, calculating assassin? She had willingly admitted to taking other lovers, had bragged about it. She would have had access to other men's bedchambers. And who would have suspected a beautiful young woman as an assassin, especially one of such accomplished acting abilities as Constanza?

An image flashed in John's mind of Constanza's small, jewel-handled knife, the one she had used on him in a fit of rage. Was that blade stained with the blood of other men? One hand absentmindedly rubbed his own scarred ribs while he glanced back over his shoulder at Oliver's still form. The fatal wound had been made with a small-bladed knife. All the pieces fit.

"He must have died in her arms," John whispered, shaking his head. "The poor bastard."

"What did you say?" Sheriff Watson asked.

John turned around. "Yes, Sheriff, in belated answer to your questions, I think Constanza is *La Serpiente,* and I think she murdered her husband. Unfortunately, I have no proof."

The room settled into silence for a few minutes. John could tell from the expressions of the other men that his theory was difficult to swallow. The thought of a young woman committing such heinous crimes was unpleasant to contemplate, even for him, and he knew Constanza better than any of them.

Inspector Todd finally spoke. "I suggest we question Mrs. Mainwaring about this."

"Do you accept Mr. Cantrell's declaration of innocence Inspector?" the sheriff asked, as if John were not standin only a few feet away.

Instead of answering the question, the inspector looked a Mercer. "Geoffrey?"

"The inspector and I have worked on other cases together," Mercer said in response to the questioning look both John and the sheriff gave him. Then he answered the inspecto "Yes, Tim, I believe Mr. Cantrell. I'll be happy to let yo read my report—you, too, Sheriff—but I am satisfied of M Cantrell's innocence, even though there is no definitive proof At the risk of sounding cold-hearted, I am not concerned wit foreign nationals killed years ago in a foreign country durin a time of war. Mr. Mainwaring's death, however, is anothe matter entirely."

The inspector and the sheriff both nodded in agreement.

Mercer continued. "Based upon my knowledge of Mr. Can trell's character and the word of his wife, at this time I d not consider him a suspect in Oliver Mainwaring's death." He leveled his gaze on Todd. "Why are you here, Tim? I wa not aware the Secret Service was investigating this case."

"I am here on an entirely different matter," Todd said "Mrs. Mainwaring has other questions to answer."

"I also want to ask Constanza about her connections to radical group in Mexico," John said, leading the way to th door. "In addition, my wife is very anxious about this whol affair. I would like her fears for me laid to rest and her ques tions about her uncle's death answered as quickly as possi ble."

Geoffrey Mercer pulled the sheet back over Oliver's body then followed the rest of the men from the room.

A few minutes later, the four men filed into the parlor Jennifer met John's gaze, her green eyes sad and haunted. He strode to her side and bent over her, placing his hands or her shoulders.

"I am sorry, Jennie. Oliver has indeed been murdered."

She nodded wearily.

He tightened his fingers for a moment, then released her and straightened, turning to face Constanza.

"I know what happened, Constanza," he said quietly. "I know everything."

"Of course you do," she retorted. "You did it."

"No, I did not." He walked over to stand in front of her. "Where is the knife?"

She stiffened. "What knife? What are you talking about?"

"What is this, Sheriff?" Alejandro demanded. "Why is he allowed to ask these outrageous questions of my daughter?"

"He is allowed, *Señor* Noriega," the sheriff said. "Let him continue."

"I want the knife, Constanza."

"What knife?" she angrily repeated, glaring up at him with hate-filled eyes.

"The one you used to kill those men in *Ciudad de Mexico*. The one you used on me. The one you used to kill Oliver." John stared at her. "Surely you remember; it is small, the blade only three inches long, with a jeweled handle."

Jennifer stared at John. *The one you used on me.* Now she knew how he had been scarred. How easily he could have been dead! How easily she could have never known him!

Arturo, who again stood at Constanza's side, started and looked down at his sister wide-eyed, while Alejandro stepped toward John.

"What are you saying?" he shouted. "My daughter is no killer!"

John did not take his eyes from Constanza. "Unfortunately, *Don* Alejandro, she is."

"I also have reason to believe she is a traitor to the United States," Inspector Todd added.

At that, Constanza's composure noticeably slipped.

John held out his hand. "The knife."

Constanza's mouth tightened into a thin line. Her gaze darted from John to her father to the inspector. When she looked at Jennifer, her eyes narrowed with furious hatred. Then she returned her gaze to John. "I am surprised it took you so long to discover the truth, Juan," she said, her tone conversational. "You should have known in Mexico. Those men were so stupid, so easy to fool, so eager to bed me. I was so simple." Her hand disappeared into the side pocket of her skirt. A moment later, she held the jeweled knife out on her palm.

"Constanza, no." Alejandro sank onto the sofa, his expression one of disbelief and deep anguish. Arturo moved to his father's side. Constanza ignored them both.

John took the small weapon from her hand and examined it. The craftsmanship involved in the design of the handle and the quality of the blade were remarkable. How ironic, and sad, that such a work of art had been used as an instrument of death.

"You had plenty of opportunity to kill me in Mexico, Constanza. Why didn't you?" John sincerely wanted to know the answer.

"You were on the list," Constanza acknowledged. "But then I learned you were a *Juarista* agent. We fought for the same cause." She shrugged. "I used the knife on you in a foolish moment of rage. Had I wanted to kill you, I would have."

"I know." He looked at her. "Why are you confessing so easily now?"

Constanza leaned back in her chair. "Look around, Juan." She indicated the others in the room with a nonchalant wave of her hand. "There is no escape, not right now. I am outnumbered. And the Inspector presents a special problem." She shrugged again. "I am a realist."

"I do not understand," Jennifer said, her brow wrinkled in tormented confusion. "Why did you marry Oliver? Did you always intend to kill him?"

"I married Oliver in a foolish attempt to appease my father," Constanza snapped. She stood up and put her hands

on her hips, glaring at her old, sorrowful parent. "He went
on and on about my lost virtue, about his grandchild having
a name, a grandchild I had already disposed of. It was easier
to go through with it than explain that I had erred in trying
to force an annulment of your marriage. I could not confide
in my father. He would never have understood why I needed
Juan, why I needed the Santa Maria." She started to pace a
small section of the carpet. "He himself betrayed Mexico.
My own father! Not only did he befriend the *Americanos,* he
did not fight them when they took California from us. As
for Oliver, sooner or later, he would have had to die; he was
a liability, in addition to being a *gringo.*" She spat the last
word.

Jennifer looked down at her clasped hands, her mind numb
with shock and horror. Constanza had given no more thought
to killing Oliver that she would to stepping on a spider. Not
even he deserved to die in that way.

"Are you a member of the Brotherhood of Mexican Na-
tionalists, Mrs. Mainwaring?" Inspector Todd asked.

Constanza eyed him coldly. "The correct title is *La Fraternidad de los Nacionalistas Mexicanos,* Inspector, and yes, I am
a proud member."

"What is this *fraternidad?*" Preston asked.

John answered. "It is an underground organization made
up of terrorists and fanatics who are dedicated to regaining
the lands Mexico sold or ceded to the United States since
gaining her independence from Spain in 1821."

"We are not terrorists and fanatics," Constanza said hotly.
"We are the true patriots of Mexico, and we will see returned
to her the lands that are rightfully hers." She arched an eyebrow at John. "I am surprised you remember. *La Fraternidad*
flourished, even though you refused to join."

"The brotherhood no longer flourishes, Constanza."

Constanza tossed her head in the habitual manner she had
used when her hair was long. "Of course it does, Juan. *La
Fraternidad* will always flourish. Even now, plans to over-

throw the weak, traitorous Mexican government are being pu
into place. We will not be stopped. Soon the people of Mex
ico will rise up, as they did under Hidalgo and Juarez, and
they will claim what is theirs." Her eyes had taken on a
heated look.

"Texas and California are no longer theirs to claim, Mrs
Mainwaring," Inspector Todd said firmly. "Nor are the terri
tories of Arizona and New Mexico. Did you honestly believe
the United States would surrender those lands?"

"The United States will have no choice. *La Fraternidad* i
stronger than all your armies." Constanza's voice carried a
ring of impassioned conviction.

John exchanged a glance with Todd. At the inspector's nod
he began to speak. "The plot was uncovered in *Ciudad d*
Mexico months ago, Constanza. Mexican and American offi
cials worked together to set a trap for the members of you
brotherhood. Most have been captured; some were killed, and
those still at large will be hunted down. Those captured wil
be tried and, if convicted, hanged for treason. *La Fraternidad*
has been destroyed."

"It cannot be," Constanza whispered, swaying slightly
"Who told you these lies?"

"I still have contacts in the Mexican ministry," John an
swered. "You may remember Miguel Herrera. He wrote to
me."

"Your name is on the wanted list, Mrs. Mainwaring," In
spector Todd said. "I am here to arrest you for treason."

"And I will charge you with the murder of Oliver Main
waring," Sheriff Watson added.

Constanza's pale face took on a sickly hue. She closed he
eyes for a moment, clasping her hands in front of her. The
she straightened. "My compatriots will come for me." He
voice cracked and she cleared her throat. "And even if they
do not, *La Fraternidad* will live on long after I am dead. You
cannot kill the spirit of the revolution."

"*La Fraternidad* never espoused a noble revolution of the

people," John stated. "It was a group of misguided fools led by greedy men bent upon enriching themselves. And now, thank God, the brotherhood is no more."

Sheriff Watson took Constanza's arm, but she shook free of him.

"I will not be led away like some common criminal," she said proudly. "I will walk alone." With her head held high, she marched across the room and out the door without as much as a glance at her father and brother.

The sheriff followed her and paused at the door. "A few of my men are outside with a wagon. With your permission, *Señor* Noriega, I'll have them remove Mainwaring's body."

Alejandro did not appear to have heard him.

"Go ahead, Sheriff," Arturo said.

The sheriff nodded and left.

Arturo turned dull eyes on the inspector. "What will happen to her?"

"She will be tried for treason and murder." Inspector Todd's expression softened. "I regret telling you that if she is convicted, she will probably be hanged, even though she is a woman."

A long, low moan escaped Alejandro's lips as he buried his face in his hands. Arturo laid an awkward hand on his father's shoulder.

Jennifer did not move. She felt overwhelmed by the events of the morning, by the revelations she had heard.

"There is one thing Constanza said that I did not understand," Preston said. "She mentioned that she had to have John and the Santa Maria. Why?"

"I don't know," Inspector Todd admitted.

After a moment of silence, Arturo spoke. "Because of the close proximity to San Francisco, Constanza's mission was to procure land to set up a military base, and she felt that the lands of the Buena Ventura were not enough. She wanted the Santa Maria as well. That was why she tried to force you off your land."

All eyes turned to him in amazement.

"Constanza was behind the acts of vandalism against the Santa Maria?" Preston demanded.

"Yes." Arturo slumped down on the sofa next to his silent father. "But then John returned. Suddenly, there was another way. She felt he had a right to the land because of his Mexican heritage." He looked up at John. "She told me she wanted you because you could give her the Santa Maria, but I believe she also felt something for you."

"Just how deeply were you involved in her plots, Mr. Noriega?" Todd asked suspiciously. "Are you also a member of the Brotherhood?"

"No, sir, I am not. Constanza confided a great deal in me, but I never believed her revolutionary army would come forth and reclaim California for Mexico. However, I would not have minded adding the Santa Maria lands to those of the Buena Ventura."

"I'll want to talk to you about that attack on my bull, and about a wildfire of suspicious origin, Arturo," Preston said sternly. "It is doubtful Constanza did everything herself."

Arturo nodded wearily.

"I want you all to go." Alejandro spoke in a weak, raspy voice.

"Of course, Alejandro," Preston said.

Bill and Mercer immediately left the room.

Inspector Todd started to follow them, then hesitated at the door. "I will have questions for you also, Mr. Noriega," he said to Arturo. "Don't plan on taking any trips."

"I will be here," Arturo assured him in a tired voice. "I will not leave my father."

John helped Jennifer to her feet and, with a steadying arm around her shoulders, led her toward the door. He paused to set the jewelled knife on the low table in front of Alejandro before he guided her out the door.

Preston stared helplessly at his old friend for a moment. "I am so sorry, Alejandro," he said quietly, then also left.

Constanza sat on the seat of the wagon into which the sheriff's men were loading the shrouded body of Oliver Mainwaring. Jennifer grabbed John's arm.

"I want to see to his burial," she said. "He was my uncle."

John nodded in compassionate understanding. "I will talk to the sheriff."

As John spoke, Sheriff Watson approached with a large carpetbag. "The housekeeper said this and that trunk over there belonged to Mr. Mainwaring. In light of the circumstances with his wife, I think you should have his things, Mrs. Cantrell."

"Thank you, Sheriff," Jennifer said dully.

John looked at her in concern. "Into the surrey with you, wife," he said as he lifted her up to the seat. "I'll take care of Oliver's things."

"They will need proper clothes for him, John."

"I know, Jen. We'll see to it." He turned away to speak to the sheriff in low tones, then joined her in the surrey. "We'll leave in a minute."

Jennifer nodded. The wagon carrying Oliver's body pulled away. She shaded her eyes against the midday sun and watched as both Oliver and Constanza were taken out of her life.

It was over.

She felt a curious combination of feelings: relief, shock, sadness. She also felt a deep sense of sorrow at the senseless waste of two young lives. If only Oliver and Constanza had been content with what they had had! But they hadn't been, and now one was dead, with no one to truly mourn him, and the other soon would be, leaving behind a broken-hearted father and a grieving brother. Jennifer's eyes filled with tears.

John put his arms around her and held her close, pressing his lips to her temple. He said nothing, seeming to understand that no words could offer her comfort.

"Please take me home," she whispered.

Bill must have heard her, for he slapped the reins against the backs of the horses and the surrey began to move.

Jennifer closed her eyes and rested her head against John's shoulder. He tightened his hold on her, and she realized, with the first stirrings of a deep sense of peace, that she was already home.

Two days later, in the middle of a cool November afternoon, John found Jennifer in the courtyard, sitting on the bench under the lemon tree.

"There you are." He leaned down to plant a kiss on her cheek. "Are you all right?"

She nodded with a soft smile. "I am." She pulled her light shawl more tightly around her shoulders. "I just wanted to be outside for a while."

John glanced up at the sky. "The wind is picking up; I think something is blowing in from the coast." His gaze dropped back to her. "Are you ready to come inside?"

Jennifer looked up at him, again struck by her husband's rugged beauty. A smile played about his mouth, and his blue eyes sparkled with anticipation. Her own eyes narrowed with suspicion. "I know that look. What are you up to, John?"

He took her hand and tugged on it. "I have a gift for you."

"Let me guess," she said tartly as she allowed him to pull her to her feet. "You must present this gift to me in our bedroom." A slow fire began to build in her lower stomach. Did he truly intend to make love to her in the middle of the afternoon? Jennifer found the idea intriguing.

"How did you know?" John's handsome face wore an expression of innocence. He led her across the courtyard to the doors of the *sala,* then stopped suddenly and looked down at her. "Mrs. Cantrell, surely you do not suspect that I have lustful intentions toward you."

"Mr. Cantrell, I know my husband for the lusty man he is," she sweetly retorted.

"Madam, you wound me." John placed his hand over his heart. "A gift such as you suggest would be a somewhat selfish one, as I would also benefit. This particular gift is strictly for you."

Jennifer laughed. "Then lead on, John."

They hurried through the *sala* and up the stairs, holding hands like two excited children. With a flourish, John opened the door to their bedroom, and Jennifer was surprised to see that a wrapped, beribboned gift did actually sit on the bed. She smiled in delight.

"What is it, John?" She crossed the room to the bed and touched the gay blue ribbon.

"Open it and see." John closed the door and leaned against it, watching her intently.

She sat on the edge of the bed and pulled the gift toward her. "It's heavy," she remarked. Her curiosity piqued, she untied the ribbon and pushed the cloth wrapping out of the way to reveal a thick book. She turned it over.

The American Handbook of Veterinary Medicine, as put Forth by the New York College of Veterinary Surgeons, Chartered 1857.

"I looked among your books first," John said. "I don't think you have that one."

Jennifer's eyes filled with tears. "No, I don't have this." She looked up at him. "Thank you, John. I shall treasure it."

John started across the room toward her. "Do you remember Dr. Lafferty, the veterinarian who saw to Buford?"

"Of course I do." Jennifer ran loving hands over the soft leather cover of the book.

"He and Preston are old friends. You may also remember that Emmett's wife died some months ago." John sat next to her on the bed.

She nodded.

"Emmett and Preston have reached an agreement about something that concerns you."

Jennifer looked at him. "Me?"

"Yes." John took her hand. "Preston has invited Emmett to make his home here, and Emmett has agreed to take you on as his student. He cannot legally grant you the title of Doctor of Veterinary Medicine, but he will teach you all he knows."

Unable to believe her ears, Jennifer stared at him. "Truly, John?" she whispered. Her heart pounded in hopeful joy.

"Truly, Jen." John kissed her fingers. "Does that please you?"

"Please me?" she cried. She jumped off the bed, clutching the heavy book to her breast, and whirled around in a circle. The ribbon and piece of wrapping cloth fell to the floor. "It is more than I ever dreamed of! Dr. Lafferty will apprentice me?"

He nodded, his mouth curved in a wide grin.

Jennifer stopped suddenly. "Whose idea was this?"

John shrugged. "It occurred to me that Emmett was probably pretty lonely, what with losing his wife and all, and I knew he and Preston went way back, and we certainly have the room—"

The book landed on the floor with a heavy *thunk*. Jennifer launched herself on top of John, pushing him back on the bed. "You did it," she whispered. "You did it for me." She felt her heart would explode from the sudden swell of love that poured through her. She tangled her hands in his thick hair and covered his face with breathless kisses. "Thank you, my love. Thank you."

John wrapped his arms around her. "You are most welcome, *mi rosa silvestre*," he murmured against her neck.

Jennifer stilled. "Did you call me Rosa?" she demanded, pulling on his hair.

"I called you *mi rosa silvestre*," John said with an exaggerated grimace.

Her hold relaxed. "Am I your wild rose, John?" she asked softly.

"You are, Jen. You are my wild rose, you are my beloved wife, you are my very life. *Te amo mucho.*"

Jennifer kissed him with all the tenderness and love she felt for him. "And I love you, *El Lobo,*" she whispered against his lips.

John kissed her deeply, then pulled away as if a thought had just occurred to him. "You know, you never have told me all the other things you like about me."

She arched an eyebrow at him. "What are you talking about?"

"Remember? One night we were in the courtyard, and you said when I kept my promise to make love to you, you would tell me the things you liked about me in addition to my *sweetness.*" He made a face. "You still haven't told me."

Jennifer laughed. "What made you remember that now?"

"I don't know. I was thinking back over the first few times I kissed you, and I remembered that night in the courtyard. You came to me later. I cannot tell you what that meant to me, that you would come to me, to offer your heart and your body."

Jennifer rolled off him and nestled against his side. "I was frightened," she admitted.

"Of what?" His hand moved over her hair, removing pins and tossing them away.

"I was frightened of how powerful my feelings for you were, that you would think me wanton, that you would not want me."

"Surely you no longer feel that way."

"Of course not."

"Good. Then tell me what you like about me."

Jennifer slapped his stomach. "Mostly, I like your modesty," she teased.

John grabbed her and for a while they lay there, content to hold each other, whispering all the things they liked about each other while the wind blew the first raindrops against the closed French doors. The approaching storm lent a safe, cozy feel to the dim, comfortable room.

"You know, I have a gift for you, too," Jennifer finally said.

"You do?" John asked with a smile.

"Yes." Jennifer's fingers played with the buttons of his shirt, leaving each one open when she moved onto the next. "But I must warn you, it is a somewhat selfish gift, as I will also benefit from it, and you must unwrap it yourself." She felt his heart pick up speed under her searching fingers.

"It sounds like a lot of work," John said skeptically. He ran his hand down her back to her hips, caressing her through the layers of her clothes.

"It will be worth it," Jennifer assured him. She tugged his opened shirt out of his pants. John's breath caught when she pressed her mouth to his chest, then to the scar over his ribs, a scar that now had truly and completely healed.

"Do you promise?" he whispered.

She looked up at him, her green eyes alight with love and desire. "I promise."

John believed her.

Epilogue

November 19, 1874

A year had passed, and again the cool November winds blew over the Santa Maria. Much had happened in that year.

Gabriel Horn and Rosa had been married in March, and now lived happily with Francisca in a tidy house the men had built for them. Preston had given them a fifty-acre tract of land as a wedding gift, while Bill and John had presented them with a bull and a cow. Rosa had conceived and would give Gabe his first child sometime after the new year.

Constanza Noriega Mainwaring had been in her grave three months, having been found guilty on all charges and executed. She went to her death with the same cool hauteur she had shown when she was arrested, showing no remorse for her actions, feeling no pity for herself, and accepting none from anyone else.

Preston decided not to press charges against Arturo Noriega for the attack on Buford and for starting the wildfire. He said that everyone had suffered enough. Arturo showed a surprisingly kind side of himself while helping his father come to terms with all that had happened. Alejandro was doing better, and had even made tentative steps toward re-establishing his friendship with Preston.

Now, on that cool November day, several people waited in Preston's *sala*. John paced anxiously in front of the fireplace, while Preston and Emmett Lafferty occasionally looked up from their chess game to watch him with concerned understanding. Bill and Gabe were engaged in a card game that neither seemed too interested in.

Conor O'Rourke sat in one of the wing-backed chairs, holding his sleeping six-month-old son Thomas. Lily Carolina, now six years old, and Elizabeth Parker, now eighteen months, played relatively quietly with David and Molly in a cozy corner of the room, under Francisca's watchful eye. Beauregarde Parker was comfortably stretched out on one of the sofas with his two-month-old son Jonathan Ambrose snuggled contentedly against his chest. He looked at John, then exchanged a sympathetic glance with Conor; they each knew the fear and anticipation of waiting while their beloved wives gave birth.

Barbara appeared at the opened double doors. "John."

John whirled to look at her. "Is she all right?"

"Everything is fine." Barbara smiled happily. "You have a lovely daughter, and both she and your wife would like to see you."

The room erupted in a chorus of cheers. John seemed dazed as Bill pumped his hand and Preston slapped his back.

"I'll go tell the men," Bill said, and ran from the room. A few moments later, a second round of cheers erupted outside, this time accompanied by a few exuberant gunshots.

Preston pushed John toward the door. "Go greet your daughter," he said, his voice warm with affection.

John needed no further encouragement. He raced past Barbara and up the stairs to the room he shared with Jennifer. He stopped before the closed door, suddenly shy, then raised his hand and knocked. A moment later, Brigit opened the door.

"There ye be," she cried happily. "Come in, come in." She grabbed his arm. "Congratulations, sir!"

John followed her into the room, his eyes anxiously seeking out his wife. Alina and Susannah stood on the far side of the bed, while Rosa leaned over it. She straightened and stepped back, her face wreathed in a wide smile, her hands resting on her own rounded belly. Step by step, John approached, unable to take his eyes from Jennifer's sweet, exhausted face. Her smile seemed to shine in the room, surrounding him with its warmth and love. He drew near the bed, and the other women congregated near the door to give them some privacy.

"Hello," John said softly.

"Hello." Jennifer reached for his hand and squeezed it briefly, conveying a wealth of emotion in her touch. She then pulled back a blanket to reveal a small red face topped with a surprisingly abundant amount of fine black hair, and two tiny hands curled into fists. "She probably looks a little funny to you right now, but everyone assures me that will change in a few days."

John stroked his daughter's incredibly soft forehead with a finger that suddenly seemed huge and awkward to him. "She is beautiful," he whispered. He looked at Jennifer and his heart swelled with love. "Thank you, my wife. Thank you." He leaned forward to place a tender kiss on her lips.

"Thank you, too, John. I wouldn't have her without you." Jennifer smiled at him. "I'd like to name her Ana Maria if that is all right with you."

Deeply moved, John nodded his agreement. "Ana Maria Novales Cantrell. It is a good name."

"Why don't you go introduce Ana Maria to the rest of her family?" Jennifer lifted the small warm bundle and placed their sleeping daughter in her father's arms.

John looked down at Ana Maria, totally captivated. A sudden, fierce love rushed over him for the tiny little girl, and he knew in that instant that he would die for her if need be. He raised tearing eyes to Jennifer. "We will be back soon," he said. "I promise."

She smiled at him, happily and wearily. He left the room, walking with slow careful steps, afraid the precious, fragile bundle he carried would break. Barbara, Rosa, and Brigit fol-

lowed him from the room, leaving Alina and Susannah alone
with Jennifer.

Susannah dipped a cloth in a pan of warm water and wrung
it out, then gently wiped Jennifer's face. "Do you remember
the very first day we ever met, on the beach in Narragansett?"
she asked. "I washed your face that day, too, when you fell
and landed with your face in the sand."

"I remember. Alina came running up to see what had happened."

Alina looked up from the blanket she was folding. "And
now we are all married, with little ones of our own. There
have been some hard times, some terrible times, but all in all
life has been good to us."

"For many years, you two were the very best things in my
life." Jennifer took Susannah's hand and held out her other
one to Alina. "I love you both like the sisters I never had."

"We all feel the same," Alina said as she took Jennifer's
hand. The three women joined in an awkward embrace, en-
closing each other in a circle of love.

John entered the *sala*. He held the baby up for all to see,
then crossed the room to his father. He placed his daughter
in Preston's arms.

"Her name is Ana Maria Novales Cantrell," he said
proudly.

"Thank you," Preston whispered.

John was suddenly surrounded by people offering congratulations. Preston stepped back, away from the throng, and
stared down at his granddaughter. Ana Maria opened her deep
blue eyes and yawned. Preston smiled in delight. "Our granddaughter, Ana," he whispered. "They named her after you,
and she will be as lovely as you were." He held the infant
close while his eyes searched out his beloved sons.

John and Bill stood together, each raising a glass in a toast
to the newest Cantrell. Preston felt inordinately blessed.

He and his Ana Maria had shared only a few glorious months, but Bill and Barbara, and John and Jennie, who had all found the same miraculous love, would have a lifetime, and Preston took deep comfort in that knowledge. It was as if he could feel his Ana Maria's love again, feel her presence as surely as if she were in the room. Birth and death. Suffering and love. Sorrow and joy. Life had come full circle.

Dear Reader:

As always, I greatly enjoyed the research I did for this book. I found the history of the Juarez rebellion against Maximilian and his French government fascinating, as was the history of the settling of California. I would like to point out that *La Fraternidad de los Nacionalistas Mexicanos* was born in my imagination, as was the movement by radicals to reclaim Mexican land lost to the United States. Given the shared history of the two countries, however, I felt that a brotherhood dedicated to such a cause was very feasible.

I experienced a strange nostalgia when I wrote the end of this book, as it is also the end of a trilogy. My characters come so alive for me during the course of writing their book that I actually miss them when their story is told. With my first two books, I could take comfort from the fact that I would meet Beau and Alina again, and check in on Conor and Susannah. The best I could do with John and Jennie was give them an epilogue in their own book, and now it is finished.

It is time to move on to the next trilogy, and as I get deeper into the research, the familiar excitement of a new story is beginning to grow. My Rocky Mountain Trilogy will consist of the stories of three brothers—Joseph Beaudine, Orion Beaudine, and Grey Eagle, a Cheyenne warrior, all sons of Jedediah Beaudine, a frontiersman and scout in the early days of the opening of the American West. The stories of the brothers are set in 1849-1851, in the area that would later become the territories of Colorado and Wyoming. The first book, tentatively titled *Brother of the Wolf,* is the story of

Joseph Beaudine, a frontiersman and scout like his father before him, and Sarah Hancock, a teacher from Connecticut who is determined to make her own way in the world. *Brother of the Wolf* is tentatively scheduled for publication in December 1996.

By writing historical romance novels, I am able to combine two very powerful facets of myself in one wonderful job—a passionate fascination for history and the deep, fervent belief in the power of love. I hope I convey those parts of myself through my work, and that my books, which are labors of love, give you entertainment and joy.

With my warmest regards,

Jessica Wulf

Jessica Wulf
P.O. Box 461212
Aurora, Colorado 80046

(If you write to me, an SASE would be greatly appreciated!)

About the Author

Jessica Wulf is a native of North Dakota and has spent most of her life in Colorado, where she now lives with her husband and two dogs. She has a B.A. in History, as well as a passion and fascination for it, and often feels that she was born in the wrong century. *The Wild Rose* is her third novel, and the last in her Rose Trilogy.

JANE KIDDER'S EXCITING
WELLESLEY BROTHERS SERIES

MAIL ORDER TEMPTRESS   (3863, $4.25)
Kirsten Lundgren traveled all the way to Minnesota to
be a mail order bride, but when Eric Wellesley wrapped
her in his virile embrace, her hopes for security soon
turned to dreams of passion!

PASSION'S SONG   (4174, $4.25)
When beautiful opera singer Elizabeth Ashford agreed
to care for widower Adam Wellesley's four children, she
never dreamed she'd fall in love with the little devils—
and with their handsome father as well!

PASSION'S CAPTIVE   (4341, $4.50)
To prevent her from hanging, Union captain Stuart
Wellesley offered to marry feisty Confederate spy Claire
Boudreau. Little did he realize he was in for a different
kind of war after the wedding!

PASSION'S BARGAIN   (4539, $4.50)
When she was sold into an unwanted marriage by her
father, Megan Taylor took matters into her own hands
and blackmailed Geoffrey Wellesley into becoming her
husband instead. But Meg soon found that marriage to
the handsome, wealthy timber baron was far more than
she had bargained for!

*Available wherever paperbacks are sold, or order direct from the
Publisher. Send cover price plus 50¢ per copy for mailing and
handling to Penguin USA, P.O. Box 999, c/o Dept. 17109,
Bergenfield, NJ 07621. Residents of New York and Tennessee
must include sales tax. DO NOT SEND CASH.*